Light It Up

Evie Blum

Contents

"God gave Adam a secret—and that secret was not how to begin, but how to begin again." —Elie Wiesel

To those who were taken, who danced their last dance, who fell when they ran into the fire to save others. Each of you was a whole world that will forever be missed.

This Hanukkah

Out of the Frying Pan into the Fire

Gabby

Jetlagged, tipsy, and making out with my ex in my parents' upstairs bathroom is the last place I thought I'd find myself on the third night of Hanukkah. It might not be what the rabbis of old had in mind, but it's certainly not the worst way to celebrate the Festival of Lights.

Ben delivers a searing kiss to my skin, and the scrape of his stubble on my neck as he slides down is the perfect balance of ecstasy and pain. The story of us in a nicely wrapped package. He hitches up my skirt and bites the inside of my bare thigh, and I exhale a not-so-quiet "Yesss" as his all-too-capable fingers stroke me.

Stretching up, he nips the skin just above the hem of my underwear. Like a puppet whose strings have snapped, my head falls back against the mirror. Outside the window to my right, the white snow falls against the dark sky. *How? How did I get here?* I blame the Hanukkah candles, now burning low in the family menorah downstairs. The kindling of a flame in the deep darkness of a cold winter night is apparently a little too inspired for my artistic soul to ignore, especially when my darling ex is in close proximity.

He hooks his fingers in my underwear and slips them down my hips. They fall effortlessly—as if they, too, have missed him and can't wait to be thrown on the floor to sit back and enjoy the show. He gazes up at me like I'm one of those chocolate desserts he loves so much. I can't help the half-pant, half-moan that escapes me as he glides his tongue over my most sensitive parts.

"Shhh, you can't be so loud," he cautions, in a delighted whisper.

"But it feels so good." I kick off my heeled ankle boots to sink down further toward his mouth.

"If you can't be quiet, I'll have to stop," he threatens. Then he slowly, torturously, slips a finger inside of me, presumably since his mouth is otherwise engaged in sparring with me.

"Oh," I exhale.

"Shhh."

"I'll be quiet," I promise in a ragged whisper. "But do that thing with your tongue again."

"This thing?" He leans in and demonstrates. I grip the counter to keep myself from sliding off it from the intensity of the sensation.

"Mmmmm," I say, melting. "See? I can enjoy myself quietly."

"You talk more than I remember."

"Really?" I ask.

"Nah, you've always talked a lot," he says, laughing.

"Speaking of which, use your mouth for other things, Dr. Adler."

He presses his forehead into my lower stomach, and I feel his eyelashes flutter on my skin and his mouth curl up into a smile. *I'm powerless against that smile of his.*

Before I can think too much about it, he composes himself and dives back in, this time with his mouth and his hands working together in perfect harmony. Harmony. *Ah, I had forgotten he plays piano.*

"You are amazing," he says. His *fingers* are amazing, doing something perverse, something they definitely should not be doing to me while my parents entertain guests downstairs at their annual Hanukkah party.

When Ben caught me leaving the bathroom earlier, he'd pushed me back inside, and we'd had neither the time nor the desire to turn on the light. Our whispered exchanges, his attentive touch, the shadows playing on his chiseled features—I'm trapped in a fever dream of longing and lust.

His voice breaks into my thoughts. "How're you doing, Gabriella?"

Without waiting for an answer, he slides his fingers into me, rhythmically. I thread my fingers through his dark curls and gently yank. *Why, why did he have to go and grow out his wild hair and come back looking so damn hot?*

"How're you?" I retort.

"Pull harder, naughty girl," he says.

His goading makes me smile, but despite the endorphins pumping through my body from his attentions, there's an undercurrent of turmoil, a swirl of painful memories. Memories of last summer, of our last time together. He'd kissed me on my stomach then, after we'd finished, and just lay there. I had run my hands through his hair—much shorter then—and he'd held me as if he would never let go. But he had let go. He had let *me* go. He had made his decision, and I didn't beg him to stay.

I couldn't. We'd only been casually dating. Our families hadn't even known, and I had my own life to think about—my own personal and professional ambitions. I had known as soon as he'd walked in the door that day that it was the end of us, if there even was an "us." I'd let him go, then mourned for months afterward.

Yet here we are, over a year later, wanting each other—needing each other. I felt it the moment I laid eyes on him a couple hours ago.

As I descend the stairs, arms full of unfolded napkins still warm from the dryer, my father opens the front door, and in walks Mrs. Adler.

She smiles up at me, her eyes warm. "Hi, Gabby. Happy Hanukkah, sweetheart."

"Hi, Tzipi," I say, "it's so nice to see you."

Just as I'm about to ask her how Ben is doing—a simple courtesy, of course—she turns back toward the front door, and it opens again. A familiar head pokes itself inside. It's covered by a knit hat, but I know in a second it's him.

"Benjamin, son, come in," my dad says.

Ben comes inside and closes the door behind him, but before my dad can shake his hand, he looks up at me, frozen on the stairs. My heart jumps in my chest. He's here. Why is he here?

He averts his eyes, just long enough to shake my father's hand, then walks to meet me at the bottom of the stairs.

"Hi, Gabriella," he says.

Deep breath. I smile, but my mouth is dry.

"Hi, Benji."

His grin possesses none of the nervousness of my own rigid smile.

"Glad to see you haven't forgotten your special name for me," he says, holding out his arms to take some of the napkins from me. "Where do these go? I'll help you."

As he takes them from me, he squeezes my hand and meets my eyes again.

I can't find words to respond, surprised as I am to find him here tonight. He follows me to the dining room, where I hastily fold napkins and add them to the place settings. He follows suit, watching me, not saying much, until I can't take it anymore.

"When did you get back?" I ask.

"Yesterday. I ... It's ... been a while."

"Yeah, it has," I reply, mentally calculating that it's been one year and four months since I've seen him.

Just then my brother walks in. "Ben, hey, man. What a nice surprise," Aaron says, pulling him into a hug and glancing at me. Aaron didn't know?

"Hey, Gabbers," Aaron says to me when he's done. "Happy Hanukkah."

"Happy Hanukkah, Aaron," I say, suspiciously.

"Everything okay?" he asks. Before I can reply, his phone pings with a text message, and he takes it out of his back pocket to check it. "Ah, it's my girl."

While Aaron's attention is elsewhere, Ben gestures with his head that he wants me to join him in the other room. I shake my head. He mouths the word, *please.*

Before he can press me further, my mom calls from the other room, "Let's *light the candles."*

It takes a few minutes for all the guests to gather in the living room, where she's placed the chanukiah, the special Chanukah menorah, on the windowsill.

"Let's see," she says, scanning the room. Her eyes land on Ben. "Would you do us the honor?"

"I'm not even sure I remember the blessings," he says.

"That's okay. Here," she says, holding out the matchbox and the shamash, the main candle that lights the others. "You can light, and Gabby can sing the blessings. I don't have many opportunities to hear my daughter's beautiful singing voice."

He looks at me in question. A bit embarrassed, I nod. Ben and I gather around the chanukiah, and my dad comes and clips a kippah on his unruly hair. I can't help but smile. He shrugs, and—ugh—he's adorable.

"I've always loved this menorah," he says, while my dad is still in earshot. It's a family heirloom, and his comment, while genuine, is also a joke. It's what my dad says every year when it's his turn to light it.

I smile. "Yeah, me, too."

Remnants of this morning's snow flurries speckle the ground outside the window. The moon is waning, barely visible at this point of the month, and I suddenly feel grateful to be inside my parents' warm home, surrounded by friends, family, and light. I recite the first blessing, and the others join in, but Ben and I are in our own world. He strikes the match and begins to sing the blessing, too. He must remember the words better than he thought. He touches the match to the main candle, and as he raises it with his left hand to light the first candle, he hesitates, then takes my hand and places it over the hand he's using to light it. We light the remaining two candles together. As he places the main candle in its holder on the chanukiah, melted wax drips onto my wrist.

We turn to face everyone, and my father leads us in a few traditional songs.

"Let's eat!" my mom says. I move to join the guests filing into the dining room, but Ben grabs my wrist and rubs his thumb over the drop of wax that has hardened.

He turns me to face him. "Gabby?"

"Yes?"

He presses his lips together, seeming uncertain about what to say or do next. "I …"

"What?" I bite my lip and stare at his. God, if this were a year ago, he'd already have me pushed up against the foyer wall, his hands up my shirt, my tongue in his mouth—all just out of sight of my mother's guests.

He shakes his head. "Nothing. I … haven't given you a hug yet."

He pulls me into him, and I relax into his familiar arms, wishing we could go back in time to last summer, to other summers past, and try again.

He tips my chin up. "Should we join everyone for dinner?"

Brought back to the present, I reply, "Of course. Cold latkes are disgusting."

When we come into the dining room, decorated in blue and silver for the holiday, there are only two seats left. And of course, they're right next to one another.

Aaron is sitting to my left, and Ben is on my right, and since they are catching up, Ben is turned toward me the entire meal. At one point, I ask, "Would you like to trade spots with me, so you can talk to Aaron?"

"No, I also want to talk to you," he says where only I can hear.

Aaron, now distracted by my Uncle Jacob, who is grilling him on the federal interest rate, turns away from us.

Ben uses the opportunity to lean in and whisper in my ear. "You look … so beautiful tonight. I-I wanted to call you, especially lately, but—"

My dad brings out sufganiyot, and everyone cheers. His fried Hanukkah doughnuts—filled with jelly, Nutella, or dulce de leche—are famous in our community.

When the platter reaches me, I ask Ben, "Nutella still your favorite?"

"You remembered?"

"Growing up, you ate at least fifty of these at our house," I say.

"I'll pass tonight."

"Awww, that's no fun," I tease, plucking a raspberry jelly doughnut off the platter and passing it on.

"Who would choose undefined red jelly over Nutella?" he asks, pulling a face.

"Anyone with a brain and good taste. It's the best."

I take a bite, right in his face, and jelly unexpectedly sprays out and covers my mouth. "Oh my God," I say with my mouth full.

He laughs as I attempt to wield the quickly disintegrating doughnut with a mouth full of jelly and try to find a napkin. He quickly grabs a plate and holds it under my mouth and I set the sticky mess on it. I grab my napkin and wipe my mouth.

"All good?" I ask, looking at him.

He raises an eyebrow and reaches his left pointer finger out to wipe a smudge of jelly from the corner of my mouth. "You missed a spot."

I expect him to simply wipe his finger on his napkin, but instead, he glances around, and noting that nobody is even paying attention to us, he says, "I should probably try raspberry at some point in my life, huh?" He licks the jelly off his finger, and I'm hypnotized. In an instant, I'm back in my apartment, the neighborhood park, the beach, and every other place we had sex two summers ago. I'm staring at his mouth so it takes me a moment to realize that he's staring at mine, too.

If there weren't twelve other people here, I'd lean in and kiss him this inst—

"Earth to Gabby," Aaron says.

"Huh?" I say as I snap back to reality.

"What happened to you? You have jelly all over your skirt."

I look down. "Oh, yeah. Um, I should go clean myself up."

Never one to miss a laundry emergency, my mom informs me that there are some special wipes in the laundry room, so I push my chair back and head upstairs.

Once I'm up there, I find my mother's wonder wipes in the cabinet and walk to the bathroom to wash my hands. I feel like splashing water on my face—something, anything to cool me down and help me reset—but it would mess up my makeup. Instead, I turn off the vanity light and lean against the counter, taking some deep breaths.

What is he doing here? Why am I so bothered? I have to pull myself together.

I open the door to leave, but a large, strong body pushes me back inside.

"Stay here," he says, gruffly, pressing me up against the vanity and pinning me there with his hips.

"What are you doing?"

"You know what I'm doing," Ben says, and he pulls me close.

I could melt up against his hard body. He's always been fit, but fuck, this is next level. He leans down and kisses my neck.

"Oh," I exhale.

"What is it about you?" he says in a low voice filled with desire.

"What do you mean?" *I wrap my arms around his trim waist and curl them up to caress his strong shoulders.*

"You're like a drug," he whispers. "An addiction. I've been here an hour and all I can think about is ..."

"What?"

He leans in and whispers in my ear, "Fucking you." *He buries his face in my neck and runs his hands through my hair, and I do the same.*

"When did you let this ridiculous hair grow out?" I tease.

"You don't like it?" he asks, sounding fake-hurt.

But I can't lie. It's gorgeous and smells amazing. "I love it."

"So run your hands through it—"

"I am—"

"—While I go down on you."

Sounds like a dream. But my family is downstairs. His family is downstairs. It's a Jewish holiday about the rededication of the second temple for God's sake. Gabby, don't do this.

"Alright, let's do this," I say. Weak. *You never would've made it as a Maccabee.*

He kisses down my body, and I stupidly blurt out, "I, uh, bought you a scarf?"

He laughs softly as he continues his way down. "Why don't you wrap your legs around my neck instead?"

And I agree. It's a fine idea to keep us both warm on this wintry evening.

That's all it took, huh? An overfilled glass of wine and seeing a hot guy lick jelly off his finger to be convinced into spreading my legs for …

"Ohhhhh, oh, God. I'm gonna come," I moan out.

"Yessss. I've missed hearing you lose it."

"Oh, Ben, yes …"

He slides one hand up and palms my breast. "Fuck, Gabby, come for me."

"Oh, ohhhhh, yessssss," I say as I orgasm.

I can barely hold myself up, and he slides up my body to support me with his strong arms, wrapped around my back. His chest and hips are pressed up against mine. *He's hard.*

"You set me on fire," he whispers huskily in my ear. "Can I … Can we…?"

His question trails off, but his hands pull my hips into him, as he places one leg between mine to finish the sentence.

There is so much wrong with this situation. The distance. The fact that I have no idea if he'll even be here next week. The fact that he left me. The fact that I haven't seen him for almost a year and a half. It's wrong. So wrong.

Yet.

I raise one leg and wrap it around his hips, and my skirt slides up my thigh. He starts to unbuckle his belt. And then, a knock on the door.

"Gaaaabby," my mom calls. He raises his eyebrows, and we grin maniacally at each other, trying not to laugh.

I exhale, trying to calm myself. "Yeah, Ima."

"Are you okay, dear?"

"I'm okay. I'll come in a second."

"Too late for that," he whispers softly in my ear, and I pinch his side to indicate he should shut up.

"Just … um … washing my hands." Ben, in a better position to turn on the faucet, reaches out and turns on the water. Then, naughty as all hell, he slips my shirt off one shoulder and begins to suck on my nipple through my lace bra.

"Well, some of the guests are leaving, so come down and say goodbye. Tzipi wants to leave, but she can't find Ben. He's not answering his phone."

Just then, there is a vibration from his pants, and honestly, it's in an excellent location, not far from where Ben recently finished some other activities.

"I'll be out in a few."

But she continues. "I thought maybe those latkes hurt your stomach. I told Aba not to add chia seeds to the recipe, but he insisted on—"

"Enough, Mom," I say, which is what I call her when others are around, and I'm losing my patience. I reach out now and close the faucet.

She mumbles, and her footsteps pad away. I lower my leg. I guess things won't proceed as planned, or more accurately, unplanned.

The moment—the mood—has shifted. A drawn-out conversation with your mother about Jewish holiday food digestive issues tends to do that.

But I can't let him go, not without saying something. "What was that?"

He buckles his belt and straightens my shirt, but before he removes his hand from me, he reaches up and touches my face.

"I don't know," he says. "When you're in the room, I lose my mind a little bit."

Same.

"You should go, I guess."

He nods, perfunctorily, and says, "You're right."

He opens the bathroom door a sliver and peeks out. "Coast is clear."

I touch his shoulder, and he looks back at me. "When do you leave?"

"I have a flight back in five days," he says.

Of course.

He was always good at leaving and not looking back, so I push past him, walk down the hallway, and do the same. *Don't look back.*

I say a quick "goodbye" to my parents downstairs. "I'm gonna drive back to the city."

"So soon?" my mom asks.

"I'm tired, Ima."

She narrows her eyes at me and then looks out the window. "It's snowing now. You could stay here and drive back in the morning."

I don't want to. My place is as full of memories with Ben as this house, but at least *he's* not there. In Brooklyn, I'm far away from him. I need the distance and the time to think.

"I'll text you when I get back," I say, kissing her on the cheek and then hugging my dad, whose brow is furrowed in concern.

I grab my coat and stride toward the front door as Ben comes down the stairs. Our eyes meet. He opens his mouth to say something, but I turn and walk out the door. I'm done. With tonight and definitely with Benjamin Adler.

Twelve Years Earlier

Ancient Jewish History

Gabby

I'm about to head upstairs with my second mug of hot cocoa when I hear my mom tell my dad in a quiet voice, "Tzipi says that she and Jonathan have drifted apart over the last few years."

We had been discussing why I came home early from the high school basketball game tonight, where Aaron and Ben must still be, so Ben must have been top of mind for her.

I stall at the foot of the stairs, curious to hear more.

"It's a shame, but there's not much we can do," my dad replies.

"Well," she says, "at least the time Ben spends here gives him a break from hearing them bicker."

"He's here all the time. They argue that much?" my dad jokes.

After a short pause, my mom says, "Maybe not that much. He just likes being here, I think. Tzipi said it's been more tense the past six months or so."

"What do you think is the problem?"

"I think Jonathan has very high expectations of himself, and she said he always seems annoyed with her. He puts too much pressure on the kids, too."

Jonathan, Ben's dad, has always struck me as a serious guy.

My mom continues. "The girls are already gone, but Ben's still there. And he's ... well, you've seen him. He's a sensitive soul. Not built for confrontation."

They're quiet. *Do they know I'm standing a few feet away eavesdropping?*

"Ben's tough," my dad says.

"You think so?" my mom asks.

"I know so. He can be quiet, but I can imagine that boy in ten years. He's coming into himself, and he's gonna be one hell of a man."

"You might be right," my mom says.

I wonder what they mean, but I've already pushed my luck sticking around as long as I have, and I continue up the stairs, avoiding the squeaky top step.

As I close my bedroom door, I hear my dad say, "Marci, you know that I love you, right?"

"I know you do, Marc. I love you, too," she replies. I smile at the sweet reminder that my parents' names are so similar.

It's almost midnight when Aaron and Ben come home after a basketball game and, I assume, the after-party. Since my escape upstairs earlier, I've been playing around on my bootlegged version of Photoshop. My love of art—encouraged by none other than Ben's mother, my art teacher in elementary school—has grown throughout the years, but my dad insists that if I'm considering a more creative route, then I at least have to learn how to use technology.

In middle school, I was in a Girls Who Code club, so the idea of creating art and designs and then learning how to build them on a webpage or create animations intrigues me.

Outside my door, Aaron tells Ben he's going to take a shower. "You can hang out in the living room if you want or grab some food from the kitchen."

"Cool," Ben says. Someone heads down the stairs, hitting the squeaky board, but then footsteps come nearer my closed door and there's a light knock.

"Gabby?" Ben says softly outside my door. "Are you awake?"

I'm sitting at my desk in a Pokémon onesie pajama set my friend Leah gave me as a joke for my fourteenth birthday, and I quickly pull the robe from the hook on the back of the door and throw it over my pajamas.

"Ben?" I say, sticking only my head out the door.

He tilts his head. "Hey." He's wearing a burgundy hoodie with our school logo, and even with the dim light in the hallway, it makes his hazel eyes look greener.

"I'm awake. What's up?" I ask.

"I saw your light on under your door. What are you doing?"

I crinkle my brow at him. *Why does he care?*

"Just messing around with some art thing on my computer."

"Can I see?"

"Um, it's just stupid stuff I'm working on," I say shyly.

"Please?"

"Fine," I say, opening the door more and letting him in.

I sit down on my bed as he takes a seat at the computer.

"Why'd you leave the game earlier?" he asks, turning to me.

He saw me?

"Oh, my friends didn't show up, and I didn't want to be there alone."

"I would've sat with you," he says.

Really? But I don't say it aloud. "So did you guys have fun at your ... party?" I ask instead. I fake disinterest, pulling a face as I say the last word, in an attempt to hide my curiosity. I desperately want to be a part of that older high schooler world, but I'm still relegated to the realm of the lowly freshmen. I'm never invited to *actual* parties, only my friends' sleepovers.

"It was ... whatever. Aaron wanted to go to see if some girl he likes would be there, but she wasn't."

"Who *was* there?"

"Nobody important," he says, then glances back at the computer monitor where some of my mocks are still displayed. "So show me your stuff."

I lean closer to click into one of my folders, some projects I've been working on recently, and become aware of how close I am to him, how sweaty and nervous I am. *It's just the fleece onesie and the robe,* I tell myself. Why would Ben make me nervous? He's been here a thousand times.

I open a few images for him to look at and quickly situate myself back on the bed, putting some space between us. He clicks around and leans in a few times, mostly silent. They're pretty good, at least for me, but watching him examine them so carefully is making my heart pound.

After what seems like an eternity, he turns to me. "G, these are amazing. I didn't know you knew how to do this stuff."

My face heats up now. Any minute, I'm going to burst into flames.

"I mean…" I stutter out. "I've been drawing for years, and—"

"I remember you winning all the art contests in middle school, and my mom said you had something special even when you were her student."

"Back in elementary art class?" I ask, thinking of the beginning art projects kids do.

"Even then. But this? This is something else. Modern. Super creative. It's like an ad campaign or something."

My breath catches in my throat and warms my insides all at once like I've taken a swallow of too-hot tea. I bite my lip, pleased with the compliment, almost forgetting that I'm sitting in my bathrobe. That reminds me that Aaron is in the shower, and he might come out soon. I glance at the door, and Ben catches my drift.

"Oh, his girl wasn't at the party, so he'll be in there a while," he said, a smirk on his face. "He probably has a few *things* to take care of."

My eyebrows raise, and he looks down, embarrassed. "Sorry, I shouldn't have said that to you."

"I have an older brother. I know what teenage boys do in the shower," I blurt out, pulling a puke face and regretting my words the second they leave my mouth.

He tries to hide his smile, but it breaks through. "I thought freshmen girls were innocent."

"We are," I say. "At least, I am."

He raises an eyebrow, skeptical.

"You just got home from an actual high school party," I say sweetly, "and I shared leftover pineapple pizza and hot cocoa with my parents earlier."

"But you hate pineapple on pizza," he says.

He remembered. "I do."

"At least you're comfy," he says. "I didn't get to wear *my* Pokémon onesie to the party."

He also has a Pokémon onesie? Wait, this is a trap.

"I'm not wearing a onesie," I spit out.

He narrows his eyes at me as if trying to see through my robe. "I see Pokémon upstairs," he says, pointing up around my neck area, "And Pokémon downstairs," pointing near my slipper-clad feet.

"Doesn't mean there's Pokémon in the middle."

"Show me then."

I shake my head and avoid his eye.

"Fine," he says, "but I know you're lying."

I am lying.

"So you guys have hot cocoa?" he asks, changing the subject.

"If I bring you some, can we pretend this conversation never happened?"

He smiles, looking younger, like the Ben I met five years ago, during his first sleepover with Aaron.

"Sure," he says, "but you also have to let me look at more of your art."

I hesitate. "There's some stuff I'm not ready to share yet."

"I promise I'll only look at what you want me to see."

I agree and go downstairs to make hot cocoa for him. When I return, I hand him the mug and he moves to the floor so he won't spill the cocoa on my new computer. I join him, and we both lean against my bookcase.

"How are things at home?" I ask, realizing too late that he might not want to share.

He glances down at the mug, then meets my eyes. "They are ... um, not great."

I have the sudden urge to reach out and touch his cheek to see if it's soft or rough. *It looks rough, but ... like something I'd enjoy.* I always notice textures. But beyond that, I have this weird thought that even through a small touch—a connection point—I can take some of the worry out of his expression.

He looks back into his cocoa, and I ball my hands into fists to curb my strange instinct. I don't know what to say, but *something* needs to be said. "Having parents that fight a lot … That must be hard to be around."

"Why do you think I'm always here?" he replies, and I notice out of the corner of my eye that he's looking at me.

I turn to him and deadpan, "It's not my brother's stellar personality?"

He smiles.

"So I don't really have any experience with marriage or fighting parents or any of that stuff, and I know you're Aaron's friend, not mine—"

"I'm not?" he asks.

"You are?" I shoot back.

"I mean, you made me hot cocoa. Isn't that something you do for your bestie?"

I laugh. "Well, usually when my besties hang out with me, we also do makeup and nails, so … " He sets his mug down on the floor and holds out his hands, waggling his fingers at me, presumably to show me his nails.

"Wow," I say, taking his hands in mine and examining his nails. Trimmed, clean. "You have nice hands."

"Is that a thing?"

"Nice hands is totally a thing. I know. I'm an artist, and it's one of the hardest things to draw. But … I'd love to draw your hands. They're smooth, but like, powerful. Must be from all that playing piano."

"You're kind of embarrassing me."

"Sorry," I say, blushing, and looking at the floor.

"I showed you mine. Now show me yours."

I snap my head up, mouth open. "Excuse me?"

"Your hands, Gabby."

Oh. Thank God.

"Or the full-on onesie you're hiding under that robe."

I offer him my hands, and he takes them in his own to look at them. "Your hands are also beautiful … like the rest of you."

Excuse me?

"I-I saw your lyrical ballet solo at the winter recital last week."

He saw me dance? My eyes flit to my open closet. The bottom edge of the most revealing dance costume I've ever worn, a burgundy number with carefully situated cutouts, peeks out at me. *Oh God. Ben saw me in that?*

"Your dance. You were …" He trails off, then starts again. "That song …"

"You know 'Creep?'" I ask, surprised. "It was a cover, actually. It's a song from the nineties I found online, and something about the lyrics really hit me."

"I looked it up afterwards," he says. "The way you danced, though …"

I swallow, thinking of the emotional movements, imagining Ben watching me perform them. "I didn't know you were there."

"I was," he says simply. He meets my eyes, then releases my hands abruptly, as if he's just realized something. He blinks, then refocuses. "Um, Liana asked me to come."

Right. Liana. Ben and Liana.

"Is she your girlfriend now?" I ask.

"Yeah."

That one-syllable admission brings me down a few notches. *I'm his best friend's little sister, wearing a dumb Pokémon onesie, and his girlfriend is the head of the dance team.*

The squeak of the bathtub faucet snaps me back to reality. Having spent so much time at my house, Ben knows as well as I do that it makes a noise when you shut it off.

He says softly, "Looks like our cocoa date is over, bestie."

"I guess you're right."

"Don't worry," he says. "I won't tell anyone that you secretly *do* like chocolate."

"Only hot cocoa," I say. "All other forms are—"

"Unimaginative," he says, completing my sentence.

I smile.

"Thanks for letting me dump my parents' shit on you."

"You didn't dump a lot."

"It was enough, though." He gets up, taking the mug with him and holding out a hand to help me up. I stand and promptly trip, setting my hand down directly on my trackpad, which clicks into another folder. My anime drawings.

Ben leans down to take a look at the well-endowed cartoon character, then looks back at me, eyebrows raised. "Did *you* draw that?"

"Yeah," I admit meekly.

"You are *really* good, G. Are you, um, into girls?"

I don't answer. I'm so embarrassed.

Ben rushes his words. "It's okay if you are. I mean, you should know I'm an ally."

"Huh?" I ask.

"My sister, Miri … she came out to our family. She's gay, and we're supportive of her."

I look at him, mouth parted, trying to understand how we got here. How I'm having a coming-out conversation, of all the conversations in the world, with Ben, my brother's best friend.

"Are you … gay?" he asks. His expression is so kind, so understanding, I kind of want to say "yes" just so I don't disappoint him.

I shake my head. "No, I just like … drawing women. I like …" *To imagine myself as sexy and as confident as the women I create.* But I will jump out my window before I admit something like that to Ben.

"You like what?" he asks.

Do I like you? Wait, what?

"Well, anyways," he says, letting me off the hook. "It's a beautiful drawing."

"Thanks," I say, my heart still pounding.

"I'm lucky to have such a talented bestie," he says with a grin.

I smile, and a trickle of sweat drips down my back. I'm going to need a shower after this conversation.

He steps outside my room, and as I'm about to shut the door after him, he peeks back in. "Thanks for the cocoa."

"That's what friends are for," I say.

"Besties," he corrects me.

"Besties," I repeat, trying it out.

"My mom said you're coming to light candles at our house on Tuesday night?"

"I am?" I ask.

"Your whole family, I mean."

"Then I guess I'll be there."

He sighs. "I still remember my first Hanukkah after we moved here. I lit candles with you and Aaron and your dad."

I roll my eyes and smile. "I remember, too. My dad was announcing the candle lighting like it was the WWE. He's such a dork."

"He's a good dad."

He's right. My dad's the best.

"Anyway," he says, "I'll leave you to your art." He turns to go.

"Ben?" I say quickly. I don't want him to go, not quite yet.

"What?"

"You wanna see something?" I whisper.

He tilts his head, obviously intrigued.

"Promise you won't tell anyone?" I ask.

At this, he raises his eyebrows and nods emphatically. I open my robe and flash him my Pokémon onesie.

"I knew it," he says, breaking into a broad smile. "You have good taste in jammies."

I cover my face and giggle.

"My lips are sealed," he says before slipping out and down the stairs, just as I hear my brother leave the bathroom.

Ben

I scroll through the photos on my phone without actually seeing them. It doesn't matter what's on the screen. It's a cover in case my parents leave the kitchen and catch me camped out on the stairs eavesdropping.

"I don't ... It's not working anymore, Tziporah," my father says in a defeated tone.

Silence, then a deep breath—my mother's. "That's certainly a diplomatic way to put it."

"What is that supposed to mean?" my father asks.

"Don't we owe each other honesty after twenty-five years of marriage?"

From my perch on the fourth step of the staircase, I can't see them. But I can imagine the stern—might I hope it's also sad?—look on my father's face. He's surely nodding his head thoughtfully, but also impatiently. Just the slightest indication of his disappointment that the people closest to him know quite well.

In a sudden, surprising burst of energy my mother erupts, "It hasn't been working for a decade, Jonny. But we've tried. We've tried, and … we've failed now. Haven't we?"

I expect my dad to respond in kind, with a raised voice, or at least frustration, but he surprises me. "I-I think we have," he replies in an uncharacteristically quiet, sad voice.

"So what does that mean?" my mom asks.

"I think it means that we begin to make arrangements. I'll start looking for a place …" he says.

Oh.

"And then we'll need to tell the kids."

One of us already knows.

I pull out my phone and text Ariella and Miri.

No further explanation needed. We've been texting for the last few months with increasing frequency. I'm the journalist on the ground, reporting news from the front to my sisters, already moved out and living their lives. I'm the one who has been stuck here, listening to my mom and dad fight for the last year.

Who am I kidding? It's been years.

I want to get out of here, go for a run, listen to some loud music, and drown out the words I've heard tonight—all the words, all the arguments.

I have a vague memory of my parents being happy once. *Weren't they?* I question my own memories. Were they still okay when we moved to Glen Rock five years ago? When did everything go downhill? Was it after my mom's surgery? I should ask Miri or, even better, Ariella, since she's the oldest. *Do I even want to know the answer? What will it help?*

I'm only seventeen years old, and I'm pretty sure that I never want to get married, not if what awaits me is this shit. There must be happy couples. I've seen them with my own eyes—people like my grandparents and the Feinmans, couples who don't seem to have any antagonism toward one another.

But can you truly know what goes on behind closed doors? And how in the hell are you supposed to know someone well enough to take that leap of faith and build an entire life with them? An entire life—a quarter of a century, a home, a family. Then, it's gone because of one person's selfishness. My dad's.

It's his fault. *It takes two to tango*, and all that, but my mom has always been the one to sacrifice, to give more. My mom's dreams went on hold, and she held down the fort at home, while my dad built not one but two different family medicine practices. Who wants a career that doesn't allow you to be with the people you love? Is that what Miri's choosing? Surely, there are doctors who see their families, who stick around. So, then, my dad is the problem. High standards for himself and every fucking person around him.

I head back downstairs quietly and look out the front window. My dad's car is gone. My mom must be in her room. I'll give her some time to decompress and check on her when I get back.

I head out the door, and I put on a playlist by Portugal. The Man as I begin my run. I was hoping for a reprieve from thinking, but the slow beat and melancholy words of the song quickly drag me back to thoughts of my parents, my dad specifically, and then ... to myself. *Will I be selfish like him one day? Is it in my DNA?* But my mom's blood also flows through my veins, and she's always told me that I have a heart of gold.

As I round the block, I pass the Feinman home. Gabby's light is on, and I remember the night we sat on her bedroom floor and talked about my parents. The look in her eyes that night … her sadness, for me. A deep well of compassion. I wish I could talk to her now.

No, it would be weird. What am I going to do? Knock on the door and tell her mom, "I need to look into your daughter's eyes?" I sprint past their house and run for another thirty minutes until I've worn myself out.

I end up at the neighborhood park and sit, sweating and exhausted on the bench, elbows on my knees and looking down at the ground. My head is hanging between my knees, and I feel the muscles in the back of my neck release. *Deep breath, man.*

"Are you alright?" a high but pleasant voice calls out.

Gabby?

I look up. It *is* her, and she's with a friend. Leah, I think. I've seen them together at school, usually after third period when I'm on my way from the gym to lunch. Once I stopped to pass on a message from Aaron that Gabby needed to ask her dad to pick her up from school and her friend had looked star-struck.

I try to smile at her now. "Yeah. What's up?"

She takes me in and turns to her friend. "Is it okay if I text you later?"

"Sure," her friend says with a knowing smile. *Does she think Gabby's trying to flirt with me?* Then she turns and walks away, and Gabby comes to sit next to me.

"Hey," I say.

"Hey," she says, then reaches out to touch my shoulder. *Ugh, I'm so sweaty and gross right now.*

I let out a long exhale, and put my hand over hers, while I stare at the ground. She scoots closer, and I glance at her.

"You're not okay," she says. A statement, not a question.

I shake my head. "No, not really."

"Your parents?"

I nod. I should go home, take a hot shower, crawl into bed, and deal with my feelings in the morning. I can't talk to Gabby, to anybody, now.

"Why don't we go for a walk?" she suggests.

Yeah, I can do that.

We don't say much, just walk. Here and there, she tells me a story from school or describes an art project she's working on. "Oh, I'm going to take Computer Science next year."

"Isn't that a junior class?" I ask.

"I guess so, but my math teacher says I can handle it."

"You can definitely handle it," I reassure her.

We walk until her mom texts her checking when she'll be home, and she looks up at me, asking a question without saying a word.

"Go, I'll be fine," I say.

"You sure?"

"Yeah, I'll walk you home."

When we arrive at her house, she stops on the sidewalk and turns to me. She pulls me into an unexpected hug, and as I wrap my arms around her, she lays her head on my chest.

"I'm sorry your family's going through this," she says in a soft voice. "I'm sorry *you're* going through this, Benji."

After all these years, she's still calling me that ridiculous nickname, and despite the terrible mood I'm in, I can't help but smile.

She leans back and slides her hands down my arms. "You're strong, though, and on the days you're not, that's okay, too. You know we're always here for you. Me, Aaron, all of us."

Her deep brown eyes, looking straight into mine, calm my pounding heart, but I can't ignore the jolt of electricity running up my arms from her thumbs tracing back and forth on my forearms.

I squeeze my eyes shut for a second, attempting a hard reset of my feelings. When I open them, she's still looking at me with a soft, patient smile on her face.

"Thanks for walking with me," I say.

"Next time, just ask. Don't wait for me to come find you."

"You saw me through the window earlier?"

She nods.

I squeeze her hand. "I'm glad you found me."

Gabby

"So you've been pulled into Aaron's big date, too?" Ben whispers to me. We've both been relegated to the backseat since Aaron's date, Hannah, gets the place of honor in the front.

"Yep," I reply, rolling my eyes. *But I don't really mind.* I was starting to get bored at home this summer and a day at Six Flags sounds fun.

"Nice pigtails," he says, tweaking one with his finger before leaning back to his side.

"Nice Jew-fro," I retort.

"This is my summer hair before we go back to school and my mom makes me cut it."

"Keep growing it out and I'll be able to give *you* pigtails," I tease.

We pick up Hannah, and I mostly ignore the conversation in the car on the hour-long drive. After scrolling social media, I open the Kindle app on my phone.

"Whatcha reading?" Ben asks.

"Oh, it's called *The Deal*."

"Is it about business or something?"

It is so not about business. It's about a girl tutoring a hockey player and them having lots and lots of sex.

"It's about … tutoring," I say, hoping that sounds boring enough he won't ask anything else.

"Tutoring? My mom keeps pushing me to do some tutoring this year, so I can put it on my college application. Can I see?" he asks, holding his hand out.

"Uhhhhh."

He furrows his brows at me, and when I don't respond, he leans in and whispers in my ear, "Is it *really* about tutoring?"

"And other things," I squeak.

His eyes light up, and he whispers again, "Is this kinda like your anime drawings?"

"Uhhhhh."

He snickers and says in a low voice, "Are they kissing or something?"

They are definitely *kissing.*

"Let me see," he urges.

I try to swipe a few pages forward without him noticing, hoping the specific steamy scene I left off at last night will be over, before handing him the phone.

He grabs the phone and looks like he's won a prize. I look over his shoulder and see the word *cock. Oh no.*

"Damn, girl."

I shoot him a murderous look.

"What?" Aaron asks from the front seat.

Ben looks at me out of the side of his eye. "Oh, uh, Gabby's reading something ... really good." The smile plastered on his face is so tight, his jaw muscle is ticking.

"What is it, Gabs?" Aaron asks.

"Emily Dickinson poems," Ben answers without missing a beat.

I shrug, indicating that I don't know any of her poems.

"You like Emily Dickinson, dude?" Aaron asks Ben, giving him a look in the rearview mirror.

"I like ... romantic stuff."

"What? Are you memorizing romantic poems to impress girls?" Aaron teases.

Hannah laughs. I raise an eyebrow at Ben and smirk, and he shoots me a warning look. *You're at my mercy,* his look seems to say.

"I heard you've been talking to Aliza," Hannah says, turning to speak to him. "You should invite her to Ari's party next week."

"Uh, yeah," Ben replies.

"Why didn't you tell him to invite her today, Aaron?" Hannah asks.

Aaron glances at me via the rearview mirror, and I know I'm supposed to keep my mouth shut. It might ruin his chances with Hannah if I were to blurt out that our mom made him bring *me.*

Ben jumps in to save him. "Aaron's a good big brother. He knew Gabby's been wanting to go to Six Flags, so he invited her. And me. He knows I love roller coasters."

You do? I mouth at him.

He responds by miming sticking his finger down his throat and fake-puking. I snicker. Ben offers me my phone back, open to the raunchy sex scene, and points at it, and then to the front seat where Aaron and Hannah are sitting.

Now it's my turn to pantomime puking, and we both crack up in silent snickers.

He looks down at my phone and begins to read again. I snatch it back. "Get your own copy."

The first couple of hours at the park, we watch—or try *not* to watch—Aaron and Hannah make out in line for the rides. Around lunchtime, I blurt out, "I can't do this anymore," and walk off.

Ben jogs to catch up with me. "I'm with you. You think I want to watch those two all day?"

I laugh.

"So what do you want to ride?" he asks, nervously looking up at the rollercoaster roaring over our heads and squinting his eyes against the bright midday sun.

"Carousel?" I suggest.

"You're not just suggesting that for me, are you?" he asks. The uneasy look on his face is adorable.

"Well ..." I hesitate because I don't want to embarrass him. "I like the carousel. It reminds me of when I was little."

He shoots me a grateful smile. "Let's do it," he says, pulling me toward it. "You think they let guys my size on there?"

The person running it is a teenage girl, so a guy as good-looking as Ben will surely be able to talk her into it. She lets us both on, but I nab the last horse.

"I'll get off and wait for you," he says, as I buckle the belt around my waist.

"Nooooo, stay," I say, touching his arm. "You can make sure I don't fall off."

He looks at the belt around my waist. "Is that a risk?"

"It might've happened when I was seven."

He wraps one arm securely around my waist and grasps my thigh in a death grip with the other. "You're not going anywhere."

His warm hand rests high on my thigh, and despite the heat, goose-bumps rise on my skin. *Can he tell?* It's never been uncomfortable around Ben before, but ever since last winter, things have felt different between us. Sharing my art with him and him confiding in me about his family life opened a door to some interesting room in our friendship I didn't know existed. Accidentally revealing my secret love of smut in the car earlier today certainly hasn't helped matters.

Three minutes—that feel like an eternity—later, the ride ends, and we get off.

"Hungry?" he asks.

"I could go for a milkshake," I answer.

"For lunch?"

"For dessert before lunch," I say. "I'm going to wash my hands. Order for me?"

"I only know how to order chocolate," he teases, and I shoot him a playful warning look and head to the restroom.

After we settle at the picnic table with our food, I take a huge slurp of the strawberry milkshake he got for me, then smack my hand to my forehead as I get a brain freeze. "Ahhhh. It's good, but it hurrrrrts."

"You're such a wimp," he says, laughing, but then he reaches out a hand to rub his thumb across my forehead, and time stops for a moment. I squeeze my eyes shut to deal with the headache—but it's actually because his soft touch rattles me. Is he ... *flirting with me?*

When I open my eyes, he's about to take a bite of his hamburger. "Wait," I say, offering my milkshake to him. "Have some before you eat your hamburger."

"Why?" he asks.

"So you don't mix meat and milk."

"Nothing here is kosher," he says. "They literally serve bacon cheese-burgers."

"Still, I don't *mix* them," I say. "Why? Your family doesn't eat kosher at home?"

"We do, but *I* don't care."

"Do *you* eat cheeseburgers?" I ask, scandalized.

"I'm not right now, but ..."

"Do you believe in God, Ben?"

He widens his eyes at me. "If I'd known this was going to turn into a rabbinic school interview, I would've just gone on a rollercoaster."

I laugh. "Fine, don't tell me. But for the record, I *do* believe in God, but not the way he, or *it*, I guess, is described in the Bible. I believe in a much more open idea of God."

He sets his hamburger down. He still hasn't taken a bite. "Open?"

"Yeah? Like, some sort of force I'm not smart enough or omnipotent enough to explain."

"I don't believe in God," he admits.

"That's okay."

He narrows his eyes at me. "You don't think it's weird or ... bad?"

"You volunteer at Jewish Family Services, so I think that means you're a good person. And you're pretty smart, so if you've determined the concept of a divine doesn't make sense to you, then you probably have a good reason."

He blinks at me like he's trying to figure me out. "I prefer evidence-based ideas. That's why I like biology. You do experiments, and you get results. There's evidence for a hypothesis or there's not."

"Makes sense." I glance down at his burger. "You should eat that while it's still hot."

He looks at his hamburger and then back at me.

"Can I steal a french fry for my milkshake?" I ask.

"No stealing necessary."

"Ben the Atheist, you're the best," I say with a grin, then dip a fry into my milkshake and hold it out to him to take a bite. "Have one. It's yummy."

He glances side-to-side, maybe checking that nobody's watching, then leans forward and takes a bite. "That is g—"

"Yummy," I correct him.

He rolls his eyes but smiles. "Yummy."

I dip another one and feed it to him. This time, he leans in without hesitation and almost nips my fingers with his straight white teeth.

"So I have another question ..." I say.

"Are you gonna ask me what the meaning of life is? I mean, we did discuss my beliefs on God," he jokes.

"Nah, this is *much* more important."

He finally takes a bite of his hamburger and raises an eyebrow since his mouth is full.

"Have you ever kissed a girl?" I ask.

He swallows. "Uh, yeah."

I could've assumed as much. I know he's had girlfriends, but I had to start somewhere.

"Have you, like, done more?" I ask, taking my questioning up a notch.

He nods, uncomfortably.

"Like ...?" I take a french fry and move it back and forth, in and out of the circle I've formed with my thumb and forefinger.

He pins my hand to the table and mouths at me, *Stop.*

While I crack up, he yell-whispers, "Why are you asking me all these questions?"

"I'm on a fact-finding mission," I say. "One of my friends is considering doing, uh, *more* with her boyfriend, and we just, I mean, *she* just needs to know if he'll expect to do everything at once, or..."

"It's not you, is it?" he asks.

"Me?" I ask, incredulous. "I've never even kissed anyone."

"Oh."

I glance away.

"I mean, that's okay," he says, tripping over his words. "You should only do that when you're ready. I mean, it's perfectly fine if you're not ... experienced. I just thought since ... you know ..."

"Since my french fry has the *mooooves*," I suggest, dancing in my seat.

He snorts. "And all the questions ..."

"I took sex ed, and I have the internet, dude."

"Right, so," he starts to say, "don't tell anybody this, but I ..."

"Haven't?" I whisper.

He shakes my head. "I mean, I've done ... other things."

I take a sip of my milkshake, give myself a moment to think, and lick my lips after. *Oh my God. He's staring at my lips.*

I glance away, but I need to know more.

"So you've ... ?" I ask, trying to get him to spill the details.

His eyes meet mine for a second, but he's not offering up any more information. Then my imagination kicks in. "Ohhhhh. Lucky you."

He stands abruptly. "I'm going to get some ice cream," he chokes out.

"But you didn't finish your burger," I call out. He doesn't turn, but I see him running his hands through his hair, his go-to move for when he's flustered.

The moment he returns, I smile at him sweetly.

"What?" he sighs dramatically. "I know you're gonna ask anyway."

I approach with caution. "So you like Aliza?"

"We've been hanging out," he admits.

"Girlfriend?" I ask.

"We're getting there."

"Have you kissed her?" I ask.

He's mid-lick of his chocolate ice cream and stops. "Yes."

Yeah, these senior girls have way more experience than I do.

He has a bit of ice cream on his lips, and I hand him a napkin. "You have some ..." I gesture with the napkin at his mouth. He wipes it.

"Ben?"

He looks at me. "Yeah?"

"Did you like it?" I ask hesitantly.

"Did I like what?" he asks.

"Kissing her."

He blushes momentarily. "You're killing me today."

"I can't ask Aaron this stuff," I reply. "And I don't have any older sisters and ... you're my bestie."

He exhales loudly. "I liked it, okay? She's pretty and ..."

"And what?"

"She's pretty. That's enough."

"I thought you were deeper than that," I answer dryly.

"Speaking of deep, G, how deep did that guy in your book put his—"

"Stop!" I yell.

"I'll stop if you stop," he teases.

"Fine," I relent. I play with the napkin on the table, folding it and re-folding it, and wonder how far Ben has gone with Aliza or with any other girl. "But do you think she liked kissing *you*?"

"Oh my God. Just drink your damn milkshake, Gabriella, and quit asking me embarrassing questions."

I get up and walk away, giggling. When I look back, he has a huge grin on his face and more ice cream on his lips.

On the drive home that night, we're all exhausted from the day, and things eventually fall quiet in the car. In the dark, safe confines of Aaron's ancient Honda Civic, it's the most natural thing in the world for me to lay my head on Ben's shoulder and for him to lean his head on my own. His scent—familiar, comfortable, warm—combined with the white noise of the drive over eighty miles of New Jersey highways lulls me into a light but comfortable sleep.

"Gabby," Ben whispers, "wake up."

"Huh?" I say, opening my eyes and finding that we've arrived home.

"Hey, guys," Aaron says to us, looking in the rearview mirror. *Wake up, Gabby. You're using Ben as a pillow.* I meet Aaron's eyes for a second and see a flicker of something I can't identify, but it passes when Hannah leans into him to kiss him on the cheek.

"Should I walk home?" she asks in a tone that's somehow simultaneously sweet but naughty. I take notes in my head.

"No way," Aaron answers, playing right into her hands. "I'll take you."

He turns around to face us in the backseat. "You two, out."

I swallow a snort and drag myself out of the car. Ben comes out my side, and he barely has a chance to shut the car door before Aaron peels off.

"Wonder what they're gonna do," I say, and Ben snickers.

He hands me my phone.

"Oh, thanks."

He looks at me seriously. "You know, I wasn't looking forward to today, but I had a lot of fun with you."

"I had fun, too," I say.

"I didn't know that you suck so bad at ski-ball," he teases.

"But I crushed 'Fancy' in karaoke, so it makes up for it."

"You do a surprisingly good Iggy Azalea impression," he admits.

An awkward beat passes, and he leans in to give me a quick hug.

"Good night," I say, wishing the hug had lasted longer. Leaning on him in the car had felt ... good.

"You going to sleep now?" he asks.

"I'll read some first," I say.

The corners of his mouth turn up. "Well, enjoy Emily Dickinson. I might have to check out more of her stuff."

I look down, trying to hide my smile.

"Night, Gabby," he says and starts to walk off when a sudden inspiration—recklessness—bubbles up in my stomach.

"Ben?"

He turns back and comes closer. I rise up on my tiptoes and kiss him on the cheek. "I bet the girls you've kissed ..." He narrows his eyes at me. " *Really* liked kissing you."

His mouth parts, but I turn and run up the steps to the front door without looking back.

"When I'm ready to go, I'm going, and if you're not ready or I can't find you, you're walking home," Rachel's sister, Amy, says. "Got it?"

"Got it," Rachel and I both reply.

We're on our way to our first real upper-classmen party. It's the party

Hannah mentioned a week ago on our trip to Six Flags. Little did I know, at the time, that I'd have the chance to go. Luck intervened with Rachel's parents going out of town for the weekend, so I'm spending the night there tonight, and we are *going*.

We spent two hours getting ready earlier. Amy even let us raid her closet, and Rach and I are both dressed in clothes my mother would never allow. I'm wearing a sequined halter top, tight jeans, and way too much makeup, a result of Rachel's motto for our upcoming sophomore year—something along the lines of "more boys" and "more eyeliner."

As we stroll in the front door of Ari Goldberg's house, there are people everywhere—sitting on couches in the expansive living room, dancing, out near the pool, some people even swimming. It's mayhem.

"This is so cool," I whisper in Rachel's ear.

She giggles. "I knowwwww."

We settle in to talk to some older girls I know from the dance team. A few minutes later, Aaron arrives with Hannah and a few of his friends in tow. His eyes widen when he sees me, but as per our "don't tell our parents about minor teenage transgressions" pact, he keeps on walking.

I get up to find something to drink, and some guys from the grade above call me over. A tall guy, with blond hair and a wide smile stands. "You're Aaron's little sister, right?"

I look up at him, overwhelmed by his height, and nod.

He holds out his hand. "I'm Sam. I'm on the swim team with him. I saw you at the meets last year and wondered who the pretty girl was."

Oh.

"Can I get you something to drink?" he asks.

"Uh, sure. Coke would be good," I say, and he winks at me before walking in the direction of the kitchen.

I sit on the edge of a couch and open up my phone to text Rachel. In the three minutes I've been gone, she has disappeared. When I look up, Ben is walking in the front door with Aliza. I happen to see Liana, one of several girls he dated last year, take note of it, too. Then a burst of giggles erupts from a group of girls near the staircase. *What is going on?*

I glance at Ben again. He's fist-bumping some guys near the front door and smiling at some senior girls who called his name. *Holy shit.* Being at this party is like walking through a portal to some fantasy world. I've been granted some rose-colored glasses I never had before, and man, do they make Ben look … really good. He's no longer the nerd I played video games with, the kid who once squirted orange juice out his nose at my family breakfast table while laughing, or even the bestie I peppered with embarrassing sex questions just last week. Looking at him now, confident and holding the hand of a pretty girl, I realize that Shy-and-Thoughtful Ben Adler has completed his transformation into The-Hottie-Every-Girl-Wants-to-Bone Ben Adler.

"It's like *The Princess Diaries*," I mutter.

"What?" Rachel asks from behind me, and I startle.

"You need a bell," I say.

"Oh, sorry," she says. "Anyway, looks like Mr. Hottie arrived."

"Who?" *Quit pretending, Gabby. You know who.*

"Ben."

"Oh, right. Like, the guy gets contacts and suddenly all the girls think he's super hot."

"He's *always* been super hot. It's not just the contacts. He's also been working out, for sure."

I think back to last week when I fell asleep on him in the back of Aaron's car. *Rachel would kill me if she knew that.* I guess he *was* pretty firm.

In any case, it doesn't matter who thinks Ben is hot because he's here with his girlfriend, Aliza, the beautiful blond girl holding his hand as he searches through the crowd.

His eyes fall on me, and he cocks his head. Our eyes meet, and he turns back to Aliza to whisper something in her ear. She kisses him on the cheek and walks out to the pool area, where a group of rising seniors greet her noisily.

Ben walks over, and Rachel elbows me. I shoot her a look, and she turns around quickly. He's wearing a pair of dark jeans and a button-down I've never seen before. The sleeves are rolled up, and—*geez*—his arms *are* pretty muscular.

"Hey, Lil G."

"Hi, Benji," I reply. If he can use my childhood nickname, I can use his. He smirks.

"New shirt?" I ask.

"Yes. Thanks for noticing."

He looks at me carefully, taking in my makeup maybe—perhaps a few other things with his quick glance at my outfit. "New shirt?"

"You like it?" I ask, trying my hand at the flirty tone I heard Hannah use with my brother.

He shoots me a smile that makes my heart pound. "I might get in trouble for answering that question."

Excuse me?

There's a playful—magnetic—look in his eyes. Is this the same guy I've known half my life?

I can't drag my gaze from his, and he leans in and whispers in my ear, "I didn't know you were old enough to come to senior parties."

My skin prickles as his breath dusts my neck. Garnering courage from I don't know where, I turn, pressing my cheek to his, to whisper back, "Maybe you haven't noticed ... but I'm not a kid anymore."

He laughs softly, amused, close to my ear. "I *definitely* noticed."

Before I can go into full meltdown mode, he leans back up and glances outside. I turn to look in that direction. Aliza is walking toward the sliding glass doors to come inside.

"Have fun tonight, *Gabriella*."

"You, too ... *Benji*."

Sam comes back and hands me a cup. Ben shoots Sam a suspicious look and turns back to whisper in my ear. "Be careful, alright? You're a ... pretty girl, and older guys are ... Well if you need anything, come find me."

I think he's done, but he turns back once more to take my cup.

"And don't take drinks from other people," he says. He walks away with the cup and tosses it out once he's outside.

Sam looks at me, and I say, "Sorry. He's my brother's best friend. He's a little protective of me."

Sam rolls his eyes. "I could tell."

Rachel starts a conversation with Sam, and it gives me the chance to watch Ben. He joins Aliza, who pulls him close, then giggles. As she guides him over to a group of their friends, he glances over his shoulder at me and shoots me a look that makes my skin feel hot.

This feeling has been creeping up on me for the past year, but I've been tamping it down, not ready to acknowledge it for what it is. That one look, though—Ben's hazel eyes framed by his thick lashes and the playful half-smile on his face—does me in. *That* is when I know for sure. Ben's not just my brother's best friend anymore. He's my first serious crush.

Ben

I'm sitting outside on a patio sofa with Aliza's tan legs draped over my lap, slowly but surely moving my hand up her thigh when I see Gabby come out to the backyard. She's looking around and then looking down at her phone. Looking up, she scans the yard and the forty people in it, and then back down at her phone again. The worried expression on her face calls me to action.

"Hey," I tell Aliza, who's having a conversation with her friend about her trip in June to Europe, "I need to get up, okay?"

"What's wrong?" she asks.

"Just need to check on something. I'll be right back."

Gabby's about to head back in when I come up behind her and touch her waist to get her attention. She turns.

"Everything okay?" I ask.

She looks at me with unsure eyes. "Not really. My friend is kind of acting like, well, I need some help. I think she needs to go home. I can't find her sister. And I tried to text Aaron and call him, but he's not answering."

"Should I come?"

She looks at me, then over to my group of friends. "You're hanging out with your friends," she says, with an uncomfortable look on her face.

"It's okay."

A relieved smile spreads across her face. "You sure?"

I nod. "Give me a second."

I leave Gabby near the back door and go tell Aliza what's going on.

"But I want you to stay. I thought we were gonna ... you know ... tonight," she whispers in my ear.

Yeah, I do know. I was planning on it being our first time having ... you know.

"I'm sorry, but I have to help her. She's like my little sister. I'll call you tomorrow, okay?"

I turn to head inside. Gabby has walked over during my conversation with Aliza. She looks all at once young and in need of help and more mature than her years.

"Ready?" I ask, taking her by the elbow and leading her inside, where we find her friend Rachel dancing with some drunk senior guys. She looks like she's having fun, but Gabby gives me a worried look. The last thing I want to do is get in a fight with these guys from school, so I lean in to whisper in Rachel's ear that I want to talk to her about something. She looks up at me like I'm a rockstar, and her lips get all pouty. I shoot a look at Gabby, like *Is there something you forgot to mention?* and she winks at me and motions with her head for us to get out of there.

We manage to get her friend out to the car, and I open the door to the front passenger seat.

"Wait, do you think she's gonna puke in here?" I ask.

"I don't know," she says. "This is my first time at a party like this."

"Alright, you sit in the back with her, and we'll keep the window open."

On the way, I keep my eye on both of them in the rearview mirror. Gabby looks like a put-upon mother—frustrated but accepting of her burden.

"You okay back there?" I ask her.

"Uh, no?"

I snicker. "You'll be okay."

When we arrive at Rachel's house, Gabby and I both take her upstairs to her bedroom. I shut the door while Gabby helps her get into bed, and I go downstairs and sit on the piano bench. Gabby told me that Rachel's parents were out of town, so I play something softly to pass the time. I want to hang out for a few more minutes in case Gabby needs help.

There's a headphone connection on the piano, so I attach the set lying there and put them on. I begin playing the Kesha song I played in the talent show this year for a group of girls who needed accompaniment. I'm trying to remember a couple of the chords when Gabby comes up behind me and scares the shit out of me by touching my shoulder.

I take off the headphones and look at her. She's visibly worn out with sleepy eyes and a weary smile, but she's still … breathtaking. Her long, chestnut brown hair is falling over her bare shoulders, and I imagine what it would be like to run my fingers through it. I'd thought about it the whole drive home from Six Flags while she rested against me with it all braided into pigtails. I drag my eyes away from her hair and meet her eyes.

"Thanks for the help with Rachel," she says, sitting down next to me. "Sorry I didn't tell you she has a crush on you. But it did help get her out of there."

"It's okay," I reply. "She's a nice girl."

"Yeah," she says, her eyes drifting to the headphones in my hands. "Can I listen? While you play?"

"Uh, sure," I say. "But I won't be able to hear, so I'm not sure how it will sound."

"Just do your best," she says to reassure me.

I need to touch that silky hair of hers, so I move her hair away from her eyes before placing the headphones on her head. The smile she graces me with makes my stomach flip.

I go back to the song, "Die Young," I was playing before. After a few measures, I realize this might not have been the best choice. I'm not singing the lyrics, but she surely knows them, and all the talk about throwing caution to the wind and an undeniable attraction … I don't know why I'm playing with fire tonight, but having her close, sitting with our thighs touching on the small piano bench, is giving me all kinds of thoughts. Thoughts I shouldn't be having.

But last week—her reading that spicy romance novel, asking me about kissing, and then falling asleep half on top of me has done something to our friendship. It has planted the seeds of something else. I'd set out this evening, excited about taking Aliza out and seeing where the night led, but it seems to have led me elsewhere. And I'm not disappointed in the least.

I try to concentrate on the music, but not hearing what I know my hands are producing is jarring. I can see out of the corner of my eye that Gabby is watching my hands, but then she closes her eyes when I arrive at the chorus for the second time. She begins to hum, and I watch her face. Her mouth is pursed the slightest bit while she hums.

How would it feel to kiss her cute, bow-shaped lips? I bet her lip gloss tastes like strawberries. I lose focus, making a small mistake, and then she opens her eyes and finds me looking at her. I stop playing.

Her lips curl up in a small smile. "What happened?"

"Your voice distracted me," I say. "You, uh, made me a little nervous."

She takes the headphones off and turns toward me with a naughty little grin on her face. "Why would your 'little sister' make you nervous?"

So she heard what I said to Aliza.

She leans into me and bumps my knee with hers. "And here I thought we were just besties."

"Um ..."

"Sorry I ruined your date tonight," she says, but the twitch of her eyebrow makes me doubt the sincerity of her apology.

Am I sorry that I'm sitting next to her instead of Aliza? No, not at all. Maybe it's the late hour, or the dark, quiet house—after hours of noise—but something is brewing between us, and Gabby is the cute little witch stirring the cauldron.

"I just—" I start to say, but I don't know *what* to say. Do I lie and tell her that, of course, she's like a little sister to me? Or do I admit the feelings I've started to have for her since seeing her in that stupid Pokémon onesie and touching her last week on top of that damn carousel horse?

Her striking brown eyes laser-focus on me, and I blurt out, without thinking, "I just said that so she'd understand why I needed to go. I don't think about you like a sister." *To say the least.*

"So how *do* you think about me?" she asks.

I try to buy some time, but instead of playing it cool—or even looking away or down at my hands—I do the worst possible thing I can, which is stare at her mouth, curled into a pleased grin, and then let my eyes rake down her body. Her eyebrows go up, and her smile widens.

Shit.

"Aaron would murder me," I say. I stand and walk toward the front door before she has a chance to ask me what exactly Aaron might murder me for.

On the drive home, I berate myself for my stupidity. *Did I do the right thing?* It was cowardly, but self-preservation is an important skill in life. Aaron *would* murder me. He's a calm, fun-loving guy, but I have no doubt he would tear me limb from limb for starting something with Gabby.

We'd overheard a couple of senior guys talking about the cute freshman girls this year, and Aaron had commented to me that they were lucky he hadn't heard Gabby's name on their lips. That was enough of a hint to me about how he felt about older guys trying to date his little sister.

I shouldn't have said that Aaron would be upset with me regarding my feelings for her. I might as well have told her straight out, "Hey G, you've gotten kinda hot recently, and I've noticed."

When I get home, I check my phone.

Aliza

> **Everything ok? Hang out tomorrow?**

I was hoping it was Gabby texting me, but then I remember that somehow we've never exchanged numbers. I text Aliza back.

Me

> **Tomorrow's good. Just got home.**

Aliza

> **Freshman girls are so dramatic, huh?**

Me

> **Yeah, they are.**

And pretty and smart and kind-hearted and ... just the right amount of naughty.

Almost spilling to Gabby that she's changed categories in my head from "childhood friend" to "girl I want to kiss" wasn't what I'd set out to do tonight. With everything falling apart at home, I need Aaron as my friend, but I also clearly need some time and space away from Gabby. *Good luck,* I think. *You spend half your waking hours at their house.*

Between swim practice, trying to keep my grades up, and college applications, I barely have time to sleep senior year, let alone think about girls, which isn't to say that I didn't make the most of the last few weeks of summer with Aliza. Time I might have spent with Aaron was taken up by "quality time" at Aliza's, and I've barely seen Gabby for longer than a few minutes at a time since the night of Ari's party.

This fall, like always, she has attended all our swim meets, and when I glance up in the stands and see her there, it pains me to know that she's only there to cheer on Aaron or maybe even Sam, who she's been hanging out with more.

It's a brutally cold, rainy day at the beginning of December, and I'm just getting home after swim practice. All I want is a hot shower and some warm clothes, but the Jewish mothers of the world have other plans in store for me this evening. As soon as I walk in the door, my mom informs me Marci told her Gabby's having trouble in biology class.

"I told Marci you'll tutor Gabby. Here's a sandwich for the road. When you come back, I'll have some hot soup ready for you," she says, taking my gym bag from my shoulder.

"Uh, okay?"

She kisses me on the cheek and pushes me right back out the door I came in two minutes ago.

I walk over there in the freezing rain, hoodie on, sandwich in my pocket, thinking about what I'm going to say to Gabby when I get there. We haven't had a real conversation in months. Luckily, Mrs. Feinman answers the door, asking if I want something to eat.

"No, thanks. I'm okay," I say after extracting myself from a hug. My stomach is in knots thinking about sitting with Gabby for the next hour and talking about biology. I hope her class is studying the Krebs cycle or photosynthesis and not human anatomy. Staring at diagrams of naked people sitting next to Gabby is *not* going to help my situation.

"You sure, Benny? I have blueberry muffins. You're *usually* hungry."

Got me. I've been eating her out of house and home, alongside her son, for the past six years.

"Okay, sure," I relent. I can't say "no" to Mrs. Feinman's decadent baked goods. She's a social worker by profession, but she must have been a baker in her last life.

She pulls me into the kitchen where she hands me a plate of muffins after pouring me a glass of milk. "You take those right up and share with Gabby. She's in her room, waiting for you."

How did I get myself into this?

"I told her if she didn't get an A on the next test, we'd have to reconsider all the extra time she spends at the art studio."

No. Gabby loves her time at the studio.

"I'm sure she'll be fine," I say. "She's a smart girl."

And she is smart. She's already in Computer Science I her sophomore year, a class usually reserved for juniors and seniors. *How does she have a low grade in biology?*

I head upstairs, trying to figure out how I'm going to knock on the door with a plate of muffins and a glass in my hands, but before I have a chance to attempt it, she opens the door.

"Hey, Professor. Where are your glasses?"

I smile. "I had my contacts in for swim practice earlier."

"I miss seeing you with glasses," she says. "But I suppose we'll have to proceed without them."

"So what's the problem?" I ask, offering her a muffin.

She takes one and bites into it, and I try not to watch her lick the blueberry juice off her top lip, like the pervert I am. "Human anatomy," she replies.

Shit.

"Did you know there are 207 bones in the human body, Ben?"

"206," I correct her.

"Look at you, teaching me already," she says, taking the plate from me and brushing some stray lint from my chest. Her hand lingers. "Have you been working out?"

"Gabby—"

"What? It's human anatomy," she says, smirking.

I sit down at her desk, where she's placed an extra chair. "Can you show me your notes from this semester? Maybe your last couple of tests?"

She bends over to dig her binder out of her backpack and hands it to me. I can feel her watching me as I flip through her detailed and copious notes.

"These look pretty thorough," I say. "They didn't help when it came time to study?"

"Oh, they helped," she says, scooting closer to me under the guise of looking over my shoulder at the binder. Her arm touches mine, and her chin almost rests on my shoulder.

"And your test scores?" I ask.

"They're okay."

"Then why am I here?"

She raises an eyebrow. "You've been avoiding me," she whispers in my ear. I take in her scent, and honestly, it's a good thing there's a binder on my lap.

I swallow. "Do you even need a tutor?"

"Maybe for ... certain subjects."

Please say "photosynthesis."

"Human anatomy *is* something I've been wanting to learn more about. I thought you'd be an excellent tutor for that subject."

I could be annoyed, but I have to give it to her. Only a high school sophomore and already a master manipulator. Also, it's more than a small compliment that she's concocted this ruse to get me over here, invited up to her bedroom by her unsuspecting mother no less.

I smile, despite myself. "And what exactly is your average in biology right now?"

She looks away.

"Gabby ..."

"Ninety-four. No, actually, ninety-six."

I meet her eyes. "And you told your mom you're having trouble because…"

"Because I knew Marci would tell Tzipi, and Tzipi would tell Ben to come over, and Ben …"

"Yeah?"

"Wouldn't be able to avoid me anymore," she says. She looks down.

"I haven't been avoiding you." I'm lying. What's even worse is that she knows I'm lying.

She looks up at me. "I thought we were … friends. Remember 'besties?'" The warmth, the depth of her dark brown eyes seeking mine makes my heart race.

"G, I just … I got a little … nervous after we talked that night at Rachel's. Things seem to have …"

"Changed?" she offers.

I nod. "Things between us have shifted."

"In a bad way?" she asks, full of innocence.

I shake my head. I need to breathe, but I can't do anything except look into her eyes. She takes the binder from me and sets it on the desk, then pulls me to sit on the bed next to her.

"I get it, okay? We've known each other forever, and you're Aaron's best friend. And you're a senior, and I'm a sophomore. But like I said, I'm not a kid. I get that it's different than it used to be. But …"

"Yeah?" I ask, interrupting her. She looks like she wants to kiss me.

I want to kiss her more.

"Don't avoid me. Please?" I take in her almost-pleading expression. "I really liked being your friend. It's … different than with all my other friends."

It is different.

I reach out to take her hand but stop myself. "I won't avoid you anymore. I-I'm sorry. I was stupid, okay? Here, give me your phone."

She hands it to me, and I type in my number. "What should I save it under? Ben? Benjamin E. Adler? Benji?"

She leans close to see what I'm typing into the phone, and her long, wavy hair brushes my hand. *Is she trying to drive me over the edge?* She snatches the phone back and holds it up for me to take a selfie. "Smile."

I look at her and smile, and she takes the picture.

"That's an awful picture," I say.

"No way. It's adorable." She starts to type in the name and save it.

"B(estie)?" I ask.

"B for Ben, Benji, *and* Bestie," she says and looks up at me through her long eyelashes.

My will is breaking. Sitting on her bed is already giving me associations it shouldn't, so I stand up. "Text me whenever you want, okay? Do I need to stay now, so your mom thinks I'm *actually* tutoring you?"

"You'd lie for me?" she asks, standing up near me.

"I'd do a lot of things for ... my bestie."

The list of things I want to do with her is swirling in my head, but I can barely form words at this point.

She mercifully throws me a lifeline. "Go. I'll tell her you're such an amazing tutor that we cleared things up from my last test in twenty minutes."

I walk to the door, and she holds up her phone. "I'll text you. But only about human anatomy, okay?" She winks.

"Don't be naughty," I warn her, but I do a poor job of hiding my smile. I can't when I'm around her. As I head down the stairs, her giggle reaches my ears.

In the spring, we celebrate the Passover holiday with the Feinmans, and things—at least outwardly—are exactly like they used to be. Gabby says "hi" to me in the hallways at school, and here and there, while I hang out with Aaron, I pop into her room like I used to. All in all, I see her almost as much as before my self-imposed hiatus from her.

One balmy May night, I'm heading out for a late run when I notice the light on in Gabby's room. I spent the last few hours filling out online forms with my mom for the summer session I'll be attending at Duke in a month, and when I thought about what I was going to miss most once I left New Jersey, Gabby kept floating up to the top of the list.

I slow to a walk and open my phone.

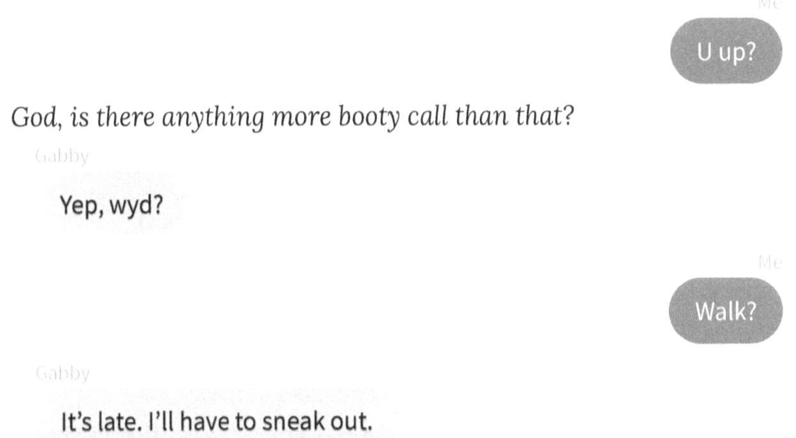

God, is there anything more booty call than that?

Before I can tell her not to worry about it, she writes me back.

I know which one she means because I've met Aaron at that side gate many times when *he* was sneaking out. The "secret" side gate at the Feinmans gets more traffic than Penn Station.

I wait near the gate, and it swings open slowly, creaking. I don't move, thinking she'll come out and join me, but instead, she pulls me inside the backyard. "I wanna show you something."

I follow her, and when we pass the kitchen window, I duck.

"Nobody's awake," she says, taking my hand and guiding me to the back corner of the yard. Her dad built a rose trellis a few years ago, and the roses on it are starting to bloom. She sniffs one and pulls me in to enjoy the scent, too.

"Don't they smell great?" she asks, looking up at me.

They do, but not as good as you. Freshly showered and in cute, pink pajamas, I want to dive into her arms and stay here in New Jersey forever. *Forget school. Forget everything.*

"Is this the surprise?" I ask.

"No," she says, pointing to the back corner of the yard, where a new hammock is hung. "Me and my dad installed it today. Wanna try?"

"Uh, sure," I say, walking closer and sitting down in it. "Wanna break it in with me?" *Shit. Did I seriously say that out loud?*

She giggles. "Okay, but lie the other way." She tugs my legs toward her. "Otherwise, I'll be on top of you."

Yeah, that would be just terrible.

I rotate my body, and she sits down carefully beside me.

"So what's up?" she asks.

"I'm … getting a little nervous about going away to school."

She sighs. "Who's gonna answer all my questions about life if you're not here?"

I smile. "But you're the one always dropping wisdom on me."

"But who will go on walks with me?" she asks softly.

Who, indeed? I glance away, and my mind jumps to earlier in the day. "I saw you flirting with Sam during lunch today." I'm not offering him up as a replacement. I'm digging for information. It's probably transparent as hell, but I don't care.

"I wasn't flirting," she says in a defensive tone. "Just talking."

She pouts her lips, and it lightens my mood enough that I switch to teasing her. "Talking while batting your eyelashes and flipping your hair over your shoulder?"

"I don't do that," she protests, shooting me that sassy little smirk of hers. I want to lean in and kiss it off her face, but instead, I meet her eye and she folds.

"Fine," she admits. "But he's a nice guy."

My body stiffens, hearing her call Sam a "nice guy." "No, he's not. He's an asshole."

"He's not an asshole to *me*. He's funny. And … cute."

Gross.

"And … I'd like to go to prom this year, even though I'm a sophomore. Not *everyone* has a mile-long line of people dying to go out with them, *Ben*. Some of us have to take what we can get."

She sits up, away from me, to get out of the hammock.

No. I don't want to fight with you.

I catch her arm and try to pull her back toward me, but she remains stiff, not giving in.

"Gabs," I say softly. "Quit talking nonsense."

"Nonsense?" she says, glaring back at me.

I squeeze her hand. "You're … You don't need to settle for any dumb guy with a crush on you. I'm sure there are a lot of quality … mature … *genuinely* nice guys who'd love to take you to prom."

"Like who?" she asks.

Like me.

She narrows her eyes at me. "Do *you* have a date for prom yet?"

Goosebumps pop up on my arms. *Here's my chance. Except Adina already asked me, and I said yes.*

I sigh. "Adina asked me yesterday."

"Oh," she says, not even trying to hide the disappointment in her voice.

Oh is right.

I touch her face, slide my hand down to her shoulder, and urge her to lean into me. This time she agrees.

We swing gently in the hammock for a few minutes, silent, and I close my eyes. *Why did I waste this year?* I could have spent so much more time with her, but soon, I'll be gone.

"When are you leaving again?" she asks, pulling me from my thoughts.

"A week after graduation."

"It's too soon," she says. She squeezes her eyes shut, turns on her side, and curls her body into me. I lift my arm and urge her to settle more comfortably into my side. *Is this the closest she's ever been?*

"I'll miss you," she whispers into my chest.

"I'll miss you, too," I say into the top of her head.

"What're you gonna miss about me?" she asks, looking up at me.

All the things I know about you and all the things I still don't. Everything.

"What?" she asks when my silence drags on too long. "You can't think of even one thing?"

Without even pausing to collect my thoughts, I say completely truthfully, "You make me laugh when I need it and sometimes when I don't even realize I need it. And you help me keep perspective about life. And I honestly don't know how you can be so wise when you're only fifteen—"

"Almost sixteen," she corrects me.

"Almost sixteen," I repeat. "I mean, I'm two years older than you, and I'm mostly confused about what I want and what I'm doing."

"I thought you were gonna say you'd miss teasing me about drawing cartoon characters' cleavage or how I walk too slowly since I'm shorter than you."

"You don't walk too slowly. I love the walks we go on together."

"Me, too," she admits. "And you're not confused. We're all just figuring things out as we go."

"You see? That's what I mean. Wisdom."

She smiles.

"What are you going to miss about me, G? The guy all the girls think is so cool, acting aloof to lure them in, but who's actually just painfully unsure of himself?"

"The guy who hates roller coasters and won't ever try strawberry ice cream even though it's the only flavor worth eating?" she asks.

I sniff out in amusement. "Yeah. What will you miss? Anything?"

She looks at me. "I'll miss everything about you." Her chest rises with her deep inhalation. "Everything."

She places her hand on my stomach and leans up suddenly. "I gotta go," she says. "Have a good night."

"Gabby," I call out, but she's already jogging to the back door and slips inside.

What was that? I wipe my hand down my face and sit up. I pull my phone from my pocket and type out a text.

Me

I'll miss everything about you, too.

But I don't have the courage to send it.

It's prom night, and I'm staring in the mirror in my bedroom when my mom comes in and clasps her hands to her chest.

"My baby," she says.

"Ima, please."

"Well, you are. What am I going to do when you go to college?" she says, bustling over to dust off my suit jacket.

"You have your work?" I offer, hoping to help.

"It'll be lonely here without you. Ever since the girls moved out, and your dad and I divorced, it's been you and me. I'll miss you."

"I'll miss you, too. But I'll be back on breaks. Don't worry."

"It's my job to worry," she replies, straightening the collar of my stiff dress shirt. "No tie?"

"No tie."

She presses her lips into a line, and I look down at her—older, wiser, and more experienced than me, but smaller and looking childlike in her workout clothes—and it suddenly dawns on me that I'm basically an adult now.

"When are you going to pick up Adina?" she asks.

I look at the clock on my nightstand. "I should go. I told Aaron I'll pick him up and then we'll go get our dates."

"It's a shame Gabby isn't going with you," she says, turning away to pick up a few stray articles of clothing, but I can see her amused—no, sneaky—expression in the mirror she happens to be facing.

"What does that mean?" I ask.

"With you and Aaron, I mean," she clarifies.

"With her brother?" I press.

"Ben," she says, rolling her eyes. "I mean that she could have been *your* date, but maybe it's for the best since you're leaving soon."

My mom has been hinting, not so subtly, for at least a year that Gabby is beautiful, smart, and talented and that I'm blind for not seeing it. I'm not blind. I know every single one of those things is true.

"I think she's going with some junior."

I know *exactly* who she's going with—Sam, the asshole. In fact, I had to restrain myself from punching him when I overheard him and his friends talking the other day between classes about getting laid on prom night.

She looks at me carefully, then replies, "Keep an eye out for her. I know her mother is worried about her going to prom with older kids."

"Sure," I say. Easy since I'm also worried about it.

"And send pictures? And please be careful. Don't drink and drive. Don't drink. But *if* you drink, stay put. And don't be stupid."

"You know me. I'm not stupid."

"I know," she replies, "but I have to say it. Have fun, *motek*."

I raise an eyebrow at her.

She lifts up on her tiptoes to kiss my cheek. "Don't give me that look. You'll always be my sweetheart."

I drive the thirty seconds down the street to Aaron's to pick him up, and I'm about to text him to come out to meet me when Mr. Feinman opens the front door and waves me in.

Inside, Aaron stands in front of his mother, who is tying his tie. The expression on his face says *This tie is coming off the second we leave*, but my look at Aaron is cut short when a flash of red catches my eye. I turn to see Gabby coming down the stairs.

Holy. Shit.

Her descent down the stairs is like witnessing an angel leaving heaven—well, maybe an angel on her way to do something naughty since she's wearing red. She is the single most beautiful person I have ever seen, wearing a red silk dress that looks like she was poured into it. Her feet are bare, and her black strappy heels are hooked over her fingers. Her smooth hair cascades down her back.

Wow.

"Benny," Mrs. Feinman says, grabbing my attention. "You look so handsome. No tie?"

"My mom said the same thing," I reply with a laugh.

Gabby sits on the bottom step and slips on her shoes. When she stands back up again, at least three inches taller, her mom turns her attention to her. "Oh, darling, you look beautiful. A little too ... mature. But beautiful."

Gabby smiles at her mom and kisses her, leaving a red lipstick kiss mark on her cheek.

Aaron runs upstairs for something, and Gabby turns to me. "You look really nice."

"You look ..." My words escape me.

"Horrendous? Awful? Terrible?"

I lean in and whisper, "Amazing. I wish you were *my* date tonight."

A pleased smile spreads across her face. Just then Aaron comes back downstairs, and their parents hustle us out to the front yard for pictures.

Since Aaron and I still haven't picked up our dates—and Sam hasn't arrived yet to pick up Gabby—it's just the three of us, and Marc takes all kinds of pictures in all combinations of individual and group possible. After a brother-sister picture, he tells Aaron to step out of the picture and for me to step in to take a picture with Gabby.

I stand next to her and place my hand on her bare lower back, suddenly noticing how low-cut the dress is. She leans into me, places her hand on my chest, and tilts her head up to whisper in my ear, "I wish you were my date tonight, too."

I smile down at her, right as her dad says, "Great pic. Good-looking kids."

After a huge group dinner at an Italian restaurant, we all end up at the prom. At the last minute, it was moved to our high school gym since the venue had some sort of electrical fire. It's not fancy, but nobody seems to care. I'm having fun dancing with Adina and hanging out with everyone, but I'm distracted. At least a few times tonight, Adina or other friends have called me out for not paying attention during the conversation. How can I pay attention to them when I'd rather be here with someone else? But that someone else is busy with her douchebag date. I suppose it's her business and her business only, but put simply, she's too fucking good for Sam.

I'm not the only one who is distracted, though. I catch her looking at me a few times throughout the night. Every time, I pull out my phone and send her a text.

> I must look amazing in a suit. You can't take your eyes off me, huh?
>
> *Me*

She checks her Apple watch and smiles. Then she holds up her hands like binoculars and peers at me.

The next time I catch her looking at me, I text her again.

> You're embarrassing yourself, G. Just because Sam is a troll doesn't mean you can stare at me the whole night.
>
> *Me*

She checks her watch, then laughs. I wish I were close enough to hear it.

While they announce the prom king and queen, I take advantage of the fact that everyone is focused on the stage and look at her, standing about ten feet away. She catches me this time and pulls out her phone from her small wrist bag to take a selfie. Pursing her lips, she looks adorable from my vantage point. Only when my pocket buzzes, do I realize she sent me the pic. I discreetly check the photo.

God, she's even cuter from this angle.

Sam leans in to tell her something, then walks away. Novice mistake. You never leave a date as beautiful as Gabby by herself.

"I'm gonna go to the restroom," Adina tells me and heads toward the exit with her friend.

I join Gabby. "Having fun?" I ask, leaning in so she can hear me over the loud music the DJ just put on for the dancing to start back up.

"So much fun," she says, rolling her eyes. "Not sure why I thought junior guys might be more mature than sophomore ones. How about you?"

"I'm okay."

"Just okay, huh?" she asks. "Adina looks pretty tonight."

"Yeah," I agree. "I still would've liked to take someone else."

"So she was the runner-up?"

I press my lips together and smile.

"Sounds like you need a better date," she adds.

"Well, neither of us can ditch our dates, but am I allowed to ask you to dance with me?"

"I think so."

"In that case, my sweet-and-snarky bestie, would you do me the honor of dancing with me?"

She clasps her hands over her heart and fake swoons. "Oh, Benji, dearest, I thought you'd never ask."

"Your Southern accent needs work, and you're a major dork," I say.

"Takes one to know one," she says, taking control and pulling me out on the dance floor.

As we sway to Ed Sheeran's "Thinking Out Loud," I hope my hands, resting on her waist, aren't sweating because the rest of my body feels like it's on fire. *Why am I nervous?*

Because she's closer than she's ever been. She's in a cute red dress and sexy heels. She's leaning in close to me, her arms wrapped around my neck, and yet, I want more. In case Aaron comes back, I keep my hands in an acceptable position on her hips—*oh man, I can feel the thong she's wearing underneath*—but what I want to do is pull her even closer and inhale her scent. What I'm dying to do is kiss her. She moves a lock of hair that has fallen into my eyes, and I fight the urge to catch her hand and kiss her fingers.

"You're wearing your contacts tonight," she says.

I nod. "Not everyone likes me in glasses as much as you do."

"They make you look like a sexy librarian. What could be better than a cute guy who likes to read? There's a whole Instagram handle for it."

I file that tidbit into my imaginary folder for "Things Gabby Likes."

"Isn't sexy librarian something people say about *women* with glasses?" I ask.

"That's kind of sexist," she remarks.

I hide a smile. *Always a feminist.*

"You look ... so beautiful tonight. This color suits you. It reminds me of ..." I trail off. I shouldn't mention the things it reminds me of.

"What?"

"It looks amazing on you."

"Ben, are you okay?" she asks. "You seem nervous." Her hands move down my chest to my waist, and I imagine them continuing even lower. "You're stiff."

Taking her words the wrong way—though to be fair, they're a relatively accurate description of the situation as it's developing on the ground—I cough out, "Excuse me?"

When she realizes I've interpreted her comment differently than she meant it, she starts to giggle uncontrollably. The slow song playing—the atmosphere of the entire dance floor—is calm and romantic, and Gabby is cracking up. Seeing her lose it makes me lose it, and people start to stare at us. I drag her off the dance floor and out into the empty hallway.

"What's wrong with you? I was just saying you should loosen up when you're dancing with a girl," she says, starting to recover her composure.

I flop down on a nearby bench, and she sits next to me and takes my hand.

"It's kinda hard when the girl is you," I say, brutally honest. Unable to keep my eyes off her, I glance down, taking her in.

"You like what you see." It's not a question, but a statement.

"Your dress ..."

"Yes?" she says, and I swear, she's poking her chest out, daring me to look.

"It's not as nice as your Pokémon onesie," I say, desperate to change the subject.

"Cute," she says with a smirk. She stands up right in front of me, putting herself on display inches from my face. "But don't you think I look better in this?"

Of course you do, but I'm trying not to get a hard-on in the school hallway.

I swallow and look down, determined not to let this get out of hand. "What do you want, Gabby?" I ask the floor.

"I want a first kiss."

My head shoots up and my eyes lock with hers. "A first kiss? With me?"

"With anyone," she replies.

"That's a lot of pressure."

"I promise I won't take advantage of you."

I laugh. I can't help it. She makes me laugh, but she takes it the wrong way.

"Don't laugh at me," she huffs out.

"I'm not. I—"

"It's been years already, Ben. Am I always just gonna be your best friend's little sister?" she spits out and turns away.

"No," I say, grabbing her hand. "The problem is ... I don't see you that way anymore."

"Really?" she replies, pulling me up by the hand and around the corner into a side hallway where the lights are low.

"You know I'm leaving soon," I say, starting to walk backward because she's walking toward me and I'm trying to maintain my distance.

"I know," she says, coming closer, pulling me into her.

"I've already registered for the summer session at Duke."

"I'm not asking you to marry me," she says, smiling.

She turns us both and presses me against a locker, and I let her because if I *really* didn't want to, it wouldn't be a problem to turn and walk away. But I *want* her body against mine. I want her hands on my chest and my neck, pulling me down toward her mouth as she whispers, "It's *just* a kiss, Ben."

Just a kiss, my ass. There have never been less honest words spoken. When her lips touch mine, I understand all of a sudden why men write songs about women, why they get into fights over them, and why the need for love and closeness is a driving force in people's lives from the moment they're born until the day they die.

Her lips are soft, but the perfect amount of insistent, as they make contact with mine. I wait for her move first, and she parts her lips, slipping her tongue into my waiting mouth. It could be awkward, or nerve-wracking, but it feels ... perfect kissing this sweet girl on her sweet mouth in the darkened school hallway. I lean against the locker, my legs wide, and she leans into me. I settle my hands on the small of her bare back and pull her into me, and all is right with the world.

We keep kissing. I can't stop, and it doesn't seem like she wants to either. Some kids explode out of the auditorium, and she pulls her mouth away from mine but stays nestled between my legs and in my arms.

She looks up at me, bites her bottom lip, and smiles, but she doesn't say a word.

"*That* was your first kiss?" I ask. There's no way. It was too good. Fuck, it was really good.

She nods.

"Whatever you say, Gabriella," I say, knowing she's lying.

She smiles more widely and winks, then leans in to whisper, "You're right. But it was the *best* one." Then, she saunters away, back toward the gym.

When did this girl I've known for half my life turn into someone who walks and talks and kisses like that?

I begin to follow her—my best friend's off-limits little sister she might be, but I need more of her—but then Aaron comes out with his prom date.

"Hey, man, wanna get outta here? There's a party at Vishal's house. Adina's looking for you inside. Go grab her and then we'll bounce."

Adina. My date. My runner-up date. Fuck.

On my way in to find her, I see Gabby talking to Sam, and he has his hands on her waist, the same place I held her two minutes ago. I take out my phone and text her:

Me

Please don't do anything with him tonight.

She looks at her Apple watch before flitting her eyes around the room, I presume, to find me. She spots me, then takes out her phone and texts me back.

Gabby

You know I do what I want.

What the hell?

I snap my head up and catch her walking out the door with Sam. I'm tempted to go over there and drag her away, so we can spend the night talking, simply being with each other while we still have the chance.

Aaron places his hand on my shoulder. "Ready to go, man?" I turn to look at him, and by the time I turn back, she's gone.

No.

I wipe my hand down my face and resign myself to … I don't know what, but it's not her. Just as I give up all hope, another text comes in.

Gabby

> **Don't worry. He's not what I want.**

Oh, thank God.

Gabby

> **Have fun with your runner-up.**

Four Years Later

Rekindling an Old Flame

Gabby

When I wake in the morning, my head aches, a semi-hangover that I'm pretty sure is equal parts emotional and physical. Having Ben Adler, my not-quite-realized childhood crush, pop up right during my hot make out session with Daniel was terrible timing, but I can only blame myself.

Bored with the sleepy college campus summer and half drunk on hard lemonade at Leah's Fourth of July party, I'd been daydreaming of Ben. Then Daniel showed up, and his well-defined chest and biceps reminded me of Ben's. I'd admired Ben plenty of times at high school swim meets, but I thought I'd left him—and my stupid high school dreams about him—behind.

Man, was I wrong.

He might have gone off to college at Duke and forgotten about *me*, but our kiss on prom night had long since settled into "core memory" territory in my brain. That kiss lasted no more than sixty seconds, but it was the first time that all my teenage wonderings about sex received a real-life answer. Well, a partial one. As my tongue had intertwined with Ben's, I remember thinking, "Wow, is *this* what sex is going to be like?" And sure, I might have a heavy class load, but luckily, college leaves one plenty of time to explore *other* subjects. Which is precisely what I was doing last night in Daniel's capable arms when Ben had snuck his way into my thoughts and refused to leave.

"I rushed into things," I told Daniel, realizing my heart wasn't in it. "I'm sorry."

He'd looked at me, bewildered, then stood up, dressed, and left me to my own tortuous thoughts, tossing and turning in bed until three in the morning.

I roll away from the wall and pick up my phone from the nightstand. I've missed a text from five minutes earlier from a number I don't know. *Daniel?* I think and smile. He must have gotten my number from Leah. I guess I *didn't* totally ruin things last night.

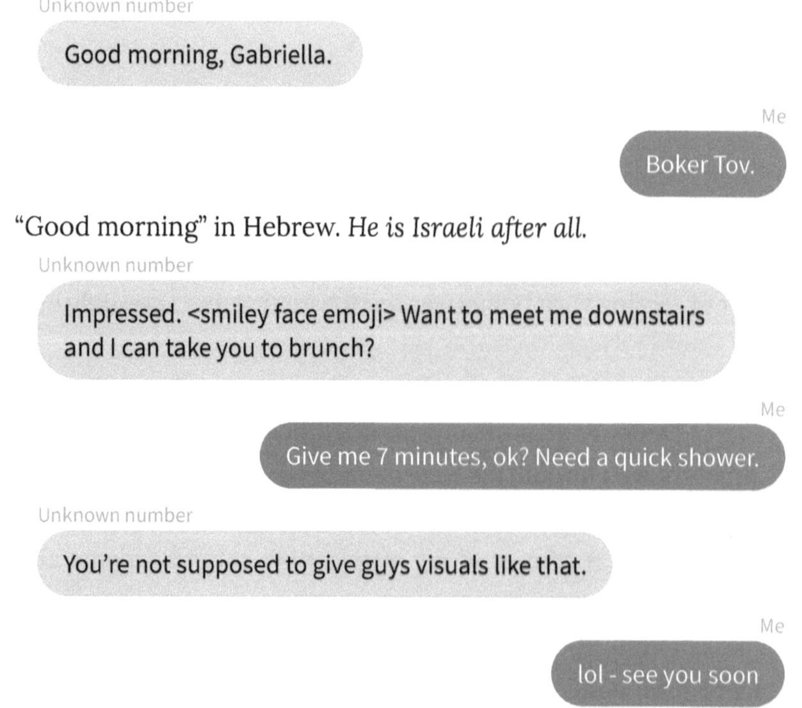

"Good morning" in Hebrew. *He is Israeli after all.*

As I take a shower, I smile. *Nice guys do exist.* I dry myself off quickly and grab a sundress from my closet. The burnt orange color looks great on me. I head downstairs, thinking about what I should say to Daniel—how to explain my about-face last night—but when I arrive in the dorm courtyard, the tall, dark, and handsome guy waiting for me isn't Daniel. It's Ben, and my heart flutters like a Goddamn butterfly.

It's been, well, in real life, it's been years. In my mind, my dreams, it's been mere hours. And he's here, standing in front of me as if I summoned him like a genie simply from dreaming about him.

"Hey, college girl," Ben says, walking over to me.

"Wh-What are you doing here?" I ask. "My mom said you're doing some fancy biology fellowship this summer in Israel."

"I am," he replies, standing a few feet away from me. "I'm leaving soon, but I ... wanted to catch up with you and see how you're doing."

He comes closer and holds his arms open for a hug. I step into his embrace, and I travel back in time four years. All of a sudden, I'm the nervous teenage version of myself that pined after Ben during his senior year of high school.

"It's so good to see you," he says in a voice that's deeper than I remember.

"I think I'm still in shock you're here," I say into his shoulder. He is bulkier than before.

He holds me away from his body now and looks me up and down. "You look great for seven minutes of getting ready. Sorry for not giving you more notice."

"It's— It's fine," I reply.

"Can I take you to breakfast?"

"That would be ... great." If I can settle my stomach enough to eat. If I can make my mouth form words.

We walk to Fritz's off-campus and sit at a table on the patio. I order a latte, and Ben orders a mocha.

"So you still like chocolate?" I tease.

"Always have, always will," he says, smiling. He sets his coffee down and leans forward on the table. "So how's the major going?"

I sip my coffee. "I'm in computer science. It's ... hard."

"Even for you?"

"What do you mean?" I ask.

"I mean, you're the smartest person I know."

I roll my eyes.

"Well, Rutgers has a good computer science program, right?" he asks. "How'd you end up taking that route? I mean ..." He looks down.

"What?"

"I feel like shit asking you these basic questions. I should have stayed in touch better. I don't even know the important things about you anymore."

"It's okay. I mean, I could have called you." *But I didn't want to be the immature high school girl chasing after the boy who moved on with his life.*

"I'm the one who left, though," he says, drumming his fingers on the table.

Yeah, you did, and it sucked there for a while.

I look up from his hands and meet his eye. "Well, I ended up in computer science for all the reasons anyone does."

"You're good at math and want to earn a lot of money in high tech?" he asks.

"Exactly," I say, laughing. "But I want to kind of explore how I might combine my art skills and programming."

"Like building video games or something?"

"Maybe," I say, shrugging. "You saw me play video games growing up. I'm not that good, but it seems like a cool challenge. Then again, I've also been taking this machine learning course. It's pretty interesting, but it's a little intimidating."

"Why?" he asks. His one-syllable question rockets me back in time to all our conversations as teenagers. Ben has been curious for as long as I can remember, and he always gave me his full attention, wanting to understand what I was thinking and feeling and ... why.

"Well, I'm one of three women in the course, and sometimes, I feel like I don't belong or maybe don't know enough." I exhale. It's hard to admit that type of thing, but his expression softens, transforming from curious to empathetic.

"But you're just starting out. You *will* know enough," he says.

"How do *you* know?"

"Because you're super smart and determined."

I pick up my coffee mug to hide my huge grin and change the topic. "What about you?"

"I graduated a few weeks ago and came back for the week before I head to this fellowship before grad school."

"Have you seen Aaron yet?" I ask.

"We texted, but no, not yet."

Why are you here, Ben? But I ask him other things instead. "So what are your plans? I mean, after the fellowship?"

"PhD at Cornell."

I widen my eyes. "That's intense."

"What do you mean?"

"Don't they have a little problem with Jews there now?" I ask.

"Don't a lot of places?" he asks sadly.

I press my lips together and nod.

"You know me," he says with a smile. "I'm no Jew with trembling knees."

"Slow down, Menachem Begin," I tease.

"Didn't Moshe Dayan say that?" he asks.

"Pretty sure it was Begin."

"You're probably right," he admits. "I mean, you usually are."

I am.

"Anyways," he continues, "that's what we do, right? Stand up in the face of hardship, bigots, I don't know, and focus on the right thing."

"What's 'the right thing' for you?" I ask.

"Biology research," he says with a grin.

"You must *really* like biology."

"I guess I do," he says, a thoughtful look on his face.

"What?"

"Nothing."

"What are you not telling me?" I ask, pouting at him the way I used to, to try to get my way.

"Fine. Remember when you tried to trick me into tutoring you about human anatomy?"

Only like once a week. That's actually one variation of my recurring sex dreams about Ben.

"I do. Sixteen-year-old me was pretty direct, huh?" *Twenty-year-old me could learn a thing or two from that girl.*

I'm saved from an awkward moment when our waiter brings our food. When he walks away, Ben admits, "You were direct, but I didn't mind. You were cute."

I smile. "You were cute, too." *And now you're mind-meltingly handsome.*

He blushes the slightest bit and takes a deep breath. "So I actually came to visit because…"

I look at him, waiting for him to continue. *Have you thought about me even half as much as I have about you all these years?* I lean forward and my dress strap slips off my shoulder. His eyes track down, his mouth parts, and I'm about to come right out and ask him when Leah walks up behind Ben. *What?*

"Hey, Gabby. Looking a little tired this morning. You two stay up late watching the fireworks last night?" she teases.

Shit.

Ben turns to look at her, and she sees it's him, not Daniel. Leah knows Ben, too, of course. Her eyes widen, but she gets her surprise in check.

"Hi, how are you?" he says.

"Wow, Ben," she chokes out. "What are *you* doing here?" She turns and looks at me, and gives me a look like *Shit, I'm so sorry.* She turns back to Ben. "I thought I'd heard you were doing something abroad this summer."

"I'm flying out tomorrow, but before I leave, I just …" His voice trails off. *Just what, Ben?* "I need to say goodbye to my dad in Princeton. He moved down there last year, and I thought I'd stop by to see Gabby and have a quick bite. Check in on her. Aaron asked me to."

Right. Of course. That's me: best friend's little sister. I should get a business card.

"Um, I need to head to the restroom. I'll be right back," he says, getting up.

When he leaves, Leah immediately sits down in his seat and appraises Ben's omelet.

"You're not joining us," I say.

"I won't, but I'm sorry, Gabs. I didn't realize it was Ben. He looks exactly like Daniel from behind." She glances toward the direction he walked off in. "Damn, he looks good now."

"I noticed."

"What happened with you and Daniel last night?" she asks in a conspiratorial tone.

"He's a nice guy, but we didn't click as much as I thought we would."

Because someone else popped into my head and un-clicked us.

"Shame, but ..." She stops and thinks for a moment. "You know, he looks like Ben. You might have a type." She raises an eyebrow, waiting for me to respond.

Since last night, I've been on a rollercoaster of emotions: boredom, sentimentality, recklessness, desire, and regret. I can't find anything clever to say.

"Just ask him," she says softly.

"Ask him what?"

"Why he's here."

I unfold my napkin and place it in my lap, then give her an uncomfortable look.

"I don't believe for a second Aaron asked him to check in on you," Leah says. "Does that *sound* like Aaron?"

"Not really," I admit.

"Right, if he wanted to know how you're doing, he'd just text you, not send blast-from-the-past-high-school-hottie Ben Adler to check on you."

I snort at her description of Ben.

"What a dumb cover story," she mutters.

She's right.

Ben joins us back at the table, and Leah stands. "It was so nice seeing you ... Ben Adler. What a blast from the past."

He gives me a perplexed look, and I try not to laugh.

She leans in for a hug, and after a minor delay, due to surprise, I think, he hugs her back.

Ben sits and starts to eat but pauses, waiting for me to join him. I cut up my omelet distractedly while I keep my eye on Leah. As she leaves the restaurant, she takes advantage of the fact that Ben's back is turned to her and mouths the words, *Do it*, before winking at me and making her way down the sidewalk.

While we eat our breakfast, I try to muster the courage to ask him if there might be some other reason he came by, like, he specifically wanted to see *me*, but we talk about other things.

"So what do you think you'll research in grad school?" I ask.

"I want to do something related to cancer research. This summer, I'll talk to the people at the Technion lab and see if I can get any ideas."

"The Technion? Impressive, Adler."

He smiles shyly. "Your mom mentioned that you might go to Israel this year with Birthright?"

"I signed up, but I'm not sure if I'll go."

"I went my freshman year of college, and it was really fun."

"I bet it was," I say. *Everybody knows what happens on those college Israel trips.*

"What does that mean?"

"How many girls did you hook up with?"

He laughs. "I haven't seen you in a *very* long time, and you're still asking me about the girls I hook up with."

I press my lips together to suppress a smile.

"How many guys have you hooked up with since I saw you last?" he asks.

I'm taking a sip of my coffee when he asks, and I choke. When I compose myself, I answer bluntly, "Enough."

He bites his bottom lip. "Anybody live up to Garrett?"

My mouth drops open. "You read it? You read *The Deal*?"

"Maybe," he says and starts to laugh.

He wipes his mouth with his napkin, then folds it on the table. The server brings our check on a small tablet, and he takes out his phone to pay.

"Let me give you some money," I say.

"No way. My treat. This has been a nice brunch. A very *enlightening* conversation."

He stands, and I join him. We walk back to my dorm, and I turn to him. "You should head out, I mean, if you're gonna spend time with your dad today, right?"

"I should," he says, his brow wrinkling. He reaches out and touches my arm, letting his hand slide down until he's holding my hand. I look at where his hand clasps mine and look up at him in question.

He swallows visibly. "Did I hear right? Are you … dating someone?"

What do I say? Admit to him that it was meaningless? That I took a guy back to my place after knowing him less than an hour? That he didn't even ask for my phone number? My stomach clenches, and I'm too embarrassed to admit that I might've jumped into bed with someone too quickly or that I was thinking of Ben half the time. I mutter, "I don't think so."

"You don't *think* so?" he asks.

I don't answer him, though, because I have a question of my own. "Why did you come here today? We've barely talked since you went away to Duke."

He blinks at me. "Because I-I think about you. I wonder how you're doing … and how your life is going … and if you're happy."

I wonder those same things about you.

"Are you really heading to see your dad later?" I ask.

"I could," he says, with a sheepish smile. "But I did see him yesterday."

"Why'd you lie?" I ask.

"I was embarrassed."

"About what?"

Now he evades *my* question. "Can we hang out today if you're not busy?"

There's literally nobody I'd rather make time for.

"What do you wanna do?" I ask.

"We could drive to the beach? I was thinking about doing it anyway, I mean, if you didn't want to hang out with me, so at least I have a swimsuit with me."

I smile. "Of course I'd want to hang out with you. That sounds …

perfect. Let me run upstairs and I'll be down in a few, okay?"

When I reach my room, the rumpled sheets on my bed stare at me accusingly. *"Another guy? So soon?"*

I rip them from the mattress and stuff them in the hamper. When I get back later, I don't want to be reminded of anything that happened before this morning. Then I quickly change into my swimsuit and grab a couple towels.

When I meet Ben downstairs, he asks, "So where are we going?"

"Belmar Beach?" I suggest. "Remember when we all went that spring break?"

"I do remember," he replies. "You always used to fall asleep on me during our road trips."

Oh, God. I did. Because I loved being close to him. That specific time, Leah had convinced Ben that the backseat of Aaron's car was simply too small for all three of us to sit there without Ben putting his arm around me.

"I guess you're just fun to cuddle with," I say, not even believing how quickly I've slipped back into flirting mode with my high school crush.

He looks down and presses his lips together. Is he hiding a smile? "I remember your cute little nose also got sunburned."

In an instant, I'm thrown back years, remembering that was the first time he'd placed his pointer finger on my nose, and it somehow had become a thing between us.

He raises his head and reaches out now to touch my nose lightly—the first time in four years. "I'll take you to the beach today, but don't burn your nose."

I pull my sunscreen out of my beach bag. "I learned my lesson."

Goosebumps prickle on my bare arms, but it's not only from the cool air blasting from the vents of Ben's car. It's the fact that I'm here—with him. I glance around, and his well-maintained crossover is ten times cleaner than my own car. *Pretty on-brand.*

While he drives, eyes mostly on the road, I admire his profile and try to neutralize my expression. No goofy smile. No glassy-eyed stare of awe. No revealing what I'm feeling on the inside.

Sentimental? Check. Nervous? Double-check.

"So any girlfriends during college?" I ask, then cringle inwardly.

Increased tendency to ask awkward, transparent questions? Embarrassing triple-check.

"A couple," he replies.

"Anything serious?"

"Not really," he says. "I mean, there was this one girl, but she didn't give good—"

"Head?" I interrupt. He looks at me, wide-eyed for a moment while he takes his eyes off the road, and my body temperature soars. "That's not what you were gonna say, was it?"

He starts to laugh. "I was gonna say 'presents.' Not that I need a lot of presents or especially good presents, but sometimes, a present is so bad that it really leaves an impression you can't get over."

I inhale and exhale slowly, giving myself a minute to think twice about my next words. *Yes, you're fine. You can continue now with normal human conversation.* "And what was this terrible present of hers?"

"Oh," he deadpans. "Really bad head."

I cackle, then snort, which makes him laugh even harder. "Tell me you did not break up with a girl over a bad blow job."

He takes a deep breath. "Nah, I wouldn't do that, but she also wasn't that nice to begin with. Pretty, but not very nice. Or smart for that matter."

"Smart *is* important," I comment.

He looks at me. "It is," he agrees. "So what smart stuff keeps you busy these days?"

"Well, I've actually done some tutoring of my own this year."

"What subject?" he asks.

"Calculus."

"Wow."

"None of my students have hit on me yet," I add.

"I'd so hit on you if you were tutoring me." He glances over at my outfit. "Especially if you were wearing *that* to our sessions."

I pose dramatically and dance a little in the seat. "So you like girls in sundresses?"

"A sundress and smart? Throw in a random fact about space or the human genome, and my heart is yours."

I smile at him, then look out the window. *I know that the sunset on Mars appears blue. I know that humans share about 50 percent of our genes with plants.*

I glance back in his direction, and he smiles but keeps his eyes on the road. "You're thinking about science facts right now," he remarks.

"I am not," I say and look back out the window.

His comfortable laugh sends a wave of happiness through my body. *How had I ever forgotten how he makes me feel?*

We arrive at the beach, and I take my bag and wide-brimmed beach hat from the car. He comes around and pulls me by the hand through the parking lot toward the sand. After we lay out the towels, he goes to change into his swimsuit.

While he's gone, I text Leah.

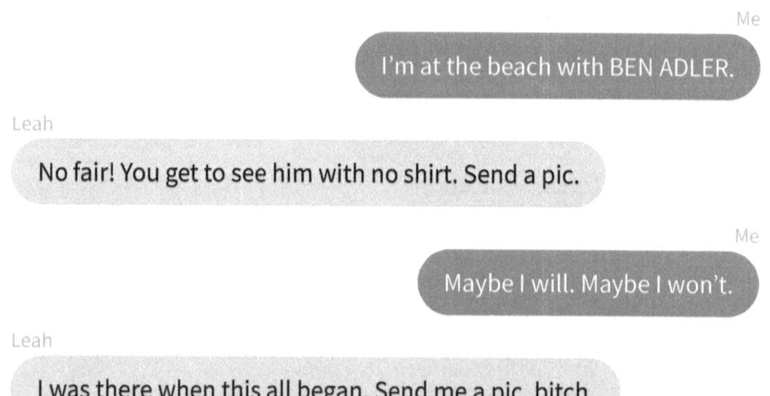

I'm laughing when he returns but stop short when I look up at him shirtless, his board shorts riding low on his hips framing swimmer abs.

He's no Ryan Lochte, but he looks damn good. I owe Leah the pic.

"Can I use some of your sunscreen?" he asks. I hand it to him. He squirts some onto his hand and puts his pointer finger in it, then wipes it on my nose. I rub in the sunscreen on my face and start to apply it to the rest of my body.

"Should I get your back?" he asks.

"Um, sure." I lie on my towel face down and try not to let my mind wander to dirty places as he rubs sunscreen on my shoulders, my back, then down near my hips. He slips his hands just inside the hem of my bikini bottoms. I'm not sure if he's *trying* to turn me on, but his hands on me feel delicious.

Deep breath. I flip over and take my hat to cover my face, giving myself a minute to recuperate from the Benjamin Adler personal massage. We don't talk, just listen to the waves and the sounds of people playing in the surf. Ben's body shifts next to me, and I remove the hat and turn toward him to see him propped up on one arm. He opens his mouth to say something, then presses his lips together.

"Yesss?" I ask.

"You look hot."

"You do, too," I blurt out, letting my eyes fall to his sculpted chest.

"I meant the temperature," he chides me.

No, you didn't. But in that case …

"Me, too," I say, smirking. "I should go for a swim and cool off." I stand, throw my sunglasses down on the towel, and remove my sarong cover-up. "Join me?"

His eyes are glued to my ass, and I'm beginning to think I know why he came to visit. A walk down memory lane and a very invested booty call—two things I'm on board for today.

He drags his eyes away from my butt and meets my gaze with an unmistakable look of desire in his eyes. Lips parted, he nods and stands. As we walk toward the water, he wraps his arm around my waist and gives me a side hug.

"I'm glad I came to see you," he says. So *sweet.* Then he smacks me on my butt.

I cry out, "What?" Before I can grab him, though, he runs toward the water and dives into the waves.

I walk, determined to either strangle him or possibly make out with him, and test the water with my feet.

"It's freezing. How do you have a smile on your face?" I call to him when he pops out from the water about ten feet away from me.

"I'm with my bestie," he calls back, and my heart flip-flops in my chest at his use of our old nickname. "Come swim with me."

"It's too rough," I call.

"Here," he says, wading closer, and I can see the goosebumps on his chest. It takes *a lot* of restraint not to reach out and rub my fingertips over his flesh. "Hold my hand. I won't let you go under."

I swim but not usually in big waves. He senses my hesitation and takes my hand. "High school record for 100-meter butterfly, remember?"

I smile. "I remember."

He pulls me out to waist-high water and turns to face me. "I forgot how much I like hanging out with you," he says. The waves continue to roll in, and every time one comes, he lifts me up.

During a lull in the larger waves, I put my hands on his shoulders, and we lock eyes. Out of nowhere, I say, "I cried."

He furrows his brow. "What? When?"

Guess I'm all in now. "When you left for college. For a few days. I think I was … young and dumb and … I guess I thought … I don't know."

He pulls me in close with his hands resting on my waist and looks at me carefully. "What did you think?"

"Stupid sixteen-year-old me thought … we could have been more than friends." I look down and shake my head, but before he can respond, a huge wave hits us and takes me under.

Ben's strong arms drag me back to the surface. "Are you okay?" he asks in a worried voice. "I'm sorry. I got distracted by what you were saying, and I didn't see it coming in."

I blink away the cold water, and he moves my mess of hair out of my face.

I'm out of breath. "I'm okay," I say, laughing.

"In that case ..." he says, then pulls me into him and kisses me. It's unexpected. *But is it?* I'm still in the middle of a laugh, which means my mouth is open and ready, waiting for the kiss I've wanted for four years. Except the man who kisses me now is no longer the boy I knew then, and the heat where our cold, wet bodies connect is something I never could have imagined when I was sixteen.

I pull back and stare at him.

"Still okay?" he asks.

"More than okay," I reply, as a rough wave hits us again, and he lifts me, then holds me close. I slide back down his body, and he must be able to feel how cold—or aroused—I am as my breasts press into his chest.

He's leaving tomorrow.

My body stiffens, and I push away from him. "I'm gonna go dry off."

I trudge through the water, putting distance between us, and jog through the sand to fall down on my towel. As Ben exits the water, I pretend to search in my bag for something, mostly to avoid looking at him.

When he draws closer, he sits down on his own towel next to me and turns to look at me, silently. I put on my sunglasses and lean back onto my elbows, examining him out of the corner of my eye.

When he doesn't say anything or avert his gaze, I turn to him to ask impatiently, "What?"

He touches my hand, and my whole arm gets goosebumps. He rubs a pointer finger over the little hairs sticking up on my forearm and smiles.

"I'm just cold," I say.

He smiles, then moves his lips back and forth over his teeth, the little tic he's had forever when he's mulling something over. "I don't know what came over me now, kissing you. You ..."

"I what?" I ask. I need to know because this whole morning has simultaneously been amazing and put me on edge.

"You looked super cute, all wet, and with your hair plastered over your sweet face. I've been thinking about you lately, and ..."

I pull his hand to my mouth and kiss the back of it.

He smiles. "What's that for?"

"You look super cute, all wet, with your hair plastered over your sweet face," I say, and rub the curl of hair falling over his forehead between my fingers.

He grabs my wrist and moves it down to his jaw, then turns and kisses my palm.

I close my eyes and swallow.

"I'm leaving tomorrow, G."

I open my eyes and sigh. "Why do you think I freaked out a little?"

He nods, thoughtfully. "We have one day, then. What would make this a good day?"

It's *already a good day just being here with you.* But I can't say that.

"Ice cream?" I suggest.

"I'd love to share an ice cream with you."

"Share? Pshhh. No way."

He laughs and stands up, leaning back down to grab his phone. "Can I take a picture of you?"

"Yeah, but you have to be in it, too," I reply, starting to get up. He offers me his hand and pulls me to my feet. The sudden weight shift throws me off balance, and I lean into him. He takes a deep breath under my hands, currently pressed against his bare chest, and runs his hand down my forearms. I wrap my arms around his neck, pulling him closer for a h ug.

Neither of us says a thing, and he moves his hands to my waist. We stand there in silence for at least a minute, and I close my eyes, listening to the waves and the seagulls and what I think is the beating of my own heart.

"I didn't think it was possible, but you've gotten even more beautiful since the last time I saw you," he finally says.

"Don't say that," I whisper.

"But it's true."

I could stay like this—close to him—until the sun goes down, until next week, until next year, but at some point, we need to leave.

"Selfie?" I ask.

"Yeah," he says, pulling away, and holding up his phone. "Say cheese."

And as he takes the picture, I lean in and kiss him on the cheek.

On the drive back, we stop for ice cream, and I peruse the options.

"You want to order for me, and I'll order for you?" he asks.

"Why?"

"It'll be fun. See if you trust me to get you something you like."

"Fine." I review the chocolatey options for him: rocky road, moose tracks, fudge brownie, and the list goes on. Chocolate lovers have it all.

Meanwhile, he goes to the other end of the cooler and looks inside. "Ooooh, I bet you'd like Marshmallow Unicorn or this neon-green pistachio flavor."

I pull a face at him. He winks at me in response. I sigh, roll my eyes playfully, and order a waffle cone with two scoops of frozen hot chocolate for Ben. The woman behind the counter hands me the ice cream, and I go sit outside to await my surprise. He comes outside a minute later with a simple cup of strawberry ice cream.

"You remembered," I say, exchanging the cone in my hand for my scoop of strawberry.

"Of course I remembered what you like," he replies, licking the chocolate ice cream that's already starting to drip down the side.

He catches me looking at him and raises an eyebrow. "Yessss?"

I realize my mouth has parted of its own will while I imagine what his tongue would feel like on my neck and ... other places.

Mischief lights up his eyes. *He did that on purpose. Well ...*

"Nothing," I say, taking a spoonful of my own ice cream, and I can safely say that it's the kinkiest spoonful of ice cream I've ever eaten. Ben's eyes shift downward to my mouth, and he licks his lips. He gulps, and I do a repeat performance, teasing him.

When I swallow, I whisper, "Your ice cream's melting."

"Huh?" He comes back to earth when it drips onto his fingers. "Oh, uh, yeah," he says, grabbing some napkins from the dispenser on the table. "It's, uh, hot out here, isn't it?"

"Very," I agree. I smile and glance away, only to catch two college-aged girls looking at Ben and whispering.

I snicker.

"What are you laughing about?" he asks.

"I think you have an admirer," I reply and flick my eyes to the cute blond who just giggled and—*oh my God*—batted her eyelashes in Ben's direction. I can't even blame her. He looks hot as hell with wind-blown hair and his tight gray t-shirt accentuating his muscular physique.

He doesn't even glance their way before replying, "I think *you* do, too." I smile, and he mouths, *Me.*

Flirting with him is so fun.

"You're different now," I remark.

"How?" he asks.

"You're more confident ... or maybe good at pretending?"

"How have you always been able—"

"To read you like a book?" I offer.

He laughs. "Something like that."

"Because I'm an artist," I say. "And artists know that what you see at first glance of a work is only one of a thousand ways to understand a piece of art." I reach out my hand out and thread my fingers through his, admiring the beauty of our intertwined fingers.

He raises an eyebrow. "So you're saying I'm a work of art?"

I press my lips together, not letting my smile break through immediately. "I like this side of you. I like your quieter side, too, but there's something about a guy who does and says silly things to get a girl's attention, to make her laugh. I like ... every side of you."

His lips curl up at the corners. "I like every side of you, too."

His hand has moved up my forearm, and I lean over the table. His eyes skate down for a fraction of a second, then his gaze locks with mine. "How far is the university from here?" he asks, his voice suddenly lower.

I slide one of my legs between his and move in closer. "Fifteen minutes?" I venture.

"We should get back," he says.

"We should." *Is he thinking what I'm thinking?*

On the drive back, Ben is quiet. I look out the window and don't say much either, but the second he pulls into a parking spot, I ask if he needs to leave right away.

"I could hang out. What did you have in mind?" He narrows his eyes at me.

I giggle. "I'm sure we'll think of something."

Ben's ahead of me, carrying my beach bag up the dorm stairs, and I can't help but admire the cute butt I see ahead of me.

He turns around, unexpectedly catching me in the act. "Are you checking out my ass, Gabby Feinman?"

I burst out laughing. "Uh, maybe?"

He holds out his hand and I take it as he pulls me up to a step higher than him. "My turn now."

I shoot him a stern look.

"Go," he orders me playfully, then snaps me on the butt with my own beach towel.

I snatch my floppy sunhat off my head, smash it down on his, and run the rest of the way up the stairs, beating him by only a couple seconds to my dorm room door. As I try to unlock the door, he crowds me from behind.

"Stop," I say, sticking my butt out and bumping him back to give me room to find and insert the right key, but he presses his front to my back and slides an arm around my waist. He peeks over my shoulder.

"Having trouble with the key?" he asks, his warm breath dusting neck.

I turn my head to shoot back at him with something sassy but find myself an inch from his mouth and quickly turn my head back. "I know how to unlock my own door, Ben. I'm just—"

"Distracted?" he asks and pulls me in closer.

Without any warning, I spin around until I'm facing him, and he pins me up against the door.

"You might not remember this about me," I say in a low voice, "but I'm very good at multitasking."

He drops my bag on the floor and braces his arms above my head, leaning in close and whispering in my ear, "Is that so?"

I turn my head, this time intentionally bringing my lips close to his. "Yep."

And just as he moves closer to kiss me, I unlock the door behind me and turn the knob, all but falling backward into the open doorway.

He stumbles in, and I dance away from him.

"I'm gonna take a quick shower," I say. "Make yourself at home."

His eyes flit around the room and land on a dresser drawer I left open earlier while searching for my bikini. A myriad of bras and underwear are spilling out of it.

The corners of his mouth turn up, but he manages to suppress a full-blown grin. "I'll keep myself busy."

I laugh as I slide the door closed to my en suite bathroom, then strip off my beach clothes and turn on the hot water. While I shampoo my hair, I take stock of the day up until now. This morning, I woke up with no idea I was going to see Ben. Now we've spent the whole day together, we've kissed, and I've given my strawberry ice cream spoon half a blow job. Did he come here specifically to sleep with me, or am I just a lucky bitch the universe is rewarding for all my charity work at the Jewish Seniors Center in high school?

Only one way to find out. I step out of the shower and wrap a towel around myself. When I come into the room, he's standing close to the wall, examining some of the art I've taped to my walls.

"It's all yours?" he asks, not turning around. "It's ... powerful. I had no idea you ..."

He turns toward me—standing there in a towel—and he cocks his head. "Well, then."

I come closer to him and lean against the desk. "Well, then."

He swallows and looks into my eyes, trying to read my thoughts.

"Tell me again," I say, "why did you come here today?"

"I thought I came here to see how you're doing, but, uh ..."

"But maybe now the plan has changed?" I reach out my hand and pull him closer.

"Gabby ..."

"Yes?"

"Close your eyes," he says.

"What are you going to do?" I ask.

He moves even closer and brackets my legs with his own. "Close them." He caresses my face and gently moves his thumbs first over my brow, then down over my eyelids to make me close them.

With my eyes closed, all my other senses are heightened. The trace of his fingertips on my jawbone, and the sound of his voice as he whispers, "What do *you* want to happen next?"

He moves his hands lower and wraps his strong arms around me. I consciously work to keep my breathing even, except I can't even concentrate on something as simple, as natural, as breathing because he's in my space. The scent of him is like a drug to me. It's his cologne—or maybe his deodorant—and it's mixed with salt water and the scent of chocolate. It's ... him, *Ben*.

I can't take the silence, as fleeting as it is, and I open my mouth to say, "What are you doing?" but before I can even utter the words, his mouth brushes mine.

His lips are soft, and he tastes like chocolate and the mint gum he chewed in the car.

"You taste like strawberry ice cream," he whispers.

"And you taste like ... " *Heaven.* I open my eyes. "How long have you wanted to kiss me before you stole one at the beach today?"

"Easy. Since high school."

"Me, too."

He smiles.

"Kiss me again," I say.

"I want to, but if I do, I won't be able to stop."

I take his hand in mine, kiss his palm like he did mine earlier in the day, and place it on the bare skin of my chest, near where the towel rests. His fingers curl under the towel, pressing against the swell of my breast. "Who says you have to?"

His hazel eyes flash at my words, and he breathes out in a huff. "I didn't come here to sleep with you and then run off to another continent. You are sexy and smart and ... borderline irresistible. I want you right now.

So much. But I'm trying to do the right thing."

I take his other hand and bring it to cup my breast. "How can it be wrong if I want it and you want it?"

His chest rises and falls as he takes a deep breath. "You want this?"

"I have for a while," I reply. "And *I'm* not throwing away an opportunity to finally see you naked."

He bites his lip and turns to the side. He seems to be thinking, coming to a decision. "Fuck it. Let's do it."

"Yesssss," I say and stand, pushing him up against the wall next to my desk.

The only thing keeping my towel up is the fact I'm pressed up against him. One sudden move and it's gone. I know it, and he knows it. I curl one of my legs around his, which makes him slide his hand down my ass and hang on, pulling my hip into him, into what feels like definite evidence he was just waiting for the green light.

I kiss his neck and the top of his chest, where his V-neck t-shirt opens. "You're such a good kisser," I whisper. "Before we get too far along, though, I have some questions for you."

"Whatever you say, Gabriella," he says, massaging my ass with both of his hands.

He kisses me again and moves one hand to my breast.

I break away from a kiss. "You still remember my favorite type of pizza?"

His face is close to mine, and he gives me a confused look. "Huh?"

"What is my favorite type of pizza?" I insist.

"Pineapple," he retorts with narrowed eyes.

I lean closer to him and nip his bottom lip with my teeth. "Wrong answer," I whisper.

He snickers. "It's olives and mushrooms."

"Correct. And do I like hot cocoa with marshmallows or whipped cream?"

He grins, catching on to the game. "Neither."

"Right again."

I move my hands up to his chest and shoulders, enjoying the hard muscles under his soft t-shirt.

"One last question," I say, looking up at him with a naughty expression. "Do you think I give good … 'presents' or not?"

A wicked smile flashes across his face, and he leans down to whisper in my ear, "I saw the blow job you gave that spoon an hour ago, and I bet the 'presents' you give are the absolute best."

I take his hand and slide it up under my towel. "A-plus, Adler. No wonder you got into a PhD program. Take off your shirt."

"Are you sure?" he asks.

I look down between us at the bulge in his pants. "Oh, I'm super-fucking sure."

He pulls his shirt up over his head and then goes for my towel, pulling it down and letting it drop to the ground. I can almost hear the sizzle of electricity between us as he slides his hands around my waist and then down my hips, grabbing my bare ass cheeks. I turn him around and push him to sit on my desk chair. I straddle him, and I can feel him hard beneath me. He leans up to kiss me, but I swerve and kiss his neck instead. He laughs.

"If you're not gonna let me kiss your mouth," he says into my ear in a low voice, "then I'll just go for other places on your body."

"Why would I ever let you kiss my mouth *now*?"

He lifts my chin and holds my jaw between his thumb and pointer finger. Our lips are less than an inch from touching, and he says, "You couldn't wait to jump my bones on prom night. Show me what you've learned these last few years."

I do love messing with him, but I can't hold back any longer. I lean into him, parting his lips with my tongue and simply get lost in the kiss. He kisses me like a starved man. His tongue tangles with mine, and he runs his hands through my damp hair.

"Oh, fuck," he moans when we come up for air. "More."

I lean in as we explore each other's mouths hungrily. His hands roam over my body. He cups my breasts, looking at them in wonder, then rubbing his thumbs lightly over my nipples.

"God, your skin is so soft," he says as he leans down to take my nipple in his mouth. While he swirls his tongue over me, I moan and realize how little power I have here.

The more we kiss, the more he caresses me and moves his hips rhythmically under me, the further and faster I want to go. My desk chair is fine for kissing, but we need more space. I'm about to suggest that we move things to the bed when I remember that I took off the sheets earlier and never replaced them.

"Um, how do you feel about the floor?" I ask.

"As in a place for carpets or ..."

I raise my eyebrow at him. "As in a place to fuck, Ben."

"Oh. Yeah, the floor is one of my top five places to fuck a beautiful woman."

I laugh. "I either pull my blanket down there and we go at it, or we take a three-minute break to make the bed. I'm not having sex on a bare dorm mattress. I don't need an STI."

"Definitely the floor. No break. Lots of sex."

I arch my eyebrow.

He smiles. "Now."

I slide off him, turn, and bend over my bed to pick up the blanket way more dramatically than needed. While bent over, I pause and glance back over my shoulder, where I see him swallow.

"I had no idea you were so direct," he says.

"Lucky you."

"Damn right." He's gotten up to untie his shorts, all the while staring at my body, now covered by the blanket I'm holding.

He pauses undressing. "Let me help you with the blanket."

We spread it out on the floor between my bed and the desk. We both stand on it, and he pulls me into his arms again and slides his hands down to stroke me, while I trail my hand down and explore what he has to offer below the belt for the first time.

"Ohhh. What have you been hiding?" I tease.

"I haven't been hiding anything."

"Surely, this is something you should have shared with your hot cocoa bestie before now?"

"You mean my fake first kiss bestie?" he counters.

I give him a pleased smile and lie down on the blanket and gesture with my finger that he should join me. "Wanna be my sex-on-a-blanket bestie?"

He starts to kneel down.

"Take 'em off, hot stuff," I say, gesturing to his shorts. "This blanket has a no pants rule."

He snickers. "A no pants rule?"

"I don't make the rules. I just enforce 'em."

He slides his shorts off, kneels down again, and crawls toward me.

Lying beside me, he asks, "Any other rules I need to know about?" he asks, leaning in and kissing me softly on the lips. "What are you in the mood for tonight, bestie?"

"Well, in my dream—" I clamp my mouth shut.

"You dreamed about me?" he asks, unable to hide his pleasure at this discovery.

"I did," I admit.

"Tell me. Did you touch yourself while you thought about me?" he asks. He parts my legs with one hand, then runs the back of his fingers over my naked flesh, and my skin prickles.

"Maybe."

He smiles. "Wanna show me?"

"Um."

"Show me," he says, taking my hand in his and moving it to my breast. It's not exactly a new sensation to feel my own hands on my body, but having Ben's hand on mine, his hard, naked body pressed against me, his legs entangled with mine, has me unsettled. I exhale a ragged breath.

"Hey, now," he says, nibbling me on my ear lobe, then kissing me in the tender space just below it. "Something tells me you're not shy in bed."

True. At least not usually.

He moves his hand to my waist and squeezes. "You know me. You're safe."

I am. I bury my nose in his neck and inhale. "Mmmm, I know."

He kisses my forehead and dips his head to kiss my jawline, then my neck. I close my eyes and move my fingers over the nipple of one of my breasts, while I run the fingers of my other hand through his hair. A sound of approval rumbles from his throat as his fingers toy with my other breast until my nipple there hardens.

"Mmmm, this is fun," he whispers in my ear, and I laugh softly.

He slides one hand down and strokes me. "G, did you also touch your pussy while you thought about me?"

"Yes," I admit, breathlessly. "I, uh, I used—"

"What did you use?"

"I used a vibrator."

"Mmmmm," he says, as he caresses me. He must be able to feel that I'm wet, and he kisses his way down my chest. "Tell me what you imagined while you touched yourself."

"I imagined you kissing me … on my breasts."

He stops his descent down my body to suck on my nipples and lick them. "Like this?"

"Yes," I say, spreading my fingers in his hair.

"What else did you imagine?" he asks while stroking me.

"I imagined what you would look like naked … while you rub your cock against my pussy," I say, suddenly gaining courage.

"You have good ideas," he says, and when he adjusts his body to lie over me, straddling me, I'm in heaven knowing that momentarily he will be inside of me.

He rubs his hard shaft against my clit. "Like this?" he asks.

"Mmmm, yeah."

"Oh, God," he says. "You're so wet … and warm. It's so … damn … hot."

You are so damn hot, Ben. I cannot believe he's here, that this is happening, and that he is talking this way to me.

He kisses my mouth and asks if he can go down on me.

I shake my head.

"No?" he asks, surprised, maybe thinking I'm shy. It's not that, though. He's here, and I want him where I can see him. I want to look into his eyes. I want to taste his mouth.

"Keep kissing me here."

"If this is what you like, then this is what I like," he says, smiling and diving in for another kiss.

You *are what I like.*

I break away from a long, deep kiss to look up at my nightstand drawer.

Ben follows my gaze. "Condom?"

I nod.

He opens the drawer and pulls one out, ripping the package with his teeth, so he can keep one of his hands moving on me. I'm slick and so ready, but I also don't want him to stop what he's doing.

"If you like this, I'll wait," he says.

"I don't want to make you wait."

"I've waited years. What's another few minutes to help you come?"

"Such an altruist," I joke.

"You have to say my name, though. That's how I always imagine it."

Oh. You've imagined this, too.

Up until now, the pleasures he's been providing have been external, but now, he slips a finger inside.

"Ohhhh," I breathe out.

"Mmmm," he responds and slips another finger inside of me.

"Gabby, please. I have to taste you."

I nod. I couldn't refuse now even if I wanted to. I barely have words for how good he's making me feel.

He leans down, and the tongue that was previously making love to my mouth begins to make love to my core. He circles his tongue over my clit, and the moan of pleasure I hear from between my legs sends me into overdrive. Within a minute, his skilled attention has me arching my back. I brace myself, my hands overhead on the wall behind me.

I groan. I moan. At some point, I think I whimper, and then I beg. I cannot control myself, and my reactions push him forward.

"Take your time," he says.

He demonstrates just how much endurance his mouth has and seems to read my mind for how fast to go, when to slow down, and when to do something different.

"Yes, right there. Ohhhhh, fuuuuck, yessss, Bennn," I mutter as I let myself go. To this. To him.

When I pat his cheek gently to indicate he *must* stop because my nerve endings can't take anymore, he scoots up and rests his head on my stomach. Though my whole body feels like jelly, I muster enough energy to run my hands through his hair.

"Can you see without your glasses?" I ask, realizing he must have taken them off at some point.

"What do you think?"

"Well, you can certainly find your way around a vagina."

He laughs, then kisses my stomach. "You ready for more or need a little break?"

"What does *more* entail?"

He slides up my body and starts to kiss my neck. "Maybe finding G's g-spot?"

"You might've found that already," I reply. "Lucky shot."

"There is no luck. Only hard work."

I exhale a tired laugh. "In any case, I think it's time to look for B's B-spot."

"It's my penis," he remarks bluntly, and I snicker.

I slide my hand down and grip him gently. "You mean, here?"

"You found it! What a good detective."

I pull him in for a kiss and move my hand up and down his hard shaft. His moan of appreciation shoots straight to whatever part of my brain is responsible for libido. If he weren't currently straddling me, I swear my legs would part for him of their own volition.

"Ben?"

"Yeah?" he replies after nipping my ear.

"I forgot how much fun I have with you."

"We've never had this kind of fun before, though."

"True."

"Wanna have even more fun?" he asks.

"What do you have in mind?"

"I was thinking of something super original."

"Hmmm?"

"Putting my cock ..."

"Yes?"

"In your hot, slick …"

"Say less, and, uh, do more."

I watch him roll on the condom, and I try to surreptitiously assess what I'm looking at. Seeing him grip himself, well, I must have a certain expression on my face.

"You want it?" he asks.

Yes, *please.*

But I take a different tack. "Nahhh, put it away."

"I'm all about consent, Gabs. I need you to explicitly say that you want this. Otherwise, well, I'll have to put it away."

He leans back to reach for his discarded shorts.

"Don't you dare," I warn.

"Sorry, what was that? I couldn't hear you."

"Don't you dare put on clothes. Bring yourself and all pieces of your anatomy toward the sexy, aroused woman you're currently straddling … "

"And what?"

"And pleasure me until I scream your name, Benjamin."

"Yeah, that sounds like consent."

"Oh my God. Get the fuck over here, Ben. Seriously." I lean up far enough to grab his hips and wrap my legs around his waist, pulling him back toward me.

As he enters me, sure, but gentle, watching my face the whole time, he asks, "What do you like, baby?"

"This," I say. "I like this."

"I should head out," he says. We've been laying on the floor, my head on his chest, for at least thirty minutes, while both of us recover.

After we finished having sex and we'd both cooled down, he'd pulled the blanket up around us, and we are currently inside a cocoon. I'm lying on his chest, and he's stroking my hair. Little by little, I can hear his heartbeat returning to what must be its normal beat.

"Today was … unexpected," he says. "I like … hanging out with you."

"I like hanging out with you, too."

I lean up to let him slip out from under me, but he pulls me back into him. "Not quite yet?"

How do I tell him I'd stay here, lying on the floor with him, until the end of time?

"Not quite yet," I agree, snuggling into him.

He tilts my head up with his free hand so it's angled perfectly for a kiss, but before our lips meet, I pull the blanket up over our heads.

"Now *this* is my kind of blanket fort," he says and kisses me softly.

"You remember the blanket forts I used to make as a kid?" I ask.

"I always hoped you'd invite me in to read a book with you."

I laugh and lay my cheek back on his chest, tracing my fingers over his ribs.

"You surprised me today," I admit. It's easier since I'm not looking at him. "I thought when I came downstairs earlier that it was gonna be someone else. I didn't have your new number."

"Who did you think it was going to be?" he asks.

I hesitate. "The guy I made out with last night …" *He's going to think that I do this all the time, that he means nothing.*

He's quiet, and I look at him. The look in his eyes is curious as he patiently waits for me to continue my sentence. No judgment.

Still … "I-I'm sorry I didn't tell you before *we*, well, this happened, and—"

"Don't apologize. I mean, you're a beautiful woman, and it seems like you're comfortable with your body and what you like … you know. It's … I get it."

You do?

"I wouldn't have invited him back here if I'd known you were coming today."

"No?"

"Definitely not."

He squeezes me tightly. "I heard what Leah said earlier today at brunch. I think I kinda knew that you went out with someone last night. But I also got the feeling that it wasn't going to turn into anything."

Not when this is what I'll have to compare him to.

He pulls the covers down and inhales deeply. "Air," he comments and laughs.

Every time he laughs or says exactly what I'm thinking, I inch that much closer to a cliff, toward a dangerous chasm into which I'm well aware I shouldn't fall.

He runs his fingers through my hair. "Should I tell you something a little ... unsavory ... so you'll feel more comfortable?"

"Yeah."

"I once hooked up with two girls in one day."

I gasp. "A threesome?"

"No," he says. "One in the morning, and one in the evening."

"Ben!" I laugh and meet his eyes, waiting for him to explain.

"It wasn't on purpose," he says, grimacing. "It just ... kind of happened."

I side-eye him, but I can't hide my amusement.

"It's terrible, isn't it?" he says.

"Well, it's not great, but I guess it is a nice testament to your sexual stamina."

He starts to laugh, and I join in. I can feel him shaking under me.

"You weren't like this back in high school," I say. "What happened to the shy, sweet Ben Adler from down the street? When did you change?"

He looks thoughtful—or hurt—for a moment, and I realize my misstep. "I'm still sweet," he says.

"I'm sorry. I didn't mean that. I just mean that you're more ... What was the word you used for me? *Direct*? Than you used to be."

"Maybe I am."

"I'm not saying it's bad to hook up with people outside of a relationship. I've had my fair share of short-term things, too," I admit.

"So what happened to you? When did *you* change?" His tone holds no malice, only curiosity.

"Well ... you're only young once, and you know, I'm this good Jewish girl in so many ways ..."

"Oh, you're good, Ms. Feinman," he says, pinching my butt.

"That's not what I meant," I say, giggling.

"I know. Go on."

"So I've always done my homework and not gotten in trouble, and this is my time in life to explore who I am outside of all that. Outside of school, outside of everyone's expectations."

He nods.

"One day," I continue, "I'll marry a nice Jewish boy. We'll have nice Jewish kids, and we'll go to synagogue and have a tacky plate that says *Love, Light, and Latkes*. And what? I won't have gotten to experience other *non-circumcised* penises?"

His mouth drops open, and then he shuts it dramatically, laughing so hard that tears come to his eyes. "Well, how did this circumcised one measure up?"

"Oh, high marks, Adler. Very high marks."

He takes a deep breath and asks, "So what does this nice Jewish boy of yours look like? What's the profile?"

"I don't know exactly, but I would imagine that he comes from a good family, who are nice to me and like me. And he doesn't want to live too far away because I love my family and want to be close to them. And he wants kids, and ..."

"That's all?"

"Of course not. He'll understand me, like really understand me. All the facets of my personality, not only the likable ones, but also the less savory aspects of me. The fact that I have a temper sometimes, or that I hold grudges, or that I hate surprises. And he'll support my dreams."

"Mmmm, that's a long list. Anything else?"

"Of course. He also needs to love going down on me," I joke.

"I mean, that's a given, right?" he replies, lazily caressing my nether regions.

I move his hand back to my waist. "I gave you *my* answer, so what's yours? How did you become such a player, huh?"

"It wasn't on purpose," he says. "I was more introverted growing up ..."

I smile, thinking of the Ben who was too shy to ever make a move on me in high school.

"And then one day, it just became easy to get girls ..."

Because you're a smart, hot, completely lovable guy. "Easy."

"And when I got to college, lots of girls were interested, and I didn't see any reason to commit to just one. Had I found someone I connected with on a deeper level, maybe I would have settled down, but ..."

"What?"

"This is gonna sound so bad."

"Say it."

"Every time I went out with a woman for longer than a month, she began to bore me."

Huh.

"I want someone who ... after three months, after a year, after twenty years still makes me think. I don't know if it's possible, but that's what I hope for if I ever decide I want to get married."

"You don't want to get married one day?" I ask, surprised.

He pauses before answering me. "I don't know. It's hard for me to believe in long-lasting love after seeing my parents' marriage fall apart. I mean, if twenty-five years, three kids, everything that comes with that isn't enough to hold it all together, to want to try, then ... what is?"

Poor Ben. I sigh and rest my head on his chest, and then all the gears in my mind—as if warmed up from our previous activities—begin to turn.

"What are you thinking?" he asks.

I don't want you to go. But what I say is something different. "Will you have time to catch up while you're gone?"

"I honestly don't know—"

"Okay," I say abruptly. I knew he was leaving when I threw caution to the wind and seduced him. I get it.

"I wasn't done," he says, running his fingers through my hair. "I don't know how much free time I'll have, but I'm going to try."

I force a smile. "I guess we have to get up at some point, huh?" I get to my knees, but before I can stand, his eyes graze over my body. "What?"

"I wish I was an artist like you," he says, "so I could paint what I see right now."

"You're so—"

"Corny, I know," he interrupts me. "I don't care. It's true. I wouldn't do you justice, though. You're perfection." As he says it, he lifts one hand and softly caresses the side of my breast, then lets his hand fall to my waist. "I'd paint you in beautiful colors, and I'd call it, 'Nice Jewish girl.'"

I snicker, hold out my hand, and help him sit up. I very obviously take in his naked body. "I don't know what you did in college, but"—I pause to exhale through my mouth dramatically—"it worked." I bite my lip and smile at the pleased expression on his face.

I wrap a robe around myself while he gets dressed. Before he leaves my room, he pulls me into one last hug, and we stand there for a minute, just holding one another. One tear escapes, but I wipe it before pulling back from the hug.

"I want us to talk while I'm gone," he says.

"Be careful in Israel, okay?"

"I will," he says and kisses my hand before leaving.

After I shut the door, I walk over to the window and wait until I see him walk out to his car.

Was he telling the truth? Does he really want us to keep talking?

He opens his car door, then looks up, searching for my window, I suppose. I move the curtain and blow him a kiss. He pantomimes catching it, curls his fist, and places it over his heart.

As he slips into his car, I close my eyes. The whole day has felt like a dream, and if I don't see him leave, maybe I can pretend he never did. In my mind's eye, I see his smiling face and his soulful eyes looking back at me. When I'm brave enough to open my eyes and check the parking lot, his car is gone, and I swallow down the knot in my throat. *I just got you back, and now you're gone again.*

Ben

As I lie back on my lounge chair on Carmel Beach and look out at the blue-green waters of the Mediterranean Sea, the sweltering heat this Friday afternoon barely bothers me. I'm thawing out from the cold lab

I've been working in since my arrival in Israel. I close my eyes and let myself daydream—just one more time, I promise myself—about Gabby. It's been two long weeks since I got on the plane and left her in New Jersey. I texted her a few times, and she always texts back, but with the time zone difference and my busy schedule during this fellowship, we always miss each other when we try to FaceTime.

I open my phone to call her now, then stop when I remember she's in class on Friday mornings. She texted me earlier this week that right after class she's heading to her cousin's wedding in Boston.

Pictures will have to be enough. I flip back and forth between the only two photos I have of her. I took one of her at the restaurant where we had brunch. In it, she's holding her coffee mug and smiling at me, and there's the tiniest bit of milk foam on her upper lip. Her hair, still damp from her morning shower, was pulled back in a hair clip, and a few strands were falling into her face. I remember thinking, *I have to capture this. I can't forget how she looks in this moment.*

The second is the selfie we took together at the beach. As I snapped the picture, she kissed me on the cheek. I had already kissed her in the water. I kissed the palm of her beautiful hand, and God knows, there were *many* kisses later that day, but that sweet peck she gave me on my cheek bridged the past—teenagers who were too young and inexperienced to know how to understand our feelings—and the present.

Ah, that problematic present—the one where she's there and I'm here, and I have no idea if there is a way forward.

The morning I drove to Rutgers, I was nervous that Gabby would be different—and she was in all the right ways. The moment she had walked out the front door of her residence hall, my pulse had sped up at the sight of her surprised, happy expression. She had grown a few inches, and as I wrapped my arms around her—our first hug in many years—then slid my hands down to her shapely waist, I realized that she had grown up.

Beyond the surface, though, I discovered that while my life had moved forward, she had also been busy discovering not only who she is, but also who she wants to become. It was like standing inside of a time tunnel. The shadow of the beautiful girl I knew from years before was still there, but as I looked into her brown eyes that July day, I caught a brief glimpse at the powerhouse of a woman she would soon become.

She's exactly who I want, who I need. But like a door slammed shut by the wind, I remember what I told her about maybe never even wanting to get married. And that is exactly what *she* wants, at least eventually—to get married, to have kids, all of it. Have I ruined my chances before I even got started by telling her the truth, by revealing all my fears and doubts?

But it was Gabby. I'd never lie to her.

I lay my head back on the lounge chair, close my eyes, and let myself imagine whether we could ever be anything. She wants someone who understands her and supports her dreams. *What are they?*

My roommate, a British guy from Liverpool, comes back from the outdoor bar balancing a couple bottles of beer and a small bowl of cracked green olives. "Goldstar?" he asks.

"Thanks, man," I say, taking one of the bottles from his full hands.

He glances at my phone and asks, "Girlfriend?"

"I wish."

"She certainly looks like she wouldn't be opposed to the idea," he replies. He holds his beer out, and we clink bottles. "*L'chaim.*"

We both take a swig, and he looks at me, eyebrows raised, waiting for me to respond.

I shrug. "We never seem to be in the same place at the same time."

He sniffs out in amusement. "If you like her so much, seems like a problem worth solving."

If only it were that simple.

I rub my tired, dry eyes, wishing I had some eye drops. I'm waiting at my gate in the middle of the night at Ben Gurion Airport for my flight back to the United States, and I read through Dr. Doron's email one more time.

Ben,

I had my reservations about allowing you into the program, not being in grad school yet, but you surpassed my expectations. I know you're interested in cancer therapies due to your mother's experience. I have a good friend in that field at Weizmann.

The world-renowned Weizmann Institute of Science?

Keep in touch over the next few years. I'd be happy to provide you with a recommendation for whatever you need.

I slouch down in the hard, unforgiving airport seat and finally close my eyes. This summer was more than I could have hoped for, at least, on some fronts. Despite my promise to Gabby, we only talked twice while I was gone. The conversations were fine but nothing special.

Maybe too much time has passed since we grew up together.

I run through my mental checklist of things to do once I'm back. With only five days before I move into my new place at Cornell, I need to prioritize: see my mom and dad, pack my winter clothes, buy a new laptop, and ... see Gabby.

I *have* to meet up with her before I drive up to Ithaca. I check her Instagram account—since finding her on there, I've had an endless supply of photos of her—and see that she's gone on some girls trip to Chicago.

Me

When are you back from Chicago?

Gabby

Stalker.

Me

<smiley emoji>

Back in a week.

Shit.

I've just left the Big Red Barn after grabbing a coffee when my phone pings.

Coming home for Thanksgiving?

Hearing from her after a pause is the perfect pick-me-up. I'm due back at the lab soon, but I have a few minutes and set my things down on the bench.

I don't think so. I'm the lead on some experiment that has to be checked daily.

So you're not coming back?

Can't <frowny face emoji>

Does she want me to?

I'd bring you some turkey, but I'm being dragged to South Florida to visit family.

Tough life, spending winter in the tropics <winky emoji>

I imagine her poolside in a bikini. If I let the daydream continue, I'm sitting near her, then I'm lying on top of her while we make out.

I wish you could come. I always enjoyed watching you swim. <winky face emoji>

Nice to know I'm not the only one daydreaming.

You just want to see me in a swimsuit.

You always did look good in one.

I smile.

But you looked even better without one … between my legs.

Goddamn, G. I chuckle.

I'll be home for the winter holidays. Maybe we can meet up then?

I see the "typing" bubble, and then she breaks the news.

I forgot to tell you. I'm going to Israel during winter break. On Birthright.

I type out my reply: *I wish I could come with you.* But my finger hovers over Send. A cloud of doubt descends upon me, and I delete it all.

What do I truly want to tell her? *I think about you all the time. I wish... we could be together.*

I run my hand over my face. Too much time has passed, and we're too far apart. *Accept it. Nothing is going to happen.*

You're gonna have such a great time. Have a safe trip.

Spring rolls around, and I hear from my mom that Gabby secured an internship at Google in the city. Gabriella Feinman—my best friend's little sister, the girl I confided my childhood fears in, the woman I still sometimes imagine coming home to—will be working as a software engineer at Google in Manhattan. It's a wake-up call. *We've both grown up, and it's time to move on.*

Little by little, my childhood crush, my "bestie," the girl who lit up my heart and made me break out into a nervous sweat from the touch of her hand on mine, becomes a memory for me, instead of what I would have liked her to be: a very real, very present part of my life.

Two Years Later

Playing with Fire

Ben

I smile at the sight of Liran, asleep and curled up in the passenger seat with my jacket, on our drive from Ithaca to Glen Rock. Excited about getting a car here in the United States, she insisted on bringing her car but got tired after driving for two hours, so I've taken over.

I noticed her immediately in the lab. She's smart, outspoken, and just the right amount of sassy. Maybe she reminded me of my sisters, or maybe ... someone else. It's too early to bring her home to meet my parents—we've only been dating a few weeks—but she didn't have anywhere to go for the holiday. I felt guilty imagining her all alone in frozen Ithaca while I was home having turkey and stuffing.

I drive over a rough patch of highway, and she stirs in her seat. "Are we there?" she asks in a sleepy voice.

I reach out my hand and rub her thigh. "No, couple more hours. Keep sleeping."

She mumbles something in Hebrew and falls back asleep. As we make our way toward my childhood home, my thoughts, too, drift to childhood memories—to one person in particular.

My last text exchange with Gabby was right after she graduated early and moved to the city. I congratulated her, and she asked if I wanted to get together. My gut reaction was yes, but then I started thinking too much. Deciding that I didn't want to navigate things with her long-distance, I'd told her I was busy. I left her hanging, and she's obviously been wise enough to keep me at a distance since.

When we arrive in Glen Rock, I drive through my old neighborhood. As we pass the Feinmans' house, I mention to Liran that that's where my best friend lived growing up.

"Aaron?" Liran asks.

"Yeah," I say, pleased that she remembers my stories about him.

"You said he has a sister, right? Abby?"

"Gabby," I reply. "How'd you remember?"

"I'm a smart woman."

"That you are," I say, as I park the car in my mom's driveway. "Ready?"

She leans in to kiss me. "Thank you for bringing me to your home," she says, and I smile both at her affectionate nature and the quirkiness of her English phrasing.

"Of course," I reply, feeling warmth in my chest, just under where she's placed her hand. "Shall we?"

She nods, and I take her inside to meet my mom.

This Thanksgiving, Ariella is spending time with her boyfriend's family, and Miri took a trip to Puerto Rico with her new girlfriend, so it'll just be us … and my dad.

When we arrived yesterday, my mom told me that she had invited him. "He didn't have any plans, and I thought …"

"It's fine, Ima. It was the right thing to do," I said, thinking of my own reasons for inviting Liran this weekend.

On Thanksgiving Day, dinner preparations go smoothly. While Liran and I tackle most of the side dishes, my mom splits her time between basting the turkey and interrogating Liran about her life and family in a diplomatic yet thorough manner.

After we finish preparing all the food, Liran goes upstairs to shower, and I check in with my mom again.

"So you'll be okay having Aba here for dinner?"

"Of course," she replies. "We talk here and there to check in on each other. We're not married anymore, but he's been my friend for thirty years. You don't easily forget such a long friendship."

Yet again, Gabby materializes in my thoughts. My mom's right. It *is* hard to forget such a long friendship.

My mom looks at me and smiles for the hundredth time today. "I'm glad you came home, sweetie."

"I missed you."

"My baby," she says, pulling me in for a hug. I'm almost a foot taller than her, and I laugh and pat her head. "Fine, my *big* baby."

"Ima, sit and rest. I'll make you some tea."

"Good idea," she says, settling down at the small breakfast table and facing me while I fill the electric kettle and turn it on.

"So what do you think of Liran?" I ask, glancing toward the stairs to make sure we're not being overheard.

I take the mugs out of the cabinet and look at her.

After a moment, she says, "She's Israeli. Israeli women are tough."

I sniff out in amusement. *She should know.* Before she met my dad, she was a soldier in an intelligence unit. I've seen a picture of her holding an M-16 during her basic training. "Israeli women are tough" is something I learned from being raised by one.

"Thanks for stating the obvious," I reply, "but I asked what you think of one, specifically."

She clears her throat. "She's ... a nice girl," she offers up. It's the most *pareve*, neutral compliment I can imagine, which means that Liran isn't her cup of tea, as the case may be. I add the freshly washed mint leaves to the mugs and pour boiling water over them.

I bring the mugs to the table and sit next to her, without saying a word.

I raise my eyebrow at her, and she smiles. "She's fine, honey. Intelligent. Extremely pretty. Striking, even. Strong-willed. I heard how she told you to butt out when she was making the mashed potatoes."

I snicker.

"Benny, if you like her, then I like her," she says and blows on her cup of tea. I do the same. "How do *you* feel about her?"

"I'm just getting to know her. She's pretty like you said, and I like her strong will.
But ..."

"Hmmm?"

I meet her eyes. "I guess time will tell if we're a good fit."

"Time does have a way of doing that," she says, looking at me intently, and perhaps waiting for me to say more.

I *want* to have high hopes, but the last time I let myself get swept away by someone, I ended up disappointed.

My mom sips her tea, then picks up her phone. "Oh, look at that. I missed a text from Marci. She's asking if I have fresh dill. Would you take it over there?"

I narrow my eyes at her, wondering if she's up to something. She casually mentioned Gabby to me this morning over coffee, while Li-ran was still asleep. I'm tempted to call her on this suspiciously timed herb-related side quest to the Feinmans', but I need to say "Hi" to Aaron. And, well, I wouldn't mind seeing Gabby either.

"Sure, let me just find my coat and tell Liran I'll be right back."

Discovering that she's already in the shower when I head upstairs, I come back downstairs and take the small package from my mom. It's a two-minute walk down the road to reach the Feinmans' house, but it's a nice, if chilly, day outside. I take a longer route, walking around the block. I remember riding my bike here as a kid. It makes me think about the winter we first moved here when Aaron and I became friends.

I ring the Feinmans' doorbell. Aaron answers the door and immediately pulls me in for a hug. "Hey, man. I thought you were gonna text me when you got in."

"Sorry. My mom's been working me to the bone cooking today. I don't know why. It's only the four of us."

"Four of us?" he asks, backing up to let me in the house, then closing the door behind me.

"Yeah, me, my mom, my dad, if you can believe that, and my ... uh... Liran. A girl, uh, friend I brought home from school."

He raises his eyebrows. "Serious?"

I cock my head, thinking. "It's kinda new." I remember the dill and hold out the bag to him. "Can you give this to your mom? She asked for dill?"

"She did? She finished cooking hours ago. She's resting upstairs."

I knew it.

"Ah, okay. Well, maybe just put it in the fridge."

"We're going out tonight, remember? Bring Liran."

"Of course. How is everyone? Is ... Gabby around? How's she doing?" Just saying her name makes me nervous. Aaron has no idea we hooked up, and I prefer to keep it that way.

"She's good. Got in this morning. She's at a friend's right now."

I nod.

"When's the last time you saw her anyway?"

"It's been ... a long time."

"She looks different now," he says. "Dyed her hair and dresses all cool now that she lives in Brooklyn and works in Manhattan." He rolls his eyes good-naturedly. He'll always be an older brother, but I can tell he's proud of her.

I follow her on Instagram and saw her post when she got her hair done. Her thick brown hair streaked with blonde was different than I remember but still beautiful.

I smile. "Sounds like she's doing well."

He leans in closer to tell me in a low voice, "She broke up with her boyfriend about a month ago. We liked him. Thought they were pretty serious, but I don't know. She just ... said he wasn't the one."

Hmmm. Sounds familiar.

"Anyway, my mom said you're coming to Friendsgiving tomorrow night, so you guys can catch up then."

I can imagine the conversation.

Hey, G. Things going well? Did you know you've ruined me for every other woman because nobody can measure up to how I feel about you?

I take a deep breath and step back toward the door. "I gotta go, man. Don't wanna leave Liran hanging."

"She's Israeli?" he asks.

I nod.

"Is she hot?" he asks with a smile.

"Yeah," I say, snickering. "She's hot."

"Cool. I'll meet her tonight. Text you later."

Gabby

I'm sitting on a bar stool in Stosh's taking in the scent of the mulled wine in front of me.

"Have a sip," Ilana says. "It's nice and warm. We deserve it after our hike."

"In high-heeled boots, no less," I say, and sip the warm wine. "Oooh, this is good."

I look around at the packed bar and recognize not a few faces. Since I graduated last winter, I've been living in a minuscule apartment in Kensington with two roommates I barely see, and being back home for Thanksgiving and seeing old friends feels good.

The beautiful woman sitting across from me now, Ilana, is a rekindled friendship. I originally met her at a Shabbat dinner at Hillel during my freshman year, and then we met again when I began working at Google. We work in the same department, and all it took was one lunch for us to realize we're kindred spirits. We've become closer ever since, and she's in town because her grandmother lives in the area.

I take another sip of the wine and lick my upper lip.

"One more like that," Ilana says, "and I'll finally get the whole story about you and David."

"I don't want to talk about my breakup. I'd rather find a distraction," I reply, letting my eyes wander over to the bar, where I saw a cute guy sitting when we came in.

"Well, you look hot tonight. I don't think you'll have any problem meeting someone. But first ... I need details."

I don't want to talk about it, but she raises her eyebrows at me.

"Fine," I relent. "Something just wasn't clicking from my side. And it seemed like I was the only one with a problem. He kept putting feelers out there about marriage—and I am *not* ready for that yet."

"Wow, after less than a year? What magic are you working?" She's been together with her boyfriend—currently at home in Miami for the holidays—for over a year, and she didn't even get an invitation home for Thanksgiving.

"Well, the magic has to be with the right guy." After eight months, it was clear to me, he wasn't.

"I hear that." She looks wistful.

"Trouble in paradise?"

"Paradise is Miami in the winter, and I'm here in New Jersey. That should be enough of a hint," she says and rolls her eyes.

I raise my eyebrow in question, but she doesn't offer up any information. Apparently, this sharing thing is a one-way street tonight.

"What was wrong with David?" she asks.

"Nothing, I guess, at least on paper. He's cute, on a good career track. He even likes animals."

"But?"

"Well, you know he was a bit older, so there was the marriage thing. And it all felt comfortable, but I guess not what ... or who ... I imagined creating a life with you know and ..."

"What?" she asks, smiling mischievously and leaning closer.

"Nothing."

"Sure. How was the sex?" she whispers.

"Um, fine?"

She raises an eyebrow.

"I guess that kind of sums it up. It wasn't that exciting. It was ... fine. But not amazing, like I know it can be with the ..."

The words *right person* are just about to leave my mouth when I look up and a woman with tawny skin and full, curly hair comes in the front door of the bar. She's laughing and turns back for a moment and holds her hand out to—fuck me—Benjamin Adler.

Ilana has noticed where my attention is and raises an eyebrow in question. She doesn't know who Ben is, or what he means to me. But something—something apparently obvious—must be written all over my face.

"Old boyfriend?" she asks, intrigued.

I let out a surprised exhale. "I wish."

"Well, looks like he's taken tonight, but I'm happy to report that someone else very cute *is* walking over here."

I turn and follow her eyes.

"Shit, that's my brother." I laugh, rolling my eyes. She starts to laugh, too.

"Hey Gabs, I didn't know you were headed here," Aaron says, as he approaches. "Didn't I see you, like, three hours ago cramming pie in your face?"

I smirk. "Didn't I see you doing the same?"

He laughs and gives me a hug.

"We ended up here after Stone & Rail was full. I think the whole world is in town tonight."

"Hell, yeah. Not everybody escapes to Brooklyn like you."

"Well, Brooklyn has a *bit* more to offer in the way of culture and excitement. Not everyone was born with the soul of a sixty-year-old man."

He kicks me under the table and glances at Ilana. *Oh, he thinks she's cute.*

"But there's a lot to be said for sixty-year-old men," I say, trying to save the situation. "They have well-established retirement funds, they understand the stock market, they know good ... bourbon?"

Ilana snorts. "Gabby, you're so mean."

He puts on his most charming smile, and says all smooth, "Isn't she, though?"

Ah, so this is Aaron flirting. It's been a while since I've had a front-row seat.

He is a handsome guy, looking especially nice tonight in a forest green ribbed sweater that complements his dark wavy hair. She responds with a smile, and he winks.

She has a boyfriend, but Aaron doesn't know that. It's not my business. Up until a month ago, I also had a boyfriend I wasn't so happy with.

"I'm Aaron, by the way, since my little sister is too rude to introduce me properly."

"I'm Ilana. It's nice to meet you, Aaron."

He extends his hand. Ilana holds hers out confidently and then she softens, as he clasps his second hand over hers. *Interesting.*

"So how do you know Gabby?" he asks her.

"We work together. I'm a technical recruiter in her department."

"ML?"

"Yeah, exactly," she says, smiling. *Did her eyes just twinkle?*

"But we originally met at Rutgers Hillel our freshman year. Where did *you* go to school?"

Oooh. She's smooth. Must be those recruiter skills.

"Ah, well, for undergrad, I went to UPenn, and now I'm doing my MBA at Columbia. It's mostly remote, so I decided to stay in the area, near my family. And not escape to the city," he says, shooting me a playful look.

"Hey, I live in the city," she says. "It's not *that* terrible."

"So what are you doing here?" he asks.

"Her grandma lives in Glen Rock," I share. "Mrs. Sokolov, from the synagogue."

I note the split-second question in his eyes. He must be trying to make the connection between Mrs. Sokolov—a frail but still feisty, light-skinned Ashkenazi woman with dyed red hair and a penchant for brightly colored pantsuits—and Ilana, with her light brown skin, dark, curly hair partially braided into cornrows and tight leather pants.

"She's my grandma on my mom's side," she says with a warm smile, "and my dad's Black."

"Sweet," he says with a small shrug.

"Sometimes when people figure out I'm Jewish and Black, they ask if I'm Ethiopian, but my parents are both American. They met volunteering on a kibbutz, and my dad converted for my mom. Now he's more religious than she is."

Aaron looks at her, and she gazes back. "You know," he says, "you don't *owe* anybody your backstory."

"I know," she says, her smile widening. "But I like my friends to know who I am—what I'm all about." *Does she* like *him?*

"In that case," he says, "I look forward to being your friend."

Holy shit. The tension between these two is palpable, and I take a sip of my drink, trying to think of something to say.

"Ilana has tons of good stories," I suddenly chime in. "She's seen the Northern Lights, she's been to the Great Wall of China, *and* she's snorkeled the Great Barrier Reef."

Aaron's eyes light up. "Those are all on my bucket list."

"My parents love to travel," she explains. "I've been all over the place."

Aaron pulls up an extra barstool and starts asking her questions about her travels. When they begin to discuss strategies for buying the cheapest flights, I consider interrupting them to tell them I'm going to get a drink, but she's laughing at something he's saying. Just because I'm going to be miserable tonight watching Ben with his date doesn't mean they have to be. Time for me to find something else to do.

I glance at the dance floor but don't want to go out there by myself, so I turn to talk to a group of old high school friends I ran into on the way in. After getting Ilana's number—*interesting*—Aaron heads to the table where his friends have settled in about fifteen feet away from us, and it looks like Ben's girlfriend is on the dance floor, dancing with some other women. I guess she makes fast friends.

Ilana joins me, puts an arm around my waist, and leans in to ask, "Are you gonna sit here all night and watch him watch her, or do you want to try to have some fun?"

I'd rather choose a third option—go home to my parents' house, put on my pajamas, and crawl into bed. But Ilana is right. I *am* looking hot tonight, and I figure, if Ben can have fun with someone else, well, I can, too.

"You're right," I say to Ilana and stand to head to the bar, charting my course to end up near the guy I had my eye on earlier. I note his broad shoulders and thick, dark blonde hair as I squeeze in next to him.

"Vodka and soda?" I ask the bartender. She nods and asks if I want lime or lemon.

The cute guy leans my way and whispers, "Go for both. Live a little."

I smile at him, then tell her, "This fine gentleman suggests I try both."

She rolls her eyes good-naturedly. She's probably heard all the terrible pickup lines in her line of work.

"What's your name?" he asks.

"Gabby," I say.

"I'm Ethan."

"Nice to meet you. Do you like to dance?"

"I'm not that good, but for a beautiful woman, I'll do my best," he says.

"Good enough for me," I say, thinking that maybe tonight won't be so bad.

I take my drink, down it in two big gulps, and pull Ethan out to the dance floor. He turns out to be more than a capable dancer. He can keep the beat, and he's not too handsy—both desirable characteristics in a dance partner. At some point, he spins me around, and I end up facing Ben and the woman he came in with earlier.

She has her arms around his neck and leans in to kiss him a lot. He doesn't deny her, but he seems stiff, and he keeps glancing at me, then away.

I turn in a different direction, and Aaron catches my eye, indicating with his head that I should join him at their table.

"I'll find you in a few minutes," I tell Ethan and walk over to Aaron and his friends. I slide into the booth next to Aaron and ask him what's up.

"Well, we were discussing the AI revolution—"

"As one does when taking shots in a bar," I say with a grin.

"Exactly," Aaron agrees. "And Noah said that the current wave of AI started at Google, and I told him it started before that at the University of Toronto."

I raise my eyebrow at him, waiting for him to continue.

"We were going to Google it," Noah chimes in.

"But I told him my sister works in ML at Google," Aaron adds, "and he seemed to think that's a more reliable source to settle this bet."

"Well, thank you for the compliment. More reliable than a search engine with hundreds of billions of results? I think you're overestimating my abilities," I joke. "I do happen to know the answer, but first, I want to know the bet."

"A round of drinks for the group," Noah says.

"Me included?" I ask with a wink.

"It depends whose side you're on," Noah answers, shooting me an adorable grin. He's attractive in a low-key "I don't even have to try" way with his long dark eyelashes and sexy, unshaven jawline.

"Well," I say, thinking, "AlexNet was the first thing to break AI out of its so-called decades-long 'winter.'"

They all look at me, mouths open, silent, not sure how to respond.

Guess I'll have to simplify. "I hate admitting it, but Aaron's right. AlexNet was developed at the University of Toronto."

Aaron cheers, while Noah dramatically throws his hands in the air. "Noooo." But I can see the twinkle in his dark eyes.

"A round of shots," Aaron declares. Noah gets up. "Gabby, wanna help me carry all the drinks back?"

"Sure," I say, sliding out of the booth. Noah follows me as I wind my way through the crowd to the bar, placing his hand on the small of my back, and I like the way it feels.

"So how long have you known Aaron?" I ask as we wait for the bartender to prepare our drinks.

"We met this year. We worked on a project together for the MBA program, and it turned out we grew up not far away from each other. He told me you guys—well, I guess he and his friends—were going out tonight and asked if I wanted to join. I didn't know he was bringing his beautiful sister."

"He didn't *bring* me, but thank you for the compliment."

"It's just the truth," he says and pulls his wallet out to hand the bartender his credit card.

I sneak a peek. "Noah Abrams. That's a pretty Jewish name there. Let me guess, middle name 'Ari?'"

"Worse. Solomon."

I laugh. "Well, at least you have cool initials. NSA."

He smiles, and I find myself liking how I'm able to make him smile.

"I can get the tray of drinks, but can you take these two?" he asks, gesturing to two shot glasses that are not quite balanced on the edge.

I take the glasses from the over-full tray, and we head back through the crowd, but on the way, Ben intercepts me. "Hey, G."

I stop and simply look at him with the drinks in my hands. "May I?" he asks, taking one of the glasses before I can say "no." He clinks my glass with his, and says "*L'chaim.*" We both drink, eyes locked on each other.

"Come on, I wanna catch up," he says, taking the glass from my hand and setting it down on a nearby table.

I shouldn't give him the satisfaction or myself the frustration, but I follow him. Noah has turned around to see where I went, but Ben winks at me and pulls me behind a pillar, then out the side door onto a patio, and into the cold night. There are portable heaters lit, but it's still chilly.

"Are you freezing?" he asks, looking me up and down, taking in the tight sweater dress with a plunging neckline and my high-heeled boots. He tries not to make it obvious, but the slight widening of his eyes betrays his thoughts. He likes how I look tonight. Though I'm loath to admit it, I quite like how he looks tonight, too, in a form-fitting dark-gray sweater and pants that hug his muscular legs and tight ass.

When he meets my eyes again, I smile smugly. "I'll be alright because I'm not staying out here. What do you want?"

"I wanted to see how you're doing."

"I was doing just fine. I danced with a cute guy and was about to have a conversation with another one."

He smiles. "I'm sure you were. You're the most beautiful woman here."

"You came here with another woman tonight. You shouldn't be saying that to *me.*"

"No, I shouldn't," he admits. He looks down but then glances up at me through his dark eyelashes and smirks. "But I'm saying it anyway."

I sniff out and roll my eyes. "Girlfriend?"

"I think so."

I scoff. "You *think* so?"

"*She* thinks so," he says. "And that guy I saw *you* with?"

"Which guy? There were two," I tease.

He raises his eyebrow at me.

"I met them both tonight," I admit.

An expression quickly crosses his eyes. *Relief?*

"I've missed your sharp tongue," he says.

"I've missed … you," I say, forcing myself out of my comfort zone. "I thought that the last time we saw each other we'd keep in touch better. But it didn't work out, did it?"

"Things were busy while I was in Israel and then when I got back and started my PhD program, I was far away again. I should've tried harder."

We should've tried harder. He reached out, then I did, but somehow … Standing close to him now, it's impossible not to feel the connection between us.

A couple of guys sitting at a patio table head inside, leaving us alone. The music playing out here is different from the loud bass they're blasting inside, and Kesha comes on.

"No way," I say. *Did he notice? Does he remember?*

"Well, that seems like a sign."

"For what?" I ask.

"That you should dance with me. I played this song for you in high school." He *does* remember.

I've been leaning up against the wall, and now I straighten, moving the slightest bit closer to him. He does the same and places his hands on my waist.

I reach up and put my arms around his neck. He pulls me into his body, and his fingers begin to move lightly on my back.

"What are you doing?" I ask.

"I'm playing you the song again," he says, and with the soft smile on his face, he is the most kissable I've ever seen him. "I know how to play guitar now, too."

"When did you learn?"

"In college when I figured out college girls love guys who play guitar," he admits.

"Just change your name already."

He cocks his head. "To what?"

"Ben 'Drop Your Panties For Me' Adler."

He laughs and simply raises his eyebrows, not refuting the accuracy of the name.

I shake my head. "Do you still play piano?"

"I don't have time. Busy with school and lab work."

"That's a shame."

"I'll get back to it."

I smile, imagining his beautiful hands on piano keys, making music. Imagining his hands on me, making me sing in other ways. "I guess sometimes we drift away from the things we love—"

"But then we come back to them?"

I meet his eyes, waiting to see if he'll say anything else. It's cold outside, but Ben's hands on me are warm. My chest is pressed up against his front, and I can smell ... him. His scent has always felt like comfort to me, and tonight is no exception.

"You smell so good, G."

"I was just thinking the same thing about you," I whisper.

"What do I smell like?" he asks.

"Roasted almonds and mint."

He snickers. "My mom's cooking. Well, you smell like ..." He sniffs my hair. "Cinnamon. Pumpkin pie."

"I had a slice earlier."

"Only one?"

"Three," I admit.

He smiles and angles his head down to sniff my hair again. His hand is on my jaw. He's close enough that if I turned my head, we could kiss. And I swallow. My body is stiff from nervousness.

"I've missed all of you," he says. "Not just your sharp tongue. I-I should've told you."

"Sometimes, showing is better than telling."

He contemplates that for a second and nods. Just then the door to my right opens, and there's a blast of loud music from the bar. Framed in the light pouring out from inside onto the darker patio is a beautiful woman—Ben's semi-girlfriend. I step away from him, bumping into the wall. After a beat, Ben comes to his senses.

"Um, Liran, this is Gabby, Aaron's sister," Ben says, dumbly.

"Hi, Abby," she says in fluent English with a slight Israeli accent. She extends her hand. "Pleased to meet you." She sounds anything but pleased, and I know better than to correct her pronunciation of my name.

"You, too," I say quickly without extending my hand. I walk quickly past her and through the door into the warm, loud bar.

Before the door closes behind me, I glance outside and see her lean up to kiss him—claim him—with a full-mouthed kiss on the lips.

Fuck.

I want to get out of here, but first I want a drink. As I head to the bar, Noah notices me and stands to join me, but I keep going.

Ethan is sitting near his friends and smiles when he sees me. "Hey, you're back. You wanna dance some more?"

"I want ..." What do I want? I want Ben like I always have, and I want to kick myself for it.

I lean in and touch his chest—it's just as hard as it looks—and say close to his ear, "You wanna get out of here?"

"Wow, uh, yeah," he replies and puts his hand over mine. He grabs it and begins to walk toward the front door. On the way out, I stop by our table and grab my coat. I tell Ilana not to wait for me. She responds with raised eyebrows.

Once we're outside, I realize that I don't have anywhere to take him since I'm staying with my parents. Turns out he's in the same situation, but his SUV has more than enough space in the backseat for us to get comfortable.

When he offers it as an option "to get out of the cold," a small voice in my head tells me to go home, but I need something to distract myself from thinking about other things—other people. I climb in the backseat, and he slides in next to me, closing the door.

"Are you cold?" he asks.

I nod.

"Here, put your legs across my lap. I'll warm you up."

I scoot closer to him, and Ethan's hands on my waist are an insufficient replacement for Ben's, but the latter isn't an option. As I make out with him and he slides his warm hands up my torso and touches my breasts, I realize that my bad record with guys is not only due to my poor decision-making. Tonight is just one more example of me not being able to let go of someone who was never mine.

While we kiss, Ethan tells me I'm gorgeous. He's turned on—insistent, but gentle—and I think for a moment that I'm lucky. He's a decent guy. I barely know him, and I all but invited him to have sex with me in the parking lot.

"Why'd you choose me, huh?" he says, kissing my neck, then pausing. "I saw you talking to a few other guys."

"I guess you just got lucky," I say tartly, and he laughs.

"I think *you* got lucky, Gabriella," he says, as he moves his hands between my legs and slides my underwear to the side, to stroke me gently. "There's nothing that turns me on more than a woman who knows what she wants. Is this what you want?" He teases my opening with one finger.

I nod, and then after a bit more attention to my clit, he slips two fingers inside, while giving me a deep kiss.

I unbuckle his pants and stroke him. It all works just the way it's supposed to on his side. He comes from the practiced movements of my hands, from my tongue inside his mouth, and then my teeth on his earlobe. And though my words indicate enjoyment, he can't tell it's all a lie, because ... he doesn't know me.

While Ethan kisses my neck and does all the things that should make me come, I don't. I can't concentrate. I'm empty inside, and the shape of the absence is very specific. There's a question in my mind that repeats itself: will I ever get over Ben?

·❤·❤·❤·❤·❤·

I wake up late in the morning, a tad hungover, but mostly fine, at least physically. Emotionally, I'm a mess. I wash my face and go downstairs. I'm grateful as my mom slides a plate with three pancakes toward me. Maybe they'll soak up some of the residual alcohol in my stomach. About ten minutes later, Aaron trudges downstairs, looking like he's been hit by a truck.

"Damn, A. You okay?" I ask before taking another gulp of black coffee.

He drags his tired eyes in my direction. "I'm fine. I was just up *really* late. Adler's girlfriend broke up with him last night, and it was a cluster."

"What?" I ask, suddenly much more alert. "I mean," I say, correcting course with a less curious tone, "what happened?"

"I don't know. She said he was looking at some other chick the whole night, and apparently, she's the jealous kind. I don't even know what she's talking about. I didn't notice anything out of the ordinary."

"Huh. Me either," I say, continuing the worst performance of "It wasn't me" ever.

"It's weird. I mean, he was either dancing with her or … I don't know. She said she went outside for some air, and he had his hands all over someone."

"Really?" I ask. "Who?" *Does Aaron know something? Is he only being vague because our mother is pretending to unload the dishwasher but is secretly listening to every word we're saying?*

He rolls his eyes. "I don't know. Anyways, she's driving back to Ithaca today, and I guess somebody's gonna have to take his ass back up there on Sunday."

I grab a pancake and my coffee cup and head upstairs. I can't be in the kitchen right now. I need to think—alone.

How does Aaron not know it was me? Did Liran not say my name? Wait, she's only leaving today. Did they make up last night?

I force myself to wait until noon to text Ben.

Me

Rough night?

It takes him an hour to respond. An hour during which I run through all kinds of scenarios in my head, ranging from he's preparing to come propose to me to them having wild makeup sex in his bedroom and he's already forgotten about me—again.

I'm lying on the floor, intermittently stretching, doing crunches, and wallowing in self-pity when my phone chirps, alerting me of a text message.

Ben

Who is this?

How dare he?

But then another text comes in.

Ben

<winky emoji>

I guess you heard then. My night was not ideal, but I'll be ok.

What about you? Have a good night with your not-boyfriend?

I lie.

Me

Nah, just went home.

Ben

I could've sworn I saw you leave with him. <winky emoji>

He *was* watching me last night.

Me

Not me. What would I even do with a guy I took home from a bar?

Ben

If you're asking that question, you didn't go home with the right guy. <winky emoji>

Understatement of the year, Benjamin. And screw you and your God-damn winky emojis.

I don't know how to respond to that, so I head into my parents' bathroom to take a long, hot bath and hope the warm water and steam will grant me magical problem-solving powers.

I sink down in the oversized bathtub into a sea of bubbles and think. Ben is flirting with me. Today's texts. Last night's conversation. I'm not an idiot, but I feel crazy inside. There's a tornado of emotions swirling in my head: a mixture of want, lust, hurt, and—*Goddamnit*—feelings of inferiority. Once upon a time, we were friends. And once—one time—we were lovers. But it never became more. *Why?*

I'm pulled out of my spiral of unhelpful thoughts by the sound of a text coming in. I purposefully placed my phone far enough away from the tub that it would be hard for me to reach over to check it. *I'm not going to check it.* It's probably something else that will drive me even crazier than I already feel right now. But then I hear it sound again.

Fuck. I'm gonna check it. I knew I would.

I reach out of the tub, wiping my hand quickly on the towel, hanging from the bar.

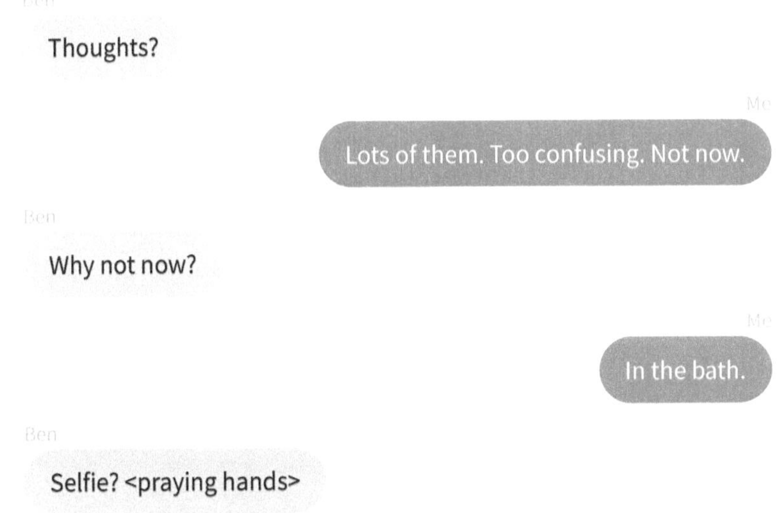

No.

I turn off the notifications on the phone, but after a few more minutes in the tub, I check and find that he sent *me* a selfie. No shirt. Messy—God, sexy—hair. Pouting his—fuck—kissable lips. Goddamnit, Ben. What sort of Instagram influencer tutorials have you been taking?

Ben

Remember that time you refused to show me your Pokémon onesie and then you changed your mind?

Me

<smiley face>

Ben

Are we in one of those situations right now? Like, is there hope?

I rinse off and get out of the tub. I take my time combing out my hair and look at my body. I'm not even considering it.

Who am I kidding? Yes, I am.

Me

B?

He writes back immediately.

Ben

Yes, bestie?

I pick up the large, fluffy bath towel my mom left in the bathroom for me, but then eye the small folded hand towel on the counter and choose the latter. The smaller towel covers just enough of my front not to be totally X-rated, but I angle my body and snap a pic that will give him quite an eyeful of my rear end.

Me

There's always hope <winky emoji>

I send him the pic.

Ben

I don't deserve her. That's my first thought when I get her sexy selfie. My second thought is *Damn, I wish she'd moved that towel a tad to the left,* but the fact that she didn't show me everything is infinitely sexier. I don't reply right away. I need to tread lightly here. *Too late for that, considering*

I asked her to send a naked selfie.

Nevertheless, I just got broken up with. I mean, Liran was fine. Before last night, I would've been willing to see where things had gone, but I learned two things in the past twelve hours.

One, the way I feel about Gabby hasn't faded over the years. And two, it's completely obvious to anybody paying attention. Probably including her.

I've jerked her around in the past, though, and I can't do that now. She just ended a long-term relationship, and she's doing well at her new job. I won't do anything to distract her from her professional success.

And I'm on my chosen path: finishing my PhD, getting a job, and proving to my asshole father that there are other ways to succeed besides becoming a physician. At Thanksgiving dinner yesterday evening, he had shown interest in my PhD research but hadn't failed to mention how proud he was of Miri for doing so well in medical school.

"I'm also proud of Miri," I told him. "But she actually *wants* to be a doctor, and I want to do research."

He looked at me carefully. "Ben, I'm not saying you made the wrong decision. I—"

"Aba, not now," I said, getting up from the table and walking into the kitchen. I've had this conversation before. How many times? A million?

"Ben, I really wish you would consider medical school."

"Yeah, Aba, but I can also help people through research, and it's a better fit for me."

Shampoo. Rinse. Repeat. Times a million.

My mom joined me in the kitchen shortly after I got up. "Sweetheart, I know he's proud of you. He doesn't always communicate well."

Right, it's so hard to say, "I love you, son. Good job on not only getting into but succeeding in a PhD program."

Why can't he just say how he feels?

It doesn't matter. I'm doing this for me. Not for him or anybody else. I'm following *my* plan. I'm achieving everything I set out to when I was eighteen years old and decided that contributing to scientific and medical discoveries is what I want to leave as my legacy.

"My legacy." Those were Gabby's words. When I couldn't choose a college major during my senior year of high school, I'd consulted with someone with even less life experience than me.

"*What do you want your legacy to be, Benji?*"

"*My legacy?*" I'd asked.

"*Think twenty years from now, or even longer, fifty. Can you imagine what you will have accomplished by then? Do you want to publish a book? Or start a charity? Or cure some type of cancer? Or—*"

Those words had hit somewhere deep inside of me. Gabby had no way of knowing, but my mom underwent a preventive mastectomy due to inheriting the BRCA gene mutation. I'd spent nights awake hoping she would be okay, even more nights awake worried about my sisters. But all those nights and thoughts—and conversations with Gabby—had ultimately sent me down a path of cancer research. And the first stepping stone was a major in biology.

Gabby's been there for so many of the challenges of my life. I'm drawn to her like we were best friends or lovers in some past life and have reunited here. Unfortunately, in this life, our paths have diverged.

I can remember when my parents loved each other, too, but I saw what my dad's ambition—and inflexibility—did to my mom. I would never do that to Gabby. She's told me in plain terms what she wants. A life with a "nice Jewish boy" who wants to get married and have children and be close to home. I love my family, but I don't know where I'll end up. Last night's mostly pleasant but ultimately depressing dinner with my divorced parents was a good reminder of how marriages that start with love and happiness can end. Not for me—and definitely not with Gabby.

I stare down at my phone. What do I write back? I can't leave her on "read," so I go with humor, hoping to defuse the situation, bring everything down a level, one step back from heading into a blackhole.

Me

Lucky towel. <winky emoji>

But Gabby has never been one to let things lie.

Gabby

I showed you mine, now show me ??

Showing her what she's done to me—something I'll have to take care of myself—can't go anywhere good, so I lie.

It's lame. It's unfair. But she takes it in stride.

Oh, shit. I forgot. We're going to her family tonight for Friendsgiving.

Friendsgiving is short and sweet this year at the Feinman house. Gabby's parents invited me, my mom, and another family over, and then all the parents drove into the city for a show called *Forever Rod*. Apparently, Marci is a huge fan of Rod Stewart, and not a few jokes were made at dinner regarding the show's name. After dessert, more friends of Aaron's showed up, and Gabby's expecting a few people to join later.

We're all hanging out in the living room, and Aaron is making drinks. I take a sip of the Moscow Mule he's offered me. "You've gotten better at bartending since high school, Feinman."

"Well, I couldn't get much worse," he says, laughing. "You guys wanna play pool in the basement?"

We make our way downstairs to the Feinman rec room and hang out for a couple hours. Despite being dumped quite dramatically at midnight last night, I could be feeling worse. Gabby comes down to the basement after answering the front door and plops down beside me on a large couch.

"What happened to all your friends?" I ask.

"Most of them went to a party in the city. And my other friend," she says, glancing behind her where Aaron is talking to her friend, Ilana, "seems to be Aaron's friend now."

I smile. "You didn't want to go to the other party?"

"Nah, I don't get to see Aaron that much anymore, and it's a nice break, being at home."

"It is. My mom did all my laundry. Of course, it also meant being grilled by her on my love life while simultaneously being forced to fold my underwear."

"Mmmm, and what, pray tell, did you say?" she asks, with a barely restrained smile.

"I told her that it's ridiculously unnecessary to fold underwear, of course."

She raises an eyebrow. I know she meant the other part of my comment. "Honestly, she did most of the talking. She obviously noticed that my somewhat-girlfriend who attended Thanksgiving dinner escaped in the night."

"And?"

"And that I wasn't all that broken up about it?"

"Why do you think that is?" She often has a twinkle in her eye when talking to me, but now she's dead serious.

I set my drink down on the coffee table in front of me. There's music and a conversation taking place behind us. I can't tell what they're saying, and I hope the same is true for the one I'm engaged in. "She probably wasn't right for me."

She raises an eyebrow.

"Okay, she *definitely* wasn't right for me," I admit, laughing.

"You need someone who understands your sensitive soul," she says plainly.

"You think I have a sensitive soul?"

A smile slowly spreads on her face. "Skittles."

"Skittles?" I ask, confused.

She nods. "When we were kids. The first time you slept over at our house. You felt bad about Aaron stealing my Skittles out of my room and you brought them back to me."

"I heard the tongue-lashing you gave him when you discovered his treachery, and I didn't want to risk the same fate," I joke.

She snickers. Her expression softens, and her eyes lock on mine. "You care about people and their feelings in a ... special way. A way not everyone does."

Is that what you think about me? Failing to find the courage to ask her, I stupidly comment, "It's been at least ten years since I've had some Skittles. I wish I had some right now."

She takes a sip of her drink. "I guess we'll have to make do with alcohol."

I run my hands through my hair to keep them busy. The longer I sit here with Gabby, the more I want to touch her and hold her. I wish it was summer and we were out on that hammock in her parents' backyard. I wish I'd told her all those years ago how much she meant to me. Where might we be now?

"She wasn't right for you," she says, jarring me from my memories.

I narrow my eyes at her. "How do you know? You barely even talked to her."

She sets her drink down and smiles, not a triumphant or condescending smile, but that smile of hers that has been bringing me to my knees for almost a decade, the one that says, *You haven't figured out that I know everything?*

"I didn't have to talk to *her*," she replies. "I saw the way *you* were *with* her. It wasn't carefree. It looked ... tight. Strained?"

She's right.

She props her arm on the back of the couch and leans her head on her hand, and the loose long-sleeved t-shirt she's wearing slides off the opposite shoulder again, but I focus my gaze on her face, looking all of a sudden vulnerable but trusting.

I incline my head, waiting for her to say what I know is on the tip of her tongue. "I guess I'm good at identifying that kind of feeling because it's how I felt with my ex. He didn't quite get me."

"In what way?" I ask softly.

She shifts her eyes down and to the side. It's signature Gabby—she's thinking, she's not interested in sharing, she feels uncertain.

I back up. "It's okay. You don't have to tell—"

"He didn't ..." She dips her head and blushes slightly.

"Oh," I say, thinking I know where this is going.

"He was comfortable, and he was kind. And here," she pauses and gestures at her head, "we connected well enough. But, like, here …" She swirls her fingers over her heart and twists her shirt in her fingers. "And, well, other places." She laughs softly and blushes again. "It was fine, okay, but not the fire I want. What I need."

She is so far beyond the girl I used to know. She has evolved into this deep well of thought and emotion, something I never knew she could become.

"Speechless?" she asks, an uncomfortable smile on her lips.

"No," I say, unable to share what I feel. That she deserves the best there is. That she deserves a partner who can keep up with her intellectually and emotionally. Someone who will challenge her and support her. She deserves her *fire*, the person who can match the beauty and depth she possesses.

"It's okay," she says. "I mean, I'm not anything that special, but—"

What the hell?

"You are *very* special," I jump in and reach out to touch her hand, resting on her leg, folded up and resting on the couch.

She looks at my hand and starts to get up.

"Don't go," I rush to say.

She tilts her head and gives me the half-annoyed, half-amused expression that has always made me putty in her hands. It's the same look she gave me last night when we were outside on the patio, and for a split second, I imagine what might have happened if Liran hadn't walked out when she did. I would've kissed Gabby. I would have embraced her—become one with her—and I wouldn't have stopped until someone dragged me away or the world ended.

The expression breaks, and, now it's a soft smile. Her eyes are once again warm and curious. She slides back down to sit on the couch, closer than she was before.

"I've been wanting to ask you something," I say.

She narrows her eyes. "What?"

"What are your dreams?"

She laughs. "What are my dreams? Seriously? Does that shit actually work on girls?"

"What?" I say, giving her a fake offended look.

She continues to laugh softly, and she looks beautiful, younger than she did last night. Maybe she's wearing less makeup, and her skin looks fresh and clean. Her hair is falling in soft waves and ...

"Ben?"

"Yeah," I say, coming back to reality.

She settles back into the couch and gives me a bemused look. "Where did that come from?"

"The last time we saw each other, I mean, the summer you were in college ..."

She smiles.

"You mentioned something about your dreams, and I realized I don't know what they are anymore. And that it's pretty important information for a bestie to know—"

Her eyes meet mine when I say the word *bestie.*

"Even if that *bestie* hasn't been the ... best. Maybe this bestie can be better? Bestie-er?" I shoot her an angelic smile. My game has improved over the years, and I know what works with most girls. Pretty sure it'll work with Gabby, too.

"I don't even know what I was referring to then." She glances away when she says it, and I think she's lying.

"Fine," I say, "then what are your dreams now?"

"Okay, I'll play. My dreams have always been focused on three areas of life: my art, my career goals, and my personal, or I guess, love life."

I love the way her brain works. Organized, strategic, straight to the point.

"And they change shape as things move forward, but the only one I seem to be accomplishing in the slightest is with work. Art, nothing. Love life, well, currently at a negative number."

That sounds right for me, too.

"Same," I say. "Work or school, moving along well. Art or I don't know, other personal pursuits, nada. And love life, well ..." I shake my head.

She squeezes my hand. "I'll be back in a minute, okay?"

She stands and turns, and I try not to stare at her ass. She is wearing some soft-looking, sexy black leggings that hug her behind. Even when she's dressed down—especially when she's not trying—she makes my pulse race.

I pull out my phone to kill some time, but when I open my messages, I find the photo she sent me earlier in the day. *Yeah, that's not helping matters.* I glance at it again quickly. I'd rather go and find the real Gabby. I get up and head toward the basement stairs when I see Aaron raise an eyebrow at me.

"Bathroom," I say, and he turns his attention back to Ilana.

When I reach the ground floor, I catch Gabby on the first step about to head up the stairs.

"Hey, where you going?" I call.

"I'm cold. Just wanted to grab a sweatshirt from my room."

I walk over to her. We're about the same height since she's one step up. "Here, take mine."

I unzip my hoodie with my school logo emblazoned on the front and wrap it around her. It's too big for her, but she looks adorable with the sleeves bunched up. She snuggles into it.

"Did you just sniff my sweatshirt?" I ask, smiling.

"Nope."

"Liar," I say, putting my pointer finger on her nose.

I step up onto the same step as her, and twist her, gently pushing her up against the wall. I lean down and rest my hands on the staircase railing behind her.

"Fine, you caught me," she admits, looking up at me.

"Second time today," I say bluntly.

"What do you mean?" she asks, looking into my eyes.

"You lied about leaving with that guy last night, too."

"It's none of your business what I do with other guys," she retorts.

She's right. I know she is. And yet.

"What if I want to make it my business?" I challenge.

She presses her lips together, not breaking her gaze with me. "Then I'd say, you should quit being a coward and make it ... your business."

I look away for a second, knowing that I'm not in the right state of mind.

She likely isn't either with her recent breakup. In the split-second our gaze is broken, I try to convince myself that she's not *everything* I want in this moment. But my body is saying something different. I'm tense from the effort of not following my most basic instincts right now. I have her loosely pinned against the wall, and I know she can likely feel *quite* clearly what my body has to say about hers.

She takes a deep breath, and her chest heaves against mine. I turn back to look her straight in the eyes. "I'm not a coward."

"You're still talking, though, instead of—"

I cut her off, my mouth crashing into hers. I taste her—ginger and lime and heaven—and there is nothing shy or cowardly about it. Her lips, her tongue tangling with mine, are a hundred times better than I remembered, and I want to melt into her. She slides down the wall, and I smile, mid-kiss. Then I shift my hands from the railing behind her to take hold of her sweet ass on both sides and prop her up, keeping her steady against the pressure of my body on hers, my mouth on hers.

She moans in my mouth, and I come undone, releasing her ass with one of my hands and moving it to one of her full breasts. Her nipple hardens under my touch, and all I want in this world is to pull down her shirt and taste it in my mouth as she moans my name.

She trails her hand down my stomach and gropes me. *Fuck.*

She wants fire, she said. She *is* fire. One of her hands presses against my chest for leverage while the other strokes up and down my shaft. I lean into her, and she rests her weight on the handrail, which squeaks and pulls me out of my hormone-induced stupor.

I snatch myself back and take a deep breath. She swallows and looks up at me, her mouth slightly parted.

"You still think I'm a coward?" I say, dumbly.

She shakes her head, all while shooting me a sexy, you'd-love-to-fuck-me grin.

I would. Love to fuck her, that is. But she deserves better than being used for one night and then left again. She should be adored, appreciated. Things I want to do, but I'm not capable of giving her right now.

I can't do this to her. I pull away, as much as I don't want to, and I turn to walk away.

"Wait, where are you going?" she asks, finding her voice.

I turn around. The look in her eyes is telling me she'd give me another chance, but I can't take it. She already gave me one, and I wasted it, totally messed things up.

That's what I do. What I'm good at. I get the girl, I lead her on, and then I mess it up. I'm not adding Gabby to my list of failed relationships. I have to be better this time. For *her*, I have to be better.

"Ben, look at me," she says.

I raise my eyes to hers. "I'm sorry, but I'll screw it up. I know I will. Y-you deserve more."

"How do you know what I need?" she asks in a ragged voice.

"You need more than what I can give you. I know that much. I would do ... so many things to you, *for* you, right now, but it wouldn't be right. It wouldn't be fair to *you*."

"I'm not some innocent girl who needs your protection," she spits out. "I-I sleep around. You know that. I'd be okay with ... *whatever* you can give me right now."

I can see her lip quiver as she makes her plea, and then she bites down on it as if to keep it still. I'm ashamed of myself for putting her in this position. This gift of a woman is begging *me* to accept *her* when any man in the world should be so lucky as to share something as simple as a conversation with her.

"I can't. Not now. I'm... so sorry, but I should go."

I turn and walk out the door in a t-shirt, despite the freezing rain, and I jog to the end of the street in an attempt to escape what I've done to her.

I slip inside my mom's house quietly and change into dry clothes before brushing my teeth and collapsing into bed. As the rain slaps against the window, I imagine how the night could have gone. Would she have taken me upstairs and let me make love to her? Would I have spent the night, hugging her close in the dark, while the storm drowned out the outside world? What I wouldn't give to know what she looks like when she wakes in the morning. I bet she's even more beautiful in those enchanting pre-dawn hours. I can picture her—her long hair tangled, face puffy from sleep, but with a sweet smile as she wakes, maybe even from discovering upon waking that *I'm* next to her.

What we could have—what we could be together—if only I knew how to do it right.

Almost Three Years Later

Stoking the Flames

Gabby

It's Friday night, and I've driven from the city for Shabbat dinner with my family. Ever since the new year, when our team took on a major initiative, things have been ramping up, and this week was particularly intense with presentations to the vice president of our org and late nights fixing bugs. I would have rather stayed in tonight, ordered takeout, and watched a movie, but I promised my mom I would come.

I'm in my parents' kitchen rinsing out and drying wine glasses before I set them on the table when I hear Aaron come in the front door.

"Hi, Son," my father calls. "Oh, hi, Ben."

I almost drop the wine glass, but my mom steadies my hand.

Just what I needed after this week.

"You okay, sweetie?" my mom asks.

"Yeah, Ima. Just a little tired."

I take a deep breath and remind myself that a few years have passed, and I've had a boyfriend or two since my last encounter with Ben, the idiot who made me swear to get my love life together and move past him.

And I'm past him. I think.

No, *I know.*

I grab two wine glasses in each hand, stems threaded between my fingers, and turn to take them into the dining room. Through the doorway, I see Aaron giving my dad a hug. Then Ben comes and shakes my dad's hand.

"What's this hand-shaking business, Ben? Give me a hug," my dad says.

I sneak a look. He looks good. No, he looks even better than the last time I saw him. *Fuck my life.*

After he hugs my dad, he turns to me. "Shabbat shalom, Gabby." *Asshole.* Coming in here acting like a fucking rabbi in front of my dad, knowing that the last time I saw him, he was sticking his tongue down my throat, not ten feet from where he's currently standing.

"Gabby, come say hi to Ben."

I muster as civil a tone as I can. "Hi, Ben. How are you?"

Before he can respond, my mom joins us. "Dinner's ready. Let's light the Shabbat candles."

We all gather in the dining room and listen as my mom says the blessing over the candles.

It's time for us to sit, but before I can position myself at the end of the table farther away from Ben, he pulls out a chair for me. And since Eagle-Eye Marci Feinman is watching, I sit, and he chooses the chair next to mine.

Aaron leads us in the blessing over the wine.

I watch Ben out of the corner of my eye, and when Aaron finishes the blessing, we say *"L'chaim"* and clink glasses.

Aaron asks, "Gabby, do you want to do *hamotzi?*"

No, Aaron. I'm trying to make Ben's hair catch on fire with my eyes.

"Sure, Bro," I say sweetly, and he cocks his head and looks at my mom, who rolls her eyes and chuckles. I bless the challah and tear pieces of it for everyone to take.

When Ben takes a piece from the plate I'm holding, he smiles at me shyly. "How are you?"

Shabbat is a time of peace, not war, I remind myself. "It's going okay.

How are you? I heard you got some award?"

"It's not a big deal."

"Sounded like it was. Can I call you Dr. Adler yet?" I ask, starting to slip back into our easy banter, much to my chagrin.

"It's just a PhD," he says with a shy smile.

I roll my eyes.

"Anyways," he says, changing the subject, "Aaron told me you moved into a place of your own?"

"Yeah, I wanted to save some time on my commute. And I found a great deal, so I went for it."

"Park Slope, right?"

I nod.

"Wow. Nice."

"Well, it's small but decent, and I got a promotion, so luckily, I can afford it."

"A promotion already?"

I nod, feeling proud of myself.

"I heard you're also writing a patent?"

Who is feeding him all this information about me? I look around the room and see at least two sets of eyes on us: my mother's and his mother's.

"I'm helping someone more senior do research for it," I clarify.

"Still impressive."

"It's *just* a patent," I joke. The corners of his lips turn up, and I have to drag my eyes back to his. "Full disclosure that anything my parents tell you about me is an exaggeration."

"Well, your mom said you're as lovely as ever."

I glance at my mom, who smiles at me warmly. I smile back at her. Why can't Jewish mothers mind their own damn business?

"And she didn't exaggerate about that part," Ben says.

"Humph."

"You're cute when you're annoyed."

"Who said I'm annoyed?" I retort.

"It's been a while, but I know that smile."

Ugh. He does know my smiles.

I stick my tongue out at him and cross my eyes like old times, and he laughs.

Damn. I know his smiles, too. And that one, right there, has tricked me before. Not tonight, buddy.

We dive into dinner, and my conversation with Ben surprisingly flows smoothly. My annoyance at my meddling mother is quickly replaced by my frustration at my own inability to maintain my justified indignation toward him. Ben deserves the cold shoulder I gave him upon learning he was joining us for dinner. He doesn't deserve my smiles, my conversation, or my forgiveness for his fuckery. But all those "He doesn't deserves" slip away, like the tide going out, and what I discover left on the shore during low tide is none other than the pull I've felt toward him for years. My memories of the times we spent together—as teenagers and later—wash away the last traces of any residual anger I had toward him, and I find myself unexpectedly enjoying speaking to him again.

As we finish the main course, I excuse myself to the bathroom, mostly to give myself a minute to think, and return to find my parents serving dessert and tea.

I sit and Ben digs into what I've been doing at work recently.

"It's been pretty challenging the last six months," I say.

"Tell me more about it," he says, and I share more about my life and my job since the last time I saw him. To my surprise, he asks relevant, insightful questions.

How does he know anything about machine learning?

At one point, I catch Aaron covertly listening in on our conversation. I raise my eyebrows at him. Yes? He smirks and goes into the kitchen to help our mom.

Dessert winds down, and Aaron comes back from the kitchen and tells Ben, "Alright, man, let's roll. Traffic to the city's getting worse, so we should head out now."

"Are you coming out, too, Gabby?" Ben asks.

I shake my head. Despite him looking like America's Next Top Biologist and our enjoyable dinner discussion, we're standing in the front hall mere feet away from the spot he left me the last time I saw him. Me, standing there like a fool, wearing his too-large-for-me sweatshirt and wishing for more.

I need to establish boundaries and make better decisions. I'm older. I should be wiser.

"No, thanks. I have plans tonight," I say, lying through my teeth. I suppose lying on my couch and falling asleep by 11:00 p.m. could be considered *plans.*

With that, I stand and take my plate from the table into the kitchen to escape. I hear the guys getting ready to go in the other room and then footsteps. I turn, and it's Aaron.

"So what did you and Ben talk about at dinner?" he asks.

"Nothing. The usual stuff."

"Okay. He seemed to be giving off a … vibe."

"What kind of *vibe*?" I ask.

He parts his mouth to say something but seems to change his mind. "Nothing. Never mind."

He turns to go but then turns back around. "But in case it *was* something, don't fall for his shit. He's my ride-or-die, Gabs, but he goes out with too many women. He's become really nonchalant about sex. You don't need that drama."

Aaron Judah Feinman, folks. The most oblivious man in the world. I take a second to appreciate just *how* clueless my brother is about my sex life.

"You don't have to worry," I reassure him.

"Fine. Be careful driving back, okay?"

"I will."

My drive home takes longer with the Friday night traffic, and when I arrive, I'm ready for a hot cup of tea and some trashy TV to take my mind off my dinner company earlier. I dump my bag on the kitchen counter, shove the containers of food my mom sent home with me into my disorganized refrigerator, and head to my small bedroom. But once I change into my pajamas, the project I've been killing myself on this week is at the forefront of my mind. I crawl into bed and open up my laptop to play around with a few new ideas I had while stuck in a traffic jam in the

Lincoln Tunnel.

When I can barely keep my eyes open, I wash my face and brush my teeth, then curl up with my favorite blanket—the plush coma-inducing gray comforter my parents gave me last Hanukkah. Just as I'm about to turn my phone to silent, I get a text.

Ben

Gabs?

Ben?

My phone starts to vibrate. *Shit, he's calling.*

I exhale and answer. "Why are you calling me?" I look at the clock on my nightstand. "It's 2:00 a.m."

"Because your brother drank too much and lost his keys, and now we're stuck."

"What do you want from *me*?"

"Can we crash at your place tonight?" he asks beseechingly.

"Uhhh ... who exactly?"

"Just me and Aaron."

"Ugh, okay. When will you be here? It's already really late."

"We're kinda outside your building already?"

"What the hell? Of all the places in New York City, and you're in Brooklyn, in my neighborhood?"

"Aaron told me you'd say 'yes,' so we came here."

"Ugh, fine. I'll buzz you in."

"You say *ugh* a lot."

"Come upstairs. You'll probably hear it again."

Ben is slouched on my velvet teal couch looking like a damn snack, and I'm sitting in the matching armchair next to it, my legs curled up and feeling exposed in my tank top and short shorts.

"Thanks for letting us stay," he says.

"Of course I let Aaron in. He's my brother. And you, well ..." I roll my eyes. All the positive feelings from dinner earlier have cooled off due to exhaustion and my unexpected guests. "It's been quite a freaking week, and it's late."

"You should go to bed," he says. "I'm sorry we woke you up." He throws an apologetic smile my way, and I soften.

After all, who can say "no" to a snack?

"I was actually awake," I admit. "Finishing up a project I was working on."

He leans forward. "You shouldn't be working so late. Doesn't your boss know it's the holy Sabbath?"

"I enjoy it, though," I say, defending my manager's honor. "I get ideas sometimes when I'm driving or in the shower, and then I want to work on them."

"Maybe you can tell me more about what you're doing. I mean, when it's not the middle of the night."

"Yeah, another time," I say. "I had just switched off my brain when you called."

"I like hearing you're happy with what you're doing in life," he says. "You deserve it. You always studied and worked hard."

I uncurl myself and place a bare foot on the floor. Feeling suddenly vulnerable, though, I snatch up a colorful pillow and hold it, tracing my fingers over the raised swirled pattern. His eyes track down.

I swallow and try to compose myself. "It can be hard to explain what I do to people outside of the field, but you asked a lot of smart questions earlier."

"My Intro to Programming course in college set a good foundation," he jokes.

I snicker.

"And when I found out that's what you're working on, I watched some YouTube videos. I wanted to know ... about you. And knowing what you work on forty hours a week—"

"Fifty," I correct him.

"Fifty hours a week. Anyway, it helps me know who you are now."

I hold his gaze but then a yawn escapes. "Oops."

"And who you are now is exhausted," he says with a slight smile.

"We need to figure out the sleeping situation since Aaron ended up in the only bed in this apartment."

We both put our fingers to our noses at the same time and say, "Not it."

"What were you saying *not it* about?" he asks.

"*I'm* not sharing a bed with Aaron."

"Me either."

"And I'm not sharing the couch with *you*."

He removes his finger from his nose dramatically, then leans in close to me and places it on mine. "Could be fun, though."

I don't doubt that.

But before I can respond, he winks at me and asks if I have blankets. "You take the couch, and I'll sleep on the floor next to you. Just try not to snore."

I swat at him and walk to the closet to get some blankets.

We get settled, and in the dim light of the room, I see Ben tossing and turning, trying to get comfortable on the flimsy yoga mat and blanket "mattress" we assembled.

"Sorry, it's not more comfortable," I say.

"Sayeth the queen atop her comfy couch throne."

"Hey, I'm freezing up here. My warm blanket is currently wrapped burrito-style around my drunk asshole brother."

"You could come down here and sleep on the hard floor with me, and I'll keep you warm ..."

"Are you sure you're not drunk?" I ask.

"Who said I'm not drunk?"

"I mean, you somehow made it all the way to Brooklyn at 2:00 a.m. I figured you were at least relatively sober. Where were you before that anyways?"

"Aaron was chasing a girl. We started out at some place called Strangelove, and then he got a text from someone named Ilana and—"

"Ilana who?"

"I don't know."

Is Aaron going after my friend? This will require some investigation.

"Anyways, since the plan was for him to drive, I had a couple more than I should have so ... I *was* buzzed, but after meeting up with her and walking about a million blocks, I was fine. I am fine ... *now*. Just sleepy," he says, gazing up at me most adorably.

He's taken his glasses off and is lying on his side, propped up in a way that showcases his bicep. He looks ... enticing, to say the least.

"You sure you don't wanna join me for a sleepover, Lil G?" he asks, raising his eyebrows and rubbing the spot next to him.

"You're gonna pull that one out of the dustbin, huh? I still remember your nickname, too, *Benji*."

He sits up, bringing us eye-to-eye. "I like when you call me that," he says, leaning forward in a way that makes me think he's going to kiss me.

I close my eyes for a split-second, expecting him to lean in and seal the deal, knowing I shouldn't be into this, but allowing it anyway when all of a sudden, he shocks me by grabbing the blanket around me and pulling me off the couch.

The way the blanket is wrapped around me means that all he has to do is tug on it, and I come rolling off the couch. In the split-second it takes me to fall, I'm sure I'll hit my face since my arms are tucked inside, but then—somehow—I don't. Because, well, because Ben's face is under mine, and without even trying, our lips brush.

"What are you doing?" I yell-whisper at him while struggling to free my arms.

"I'm just playing around," he says, rolling us both to the side and depositing me on the ground next to him where I can finally get my arms out.

I'm breathing hard from the shock of starting out on the couch and ending up on the floor—no, ending up on top of *him*. "You're always just playing around, and it ... it sucks."

He keeps doing this. Getting so close—too close—and then pulling away.

He looks at me with unease evident on his face, even in the dark. "You're right. I-I'm sorry."

He props himself up again and looks down at me. His stare is intense, so much so that I focus my attention on the buttons of his Henley, a few of them open, revealing the top of a smooth, hard pec muscle.

"Aaron warned me to stay away from you," I whisper. "It's like he knew nothing good could come from us hooking up—"

"What exactly did he say?" he asks, eyes narrowed.

I exhale. "That you date a lot of women. That you're not serious about relationships."

"What Aaron *thinks* he knows about me and the truth are two different things," he says in a low voice.

"What does he think he knows?" I ask.

"That I sleep around a bit."

"What's the truth, then?"

He looks away and then locks eyes with me. "That I sleep around *a lot*. Or at least, I used to. He remembers how I was in college, and, I guess, until last year."

"What happened then?"

"I realized that wasn't the best approach to ..."

"To what?"

"To find something meaningful in life, or someone, I guess."

"It didn't work?" I ask.

He exhales. "No, it didn't."

It never worked for me either.

A wave of sympathy—maybe also guilt—washes over me. "I'm sorry. I didn't mean to accuse you of ... well, some of the same shit I've done, I guess. I, um, kind of like sex, too."

He smiles. "Oh, do you?"

"We might've done it once before." *What am I saying?*

"Once? I remember you having two orgasms that day, G. Or was that a girl who looked like you?"

"Asshole. There's nobody like me."

A slight smile traces his face. "When you're right, you're fucking right."

I look at his lips, and for some reason, I think about the time in high school when I told him I wanted him to be my first kiss. But a lot has happened since then. The last time, I stupidly thought something might come of it.

"I need to apologize for something," he says, pulling me from my thoughts.

I wait for him to continue.

"I'm sorry for coming to Rutgers and sleeping with you and then not staying in touch. And then for kissing you *again* and disappearing. I haven't been fair to you."

No, you haven't.

"I ... I saw the way you looked at me earlier. I thought maybe, maybe I have a special place in your heart, the way you do in mine—"

"Ben—"

"But it's okay if I don't," he says, searching my eyes.

You do. You always have.

Even if my mind is telling me to hold back, my body is involuntarily leaning into him. I'm consciously steadying my breathing. *Can he tell?*

"Can I kiss you?"

"It never ends well," I whisper.

"Just one?"

"Just one, huh?"

"You're hard to resist, Ms. Feinman."

God, he looks sweet right now, like the Ben lying here with me is one who never hurt me, never left me waiting, hoping he'd get back to me.

Against every logical and responsible cell in my body, I reply, "Okay, just one."

"Then I better make it a good one," he says.

He starts to scoot down, and instead of putting his face near mine, to kiss me on the mouth, he slowly moves the blanket down my body. His slender but powerful hands slide down my side, tracing first my shoulder and then moving slowly down to the side of my breast and then my waist. He continues down and lifts the hem of my shirt, and then looks up at me, to see what my response is. I can't help but smile, and he takes it—correctly—as a yes.

He's so close to my skin I can feel his breath, and I anticipate the kiss he's about to place on the bare skin right above my belly button. But then I hear him murmur, "No, no, no. That won't do. I only get one."

I giggle, and the movement of my stomach makes his lips brush my skin. He looks up at me questioningly.

"That one doesn't count. That was my fault," I say.

"Phew," he says and smiles. He starts to move my shirt up, bit by bit. Every bit of skin he exposes, he nips me with his teeth, moving further and further up my torso until he's seconds away from baring one of my breasts.

His eyes zero in on my nipple—now hard from his mouth traveling up my body. "That one's tempting." He bites his bottom lip as he considers his options.

"Choose wisely," I advise. "You only get one."

"In that case, I choose your beautiful mouth. If I remember correctly, it tastes amazing."

My hands, which have been mostly idle suddenly come to life, and I reach to pull him up to me. He comes willingly, and our mouths collide.

His lips—full, firm, perfect—part, and I let my tongue explore *his* beautiful mouth. He tastes like my toothpaste, which he used with a new toothbrush I gave him once I found out we'd be having a sleepover tonight. We kiss hungrily for a few minutes—which might also be an eternity. Time has no meaning right now.

He rubs his body against mine, and I can feel his firm muscles under his shirt and the boxers he wore to sleep. It might have taken me a minute to be convinced, but now that we've started, I'm so turned on that I want his body on mine, no barriers.

"That was way more than one kiss," he says, breathlessly.

"You're right," I say, coming to my senses. "We should stop."

"That's *not* what I was saying."

He's balanced above me now, propped on his elbows, but I can feel him hard against me below. He takes one hand, touches me through my thin pajama shorts, and leans in to kiss my neck.

"Oh," I pant out.

"That certainly sounds like you want to stop," he teases.

He slowly traces my clit with his pointer finger, and I press into him, seeking the pressure I need.

"It's no good, Gabby? You're not turned on?" He bites my earlobe.

"It's good. I just… I don't know you that well anymore."

"Then let's get reacquainted, old friend."

"Mmmm," I say noncommittally.

"Are you having a good time now?"

I swallow. "I am."

"Good. Then tell me what you want."

I want your fucking body on mine.

"Take off your shirt," I say.

"You first," he quips.

"Take off your fucking shirt, or you're sleeping on the floor alone tonight." I raise my eyebrow at him, and we both know who's calling the shots right now.

"You're evil," he says, leaning back and pulling it off in one fell swoop. I smile, knowing I have the upper hand, and lean up to remove my own shirt.

"Now, come warm me up," I say. "You did promise."

"I'll keep you warm all night, baby," he says. "Just tell me where to start."

"You need instructions? Oh, right, you're a reformed man. You don't sleep around that much anymore. Must be out of practice."

He smirks. "I knew my little smart-ass was hiding behind that shy girl from before. I think I have something that'll shut you up."

"Show me then."

His eyes lock with mine, and then he pulls his boxers down. I break eye contact with him and glance down.

"Made you look," he teases.

I snicker, despite myself. I nod with what is surely a stupid grin on my face.

"Ooooh, you're speechless. Quite the compliment for my cock."

"You know when I can't talk?" I ask, reaching for his hard shaft with one hand and grabbing his ass with the other to pull him closer. Trying to accommodate my wishes, he straddles my torso, just over my ribs. He looks down at me, biting his lip, and shakes his head.

"When I have something in my mouth."

His lips break into a smile, and he laughs. "You're gonna kill me on the spot."

"You'll be alright."

I scoot out from under him to sit up and twist my body so I'm leaning my back against the couch. "Come here," I say, glancing in the direction of my closed bedroom door, where Aaron is hopefully sound asleep.

I grab him behind his leg, discovering a strong hamstring muscle, and pull him toward me.

"You sure you wanna do this first?" he asks. He's hard, and it's brushing my throat, just below my chin. "You don't want me to go down on you?"

"I like your cock, Ben. You don't like blow jobs?"

"Fuck, hearing you talk like that is—"

"Come. Here," I cut him off before he can finish his sentence.

I take him into my mouth, and he braces himself on the back of the couch behind me. I can tell he's trying to restrain himself—not pump his hips or get too excited—by the look on his face, the rigidity of his body, but I take him deep in my mouth and massage his balls.

He exhales, a soft moan escaping his lips. "Ohhh, G."

Ever since I gave my first blow job during my freshman year of college, I've always enjoyed it. Maybe guys feel powerful getting one, but I feel powerful knowing a man is at my mercy, out of his mind due to the pleasure I can give him.

I consider my next move, but before I can decide, he groans, pulls away from me, and slides me down to the floor on my back. Without asking, he yanks my shorts and underwear down, baring me to him. He kisses my breasts and then lightly bites a nipple.

"Oh, God," he moans. "The last time we kissed, I wanted these in my mouth. I wanted to lick you and suck you and tease you."

"Ohhhh ... it's good."

"Do I remember correctly that you like me going down on you?"

"Only one way to find out," I say, taking his head and shoving it downward.

He laughs. "So entitled. You have such a bad attitude."

"I bet a little bit of oral would fix me right up."

"Oh, I am just the man for the job," he says, trailing kisses down my body while using one hand to explore me below. Sounds of enjoyment come from his throat. "Yessss, you're so soft ... and wet."

I release a small moan. Then he's between my legs, and I part them even more, giving him full access. His tongue slides across my clit, and he slips a finger inside of me.

"More," I exhale.

My experience in the present, my memories from the last time, and all the fantasies I've had about Ben—doing this, doing more—are converging. We're surrounded by a mess of pillows, blankets, and discarded clothing. He's working hard. With my hand on his shoulder, I can feel a light sheen of sweat. One of his hands is under my ass positioning me so he can use his tongue on me in a way that is slowly melting me into the floor. I try to be quiet, but it's hard.

"Shhhh," he says, between licks, but his fingers don't stop. "Be quiet, G."

I can hear the smile in his voice. He's probably getting off on the fact that I can't control myself in his hands. He goes back to what he was doing. His right hand—the one holding my ass—disappears.

"What are you doing?" I ask, suspecting he's starting to pleasure himself while all this is going down.

"You know what I'm doing. I'm so hard right now. I need to ..."

"Come here."

He crawls up and props himself on one elbow, chin on my chest, while he continues to stroke me below.

"Are you ... You're sure?" he asks, breathlessly.

"Ben, you of all people, know I've had one-night stands ..."

"Is *that* what this is?"

"I have no idea what this is. I've never known what ..." *We are.* I leave it unsaid.

"I want you, though."

"I want you, too."

He bites his lip. "Do you have a condom?"

Fuck. They're in the nightstand. In my bedroom. Where my older brother is currently asleep.

I let my head fall to the side in disappointment and, holy hell, if I don't see a shiny metallic condom wrapper under the couch.

"What are you looking at?" he says and leans down to look at where my gaze is focused.

"Ha! It's a sign from God," he says and grabs it, ripping it open with his teeth.

"You're not even gonna ask why it's there?"

"I'm a man of faith, Gavriella bat Micah v'Miriam," he teases.

I cackle, then quiet my laugh. "You're invoking my formal Hebrew name now? We're about to engage in some very pre-marital sex. Don't you think that's a tad sacrilegious?"

He looks quite pleased with himself, and I try to stop snickering but I can't. He pauses, looks up, letting his eyes wander, rolls the condom on, and declares quite decisively, "I do not." Then he swoops down to kiss me dramatically.

The laugh bubbling up in my throat from his theatrics is cut short by the kiss he gives me—deep, sensuous, genuine.

He's hard, rubbing against me below, and I pull his hips closer to mine. When he enters me, I close my eyes. "I've imagined this," I let slip as he slowly moves in and out of me.

"Not as many times as I have," he whispers into my ear.

I breathe him in. He's here. The object of my teenage daydreams, my more adult longings, is here with me. I don't have to instruct him how to touch me or tell him what I like because somehow, everything he does is what I like.

"Mmmmm," he says, moaning into my ear, while he fucks me slowly—Goddamn, thoroughly. He kisses the spot right behind my jaw and continues to move his hips in and out, in ...ahhh ... and out.

And I rock with him, slowly. He is deep, so deep inside of me. "Ohhhhh, God, that feels good," I breathe out.

He doesn't ask what to do, or if he should go faster. He listens to my body with his own. My eyes are closed, and when I open them, curious to see what he looks like in this moment, he's already looking at me and gives me a small smile.

"Move the way you like, G. Lead me where you want to go."

I grab his ass with one hand and pull him into me, and with the other, I pull him down into a breathtaking kiss. I can barely breathe, but I don't need air—I need him. I need his mouth on mine and his body crashing into me, elevating me to some otherworldly high.

"Faster," I whisper hoarsely, and he braces his arms near my head, thrusts into me, and continues to kiss me.

"Oh, Gabby. Oh, God."

"Don't you dare come before me," I say and lightly bite his lip.

"Not happening. I bet you another twenty-five orgasms, you'll come before me."

"I'll happily lose that bet," I tease back.

"Wrap your legs around me and hold my shoulders."

I do as he says, and then he does a sort of push-up from the ground with one hand and puts one hand on my lower back to pull me up. He turns to sit down, so he's leaning against the couch, and I'm straddling him. He's deep inside me, and he's grabbing my ass, pulling me into him, over and over and over.

We just started, and I'm already so turned on I don't know how long I can last.

"What magic are you using on me?" I pant out.

"We're just compatible."

"Ohhhh," I moan out. *Compatible is fucking right.*

"Use me. Come on."

I rock my hips into him.

"Is that good?" he asks.

I'd respond, but I can't because he's hitting a spot inside of me that makes me feel like any minute my limbs will stop working. I want to yell, to scream, but somehow the 1 percent of my brain that is still working knows my brother is in the other room.

"Is it good?" he asks again.

"Yessss."

"You wanna scream?"

There really is no other response for sex this good. And he's not letting up. It's written on my face—my whole Goddamn body—that I'm about three seconds away from coming. So, yeah, I wanna scream.

I grab a pillow, put it behind his neck, and lean over him, moaning. "Yes, Ben, yessss," I bellow into the pillow. "Yesss, fucking yes."

When I think I can control myself, I look at him.

"You came, right?" he asks, breathless.

"Fuck, yes," I pant out, laughing softly, trying to catch my own breath.

"Thank-fucking-God. I can't hold on any longer," he says, laughing. He lays me on my back and within seconds has pushed himself into me.

I can barely think straight, but I lean up and kiss him. Words aren't needed. My kiss, at least for this moment, tells him everything I need him to know.

He thrusts into me, braced above me on his forearms with his face close to mine. He closes his eyes, concentrating, and then tucks his nose into the side of my neck and inhales.

"God, you're good, Gabby," he breathes out.

I turn to kiss him, only able to graze his jaw with my lips. His breathing speeds up, and then his face tightens, relaxes, and he releases in me. He lies down next to me, leg draped over my body.

"You afraid I'm going to escape?" I joke, turning to face him.

"Nah, it's ... been a long time since I've had the chance to hold you. I always liked being close to you."

"Me, too," I whisper and lean in and peck him on the nose. "I'll be right back."

I go to the bathroom, keeping the light off, and when I get back, I pull on my shirt and shorts.

I lie down next to him on the floor—*what the hell?*—and he snuggles into me.

"*Laila tov*, G," he says. *Good night.*

I smile. "*Laila tov*, B."

Morning comes too soon. I'm dozing, spooned comfortably with Ben, when I hear the click of my bedroom door opening.

Shit. Aaron.

I jump up and run to the kitchen and try to pretend that a mere fifteen seconds ago Ben's hand wasn't cupped around my breast as he slept with his morning erection poking me in the ass.

Aaron comes into the kitchen, eyes squinting against the morning light streaming in from the window, and I ask him if he wants some coffee.

"God, yes."

"Rough night?"

"Good night, rough morning," he says and a sliver of a smile sneaks out.

When the coffee maker finishes filling his mug, I turn and set it on the counter, where he's sitting on a bar stool.

"Thanks for letting us crash here last night, Gabs."

"It's fine," I say.

"I know it was late when we came up … And I stole your bed."

"That *was* pretty lame." *But also pretty serendipitous.*

"I hope Ben didn't keep you up last night."

He did.

"Sometimes he talks in his sleep," Aaron says.

Really? That's adorable.

"I didn't hear him if he did." I would have since he spent most of the night cuddling me.

"He didn't … try anything with you, did he?"

Define "anything." For that matter, define "try."

I look into my coffee mug and shake my head.

"I don't know. I had this weird dream that we were all out and then he kissed you, and I had to punch him for hitting on my little sister," he says, laughing.

I choke on my coffee. "That's weird. What'd you drink last night, Aaron?" I ask, attempting to change the topic.

"I wasn't all *that* drunk. The main issue is I lost my keys which I still don't know how I'm going to solve."

"You have a spare set?"

"Yeah. Can I take your car to drive to my place and get them, and then I'll bring your car back?"

"Sure."

"In that case, I'll leave Sleeping Beauty here and be back in a couple hours. Might shower while I'm there unless you have plans today you need your car for?"

"No, no plans."

Aaron gets ready to leave and gives me a hug. "Tell Ben I'll be back in a few hours and then I can give him a ride back, okay?"

As soon as Aaron leaves, but like as *soon* as he leaves, Ben sits up from where he was seemingly dead on the floor minutes before.

In fact, I'm heading to the bathroom to get in the shower when he reaches out and grabs my leg, and I just about pee in my pants from the shock.

"What the hell are you doing? I thought you were asleep."

"I was waiting for Aaron to leave."

"How long have you been awake?"

He stands up and stretches, and his shirt raises up and I think about how it felt kissing that hard stomach last night.

"Fifteen minutes?"

"Why did you wait?"

He comes closer to me and puts his hands on my waist. "Because I want to spend more time with you."

"Well, I was just on my way into the shower."

"What a coincidence. That's where I was heading, too," he says, laughing.

"You wanna take a shower with me?"

He shakes his head. "I was already going to the shower, so it sounds like *you* want to take a shower with *me*."

I could say, *I don't think this is a good idea*, or, *I was literally just told not to get involved with you*, or *Maybe we should at least talk about this first,* but I can't help thc giant smile that breaks out on my face.

He leans in and kisses my neck. "That smile looks like a yes."

"Let's brush our teeth first," I say while pulling him by the hand toward the bathroom.

He skips ahead of me, and I hear the clatter of the toothbrushes and the sound of the faucet already running.

I join him and put toothpaste on my toothbrush, then lean up against the sink next to him. My bathroom is minuscule, so our legs are touching, and we watch each other while we brush our teeth. It's awkward but exciting because I know we're about sixty seconds from getting naked. He finishes first and waits for me, and as soon as I put my toothbrush in the holder, he pulls me in close and leans down to kiss me.

"You've fallen asleep on me a few times, but I've never seen you right after you wake up in the morning."

"Am I everything you dreamed of?" I ask, sarcastically.

His mouth opens, and he blinks. "And more," he says simply. "You're gorgeous."

When did he become so Goddamn smooth? Part of my brain knows it's an act, but another other part of me—some lower, lustful region that wants to hear more—allows me to be reeled in by him.

I pull him in for another kiss and take off his shirt so I can see in the light that amazing body that I caressed and kissed last night.

His body has changed since I last saw him shirtless in my dorm room the summer we hooked up. He looked great then, but he looks more like a man than ever. Any vestiges of teenage Ben are completely gone, and I run my hands down his tan, fit torso.

His shirt is on the floor, and he removes his boxers. I turn to twist on the shower faucet to allow the water to heat up, and before I'm even fully turned back around, he starts to tug down my shorts. They slip off and hit the floor next to his own clothes. I start to take off my shirt, but he stops me.

"Give me a second," he says.

I shoot him a confused look. "For what?"

"To prepare myself."

"You saw me naked last night. You saw me naked ... before."

"Well, last night it was dark, and I like the build-up. The anticipation is part of the fun," he says.

He pulls the leaf-patterned curtain back and steps into the shower, and my eyes fall from his face to the water flowing down his chest, his stomach, and lower.

He notices where my eyes are, then reaches out with his pointer finger and pushes my bottom jaw up. *Oh God. My mouth was open.*

He smiles. "Alright, I'm closing my eyes now and imagining what it's gonna be like when you join me under the warm water."

"What if I abandon you here?" I tease, pulling my shirt over my head and stepping out of my underwear.

"You wouldn't do that because I think you enjoyed yourself last night, and I'm pretty sure you didn't get quite enough of me yet."

I look at him with his eyes still closed and a smug grin on his face.

He's right.

I place a hand on his shoulder and step in to join him under the warm shower spray. "Keep them closed, okay?" I whisper in his ear, pressing my chest up against his body.

I hear his intake of breath. "I promise."

I wrap my arms around his neck and pull him into a kiss, then take his hands and move them to my breasts. He elicits a sound of pure pleasure.

"Keep them closed," I say in a sing-song voice.

And then, without warning, I drop to my knees and gently place his semi-hard cock in my mouth.

"Ohhhhhh, Gabby." His eyes are still closed, but he says, "I can't not look at this. I'm opening my eyes now."

"No. I'll stop."

"Please don't do that," he pleads.

I laugh, moving back and forth on his hardening erection, loving the feel of him on my tongue. I look up, and he's keeping his word. His eyes are still closed. He's braced himself with one hand on the tiled shower wall while the other has come down to support my head.

"Do you want me to keep going?" I ask. I'm enjoying his reactions to what I'm doing for him, but I'm also kind of drowning down here.

"Can I open my eyes now?" he asks.

"Fine," I relent and slide up his body, making contact the whole way. When I kiss his jawline, his eyes pop open, and he smiles a naughty grin.

"Now you're in trouble," he says in a low tone.

"Oh, am I?"

"You think being sassy will work with me? I know you," he says, maneuvering me up against the shower wall. The tile is cold and slick on my back, but immediately, he presses up against me, keeping me from slipping. The water is hitting us from the side now.

"You okay?" he asks.

"More than okay." *Amazing, in fact.*

He gives me an unexpectedly innocent smile. "Good. Me, too." He grasps my face in both of his hands and kisses me, deeply, fully. His left hand trails down my body, stopping to caress my breast, but then he reaches lower and parts me with his gentle touch. He moves his finger slowly up and down my clit, and I squirm under his touch, saying with my body *do it already.*

"Tell me what you want," he says. "It turns me on so much when you say it." He kisses my neck, and his stubble scrapes my collarbone.

I know what I want. It's simple, but what's happened in the last twelve hours is the stuff of dreams. Simple will more than suffice.

"I want you to kiss me, and make me come, and tell me …"

"Tell you what?" he asks.

I don't know what this is or how much time we have or whether this is a one-night stand or something more, so I go for broke. If he's my fantasy-maker, then my fantasy is that I'm everything he needs.

"Tell me how much you want me."

"Let's get out, and I'll show you how much I want you. It's way too slippery in here for me to fuck you hard and make you come like I want."

My eyes widen. I swallow. With my eyes still trained on him, I reach over and turn off the shower. "Let's get out and you can, um, *fuck me hard and make me come like you want,* huh?"

He reaches out and grabs a towel to wrap around me. "Sounds like a perfect Saturday morning."

·❤·❤·❤·❤·❤·

When I leave the bathroom, I find Ben in my bedroom, a towel wrapped around his waist. The sun rays shining through the crack of my sheer lilac curtains highlight his toned torso, and something low in my body clenches.

Holy shit.

He comes closer and helps me dry my hair with my towel, surprising me by taking the towel and throwing it on the floor of my bedroom.

"What're you doing?" I ask.

"Well, I'm guessing your sheets still smell like the guy who slept there last night, and that's the last place either of us wants to have sex."

Good point.

"Lie down."

Direct.

I spread the towel out and sit on it. I don't love the position my body is in, especially when he's looking down at me. As if reading my mind, he says, "Your body is the most beautiful thing I've ever seen."

Take my money.

One of my legs, betraying me, involuntarily falls open. I raise my eyebrows, and he laughs softly.

"Someone made some big promises a minute ago in the shower," I say, and almost before I've finished my sentence, he's taken his towel off and joined me on the floor.

He lays me back and kisses my whole body, starting with my mouth and moving down my neck until he's reached my breasts.

"So much better in the daylight. Oh my God," he groans as he kisses and licks my nipples. I feel them harden at the contact.

"Benji," I say, playing with him.

"I like it, but not during sex."

"Benjamin?"

"Acceptable, but not ideal."

"Big Ben?" I joke.

"Accurate description, but too British."

I laugh.

"Hottest lover of my life?"

"Ah, that one works great," he replies, positioning himself between my legs. He guides one of my ankles closer to my hip, opening me up wider.

As he reaches down and grips his hard-on, readying himself to enter me, he asks, "Do you want it gentle or—"

"I want it covered," I reply.

"Oh, right," he says, sheepishly. "Nightstand?"

I nod.

He crawls over there and opens the drawer, finding a small but varied assortment of contraceptives and, well, my vibrator.

"Gabriella Feinman, you little minx. So many options. What will it be today?" He holds up three different boxes of condoms, then waggles my vibrator back and forth, watching it sway and acting as if he's hypnotized.

"Ben," I say in a dry tone.

"Yes, Gabby?" he says, not stopping the vibrator dance.

"Will you choose one and come fuck me already?"

His eyes flick to mine, and he looks downright gleeful. He tosses the vibrator on the bed. "You, sir, will have to wait your turn," he says, and I burst out in laughter. He snatches a condom at random and examines the package. "Ah, here we go. The quadruple-X super-duper jumbo size."

I roll my eyes and giggle as he opens the packet and rolls it on.

When he's ready and hovering over me once more, he asks, "So back to where we were before I encountered Gabby's Drawer of Pleasure …"

I look up at him and can't keep a straight face. "Yes?"

"Do you want it gentle?" he whispers, in my ear. "Or hard?" He bites my neck.

"I think hard is what was promised," I reply tartly.

"Then *that* is what you'll get," he says, entering me in one motion.

"Ahhh," I exhale. It feels different than yesterday, but good.

"Are you alright?"

I meet his eyes and nod.

Still inside of me, he braces himself on his forearms on either side of my head and begins to move back and forth. I turn my head to kiss his bicep and then bite one, hard.

"Aye," he yelps.

"Harder, Ben."

He listens and grabs my ass to keep me in place as he pumps into me.

"Yeah, like that," I say. "Oh, that's good."

I raise my hips, exploring the angle, and it's good, but I'm having a hard time holding my own weight and his.

"Let's flip over, okay?" he suggests. "Sit on me?"

We take a moment to readjust, him on his back and me on top. I slip down on him and the sensation of him filling me takes my breath away for a second. Before I can even inhale again, he's moving under me.

"Put your hands on my chest," he instructs.

I do as he says, and then he begins to move his hips up and down, and the feeling of him—hard but slick—inside of me begins to take me to another level, beyond any fantasy I've ever had about him.

He's holding one of my hips and the other reaches up to grab my breast while he continues to shift up and down, hitting just the right spot.

"Should I do something else?" he asks, but I can barely answer him. All my attention is focused on what feels like electricity hitting the same spot over and over, and I'm trying not to scream. It's amazing, so much more than amazing. And it's what I want, *he* is what I want.

I look down at his face to find an expression of pure ecstasy, and he grabs my hands and scoots them up his body until I'm lying on him and my breasts press against his hard chest. I caress his shoulders while we rock back and forth.

"Is this position good for you?" he asks.

"It's good, but I can't ... oh ... move fast enough," I respond.

"Let me help you," he says, starting to lift his hips, pounding himself into me.

"Ohhhh, shit."

"No?"

"Yessss." So. Thrust. *Much*. Slap. Yes.

It only takes about thirty more seconds in this specific position before I cry out. Any shyness I might have considered exhibiting, any restraint I had planned on showing, is nowhere to be found. Given a few more seconds of an orgasm like this one, I'd agree to join a Benjamin-Adler-dick-worshiping-cult, but thankfully, he comes shortly after me, apparently enjoying the show I put on. I lie on top of him while he comes and moves gradually slower.

He rolls me to my side, lying next to him, and looks into my eyes. "You're pretty good at this."

I laugh. Then, I imagine the bird's eye view of the current scene in my bedroom—Ben and me, splayed out naked on my floor, two towels somewhere in the near vicinity—and laugh harder.

"What's so funny?" he asks.

"We've now had sex on the floor three times," I say. "We've yet to do it in a bed."

"I guess you're right, but give a guy a minute to recover."

"I can wait a minute," I joke.

"Breakfast wouldn't hurt either," he replies. "The last thing I ate was your mother's chocolate babka fourteen hours ago."

"Get up, and I'll make you something. Right after I rinse off."

"Are you inviting me to join you in the shower?"

"You think you can keep your hands off me?" I reply.

"Hell, no."

"Then why don't you give me a two-minute head start so we can put on our clothes sometime this morning."

Just then there's a knock on my front door, and he looks at me, a question in his eyes.

"It's too early for Aaron to be back," I say, but then my phone buzzes. "Shit, I bet it's him."

"Get in the shower, and I'll get dressed and open the door."

"You sure?"

"Yep, no problem," he says, taking my hand to stand up.

I head into the bathroom, and he smacks me on the butt. I turn back to fake-sneer at him.

"Best ass ever," he comments.

I would respond, but Aaron is calling my name through my front door, "Gaaaaby, Gabriella, Gavrioli, Gggggggg."

Go, I mouth at him. He pulls on his t-shirt and shoots me a million-dollar smile, then jogs to the front door. I slam the bathroom door shut and turn on the shower.

I take my time in the shower, hoping that Aaron will simply leave my keys, and I can avoid having a conversation with him—a conversation that might lead to questions and more warnings against getting involved with Ben.

When I get out of the shower, my apartment is quiet. Everything is as I left it in the bedroom, and the blankets Ben and I used last night are folded neatly on the couch, the yoga mat put away carefully in the corner.

I get dressed, then find my phone. There are three missed calls from Aaron and a few text messages as well:

Aaron

> Thanks again for last night. Ilana called me on my drive home. She found my keys in her purse this morning, so I turned around.

> Now would be a good time to tell you that your friend Ilana and I have gone on a couple of dates.

> Me and Ben are taking an Uber to her house and then my car. Hope it's not towed.

And in a separate thread:

Ben

> Next time, not on the floor.

I smile.

Me

> So that means there will be a next time ?

It takes him half an hour to answer, and I assume it's because he's in a car with my brother and doesn't want to get caught texting me.

> I'm already thinking about the next time … and the next time
> … and the … well, you get the point.

Me, too, Ben. Me, too.

Ben texts me on Saturday night and asks if he can take me to brunch the next day, but I know if I go to brunch, I'll drink mimosas. And if I drink mimosas, we'll end up back at my place and well, there goes the whole day. I have an important presentation early Monday morning, and I want to integrate a few of the new ideas I had last night. Performance reviews are in full swing, and this is a great opportunity to showcase some of my work.

I buckle down and work for a few hours on Sunday morning. Afterward, I head to the supermarket, daydreaming on my walk up Fourth Avenue about taking a shower with Ben. When I get back, I eat a quick lunch and get back to work. In the evening, I get a text.

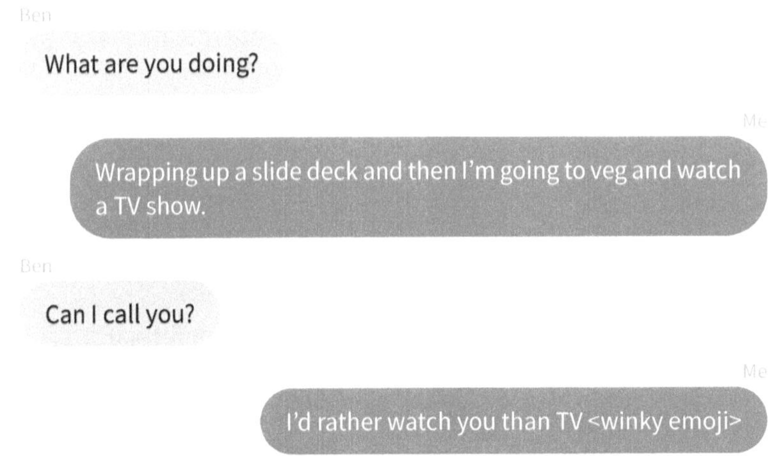

Oh no, he's Facetiming me.

I tap on Accept.

"Hi," I say. "I was joking about watching you." But I can't say I don't like the view. He must have the phone propped up, and he's lying down on the floor.

"What are you doing?"

"I was doing some sit-ups and push-ups and other super manly stuff that girls like."

I snort.

"Turn on your camera," he says.

"No, I exercised this morning, and I'm disgusting. I haven't even show-ered yet."

"Don't mention showering."

"Why not?"

"Because I recently had the hottest one of my life, and I don't want to embarrass myself begging you for a repeat."

I laugh.

"Anyways," he says, "I'm sure you don't look disgusting. In fact ..."

"Yes?"

"I can't wait to see you again."

Sigh.

I turn on the camera.

"You still want to see me again soon?" I ask, holding the phone out at arm's length at what I hope is a complimentary angle. I'm still in my sports bra and yoga pants, but I surmise there's not much to be shy about considering our recent escapades.

"Well, I *thought* so—"

"And now?"

"Now, I *know* so."

I smile.

"What were you working so hard on today?" he asks.

I tell him more about the project I'm trying to push forward.

"One day you'll have to tell me how you pivoted from video games and graphic design to machine learning."

"It was you," I say. "I mean, kind of."

"What?"

"That time you came to visit me at Rutgers, I had taken, like, one course in ML, and I told you I was intimidated and ..."

"And I told you you're the smartest person I know and those guys better watch their backs because you'd show them who's boss?"

I sniff out. "Approximately. I mean, it was a process, but you saying that helped. I took the course, realized there's so much to learn and discover, and got hooked."

"That's how I feel about my research as well," he says.

"And what did you discover?"

"Nothing huge yet, but you know, all science is building on top of other discoveries. You start with a good foundation of knowledge, and you keep moving it forward, little by little, until you reach the big thing. And everyone says, 'What a miraculous discovery. How amazing.' But as a researcher, you know how gradual it all was. Sure, sometimes there's a breakthrough, but sometimes, you just keep working toward a goal and—"

"And it happens," I chime in.

"Exactly. You're not sure when will be the day it all comes together, but you have faith that it will."

What are you really talking about, Ben?

He clears his throat, and it brings me back to the present.

"Sorry, I was checking the time, and—"

"You should go," he says. "You have an important meeting in the morning."

"I do."

"Have a good night. I ..." he trails off.

"What?"

"I was just thinking I'm glad Aaron lost his keys on Friday night."

"Me, too."

On Monday, I head into work with a lilt in my step. With the progress I made on my project this weekend and the turn of events related to my love life, I'm feeling like a new woman.

I prepare my coffee and grab an apple from the kitchen. My coworker Marissa is sitting at one of the sleek dining tables with her laptop open.

"Hey, how was your weekend?" she asks.

"Great, how about you?" I reply.

She raises a perfectly-shaped ginger eyebrow at me and says in a suspicious tone, "Did you meet someone?"

"What? Why?"

She stands and approaches me, eyeing my hair, then my outfit. She brings her piercing gaze back up to my face. "You look *a lot* happier than you have recently."

"I'm ... happy," I retort, turning to the sink and rinsing my apple.

"Right, and you haven't been since—"

"Don't mention it, please," I say, knowing she means Adam, the last guy I dated who decided to get back together with his ex and ended up engaged to her less than a month later. I turn off the water and face her.

"Fine, anyways, you're happy but generally snarkier. Today, you're downright ... gleeful."

I look gleeful?

"Did you get laid?"

I almost spit out my coffee but manage not to dribble it on my green silk blouse.

"Ahhh, well. It was a shot in the dark, but—"

"What was a shot in the dark?" Ilana asks, suddenly popping up in the kitchen.

"Nothing," I say.

"Gabby found her rebound guy," Marissa shares.

"Ooooh, who?" Ilana asks, her brown eyes glittering.

"Just ... someone I used to know. It's nothing," I say. But I kind of hope it's *not* nothing. I gather my coffee and my apple and head in the direction of my desk, but then stop and look at Ilana.

"Aaron, really?" I say.

She gives me a hesitant smile. "I should've told you already. I'm so—"

"Don't apologize. You know I love you, and I guess he's okay, too."

She grins. "Really?"

"Of course," I say. "We'll talk later, though. I gotta get to a meeting."

•❤•❤•❤•❤•❤•

Around lunchtime, Ben texts me.

> **Ben**
>
> How'd the meeting go?

> **Me**
>
> Great.

> **Ben**
>
> I knew it would. You're a rockstar.

A girl could get used to this kind of praise.

> **Ben**
>
> Soooo, I know you're busy with work, but would you like to meet up this week?

> **Me**
>
> I'm swamped.

> **Ben**
>
> Is this your nice way of saying you had enough of me and I should leave you alone?

I haven't had enough of you. Not even close.

> **Me**
>
> No. I really am busy. Have to tweak a lot of things we presented today.

> **Ben**
>
> <heart eyes emoji> In that case, would Friday work? We could do Shabbat together at your place? I could cook for you.

I forgot. He also cooks. *Of course he does.* A pianist, a biologist, and a chef ... who also has a magical penis. I never stood a chance. We still haven't talked about what happened on Friday night on my living room floor, or Saturday morning in my shower, or Saturday morning on my bedroom floor ...

Are we dating now? Or are we just having sex? Do I care? I have no idea what his plans are after this summer. I'm not sure if he does either since he's still waiting for answers from a few post-doc programs.

Aaron told me Ben's a player—and I certainly have my own experiences to go on regarding his unpredictable nature—but Ben claims he's changed. I've had a thing for him for close to a decade now. I *can't be making an objective decision right now. I don't want to anyways. I want to kiss him more and screw him and laugh with him like I used to.*

My decision is made.

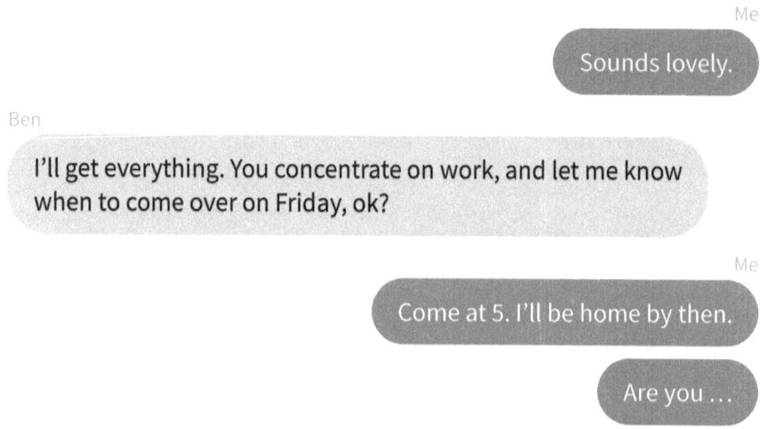

God, am I just gonna come out and say it? Yes, yes, I think I am. I can't drive myself crazy this week wondering.

I see the typing bubble and then it stops. *Deep breath.*

I certainly hope not.

Friday afternoon rolls around, and I leave earlier than usual so I can buy a fresh challah and some wine. I get home at 4:40 p.m. and hop into the shower. I'm pulling an off-white sundress over my head when I hear a knock at the door. 5:04 p.m. Punctual.

When I open the door, he's standing there with a small black duffel bag over his shoulder and a canvas bag of groceries in each hand. *Should I hug him or kiss him or something else?* His hands are full in any case, so I do the most logical thing and take the groceries. He sets his duffel bag on the floor, and I turn to head to the kitchen to place the groceries on the counter.

"Hey, where are you going?" he asks, catching me from behind by the waist and spinning me around.

"I was gonna put the groceries away."

"That can wait," he says, pulling me in close and leaning down to kiss me on the lips. I guess that answers my question.

He slides his hands down, takes the grocery bags, and sets them on the floor. "I've been thinking about doing that all week."

My hands now free, I place them on his shoulders, feeling his warmth through his dark green t-shirt. "Do it again?"

His kiss is soft, different from last weekend. He takes his time and parts his lips, slipping his tongue into my mouth and confidently but lightly exploring. One of his hands slides down and presses into the small of my back while the other cradles my face, angling it just so. I expect this kiss will lead to more and those kisses will lead to even more, but he pulls away slowly and heads into my very small, very blue kitchen.

"So," he says, leaning down to begin unloading the bags, "I didn't check the menu with you, but I remembered that you prefer vegetarian and that you hate radishes, so ..."

"Why don't we just start cooking?" I say.

"We? I wanted to cook for you and let you relax." He washes his hands at the kitchen sink and dries them.

"I'd like to do it with you unless you're a control freak in the kitchen?" I ask, raising an eyebrow, and joining him.

"In the bedroom, you can be the boss, but in the kitchen, I'm in charge." He snaps the kitchen towel he's holding at my butt, and I jump back, too late.

"Ouch," I say, snatching the towel out of his hands.

He grins at me and winks. "Let's cook, baby."

Tzipi apparently trained Ben better in the kitchen than my mother did me. While Ben does all the work, I drink wine and fill him in on my life now. It's like a really bad cooking show. As the attractive contestant washes and chops vegetables and sautés onions for homemade tomato sauce, the half-drunk host adds generally unhelpful commentary and unrelated stories about work and life, while also sexually harassing the contestant who looks amazing in a pair of well-worn jeans bending over to place the veggie lasagna into the oven.

Before I know it, we're sitting to eat said lasagna accompanied by the colorful salad he prepared.

After we've said the blessings for the wine and the challah, we dig into the meal. While chewing, he glances around my apartment which is decorated in soft earth tones with splashes of color—dark magenta, deep blues, and my personal favorite, burnt orange.

"It's exactly how I would have imagined your place," he says.

"Really?" I ask, pleased by his comment. "How would you describe it?"

He sips his wine before answering. "It's like you. Bold, but warm and inviting. A little wild."

His thoughtful description brings a smile to my face. "Thank you. It all kind of grew out of my favorite piece."

His eyes flick to the large mixed-media piece in the center of an otherwise blank wall, a collage I spent a year making. The idea came to me one night in the Judean Desert in Israel while I stared into the flames of a campfire. Upon returning home, I'd started the piece based on a picture of the flame. Then I'd branched out, adding acrylics, bits of paper, all sorts of things.

"It's different than the art you used to make," he observes.

"That's why I like it so much. My art grew."

"Because you did," he says.

Our eyes meet, and I glance away to avoid the intensity of his gaze.

He leans back in his chair. "So how can you afford your own place in Park Slope in your twenties?"

"It's not cheap, but I manage," I say. "Working in high tech is more lucrative than biology."

"Maybe I chose thc wrong profession."

"That came out wrong," I say. "I mean that I'm lucky that I chose the field I work in and that it pays well. It means that I won't ever have to be dependent on a man and his career."

He looks at me thoughtfully. "That's smart."

I reach out and take his hand. "But it's amazing you found something you're passionate about. You've always loved science. I still remember the assembly when you got an award for excellence in ... teaching rats how to do stuff?" I smile.

"They were mice, and I taught them how to run through a maze. I mean, not my finest work, but ..."

"The point is, you found something you loved early, and you've stayed the course. And look at you. You have a PhD. You're going to cure some disease or ... what *are* you going to do exactly?"

"You know about my mom?" he asks.

"What about her?"

"She inherited the BRCA gene mutation from one of her parents, and she was so scared she would get breast cancer that she had a preventive mastectomy when I was in eighth grade."

"I had no idea," I breathe out. *Poor Tzipi.*

"She didn't want a lot of people to know, so we told everyone it was an appendectomy."

"I remember that."

He nods. "Everyone thinks only Ashkenazi Jews have the mutation—and it does have a higher occurrence in that population—but it also happens to other people, like Moroccan Jews, non-Jews ... So she went that route. Even though my dad was an asshole about lots of other things, he had her back on that, but things went south for them a couple years later."

"Unrelated?"

"I think so? It's hard to know sometimes what's going on between two people. Especially as a self-absorbed teenager."

I nod.

"Anyways, that helped guide me toward what I research now."

He goes on to explain how what he's researching could have an impact on cancer treatment. It must be way more complex than he's letting on, but he explains it in a way I can understand.

When he finishes, he looks at me, eyes narrowed. "Why are you looking at me like that?"

"It must be true what they say," I say, unable to hide my smile.

"And what do *they* say?"

"Big cock equals big brain."

He snorts. "Nobody says that."

"True," I agree, "but maybe I should start."

"How do you kick ass so much at work when you obviously have a one-track mind?"

"Two tracks," I correct him. "Machine learning models focused on predicting consumer behavior and ... your cock."

He holds out his hand and pulls me to standing, placing a kiss on my mouth. "I can live with two tracks."

"Do you wanna watch a movie or something?" I ask, going to sit on the couch.

"I was thinking *or something*," he says, laughing.

"Oh, Monopoly, of course."

"Closer to Twister actually."

"Are you gonna tell me that every time we played that growing up you were thinking about getting in my pants?" I ask.

"Only after you started flirting with me."

I snicker. "Dirty old man."

"I'll remind you that I was only a teenage boy at the time."

I scoot away, teasing him.

He grabs my ankle and pulls me back closer. "You remember that party before my senior year at Ari's house when I told you you're a pretty girl and need to watch out for older guys?"

I think back and do remember it. I nod.

"I was trying to tell you—however ineptly—that I thought you're pretty and you should watch out for *me*."

I laugh. "You could've just said, 'Hey, I think you're cute.' I would've followed you to the ends of the earth at that point."

"And your brother would've pounded me into the ground."

"He might try to pound you into the ground now if he knew."

"Now, I'd let him know it's none of his business ... if that's what you wanted me to do." There's a question in his voice.

"I ..." I hesitate. How do I tell him, without sounding like an asshole, that I don't want to tell Aaron or my family about us right now?

But he saves me. "I won't tell him. Not if you don't want me to."

I nod.

"But to buy my silence, you're gonna need to let me kiss you some more." He leans me back and kisses my neck. I tip his chin up, bringing his lips to mine.

"Mmmm, you taste like tomato sauce and red wine," he remarks.

"I drank a lot. I think I was nervous."

"I make you nervous?" he asks.

"You've always given me butterflies in my stomach."

"So now with all the wine, your butterflies are drunk?"

I smile. "That is a perfect metaphor for how you make me feel. My butterflies are drunk."

He gives me a soft smile. "What are you nervous about?"

"I just ... still don't understand where all of this came from. And I guess I'm worried or unsure or—"

"Try not to worry, okay? I know we have a little ... history. But we'll just do things however *we* choose to do them. Just do what *you* feel is right. Got it?"

I look at him and open my mouth to protest, to say one more thing, anything, but the familiar look on his face, it's the same candid, sweet look I remember from my childhood.

He squeezes my hand, bringing me back to the present.

"What I feel like doing is making out with you, Ben. I want to take a step back from ..." I lean in to dramatically yell-whisper the next part, "Your cock down my throat while my brother is asleep in the next room."

He snorts. "Do you wanna watch a movie?"

"What?"

"Well, we've liked each other since high school, so let's watch Netflix like some high school kids who are pretending they're both into the show, but they're both secretly plotting how to start making out with each other. And then, we'll ... make out."

"Hmm," I say, considering this cute little plan of his. I'm giving myself more credit than I deserve if I think this is actually gonna work, that we'll only end up making out and not doing more. *Worth a shot.* "Okay, what do you wanna watch?"

"A horror movie so you can grab onto me during the scary parts?" he says, raising an eyebrow.

"Where am I allowed to grab?" I ask naughtily.

"Uh, anywhere, but aren't *you* the one who said you want to take a step back and cool things down?"

"I'm allowed to have complex feelings on the subject, Benji."

"Why do you keep calling me that?"

"I don't know. Maybe because it makes your blood pressure spike, and I like seeing you hot and bothered."

"There are other ways to get those same results, you know."

"Soooo ... no movie?" I ask, looking at him with a mischievous grin.

"You know," he says, "movies are overrated."

"Yeah, people spend way too much time looking at screens these days," I agree.

"They should spend time looking at other things ..."

"Like well-defined abs," I say, sneaking my fingers under his shirt and exploring.

"And soft, perfect tits," he adds, squeezing my breast.

"And hard, smooth ..." I say, beginning to kiss his neck and trailing my hand down to *his* hard, smooth—

"Cocks?" he supplies.

"I was gonna say something else."

"No, you weren't," he replies and pushes me down on my back on the couch. I dig out a pillow that's in my back and toss it onto the woven rug.

"Sure I was," I say, grinning up at him.

"I'll give you a million dollars if you can tell me what you were gonna say," he says. But he's rubbing his hard shaft along the inside of my leg, and there is literally nothing else I can think about *except* his cock.

I give him an innocent look and shrug.

"I should've known after I read that book of yours in high school that you have a naughty side to you," he says, amused. "And then, going all temptress on me in your dorm room, coming out wet and sexy in just a towel. You like dirty talk, and you like sex, and—"

"Is it too much for you?" I ask. "Knowing me then, and finding out who I am now?"

I know what I like, and I'm not embarrassed about liking sex, suggesting it to the guys I date, or even just go home with. But Ben knew me long before this side of me developed, before I was brave enough to own it—at least in private. *You knew me then. Do you accept me now?*

He leans down, pressing himself even harder into me, and I crave his body on mine. He braces his forearms on either side of me and whispers in a deep voice in my ear, "I think you're a modern, sexual woman who knows what she likes and isn't afraid to say it. And it's a fucking turn-on."

Damn, Ben. Feminist award forthcoming. Growing up with sisters apparently can make a difference.

"What else are you thinking?" I ask, desperate to keep him talking this way.

"I *think* I want you to sit on my cock so I can fuck you the way you so obviously want."

I exhale a small laugh. "That sounds downright lovely. *And* you owe me."

"I owe you?" he asks, as he pulls down his jeans while I raise up my dress.

"I've had lots of sex dreams about you. So ... many ... dreams," I say, touching myself and letting him see what I'm doing, "I've made myself come while imagining you without clothes, which reminds me ... take off your shirt."

He nods and watches me stroke myself through my sheer underwear, while he rapidly removes his clothes.

"You're right," he says, now completely naked. "I do owe you." He scoots down and parts my legs. Moving my fingers aside, he kisses me through my underwear, and his warm breath is enough to make me wet in an instant.

"May I?" he asks, and I hear the smile in his voice.

I rest my hand on my inner thigh, and he kisses it, then bites my thigh.

"Oh," I breathe out.

He slides my underwear to the side and licks me, lightly. After a few strokes of his tongue on me, he pauses. "Take off your dress. I want to feel your whole body."

I nod and sit up to slip off the dress.

"You weren't wearing a bra this whole time?" he asks, surprised.

"No."

"Make out, my ass," he says, laughing.

I give him a sheepish smile.

He slides my panties down my legs and dives in, like he's trying to pay penance for all those times I had to please myself and didn't have him to do *this* for me. He reaches up and massages my breast while he continues to tease my clit. He plunges his tongue deeper, and I come unglued.

"Fuck, Ben, what are you doing?"

He stops. "You don't like it?"

"Stop talking. Do it more!"

He laughs, somewhere inside of my vagina, and I reach down to touch whatever I can reach of him. I could come this way, but I want him by my side. I want to touch him, too. I *need* to run my hands over his warm body. Stop or continue?

"You aren't focused. What's wrong?"

"I, uh ..."

He kisses his way up my stomach, rests his chin on my chest between my breasts, and gazes at me.

"Do you want something else? Ask for it. Don't be shy."

I wrap my legs around him, and he scoots up even farther.

"I just ..."

Why am I stuttering? Why can't I just say what I want?

"Do you want kisses? Do you wanna screw? Do you want me to dance to 'Hava Nagila' naked in your living room?"

The last one makes me laugh. "Please, God, not the last one. Come kiss me. It's all good, but I think that's the best part."

I feel raw admitting it. I've had sex with a lot of people, but when I kissed them, it was often him I was thinking about.

"Of course," he says, kissing me on my chin and then positioning his mouth close to mine. "I love kissing you."

The next kiss is one for the history books. As he moves his tongue over mine, I feel everything at once—ecstasy that I have him in my arms, doubt over what we're doing, longing that this might not last forever.

"I can feel you thinking too much, G," he whispers. "Just enjoy the moment."

"I'll try," I respond and reach down to touch him. "This was a very pleasant surprise," I say, referring to the part of his anatomy that I'm holding.

"But you've seen it before. Did you think it would've changed? What did you think you'd find?" He laughs.

"A unicorn."

"Quit joking, or I might lose my hard-on."

"Sorry."

"I was joking. You're naked, and I have your ass in my hands. I'm not getting soft anytime soon."

"Then let's take advantage of the situation."

I guide him to my opening, and he looks at me, narrowing his eyes. "No condom?"

"I have an IUD. And I was monogamous with ..." My ex.

He nods. Good. I don't have to say his name. "And you?" I ask.

"I'm clean. Not a man-whore like Aaron claims."

I smile at him.

"Are you sure, though?" he asks quietly.

I nod.

He smiles, leans down to kiss me, and enters me slowly. "Goddamn, Gabby. You're amazing."

"You're just pussy-drunk."

"Likely," he replies in a satisfied tone. He buries his face in my neck and begins to move back and forth.

"You know, your cock is … delightful."

"Cock-drunk Gabby is such a compliment to my masculinity."

"Let's stop talking."

"But what will we ever do instead?" he says, thrusting into me and leaning up so I can see the broad smile on his face.

"I … have … a few … ideas," I say, pulling his shoulders to press him harder into me.

"Wrap your legs around me, baby."

I do, and he picks me up and sits back on the couch. "Now …"

I raise my eyebrows, curious.

"We go deep."

And "deep" is where it's at. By it, I mean, my sanity. Where I left it because the way he's fucking me right now is enough to make me lose my mind. I whimper and beg and scream until I completely lose it. And there's a moment right after he comes—a lot more quietly than I did, for the record—where I feel embarrassed. I had a full-on high school crush on this man, this man who used to be the boy down the street. He's seen me in a Pokémon onesie, for God's sake. I've thrown myself at him not only as a horny teenager but also as a, well, horny but slightly more mature college student. And here I am, full-on losing my shit as if I've never had an orgasm before.

"Sorry for being so … loud," I whisper. I peek out of one eye at him.

He leans up to peer at me closely, and I open my other eye.

"Don't apologize. You are *wild* in my hands, and I fucking love it." I lift up so he can pull out, and after, he pulls me back into a hug. "You're … you. Don't apologize for it."

Damn, Ben. Just … damn.

"I'll be right back, okay?" I say, standing. I go to the bathroom for some quick cleanup and come back out with a towel wrapped around me.

He's stepping into his boxer shorts, and I take a moment to appreciate his beautiful body—strong shoulders, a narrow waist, and an ass that just begs to be squeezed. He looks up and sees my smile.

"Yes?" he says.

"Oh, nothing," I say with a giggle. He rolls his eyes and heads to the bathroom, and I switch out my towel for a throw blanket on the chair. When he comes back, he sits down on the end of the couch and begins to massage my feet. "Should we watch a movie *now*?" he asks.

I nonchalantly scoot the blanket down to my waist and look at him, bare-chested, and prop my head on my crossed arms behind my head. He bites his lip as he takes in the view, and I rub my foot over his crotch.

"Yeah, but, like, try to control yourself, man. You can't keep your hands off me," I tease.

"We'll watch a movie tomorrow. Tonight," he says, standing up and pulling me to my feet, "it seems like you have other things on your mind."

"Think it might be time for us to finally spend some time together in a bed?"

"Do we have to sleep?" he asks me for the second time this week, desire glittering in his eyes.

This time, I voice my thoughts. "I certainly hope not."

Ben

On the train ride home from Gabby's on Sunday evening, I think about the week ahead, but what awaits me is far less exciting than the weekend I just finished.

Since I've been back from Ithaca, my weekdays in New Jersey have been filled with reading scientific literature and writing, on the one hand, and helping my mom with cooking and house repairs, on the other. Which isn't to say I'm not enjoying the time with my mom. When she and my dad divorced years ago, and I was the only kid still at home, we became closer. Things in our home became less tense without my father's strong personality present, and we established a sort of peaceful partnership. Being home now is like revisiting that period of my teenage years, and we've both fallen back into our roles in some ways. There's also the practical aspect of living at home, which is that my mom ... is in my business again.

The announcement comes on that the train has reached Glen Rock, and I stand and walk toward the exit doors. It's a nice night out, so I walk home from the train station since I only have a small bag with me, and when I walk in the door, my mom is in the living room.

"Hi, Benny. *Where* were you exactly, sweetheart?" The look on her face is mischievous.

I set my bag down. "In the city."

"How nice. Do anything fun? How was the weather? Who'd you stay with?"

Just sneaks that last one in, like I won't notice.

"A friend—"

"Where?"

She's trying to pull her innocently curious Jewish mother act on me. *It won't work. I know this one.*

"In Manhattan," I say, lying through my teeth. *It doesn't have the same feeling of accomplishment it did when I was a teenager, and I feel a little guilty.*

But if I told her I was in Brooklyn, she'd guess in a second that I was visiting Gabby. Aaron told his mom about us staying there last weekend when he lost his keys, and I'm sure Marci told my mom, even though she hasn't mentioned it.

My mom has been hinting for years that I should date Gabby, and the fact that we're both single and in our mid-twenties now would only make it worse. Gabby asked me not to say anything, so I don't.

"Hmmm ... anybody I know?"

"Just an old friend from school." *Not entirely a lie.*

"Well," she says, standing and grabbing her tea mug and book from the side table, "I'm glad you had fun." She kisses me on the cheek before heading into the kitchen.

My phone buzzes in my pocket, and I open it to find a cute selfie of Gabby.

Gabby

> Glad we finally made it to a bed. <winky emoji>

She's leaning against her headboard, and the slouchy light-gray sweat-shirt she was wearing when I left has slid off one shoulder, revealing a red bra strap. Her full lips are curved into a half-smile, and she looks all sorts of sexy.

I'm about to text her back when another few texts roll in.

> Here's some soft...

> Perfect ...

She wouldn't.

But apparently, she would, because the next text is a close-up of her in a red lace bra—no face, just cleavage. My phone clatters to the floor.

"Everything okay?" my mom asks, popping her head into the foyer to find me bending down to snatch up my phone, which has very conveniently fallen face-up.

The photo is still open—thank God she didn't include her face—and my mom's mouth drops open. "Ummm ..."

"Everything's great," I choke out, snatching up the phone and stuffing it into my pocket.

She tries, but fails, to hide a smile. "Good night, Benny. I'm glad you, uh, had fun this weekend." She snorts as she walks back into the kitchen.

"What was up with the hot selfie yesterday, huh?" I ask Gabby on Monday night when we talk.

"You didn't like it?"

"Oh, I liked it. But you can't do that to me. I don't know when I'll see you again, and it's not fair."

"I thought we'd see each other this weekend, no? And I wanted to give you a little something to tide you over."

Do I tell her my mom saw it? I don't want her to be embarrassed, but I go with full transparency.

"So my mom kinda saw your pic yesterday."

"What?" she spits out.

"Not the one with your face. Don't worry."

"So she *only* saw my tits? What is wrong with you?"

"I was surprised—pleasantly—and I dropped the phone."

"So now your mom knows we sext?"

"That wasn't *really* sexting ..." I pause.

"Ben, I don't need a tutorial on what sexting is, but like—"

"Hey, it's okay. She only saw your boobs. Your name and face weren't on the screen. So unless you've been showing her your boobs in real life, she doesn't know those specific soft ... perfect ... tits belong to you."

It's a Hail Mary pass. I know that.

She exhales. "I'm gonna strangle you the next time I see you. You know that, right?"

"As long as you do it while you're riding my cock—"

She bursts out laughing.

"So you want me to come see you again on Friday?" I ask, moving the conversation into what I hope is safer territory. "You're getting used to me, huh?"

She sighs. "I don't think I ever got un-used to you."

Same, girl. Same.

"What are you thinking about this fine Monday evening?" I ask.

"Remember our famous tutoring session?"

"The one where you tried to jump me?"

"God, I was a horny little teenager, wasn't I?" She laughs. "I even told you a dirty joke that you didn't get."

"Wait, what?"

"I said that the human body has 207 bones."

"Two hundred and six," I reply.

"That's what you said then, too. But I'm pretty sure that you were holding a binder over number 207."

I crack up. "You're right. I did *not* get the joke then."

"No, but you did get a boner."

"Number 207," I reply, snickering. "So I don't mind coming to you, but are you sure you don't want to come here?"

"I-I feel more comfortable here."

"Okay," I say, "I'll come see you this weekend."

As the words leave my mouth, my mom comes into the room to dump some clean clothes from the laundry basket on my bed to fold.

"Oh, sorry," she whispers. "I didn't know you were on the phone."

I smile up at her. "It's okay, Ima. Thanks for the laundry."

She walks out the door and mutters to herself, "That's something he never would've said in high school."

"Your mom came in? Did she know you're talking to me? Or just the owner of the red lace bra?"

"Neither," I say.

She sighs audibly. "I miss you."

I miss her, too, but something keeps me from saying it out loud.

"So does that bra have a matching thong?" I ask.

"I guess you'll have to come visit me and find out."

"Can't wait," I say. "I'll let you go. Sleep well, tonight."

"Night, B."

When I walk into the kitchen on Tuesday morning, I fully expect my mom to ask why I was chatting with Gabby last night. I have a weird feeling that she knows we've been talking.

To her credit, she waits until I've poured some coffee into my mug before jumping in. I'm adding the cream when she says in what she probably thinks is an off-handed tone, "Two weekends in a row in the city, huh?"

"Good morning to you, too, Ima."

She raises an eyebrow that I know means *answer me.*

"Uh, yeah, I guess so," I say, not giving an inch.

"Someone special?" she asks.

Yes, the most special. I'm a millisecond away from blurting it out, maybe even telling her that she knows and loves this special person. *God, what is it with that inquisitive eyebrow of hers?* But I catch myself.

Gabby doesn't want anybody to know we're ... What are we? Are we dating? I mean, we've had *a lot* of sex the past couple weekends, but she and I both know that mind-blowing sex does not a relationship make. But the facts at hand, at least from my standpoint, are: one, we've always had a special connection, and two, it's only been two days since I saw her and I can't stop thinking about her.

There is something about her—about us—that is beyond my control. I've felt it for years. She's letting me get closer to her, but she doesn't completely trust me. She's holding something back. But so am I. I can't bring myself to talk to her about our "expiration date." I'm finally getting the opportunity to experience her, to experience an "us," and I don't want it to end before it's even begun.

"Benjamin," my mom says, bringing me back to the present. Her lips are pursed, I think to avoid smiling, and she widens her eyes indicating I should answer.

"I–I've just been hanging out with some friends. I mean, I figure it's my last chance to take in the New York City atmosphere before I head off to my post-doc," I reply, joining her at the table.

She rolls her hazel-colored eyes, the ones I inherited from her. She knows I'm not telling her the truth. It's the same look she used to give me when I was a teenager, lying to her about what I was doing with my friends on a Saturday night.

"Anyways," I say, basically admitting that I might have been seeing someone in particular, "it won't turn into anything."

My gut clenches as I say it. *Do I mean it? Is that what I want? Or have I just already accepted that's how Gabby and I will end up?* "I need to stay focused on my post-doc, not get off-track."

She sniffs out, annoyed. "You sound like your father." My eyes meet hers. She knows how much those words sting, but she chose them anyway.

Her face softens, and she reaches out a hand across the table to pull one of mine away from my coffee cup. She squeezes my hand. "I'm sorry. I didn't mean that, or at least, I meant it in a different way."

I raise my eyebrows.

"Sweetheart, your mind and heart are big enough to be driven in your career and also find love. Life isn't only about working." Her eyes dip, looking at our hands, instead of directly at me.

"Is that what it was?" I ask.

"What, what was?" she asks.

"What the problem was between you and Aba? That he worked too much."

"He worked a lot, but no, that's not what it was. Your father, he's … a difficult person. A smart, successful, and good-hearted person, but … a very difficult person to live with, to be married to."

"You genuinely think he's good-hearted?" I ask, not believing her and thinking maybe she's trying to save face for him since I'm his son.

She lets out a small but noticeable sigh. "Of course he has a good heart. You know how we met."

"But that was a long time ago," I protest. "He was in his twenties, volunteering for a few months in Israel—"

"Volunteering for *six* months treating children and elderly people in southern Israel and Bedouin villages *while he put his career on hold* … is no small thing."

She's right. They met in a community center in Be'er Sheva. She was running an arts program, and he was there checking in with the director of his program. My dad told me and my sisters, embarrassingly, about the moment he first saw her. *She was teaching a painting course to some kids, and I swear my heart stopped beating when she turned around.*

"I know, Ima. I know."

"He's a good man," she says, "but he has his own demons. Being the child of Holocaust survivors is … Well, you've read about intergenerational trauma in your line of work."

I have. Whether it's something physiological or environmental—or both—traumatic experiences can impact the minds, feelings, and relationships of people several generations past the survivors themselves.

"He has his issues, his challenges. I wanted to be there for him—I *was* there for him, for many years—but he could be … well, I won't say more. He's your father. I loved him. I spent half of my life with him, and it was hard. You know that."

She exhales loudly, and I rub her shoulder.

"Well, I won't say *much* more," she says, "but for you to understand, I'll say this: I think I lost myself in our marriage, and I'm still working on recovering *me* after so many years of giving to others."

I look at my beautiful mother—her dark complexion, high cheekbones, and striking eyes—and I see the face of my own sisters in thirty years. Has Ariella chosen her own partner wisely? A man who will encourage her to fulfill all her dreams, who will help her carry the heavy load that comes with being a mother? What about Miri?

What kind of partner would I be? The kind I want for my sisters or the kind my dad was?

"I'm sorry, Ima." *Am I apologizing for my father or for some future transgression of my own against the woman I end up with?*

She pulls her hand back and sighs. "You don't need to be sorry. You have been my beautiful, kind boy since the day you were born. Even before. Only one day of nausea while I was pregnant with you."

I smile at her, wanting to believe what she says, but she doesn't know *all* of me. The careless way I've treated some of the women I've dated, even Gabby. I've never been cruel or abusive, but a serious relationship—a marriage—requires more. I've seen firsthand what happens when there's an imbalance of power, of respect.

"Ima, I love you. I don't always say it, but I do. You did everything for us so we could succeed, but what about you? What about your dreams?"

A tear slips from one eye, down her cheek. "Listen to yourself. Your heart is big enough for anything you want to go after ..." She meets my eyes. "Including love. Don't let mine and your father's experience jade yours."

I still feel uneasy but a little more heartened. "I won't," I say. "But it's ... still complicated. You know I'm leaving soon. And she ... she can't leave. She's doing well at work, and I don't want her to give that up."

"Ben, you've lived with women long enough to know that we don't like decisions to be made for us. You should leave it up to *her* to decide what's best for her."

But what's best for Gabby might be staying the hell away from me.

Gabby

It's only been a couple weeks, but I've already begun to think of my weekends as "Ben time." It's an imaginary world in which I explore, *What would it be like to date Ben?* I'm trying to be realistic, though—something I never did in the past concerning him. I don't know where he's going this fall—neither does he—but it certainly isn't Long Island.

Should I stop seeing him before we get too entangled? Should we be more careful?

But I don't want to. I want this time with him. I feel so, so good when he's near.

I'm contemplating when—or rather whether—I should ask him what he thinks about what we're doing when my phone rings.

Ima, pops up on my phone screen. I accept the call on speaker since I'm sitting in my living room working from home.

"Hi, Ima," I say.

"Hi, sweetie," she says. "How are you doing?"

"Okay, just in the middle of a project. Trying to finish it up by the end of the week."

"Speaking of the end of the week," she says, and I can hear the smile in her voice. "Tzipi's invited us for dinner on Friday night. Can you come home?"

"Ummm," I stall, thinking that Ben and I had planned on seeing each other this weekend. "I ... uh..."

"Do you have plans?"

"Um, no," I lie.

"Aaron is bringing a girl he's been dating," she says brightly. "And Ben will be there, too." *He will?* "I know he was at our house a couple weeks ago, but it might be nice to catch up."

"You're right. That would be nice," I say, thinking of how much *catching up* we've been doing lately.

"I saw him out running the other day. He helped me take the trash cans in. He's such a nice young man. Always has been. And handsome, too. Do you think he might be gay, honey?"

I snort, amused by my mom's insane stream-of-consciousness monologue, but cough loudly to cover it. When I recover my composure, I reply, "I'm pretty sure he's not gay."

"Well, I mean, it's okay if he *is*, but I do wonder why he doesn't have someone special in his life."

Someone special. Are those his words or my mother's?

"Did he tell you that?" I ask.

"No, but Tzipi says she tried to set him up last week with Mrs. Moskowitz's daughter who's here for the summer, and he said he doesn't have time for dating right now."

Good. He better not.

"Though," she says, continuing with her theorizing, "come to think of it, he can't be gay."

"Why is that?" I ask, indulging her and standing up to stretch my legs.

"Well," she says, lowering her voice. *Here she goes. That's her gossip voice.* "Tzipi told me that he's been staying in the city the last couple of weekends." *Oh boy.* "And she even saw a *very* risqué selfie on his phone that an adventurous young woman sent of her—"

"Mom," I interrupt. "You know, that's Ben's business. And sending sexy pictures to people, as long as they remain private, isn't all that bad. In fact, most people in their twenties have done it at some point—"

"I certainly hope *you* haven't."

I flop down on my couch, face-first, and bury my face in a pillow.

"Of course not, Ima," I lie.

"What?" she asks. "You sound muffled."

I turn my head so it's not in the pillow anymore. "I said, 'Of course not.' I'd never do something so ... 'adventurous.'"

"Anyways," she says, getting back to the reason she called, "why don't you come and stay the night? We can spend time together, you and me, on Saturday morning. I miss you."

"I'll think about it. I mean, I'll come for dinner. I'm not sure if I can stay over."

"Okay, well, make sure you wear something pretty."

"Of course," I say. "I gotta go. Love you."

When I get off the phone with my mom, I head to my kitchen. I could use a strong drink after that call, but jasmine tea will have to suffice since I'm only halfway through the workday. I sit back down at the computer and call Ben.

"Hey," he says, "I didn't expect to hear from you in the middle of the day. How's it going?"

"Well, I mean, the Jewish Mother Network strikes again. Word on the street is you're getting, and I quote, 'risqué selfies from an adventurous young woman.'" I exhale loudly while I listen to him crack up.

"Thank God for adventurous young women," he replies.

I chuckle. "So it sounds like this week, it's dinner at your mom's?"

"I meant to tell you. She's trying to call my bluff and see if she can get me to invite the beautiful woman I've been spending time with each weekend in Manhattan."

"You have a beautiful woman in Manhattan, too?"

"Oh, yeah, in all the boroughs. One in the Bronx, one in Queens. I'm still looking for my Staten Island bae, though."

I snicker. "So I guess I'll come."

"You always do with me, G."

"Ben, seriously not in the mood after that conversation with my mother."

His rich laugh fills my ears, and I wish he were here with me.

"My mom wants me to spend the night," I say.

"I want you to spend the night, too."

"We can't have sex in your mom's house."

"Why not?"

"Because … nobody even knows we're together."

"Would that be such a bad thing?"

Tread lightly. "It wouldn't be a bad thing, but I'm still … wrapping my head around … whatever it is we're doing. Your plans are up in the air, and well, my plans are … here. Let's just wait a little bit?"

He breathes out, not quite a sigh. I've said the wrong thing. Of course I have. Nobody wants to be someone else's secret. I don't want him to be my secret either, but it's hard enough to know he has left me before and that he'll likely be doing it again. I can't take the compounded challenge of him being gone *and* having to deal with my family's questions about it.

"It's okay, G. I understand."

Does he?

But I don't push it.

On Friday afternoon, I cut out from work early. My hostess tonight, Tzipi, doesn't know I'm dating—screwing?—her darling son, but the woman has seen more of me than I would like. Whatever she knows, or doesn't, flowers can't hurt, so I pick up some tulips at the flower shop near my place.

After a quick shower at home, some light makeup, and a supersonic blow-dry, I pull on the royal blue A-line dress I bought on Wednesday. It's a bold choice, but it looks great on me, especially with my hair lightening up this summer.

On the drive to Glen Rock, I listen to *Normal Gossip* but barely hear it. I'm twisted up in thought about my upcoming dinner invitation. When I arrive at my parents' house, I take my overnight bag and the flowers into the house, where my dad greets me at the front door.

"For me?" he jokes, holding his hands out for the flowers.

"Sure, Aba. I know you love tulips," I say. "Sorry, I'm late. Traffic was bad."

"It's okay. We're only a few minutes late," he says, taking my bag instead.

"Is that Gabby?" my mom calls from upstairs.

"Yes, dear," my father calls back up. "Ready to go?"

"Of course!"

"Where's Aaron?" I ask.

"He already headed over with Ilana, this new girl he's dating. You know her?"

"She's *my* friend."

"Well, Aaron thinks she's *his* friend," my dad says, winking.

I look away, thinking about what this means, the fact that Aaron's going out with my friend, and I'm, well, *something* with his. But Ben is so much more than just Aaron's friend. He's—

"Everything okay?" my mom asks, coming down the stairs. "Oh, Gabby, dear. You look beautiful."

I smile at my dad. My mom always says that. If she doesn't like something about the way I'm dressed, she never says it in front of anyone else. She pulls me aside afterward to tactfully tell me something is too revealing or the wrong color.

"Really?" I ask, looking at her carefully.

"Really, darling. You only bring me *naches*." *Joy.*

I give her a side hug and walk back out the door, waiting for my parents to join me. "Shall we go?"

When we arrive at Ben's house, he greets us at the door. "Shabbat shalom," he says to my parents. He leans in to hug each of them and ushers them inside, then steps out and closes the door slightly.

"Hey, there," he says, embracing me.

"Hey," I say, sighing, suddenly feeling lighter now that I'm with Ben in the flesh. "How was your week?"

"We just talked last night," he whispers in my ear.

"Fine. How was your day?"

"My day was good. I went for a run, fixed the front door—"

"You know how to fix doors?" I ask.

He nods.

"That's kinda hot," I say.

"I didn't know you had a handyman kink," he says, then rakes his eyes down my body. "You look gorgeous, by the way."

"Blue's your favorite color." *It's for you.*

"Especially on you," he says, and my insides warm. "We should go inside, but just so you know, I'd rather stay out here and kiss you for a few minutes."

"Let's go, smooth talker," I say.

As I walk through the door a step ahead of Ben, he traces his pointer finger down my spine, sending shivers through my body. Since my mother and Tzipi are still in the foyer, I make a mental note to pay him back later.

My mom raises an eyebrow at me, then smiles. "Thought we lost you, dear."

"Ben and I were catching up," I reply.

"Why don't you give Tzipi the flowers you brought for her?" my mom suggests.

I walk over to Tzipi. "I remembered that you like tulips because they're my favorite, too." As luck would have it, on the wall behind her is a painting of hers, orange tulips, not so different from the ones I've brought her.

She takes the flowers, sets them on the table behind her, and pulls me in for a hug. "Thank you, sweetheart. You've always had an eye for beautiful things." She inhales. "What is that wonderful scent?"

I pull back from the hug. "Oh," I laugh. "Um, it must be my moisturizer. It's made with lavender."

"Ah, it seems … familiar," she says, and I look into her eyes, framed by thick, dark eyelashes, and notice how much like Ben's they are.

"Well," my mom says, "can we help you in the kitchen, Tzipi?"

"No need," she says. "Ben and I already prepared everything. We can sit to eat, but let's light the Shabbat candles first."

We walk into the dining room, and I turn to hug Ilana.

"Gabby, Ilana," Tzipi says, "would you like to light the candles for us?"

"Sure," we both say, and we join her at a side table with several sets of candle sticks. Ilana and I open the box of candles, each taking two, place them in the candlesticks, and light them. I nod at Ilana, and we wave our hands over our eyes three times in circles, then close them, and say the blessing.

I open my eyes to look at the candles and turn to give my mother, who is standing nearby with a warm smile, a hug. "Shabbat shalom, Ima. Shabbat shalom, Aba." Aaron is holding Ilana's hand, so I turn to Ben. "Shabbat shalom, Benji," I say and wink.

After the blessings over the wine and the challah, we dive into a full-on feast. My mom's food is great, but Tzipi has a way of making everything taste good and look like a work of art.

"Tzipi," Ilana says in awe, "this fish is fabulous."

"It's called *chraime*," she says.

"Oh, I've heard of that, but I never knew what it was," Ilana says with a smile. "And the salads are lovely, too. How did you prepare all of this yourself?"

"I didn't," Tzipi says, reaching out to squeeze Ben's hand. "Benny helped me with everything. He's a great cook. I made sure he always helped me so one day when he gets married, he'll be able to pull his weight in the kitchen." Our eyes meet and she winks.

Oh, God.

"Benjamin," my father asks, saving me from the awkward silence, "when are you heading out to your post-doc? Your mom said you still haven't decided?"

"I should know pretty soon, actually," he replies. "It'll be sometime near the end of the summer. I applied to about five or six programs, and, uh, I'm waiting to hear back from a couple more—positive or negative—before making a final decision."

Ben's eyes flick to me before he tells my dad the programs at the top of his list. Two in California and another on the east coast.

North Carolina? No, he has to be closer. Otherwise ...

I reach out for my glass, hoping a well-timed sip might hide my crestfallen expression. But my shaky hand knocks it over, spilling half a glass of red wine onto the beautiful white Shabbat tablecloth.

"Oh, God, I'm so sorry," I say, righting the glass as Ben throws his napkin over it to soak up the liquid.

"It's fine, dear," Tzipi says, standing and taking a dish towel from the side table to assist with the cleanup.

"I don't know what's wrong with me," I mutter.

Ben's eyes lock with mine. "There's nothing wrong with you."

"I just—" I cut myself off. *I just got a dose of reality.*

In that one short exchange, I've learned more about his plans than he's shared with me during all our conversations, FaceTimes, or texts the last couple of weeks. I only had to ask. *But maybe I didn't want to know the answer.*

The conversation around me moves on, and when it's time for dessert,

I stand to help Ben clear the dishes. Tzipi starts to get to her feet, but I tell her to sit.

"We'll handle it. You've done so much already." I walk into the kitchen and set the dishes on the counter near the sink harder than I intended to.

Ben comes up behind me and places a hand on the small of my back. "You okay?"

"Of course," I lie, not turning to face him.

We jumped into all this. Zero to sixty miles per hour in one week—one night—and I feel unsteady all of a sudden.

"No, you're not," he says, "but have some strawberry cake."

"Strawberry? Not chocolate?" I ask, turning around.

"It's your favorite." He shrugs and gives me a shy smile.

He made it for me.

He hands me the dessert plates and forks from the kitchen island. "I'll bring the cake."

When we rejoin everyone, my parents and Tzipi have settled in the living room.

"Oh, do you want dessert in there?" I ask.

"I couldn't eat another bite," my mom says.

Tzipi and my father agree that they'll pass on dessert and just have coffee.

Aaron and Ilana are getting ready to head out the front door. "Sorry, Ben," Aaron says, as Ben walks into the room carrying the cake. "I got us tickets for AJR tonight, and there are a couple of opening acts, but I don't want us to miss the main show. Rain check?"

"No worries, man," Ben says. "Have fun."

He sets the cake down on the table and gives me a serious look. "Can you eat half a cake?"

I smile. "I will do my absolute best." He serves me a large piece on a plate, takes a much smaller one for himself, and asks if I want to sit out back with him.

I smile and nod. I follow him out to the back porch, and we sit on the patio sofa. Ben scoots close to me.

"Why are you on top of me?" I ask.

"You, of all people, should know what it feels like for me to be on top of you, and this," he says, scooting an inch closer, "is not on top of you."

I roll my eyes and take my first bite. "This is … mmmmm … very good."

"Stop talking like that," he whispers, looking at my mouth.

"Like what?"

"Moaning in ecstasy like you're having an"—he glances around—"orgasm," he whispers.

I laugh loudly. "Mmmmmm, but it's soooooo good. I just … mmmm … want more, Bennnn."

He shakes his head and snorts quietly. "You're so naughty," he says, watching me take another bite. "Stop it."

"Am I allowed to express *any* pleasure about how good this is?"

"No," he says.

"No?"

"Save all your pleasure sounds for later," he orders me.

"Oh, is there another cake?" I ask, laughing.

He shakes his head and very obviously flicks his eyes down to my chest, licking his lips playfully the whole time.

I laugh even more. "Stop it. You're gonna make me choke on cake."

"And here I thought you might choke on my—"

"Benny," Tzipi calls, leaning out the patio door.

At this point, I basically snort cake up my nose. I cannot stop giggling, and Ben hops to a standing position while shooting me a fake dirty look. His mom asks him if he can get something down from the top cabinet for her, and he follows her inside. I set my plate down. It really is too much cake for a person to consume in one sitting. When Ben returns, he tells me that my parents are getting ready to walk home.

"I should go with them," I say.

He nods and holds out his hand. I take it and stand.

"They'll probably go to bed soon," I say casually.

"Does that mean …"

"It means if you want to go on a walk with me later, I'll change my shoes, and we can … go on a walk?" I smile.

"You know what *walk* rhymes with?" he asks in a sing-song voice.

"And you say I have a one-track mind."

"I'll text you when I finish helping my mom clean up."

An hour later, I'm lying in bed re-reading *The Deal* and thinking about the time Ben caught me reading it in Aaron's car when I get a text from him. We've been texting back and forth the last few weeks, but sitting here in my old childhood bedroom and seeing that name pop up triggers my nostalgic side, and I change his name from "Ben" to "B(estie)" like the first time he ever gave me his number.

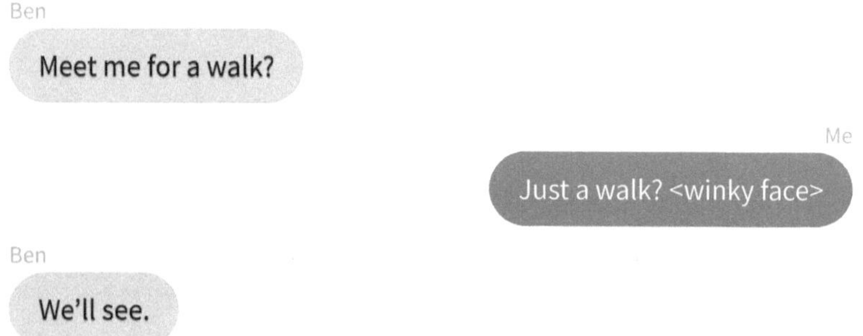

When I go downstairs, he's waiting for me near the side gate.

"You remembered our old way of sneaking out of the house?" I ask.

"Yes, I remembered the worst-kept secret side gate in history." He leans in and kisses me. "Mmmm, you taste like toothpaste and … strawberry cake."

"Yeah, well, it's still stuck in my nose from earlier."

He pecks me on the nose. "That nose of yours is irresistible. No wonder."

"Park?"

"Sure."

We walk holding hands, and the simplicity—the everyday, no-pressure goodness of it—sends a swirl of mixed emotions through my insides.

"So," he asks, "you changed your shoes but you kept the dress?"

"I like it, and I thought you liked it."

"I like it a lot. Why do you think I kept touching your legs at dinner underneath the table? It's the perfect dress. Just long enough—"

"Not to be slutty," I interject.

"Yeah. And just low-cut enough to—"

"Showcase my rack?" I suggest.

He snickers and takes in the aforementioned rack. "If *that's* what you were trying to do ..."

It might have been.

"Then it worked."

We arrive at the park, and I pull him toward the swings. I sit on one and encourage him to get on, too.

"I'm not sure I'll even fit on these anymore," he says.

"Oh, come on. You're not that big," I tease.

He acquiesces and pumps his legs, going much higher than me.

"For a guy who doesn't like rollercoasters, you're certainly a strong swinger," I call out.

"You remembered I don't like rollercoasters?"

"I remember lots of things about you," I reply and blow him a kiss.

We swing for a few minutes in silence. Hearing him detail his plans earlier at dinner when my dad asked shook me. A few post-doc offers. A few more still undecided. *Like me and Ben. Undecided.*

I'm jolted back to the present by Ben shooting out the front of his swing. He lands perfectly in the sand and spins around, gesturing with his hands for me to jump out.

"No way," I say.

"Come on," he says. "I'll catch you."

"It's been a while since I've done this," I say, letting the swing slow down. Then I let go, stumbling into Ben's waiting arms.

"See? I got you."

But do I have you?

He takes my hand, and we continue walking until we reach the ancient gazebo in the middle of the park. As we make our way under the old wooden roof, Ben looks up. "A little worse for the wear but still standing."

What a perfect metaphor for me.

He places his hands on my waist and guides my arms up around his neck. Then he begins to sway.

"Like a high school dance?" I ask.

"I guess so," he replies. "We never got to finish that dance at prom, did we? You made a dirty joke—"

"I did *not* make a dirty joke. You just understood my perfectly innocent words in a dirty way," I retort.

He laughs. "But you still ended up kissing me."

"You wanted me to," I reply, looking at his lips, then shifting my gaze up to his eyes.

"Hell, yeah, I did," he agrees and tips my chin to kiss me softly on the lips. *So good. So simple. Why couldn't things just ... work for us?*

He turns and pulls me gently over to the bench at the edge of the gazebo, then sits before I do and pats his legs.

"Sit on my lap," he says. If there were enough light, I'm sure I'd be able to see a twinkle in those beautiful eyes of his. "So you don't ruin your beautiful dress, of course."

"How thoughtful of you," I remark, twirling so he can admire the dress before sitting down and snuggling into him. He wraps an arm around my waist to keep me from sliding off his lap.

"It feels weird being here now, doesn't it?" he says.

"A little bit. I haven't been in this park in years."

"We used to walk here a lot, didn't we?"

I swallow, thinking of the hard years he had in high school while his parents' marriage broke down. "I always loved those walks with you. I'm sorry you had to escape your house, but ..."

"What?" he asks.

"I'm glad that when you escaped, you escaped to me."

"Me, too."

An awkward beat passes, and he twirls a lock of my hair in his fingers.

"So why is it weird being at home?" I ask. "Have things changed too much?"

"I guess some things have changed a lot. And others," he says, catching my gaze, "have stayed the same."

"You sound like the Sphinx telling a riddle," I say, giggling.

He shakes his head as if clearing his thoughts. "Sorry. Been having some deep thoughts lately, I guess."

About what?

I reach up and run the back of my fingers along this jawline, loving the texture of his face, even—or maybe especially—when it's not smooth.

I sigh. "I guess once you've been out in the big world, things back home feel small, less important. I mean, you went away to school—twice—and traveled. I've barely left New Jersey."

"You live in the greatest city in the world."

"You know what I mean. New York City has a lot to offer, but I wonder sometimes whether I should've gone farther afield."

"To do what?" he asks, tilting his head, listening carefully.

Do I tell him? The dreams I buried deep inside once it was clear the path I was going down?

"To ... explore," I reply, simply.

He smiles. "And what do you want to explore?"

Myself.

"Maybe to paint," I say. "Maybe I missed my calling as an artist in Venice or Paris?" I look up at him shyly through my eyelashes, and he tips my chin up.

"You haven't missed anything. You'll go one day," he says. He runs his hands through my hair. "And you'll create beautiful art, a beautiful life. You ... you bring beauty wherever you go."

"You do, too."

"Beauty?" he asks, surprised.

I run my fingers over his brow, then kiss his nose. "I don't know if the right word is beauty, but I know that when you're around, things feel ... good. And when you're gone..."

The weight from before, the burden I felt hearing him tell my dad his plans at dinner, returns, and I glance away.

"I'm here right now," he says, turning my head gently back in his direction with his hand. "Let's focus on that."

But what will happen to us?

I look into his eyes now. *Does he feel what I do? Am I the only one* it's obvious to? We're here together, after all these years. It can't be just chance, or if it is, it has to be one we could take, together.

We have something different, a special connection that despite the distance, the years, doesn't seem to fade. We've jumped into this summer fling, but couldn't we create something that lasts longer?

I kiss him, parting my lips, and our kiss deepens. He pulls me into him tightly. I *feel* him telling me this is something more, but am I misreading him? Too scared to utter the words, I show him, through touch, through physical connection, what I feel. *We could be so much more,* my kiss says. *We could be everything to each other.*

His hand moves from my face down to my breast, and he traces my nipple with his thumb. Goosebumps pop up on my arms and legs. "That feels good."

"I love making you feel good," he says.

But what I actually feel is mixed up: my previous uncertainty and longing for something with Ben—not just for the summer, but for longer—jumbled together with the events of right now, the very real, very sweet man parting my lips with his, granting me the smallest taste of what a lifetime with him could be like.

I pull away, breathless—from his kiss, from the weight of my feelings.

"What happened?" he asks, meeting my eyes.

I can't say it. It's only been a couple weeks.

He puts his pointer finger on my nose, and I look down, cross-eyed, at it.

"It's not fair how adorable you are, G. Even with your eyes crossed like that."

He slides his finger down lightly across my lips, then continues down further, reaching the tie holding the top of my dress. Holding my gaze, he pulls the string. Once loosened, he can see the lace hem of my bra.

"You are the Goddamn sexiest woman I've ever seen," he says, breathing heavier than before. He slips his hand inside my dress and cups one of my breasts.

I slip off his lap onto the bench and undo his pants, reaching my hand inside to feel with my hand what I felt under me before.

"You really do like this dress," I tcase.

"I like what's in it more," he replies.

I laugh. He can always make me laugh, and the bad feelings from before dissipate as I concentrate on the here and now. He wraps his free arm around me to keep me from falling and tries to kiss my chest, but the angle of this bench is not ideal.

"What exactly was your plan for this gazebo?" I ask.

"I didn't really have one."

"Well, my plan is to go high school style and give you a hand job."

"Here?" he asks, surprised.

"Like this would be my first time giving a hand job in this park?"

"Gabriella Feinman," he says in a matronly tone.

"Like this would be your first time *getting* a hand job in this park?"

"Ummmm…"

"That's what I thought," I say.

"But it's our first time together," he says, caressing my face as he slips his tongue into my mouth. He laces his fingers in my hair. "You …" he breathes out.

I slip my free hand up his shirt and caress his hard stomach.

"I what?"

"You … I want to be inside you," he whispers.

"Soon."

"Let's go back," he says.

"Where?"

"We'll figure it out," he says, pulling his boxers and pants up to button them and pulling me up into a hug. I can feel he's still hard between us, and I let my hand trail down to stroke him.

"No, don't do that. I only have so much restraint and …"

"What?"

"I have an idea."

Ben

My idea is that Gabby is coming back to my bedroom at my mom's house.

Twenty-seven-year-old Ben is about to do something that would've blown seventeen-year-old Ben's mind.

"So we're doing this?" she asks as we walk quickly back to my house.

"Oh, we're doing this."

"Your mom is there," she says.

"Don't worry. She's already in bed, and her bedroom is downstairs. We're about to light it up, Lil G."

She snorts. "Oh my God. Okay. Okay."

I think she's talking herself into it.

We'll have to be quiet, but I'm getting turned on just thinking about it. I walk behind her and kiss her neck while I grab her ass.

When we reach my house, I take her to the back door. It's farther from my mom's room. We're about halfway up the stairs, trying to be quiet, when Gabby trips and lands on her knees a stair above me. We freeze.

My mom calls, "Benny, *hakol b'seder?*" *Everything okay?*

Gabby's eyes are the size of saucers, and I hold a pointer finger to my lips and answer. "I'm fine, Ima. I went for a walk. Going to bed now."

"Do you need anything, *motek?*"

Gabby's face lights up, at least as much as it can in the darkened stairwell.

"No, I'm okay. *Laila tov*, Ima."

We stumble into my room.

"Do you need anything, *motek?*" Gabby asks, imitating my mom and releasing mostly silent giggles.

I shoot her a stern look. "You're acting like you're drunk," I yell-whisper at her.

"I feel drunk," she says with a delicious smile on her face.

"Didn't you spill most of your wine at dinner?" I ask.

"It doesn't matter. I'm drunk on *you.*" She spins around, her arms up in the air, then falls back on the bed. "What I wouldn't have done to be invited up to this bedroom when I was a teenager."

I jump into the bed beside her. "If it makes you feel any better, I fantasized about you often enough in this bed."

"Oooooh, do tell. What was your favorite fantasy about me?"

I look at her, silent, hesitant to share all my deepest, darkest secrets.

"C'mon, tell me," she says, trying to convince me. "I promise I'll make it worth your while." She trails her pointer finger down my chest, and I shiver.

In that case.

"Fine. So I had this fantasy where I would be asleep, and then you'd come in through the window from the roof..."

Her eyes light up. "I know how to climb like Spiderman in this dream?"

"Shhh... you're ruining it."

"Okay, okay. Go on."

"And then you crawl into bed with me wearing only your bra and underwear."

"So tame, Benji. Why not naked?" she teases.

"Because back then you were sixteen, and I figured you weren't quite as, uh, *advanced* as you are now."

"Fair," she replies, getting up from the bed. She peels her dress over her head and—*holy shit.* I thought I caught a glimpse of that red bra earlier, but seeing it on her in its full glory with the matching red lace thong beats anything I could have imagined as a teenager.

"You did not have *that* when you were sixteen," I say.

"True, but I thought since I teased you with a pic earlier this week, it was only fair to let you see the real thing..."

"Come here."

"No, keep telling me about your fantasy. Let's act it out."

"So I get to tell you what to do?" I ask. *Is my breathing getting shallow?* She nods.

"And you'll do it?" I confirm.

"Yep."

Shit. I did not prepare for this.

I bite my lip and only realize my hand has moved down to cup myself when I see her gaze drop. "Getting a little ahead of myself. Sorry."

"Don't be sorry. Unzip your pants. I like watching you."

This woman.

I remove my pants and start to stroke myself through my boxers.

"Take everything off, Ben."

I stand for a second to rip my shirt and underwear off.

"Now," she says, smiling and crawling on the bed toward me. "Touch yourself while you tell me your fantasy."

I glance at her breasts, filling her sexy bra, and want to touch only her, but I don't dare stop doing what she instructed me.

"Well," I say, "one is that I'm asleep and you wake me by going down on me, but ... can I switch fantasies?"

"In the middle? How many did you have?"

"Plenty. I was a teenage boy, and there was a hot girl living down the street who I think kind of liked me?"

She nods.

"But I wasn't allowed to touch her."

She leans closer, takes my free hand, and places it on her breast. "You're allowed to touch me now."

I kiss her collarbone. I want to keep going, but telling her my fantasy—having her act it out with me—is also pretty damn hot.

I gesture toward my desk with my head. "Go lean over the desk, like you're looking at the computer screen, trying to understand something."

She raises an eyebrow but gets up. She leans over the desk, giving me a perfect view of her luscious ass, and then peeks over her shoulder. "Like this?"

Fuck.

"Just like that."

"And?"

"Ask me a question. Um, pretend—just for a minute—that you're not ten times smarter than me."

She laughs, then takes a deep breath, getting herself into character.

She says in a higher-pitched, breathier version of her voice, "Oh, Ben. I'm usually so good at science, but tonight, I need to study for finals, and I just can't remember how many bones are in the human body. Do you think you could help me?"

I can see the barely restrained laughter in her expression, and I get up and walk over to her, pressing my front to her back, letting my hard-on rub up against her ass, and cupping her breasts.

"You know, I was once tricked by a pretty girl pretending to need help in biology. Human anatomy, specifically. How do I know you even need a tutor?"

"Do you think I'd show up in your bedroom dressed like this if I didn't *truly* need you?" Her eyes glimmer with amusement, and she reaches behind her back to stroke me. "I once had a biology tutor who was too scared to make a move on me." Her voice returns to its normal pitch. No, lower. Throaty and sexy as hell. "That won't happen tonight, now will it?"

I bite her shoulder and kiss up her neck to whisper in her ear, "No, the fuck, it won't."

I yank her underwear down and bend her over, so she's resting on her elbows. "You ever done it on a desk?"

"Nope."

"Want to?"

"Oh, yeah."

I slide my hard shaft close to her entrance and slip my hand in front of her between her legs, to stroke her clit. "You are the hottest thing I've ever seen, bent over, opening yourself to me."

"Is that part of the fantasy?"

"*You* are my fantasy, baby."

"Less talking," she starts to say, and I slide the tip of my cock into her. "Ahhhh ... more ..."

I pull her in close. "More ...?"

"Yes, more. Always more."

And I learned my lesson long ago that when a beautiful, smart woman offers you the chance to, uh, tutor her, you take it.

It's 1:00 a.m., and Gabby snuggles into me under the covers. I can't sleep. I should be dead to the world after what we've been doing. Physically, I'm exhausted. I ran earlier, I helped my mom cook for half the day, and Gabby and I went a couple rounds of shushed, fun lovemaking before she passed out.

But my mind is buzzing. I'm lying on my back, and Gabby's warm naked body is curled into me. Where our skin touches, I feel a light sheen of sweat. It could be gross, but God, nothing about her is gross. Backlit from the moonlight shining in my bedroom window, she is indescribably beautiful.

She shifts in her sleep and opens her eyes. "What time is it?" she asks in a groggy tone.

"One o'clock."

"I should go," she says, starting to stretch.

I slide my hand down her naked back and pull her closer. "Do you have to?"

"My parents will worry. I still have to wake my dad when I come home late at night."

"Even now?" I ask.

"Even now."

"Okay, get dressed and I'll walk you."

"You don't have to," she says.

"Of course I do."

She smiles up at me and kisses my chest. *This girl is gonna be the end of me.*

She sits up. "Where'd you throw my thong when you ripped it off me earlier?"

I smile and get up to search to no avail. "I can't find it. Can I bring it to you next time I come to your place?"

"Are you trying to make sure you get invited again?" she asks in a still-sleepy voice.

"You mean tonight's services rendered didn't already guarantee my next invitation?"

She presses her now-clothed body up against mine. "You are a wild animal in bed, Benjamin, and I'm going to be sore for days."

"Shit, I'm sorry." I don't tell her that while I have my fair share of experience, it's never been like this with anyone else. The looks she gives me, the sounds she makes, the ... connection between us makes me insatiable. I *do* turn into a wild animal. I scrunch up my face and try to look contrite.

But she just smiles. "Don't worry. It's a *good* kind of sore."

I kiss her on the forehead. "Let's go."

When I drop her off at her house, I wait until I see the curtains to her bedroom move to the side to check if I'm still there. It's something I used to do when we were in high school after we'd go on all our walks together. She blows me a kiss and closes the curtains.

As I continue down the street in the opposite direction from my mom's house, heavy thoughts descend upon me, dampening my earlier euphoria. *What would it be like if we were truly together? If we weren't just pretending?*

Upon encountering her a couple weeks ago, it only took a few minutes for me to fall back into the comfortable place her presence creates for me. But my presence in *her* life has a different effect on her. The scared look in her eyes earlier when her dad asked me about my plans cut me to the core. I want to promise I won't leave her, but I can't do that. *What am I doing to her? To us?*

I pick up my phone to text her "Good night" one last time and see that she's already texted me.

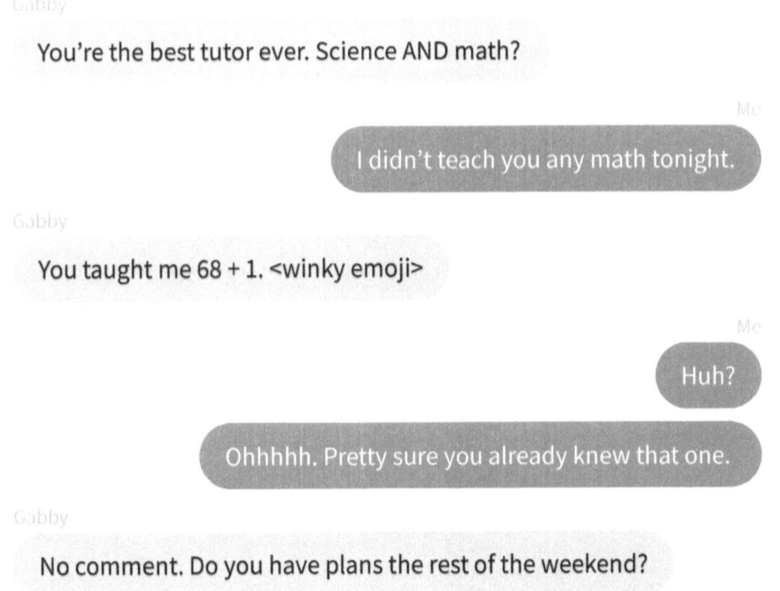

I call her.

"Yesss?" she whispers.

"Well, my Staten Island woman got back to me ..."

"Tell her you already have a date in Brooklyn."

"What does this date *involve*?" I tease.

"Wine, good food—"

"You're *cooking*?" I ask.

"I'm *paying*."

"I approve. Anything else?"

"Well, if I get lucky, then ..."

"You think you can get lucky just by wining and dining me?" I challenge.

She snickers. We both know the answer to my question. A resounding "yes."

"I'll see you tomorrow, B."

Gabby

On Sunday morning, I pull the blanket over my head to block the sunbeam that feels like it's piercing my brain, and I accidentally nudge Ben.

"You awake already?" he asks in a just-pulled-from-slumber voice that's so gravelly and sexy it *almost* distracts me from the hangover I'm becoming increasingly aware of.

As promised to Ben, last night started with wining and dining, but then it continued on to drinking and dancing and making out in a club and—*Oh, shit.* I saw Marissa from work while Ben and I were drinking and dancing and *making out in a club.* He was kissing up the side of my neck and whispering sweet-nothings in my ear when a red-head in stilettos bumped into me and ... *Ugh.*

My brain is in a complete fog, but it's starting to clear enough for me to work out that Marissa knows Ilana and Ilana is dating my brother. How soon until the whole world—well, my family—knows?

"Still tired?" Ben asks, pulling me from my tornado of worry. He snuggles in behind me and dives under the blanket to kiss my shoulder.

Oh. That's nice.

I sigh. "We went to bed late, and I didn't sleep well."

He kisses my neck softly. "You can always wake me up, and I'll listen if something's bothering you."

He snakes his arm around me, pulling me close to him, and warmth spreads throughout me. Ben knows I've been a bad sleeper for a long time. Even when I'm able to fall asleep alright, I wake in the night, my worries visiting me and preventing me from falling back asleep. This summer, my worries have been of a different nature. Once school or test anxiety, then more related to projects at work, my daytime happiness with Ben has been counterbalanced by nighttime worry about it all ending too soon.

"I'm alright," I say. "Probably too many ... What were we drinking? Wine? Margaritas? Mules?"

"All of the above," he says. "No wonder you're hungover."

I groan and close my eyes.

When we came home last night and fell into bed, promises of Sunday morning sex were made since we were both exhausted. Ben crashed immediately, but I was awake for at least two hours, listening to his rhythmic breathing beside me.

At some point in the night, he had snuggled into me in his sleep, cupped my breast, and made a sort of happy sound. I'd turned over and watched him, sleeping peacefully, then started to breathe in and out myself to the same rhythm. I had eventually fallen asleep, but it wasn't nearly enough.

"Do you want to sleep more?" he asks me softly.

"No, I'll get up."

"Can I take you out to brunch? My friend told me about a good place nearby."

I grumble about the prospect of having to get dressed and make myself presentable for the public.

"They have breakfast burritos," he says, trying to entice me.

"You know my weakness," I admit, and he laughs. "But I need a hot shower first."

"Can I join you?" he asks.

"We'll never make it to breakfast if you join me. You know that."

"At least not before breakfast is over," he says. "But after brunch, we're coming back here, and you're gonna orgasm and then take a nap."

I giggle. "That's quite possibly the most perfect Sunday plan ever."

How am I going to give up these weekends, this time with him, when the summer ends?

His brows draw together as he traces his pointer finger over my jawline. "What?"

My expression must've changed. I shake my head. "Nothing. I'll be quick," I say as I scoot out of bed and head toward the bathroom.

"Gabby?"

I turn. "Yeah?"

"You're always beautiful, but I think you might be most beautiful in the morning."

I scowl. I hate mornings.

"Especially that face," he says, his lip twitching.

We get lucky with an outside table on the restaurant's patio. The heat wave of the last few days has broken and the weather is glorious—clear skies and miraculously low humidity for July. I lean back in my chair, holding my hot cup of coffee.

"This is exactly what I needed this morning."

"What's that?" he asks.

"A delicious latte, good weather ..."

"And a strikingly handsome breakfast companion?" he asks hopefully, stabbing a piece of waffle and bringing it to his mouth.

I blow him a kiss. "Yes."

"So your birthday's coming up," he says.

"You remembered?" I ask.

"Your mom said something about it to my mom," he admits. "She's getting you something good."

I lean in. "Is it the dark red leather tote bag we saw at Nordstrom?"

He tilts his head and narrows his eyes. "That's … strangely specific."

I dance in my seat. I've wanted that bag for a year but felt guilty splurging on it. "It is, isn't it?" I ask, waiting for him to confirm.

He shrugs. "Can't tell. I was sworn to secrecy."

"Who's your allegiance to anyways?" I huff out. "Me or my mother?"

"You, of course," he says, smiling sweetly. "But I can't screw over Marci. She'll know. She's a Jewish mother. And then she'll never cook for me again."

I pout at him but ultimately agree. "You're right. She's damn good at ratting out a liar."

He laughs and takes my hand to kiss my fingers.

"But if you're not going to tell me what she's getting me," I say, "I think I deserve a consolation prize."

Ben leans back in his seat, then slides a strawberry off the decorative toothpick resting in his mimosa glass and takes the sexiest bite in the history of Sunday brunches. Fully aware my eyes are trained on him, he licks his lips.

"I'm sure I can think of something," he says suggestively, reaching under the table with his other hand and rubbing the inside of my knee.

"Someone's certainly getting ahead of himself."

"Getting head, I mean, a-head, is always good," he jokes.

I snort a little.

"But I do actually have a present for you," he says in a much more earnest tone.

"A non-sex-related present?"

"It's a gift certificate for a massage with a happy ending, but I guess if you want something non-sex-related, it's back to the drawing board."

"Quit messing with me," I say. "What is it?"

"Well, I'd like to take you somewhere nice for your birthday. Beach? Fresh air? Good lovin'?"

I raise an eyebrow. "Sounds pretty sex-related."

"You got me."

I laugh.

"Am I allowed to surprise you?" he asks, giving me an adorable smile.

I hate surprises.

"Come on," he says, reaching across the table and taking my hand. "Let me surprise you."

I exhale. "Fine, but you have to tell me details on when, the duration, and what I need to pack."

"Easy," he replies. "Two weekends from now, duration Friday afternoon to Sunday evening, and packing list: that hot red thong of yours."

I snort. "That hot red thong of mine is still lost in your bedroom somewhere, I think."

"Then I'll be in charge of packing the thong. *You* just show up."

"Ben. Seriously. I like to be—"

"Prepared for things," he says, finishing my sentence. "Don't worry. I'll give you the approximate location and agenda so you're prepared ... for *anything.*" He makes a discreet but unmistakable rude gesture with his fingers, and I burst out laughing.

"Okay," I agree when I stop giggling.

The idea of a bed and breakfast with Ben on my birthday sounds amazing, but isn't that the sort of thing couples do? Does that mean we *are* one? I'm about to ask him when the entire waitstaff shows up. Our waiter is standing next to the table with two shot glasses in his hand.

"Happy birthday!" he says cheerfully. I look at Ben who has a goofy grin on his face and shrugs.

They jump into a raucous version of the birthday song and then convince us both to take a shot of tequila at the end. It brings tears to my eyes—Ben's, too—after I bite the lime.

After they walk away, I ask him, "Did you tell them it was my birthday?"

He shakes his head and laughs. "I guess they heard me talking about it and got a little over-excited."

I'm laughing between taking sips of water to wash down the tequila taste. Ben pays and stands, holding his hand out for me. I take it, and we head down the street. Walking this way with him, holding hands, it's almost like he's ... mine.

I lean into him. "You know, the last time I took a shot with you, things went a little crazy. Remember Thanksgiving a few years ago when you brought your 'sorta-girlfriend' back from college?"

"That *was* a crazy night," he agrees.

We walk for a few minutes on the west perimeter of Prospect Park.

"Want to explore?" I ask.

"Sure," he says, and we turn onto a small lane around Litchfield Villa.

It's warmed up since the morning, and I head into a small wooded area to escape the sun. After a minute or two, I stop short and turn to him.

"I wanted you to kiss me that night," I say, jumping back into our previous conversation.

He must still be thinking about it, too, because he answers me immediately. "I was working up the courage to, but then we got interrupted."

"You would've cheated on your girlfriend?" I ask, brushing his hair off his forehead.

He dips his head, then looks up at me through his eyelashes, throwing me one of his otherworldly "beg on your knees" gazes at me. "She wasn't exactly my girlfriend. I mean, the situation was far from ideal. I would've preferred to be completely unattached when I saw you. But ..."

"What?" I challenge.

He takes a deep breath. "The truth?"

I nod.

"Even if she and I had been more serious, I might've risked it."

I don't know how I feel about that.

He moves closer to me, placing his hand on my waist and guiding me backward up against the trunk of a large tree. "For you, I would've done all sorts of stupid things."

I can't even fault him because he makes me do all sorts of dumb things, too. Like convince him to sleep with me not twenty-four hours after another man left my place. Or throw myself at him in my parents' hallway, knowing things won't work out. Or let him—no, invite him—into my life for an entire summer, knowing we're a train heading down an unfinished track.

I sink fully into the tree behind me, suddenly feeling weak in my knees. "I don't know if I'm still drunk from last night or—"

"From the tequila we had at ten in the morning?" he asks. He moves his hips against mine, pinning me to the tree, and bites my neck.

Electricity runs through me, and I inhale sharply. "You make me want to do stupid things, too."

"Like what?" he says softly, and his warm breath on my neck melts my insides.

I take his hand and slide it up the skirt of my dress, so he can feel what I'm wearing underneath.

"Ah, like not wearing underwear out to brunch?" he asks.

I meet his eyes. "For example."

He slides his hand around to the front and cups between my legs. I move closer to him. There's nobody around, but I hear voices in the distance. *What if someone catches us?*

"You like being naughty, don't you?" he asks. "You always have."

"Who, me?" I tease.

"Do you see someone else here with my hand up her skirt?"

"I told you. I can't do everything by the rules now, can I? Jewish American princess. Get good grades, make parents happy, marry a nice Jewish boy—" I raise a finger each time I name another item on the checklist.

"*I'm* a nice Jewish boy," he says, taking my hand and kissing the base of my thumb.

Don't say shit like that.

I'm too vulnerable to have this conversation right now, so I crack a joke. "You're a Jewish boy with his hand on my very sensitive places. I wouldn't consider that nice."

"This falls into the category of *very* nice," he says, slipping one finger inside of me as I lean into him and exhale his name into his ear.

"Goddamn, you're good at this."

"You want more, naughty girl, or do you want me to stop so you can go look for a nice boy who doesn't know how to fuck you the way I do?"

What the hell is he doing to me? I can *hear* how wet I am as he slides his finger in and out of me while rubbing my clit with his thumb. He's holding my bare ass under my dress with his other hand, pulling me into him at the perfect angle.

"I *should* stop, huh?" he whispers daringly into my ear. "We're in public, after—"

"No, *don't* stop."

"More, baby?"

I moan softly. "I told you. Always more."

As if he was just waiting for me to say it, he slips another finger into me, and I close my eyes. "More ... please."

"I love it when you beg a little. Feel me, G. I'm hard as steel right now."

With a shaky hand, I stroke him through his pants. As he groans softly, I grasp his shoulder tighter and rock myself on him, praying that nobody walks this way, while I unabashedly let him bring me closer to orgasm with those magical piano-playing, test-tube-flicking fingers of his.

He leans even closer and whispers in my ear, "I'm gonna get you off now, and then when we get back to your apartment, I'm gonna bury my face in you until you scream."

"And then?" I manage to whisper between my ragged breaths.

"Mmmm," he says, in a low voice. "And then ... I'm gonna fuck you hard until you scream again."

Hearing those words, those dirty, dirty words, is all it takes for me to explode. Am I a super-tramp? Maybe. But do I care? No. *Correction: hell no.* Knowing he wants me that bad, that he'll do anything I want—including finger-fuck me on a quiet Sunday in a public park—is such a turn-on that I can't hold back.

The urge to cry out in release is strong, but I bury my face in his neck and moan, low and guttural, like a wild animal.

When I can breathe again, I exhale loudly. "What the hell do you do to me?"

"You said I make you do stupid things," he says with a smug grin on his face.

I laugh softly. "Let's go back."

He looks down, then back up at me with a raised eyebrow. "You're gonna need to walk in front of me."

"I turn you on that much?"

"G, you fucking *purred* in my ear."

I grin. *I did. Who am I?*

I squeeze his hand. "It's a five-minute walk, and when we get back …"

"Yeah?" he asks.

"I have a few plans of my own."

He smirks. "Stupid things?"

"Soooooo stupid. You're gonna love it."

Ben

I lean against the counter of the coffee stand in Bryant Park while I wait for the barista to call my name. Gabby and I spent hours traversing MoMA earlier. When she caught on that I had zoned out, she mercifully offered coffee, and I jumped on it.

I glance toward the back steps of the public library where she's sitting at a small table sheltered from the sun by an umbrella. She's looking at her phone, flicking through photos, I guess, and she smiles. Something twists in my stomach. *What are we doing here? What have I set us up for?*

She looks my way and catches me watching her, and I wink at her. She blows me a kiss, but before I can reach up to catch it—like a love-smitten dork—the barista calls my name.

"What were you looking at?" I ask when I set her latte down on the table and remove the lid for her. She always does that for some reason, and she thanks me with her beautiful smile.

"I was checking out the pictures from the museum," she says, taking a sip of her coffee. She holds out the phone to me. "Look at this one."

I take the phone and snort. It's me in front of a 3D art installation of sewn-together stuffed animals with a sarcastic *wow* expression on my face. "I love modern art so much, you know. It's hard to contain my excitement."

She snickers.

"I did my best," I say. "Sorry I spaced out."

"I could tell I'd lost you when I made a dick joke and got no response," she says.

"I missed a dick joke?"

"A *stuffed-animal* dick joke," she says. "I'm sure there will be other opportunities." She traces her pointer finger around the rim of the cup, then looks at me. "I know it's not your favorite thing, but I'm glad you came with me."

"Well, it's better than when my mom used to drag me to museums." I'm not completely untrained in this form of torture. In fact, I spent an entire month in Paris one summer during high school with my mom. I think we visited every museum in the city. At least with Gabby, I try to pretend I'm interested.

"Why better?"

"Well, I love my mom, but she only bought me chocolate crepes after, and you …" I raise my eyebrows suggestively.

"You say I have a one-track mind, but …"

"What do you expect me to think about when half the garden there is sculptures of naked people?"

She suddenly closes her eyes as if imagining it all again. "It was beautiful, though, wasn't it?"

I look at her, eyes still closed. "It was beautiful," I say, simply, mostly because of her.

She opens her eyes and takes a sip of her coffee.

I look out at the green expanse of the park lawn and, inspired, I suggest, "Let's get out of the city tomorrow and go on a hike."

"Sure. Where do you want to go?" she asks.

"I was thinking Franklin Lakes. I went there this week."

Between reviewing articles and worrying about the future, I take hikes. Sometimes I worry about the future *while* I take hikes, but I'm mostly able to disconnect and give myself a break.

"Let's do it," she agrees and leans over to take my hand in hers, caressing the top of it with her delicate fingers. "You still have beautiful hands. You should let me draw them."

"If you must."

"I must. I wish I could listen to you play piano, too. It's been a long time."

I think for a moment. "I could Facetime you this week when I'm at home?"

"That sounds nice," she says, pulling my hand up to hers to kiss my fingers.

She stares at my hands, and I move my head into her line of sight which makes her look at me. "Sorry, I was just thinking about something," she says.

"What?" I ask, but I think I know.

"What are the post-doc programs you're considering again?"

It's what I thought.

"I have to give an answer to Stanford and Duke soon, and there's one more I'm holding out on."

She raises her eyebrows.

"UC Berkeley."

"Oh, so *two* in the San Francisco Bay Area?"

Gabby works in high tech, and that's the epicenter of it all. I *could* choose one of those programs—they're both amazing—and I could ask her to come with me.

But Duke is offering me a much sweeter package than Stanford, and there's a researcher there I collaborated with during my PhD. Google has an office in Durham, but it's nowhere near the size of the Silicon Valley or New York hubs. I checked, because ... *No, I can't derail her career by limiting her exposure to the right people.*

There's also the fact we've only been together for a month or two. But *are* we even together? It's still a secret to most of the world, and her not wanting to tell the people we both know is a sore spot for my ego.

"Yeah, I have some more time to decide. We'll see."

She presses her lips together and nods. "Yeah, we'll see."

On Sunday, we pack a picnic lunch and head to New Jersey. As we near Glen Rock, she raises her eyebrow at me, but I drive past the exit.

"Don't worry," I say. "I'm not going to pull into your parents' driveway and embarrass you."

She crosses her arms, and I turn down the air conditioner, thinking she's cold, but out of the corner of my eye, I catch her looking at me intently.

"It wouldn't embarrass me," she says.

I reach out and pull her arms apart, taking one of her hands in mine. "Good to know."

At the state park, we set out on our hike. We don't talk a lot while we walk—nature speaks for itself. The trees, green and full this time of year, provide us ample shade as we wind our way through the woody areas around the main lake.

After an hour, we take a break and sit to unpack the sandwiches and fruit we brought.

"You're quiet today," I note between bites of my apple.

"I guess I am," she replies, picking at the crust of her sandwich.

"Thinking about anything in particular?" I ask.

"Just that summer is flying by this year."

I run my hand down her arm, and she sets the sandwich down and lets me hold her hand.

We both know that we don't have a lot of time left together. *Together.* It's a weighty word, and my thoughts drift back to yesterday's conversation.

I could ask her hypothetically. No. *That's no way to handle an adult relationship, you coward.*

I can imagine the conversation. I would tell her something she already knows, that none of the programs I'm considering are close by. I would say, *But if you wanted to try long-distance, I would do it.*

Is it naïve to think we could do long-distance when we haven't been seeing each other that long?

What if we grew apart? We would grow apart.

But she could visit. Maybe she could even work from the Bay Area to try it out.

But what if it didn't work?

What if I'm just like my dad, and I begin to focus on my career more and more and …

"Ben?" Gabby's voice pulls me from my endless loop of arguing with myself. "You okay?"

I look at her. I don't want the conversation to take a wrong turn. I don't want us to admit we've been playing pretend this summer.

What if all we have together is a couple more weeks?

It doesn't matter. I want those weeks. I want every day, every damn hour that's left, to be ... happy. To be with her.

I scoot closer to her and put my arm around her.

She snuggles into me and says, "Tell me something I don't know about you."

I sniff out, not sure what she wants to know.

"Come on. In return for me letting you surprise me on my birthday?" She looks at me hopefully.

"Ummm ..." I try to think of something that fits the bill. "I like playing piano—"

"I already knew that," she interrupts.

"No, listen. I *really* like playing. I always have, but growing up, I never admitted that to my parents because they would bribe me to practice and I liked getting extra spending money."

She laughs. "So how big is your horde of piano-playing cash?"

"Oh, I'm independently wealthy from the whole ruse. I hide it by wearing regular old Nikes and ballcaps. Can't let the masses know."

She takes off my hat, smiles at my crazy hair underneath, and shoves it back on backward. "There. Now nobody will know."

I lean in and kiss her.

"What scares you?" she asks as soon as our lips part.

You do, G. Being with you. Losing you. Everything ... you.

But I can't say that to her. That what I feel for her is more than what I can allow myself right now. So I confess another fear. "I'm scared I won't live up to my own expectations, or ... my dad's."

My mouth is dry. I've never truly admitted that one to myself, let alone another person. But her eyebrows furrow, and she presses her lips together. I recognize the understanding, the empathy in her eyes. I *feel* it in the touch of her soft fingertips on my hand.

She doesn't say a word, but her heart is telling me that it's okay to open up.

"He thought that what we did or didn't do was a direct reflection on him," I say. "It's why he was always pressuring us to go down the path he chose himself. It's narcissistic."

"Are you sure?" Gabby asks.

"About what?"

She narrows her eyes at me. "I don't want to act as if I know your father better than you do, or overstep …"

"What?" I ask. "I'm curious what you think."

"How's your relationship with him now?" she asks, rubbing her thumb across the inside of my wrist.

"Better than it used to be. He's more self-aware now."

"What if his behavior didn't stem from narcissism?" she asks. The look on her face is so hopeful. "What if he was just … doing his best?"

I crinkle my brow.

"Hear me out," she continues. "What if he was just worried, and he only knew how to guide you down a path he already knew could be successful? And …"

I raise my eyebrows

"Not everybody is able to understand their own feelings," she says, "let alone verbalize how they feel."

Well, if that doesn't hit the nail on the head.

"Am I ever going to catch up with you?" I ask.

"Riiiight, you think I'm so wise." She snickers, but her face turns serious quickly. "So why do you think it didn't work out between your parents?"

"Did you miss the part about my dad being an asshole?" I joke.

She grants me a courtesy smile but stays silent, waiting for more.

"My mom says that he used to adore her, but at some point, he became hyper-focused on work and … well, self-centered. He was bitter and unhappy at home. He was a little less critical toward Ariella and Miri, but he was always harder on me and definitely on my mom."

Gabby's face is scrunched up in thought.

"He never hurt her physically, or anything, but he was an asshole. And I-I never wanna become that."

"You're so warm. I can't even imagine it."

"Maybe," I say, but I don't meet her eyes. I've *already* done some things I'm not proud of. I put myself first and held back when I should have reached out to her, and here I am, about to mess everything up again. I can't change where we are in life or the fact that both of our careers—the trajectory of our lives—are highly dependent on what happens over the next few years. But I can apologize to her for what I've done up until now.

Maybe a small part of her will remember that when I ultimately screw all of this up. "I'm sorry if I was an asshole to you. I try to be a good person, but sometimes, it's like the Adler family DNA is being expressed without me even realizing it."

"We all make mistakes, B. The point is to learn from them, right?"

"Right," I say, tipping her chin up to kiss her. *But have I?*

A flutter of birds in the trees above draws her attention, and she looks up. "I should paint a bird. It's been a while since I've painted." She meets my eyes and smiles. "Maybe I'll name him Benji."

"Do you always name your art?"

"Usually, but it's more like they name themselves and let me know what they're supposed to be called."

The bird above us flies away. *That's me, alright.*

"Do you want to keep hiking?" I ask, my throat suddenly dry. I need to move. I need to distract myself from the ache slowly spreading from my stomach to the rest of my body.

"We could rent a canoe," she suggests.

"Sure," I say, standing and offering her my hand to help her up.

She looks around, then laughs. "Do *you* know how to get back? I'm a little turned around."

When have I ever been the one who knows the way forward?

"Do you mind getting a little lost this afternoon?" I ask.

She wraps her arm around my waist and leans into me. "I guess we're not lost if we're together." She looks up at me and her sweet, trusting expression almost pushes me over the edge. On the tip of my tongue are the words my heart yearns to share. *I love you.* But before I can utter a word, she bends to pick up the backpack, and the moment, so ripe with opportunity, passes.

"Ready?" she asks, straightening back up.

"Yeah," I say, "let's get lost together."

We stand on the platform of Glen Rock train station while I wait with Gabby for the 6:14 back into the city.

"So are you ready to divulge the top-secret location of our adventure next weekend?" she asks.

"There will be sun, there will be a breeze, there will be lots of kissing, and you are allowed to bring a swimsuit and a few summery outfits plus one light sweater."

"And sexy lingerie," she says.

"And sexy lingerie," I confirm.

She giggles.

"I'll pick you up—"

"I'll work half a day, so we can beat traffic."

The train pulls in, and I pull *her* into me for one last kiss.

"Perfect," I say. She thinks I mean next weekend's plan. But I think I mean her.

I pull out after an especially intense orgasm, roll Gabby onto her side, and snuggle into her, spooning her sweet ass and cupping her breast.

"You didn't come yet," I say, burying my nose in her hair. "Let me do something for you."

"Remind me again why you paid for an expensive bed and breakfast near the ocean if we're gonna spend all day in bed."

"Worth every penny, and it's called Point Pleasant for a reason. Isn't this pleasant?" I ask, stroking her between her legs.

"Very," she says and scoots her ass back into me, suggestively.

"Thank you for the compliment," I say, "But I'm gonna need a little longer than thirty seconds to recover."

"So keep doing that. Ahhh ... it feels ..."

"Pleasant?"

She giggles. "Amazing. Keep going, just like that."

She's never afraid to ask for what she wants, and I love it. If only I had the same courage. Not in sex, but in life.

I crawl over her and lie down again, this time facing her. I lift her leg and rest it on my hip, opening her up, so I can touch her the way she likes. Two months in, I know what will make her come. I can take the slow route or the fast one.

She gives me a slow, lingering kiss. *Ah, she's in the mood for slow.* Me, too. I want to stop time and stay with her forever.

I pull her close into my body, angling her hips just the right way for me to slip my fingers inside of her. While I enjoy her slow, sensuous kisses, my mind wanders. *What comes next?*

The finish line is quickly approaching. I knew we'd get here, but how did it happen so fast? Do I regret letting all of this get way out of hand? I *don't regret one minute. One day with her is worth a thousand with anyone else.*

I move my fingers inside her warmth, and she pants, "So ... so ... good."

I kiss her more and toy with her, bringing her close and then pulling back, warming her up for what I hope is going to be a killer orgasm.

"Ohhhhh. I can't take it," she says, whimpering.

I trace my tongue over her nipples and thrust my fingers into her at the pace that will drive her over the edge. "Yes, you can."

"Ahhhhh," she exhales. "Ben, it's ... I can't take it."

Please be strong enough. Because I'm not.

She calls out my name as she comes, and I lay my head on her soft, warm body, trying to absorb every last bit of her. *If I leave her here, I won't get another chance.* She'll find someone while I'm gone—someone who knows how to put her first for real.

Gabby's known for a few weeks that it's down to three programs: one closer, two farther away. A couple of them agreed to give me until the first week of August to make a decision. I'd promised I would give them an answer on time, and I was planning to send UC Berkeley my answer tomorrow. The email is sitting in my drafts, ready to go: *I'm happy to accept the offered postdoctoral position with your university, and I'll begin making living arrangements soon.* And then—*ah, then*—I would tell Gabby that this has been the best two months of my life, and I want to try long-distance with her.

It was the perfect plan, a way for me to get most of what I want professionally and everything I *need* to live my life with someone I'm pretty sure I'm in love with.

But then I checked my email this morning, and it changed everything.

I arrive at Gabby's apartment, and when she opens the door for me, she pecks me on the lips.

"Come in," she says, pulling me inside. "What's going on? Big news?"

I nod. I try not to look worried, though that's exactly how I feel.

"Come sit on the couch with me," I say, taking her hand and leading her over there.

She nods and follows me to sit down.

I jump right in. "So I was about to accept one of the post-doc offers, and then I got an email today with a new one."

"That's great," she says, a broad smile appearing on her face. *God, the energy in her smile could create worlds.* She takes my hands and squeezes them. "You're so smart. Of course one more place wanted you. So where is it?"

I squeeze her hands back and look down at my lap.

It could be so good, couldn't it?

I don't answer her. Not yet. Because as soon as I tell her, that will be all we talk about, and I have to make her understand how I feel about her. "I need to tell you that ... I have loved every minute with you the last couple months. Spending time with you, getting to know you—the real you, not this idea I had of you—has been ... unbelievable. And—" *Shit. Moment of truth.*

"Just tell me," she says bluntly but not unkindly.

I swallow, wishing for ... I'm not sure. Something different than this.

"Did you happen to get an offer close by?" she asks in what sounds like a wishful tone.

I shake my head.

"So what's it gonna be? North Carolina? California? Somewhere else?"

I sigh. "There's this program I applied to, and it was a real long shot. I mean, I applied last year, and I'd written it off. But I got an email today. They originally chose someone else, but that person ended up taking another post-doc, and they're offering me the spot."

She raises her eyebrows. "Ben. Where?"

"The Weizmann Institute."

"Israel?" she asks with a confused look on her face. She's confused because it never came up. It never came up because I didn't even think it was a possibility. I still feel shell-shocked myself after receiving the email this morning.

She exhales. "I-I always thought you'd be here in the US for your post-doc."

"That was the plan..." I lose my words, looking into her eyes. She's biting the inside of her cheek, a nervous tic of hers she's tried to quit over the years.

"*Was* the plan?" she asks.

"I wanna go," I say.

Until this moment, I wasn't sure what was going to come out of my mouth when I told her. On the drive to her place, I'd gone back and forth at least twenty times. I'm almost as shocked as she is. I could just as easily have said, *I love you, Gabby, and I want you to come to California with me.* Somewhere, in some alternate universe, we're hugging and kissing, and we're beginning to plan the rest of our lives together.

But here in this universe, she says in a whisper, "Oh."

The ever-present sparkle in her eyes is dull. Her gaze shifts and her mouth parts, but she swallows down whatever she is about to say. She pulls her hands from mine and wraps her arms around her own middle.

"Mazel tov, Ben."

That's it? Of course it is. What did you expect? For her to profess her undying love for you? You're proving right now that she can't count on you.

I need to explain. Maybe she doesn't want to hear it, maybe she would even prefer I leave, but I have to know she'll be okay. That *we* will be okay. That she won't hate me.

"I knew I'd be moving, but I thought I'd still be in the US. I didn't even realize I wanted the position at Weizmann until it became a reality, and now that it is, I feel like ... I have to take it. To try."

"You've dreamed of living in Israel ever since your bar mitzvah trip," she says. "I get it."

"You do?" I peer at her face, but it's a wall, blocking me from any emotion she's feeling right now.

"I do." Her voice sounds colder, almost robotic, like she's forcing the words out. *Is she even disappointed?*

"G, this summer—with you—came as a surprise to me, but it was ..." *The best summer of my life.*

"It was so good ..." she says.

I nod.

" ... while it lasted."

And I'm the one ending it. I look at the floor. Before this, I could have looked into her eyes for eternity, but I can't right now. They're too sad.

"It was a good summer," she says again, and I look up. "Really." She locks eyes with me and touches my shoulder.

Ask me to stay. I'll do it. Tell me that I mean as much to you as you mean to me.

"But we're both still young, right?" she says instead. "We have to move ahead in our careers and not get distracted."

"I thought—"

"Ben, it's okay. I'll be fine. You go after your dreams, and I'll ... go after mine."

Gabby

In the deafening silence are all the questions I wish I could ask, all the confessions I wish I had the courage to make. What if I tell him that this summer has been a dream come true, getting to spend hours upon hours with him, touching him, and talking to him about my worries and my dreams? What if I beg him to stay in America, to choose me—to choose us—and he still says no? What if I pour my heart and mind out to him on a platter and he tells me that he's still leaving like he has every other time?

I won't ask. I won't beg. I can't.

He's told me that he's had fun. He's told me in the throes of passion that my body was made for his. But what he hasn't said is that he loves me or that he wants a future with me. What he's saying by making this choice is that a future with me isn't even important enough to sleep on it. He found out this morning, and he has already decided he's going.

Maybe he is right. Maybe there *is* a part of his callous, selfish father in him.

I suddenly feel vindicated that I never told anybody about us seeing each other this summer. What I thought could happen—what I hoped wouldn't—has happened.

He touches my arm, and I look up.

"I have to participate in a symposium right after the High Holidays at Tel Aviv University, so I need to find a place as soon as possible in Rehovot. It means I'll leave in a week."

A week.

A tear slides down my cheek. *Damnit, Gabby.* I turn away.

"I'll miss you so much, G. I'm sorry. But I-I have to take this opportunity."

You don't have to do anything you don't want to. But instead, on auto-pilot, I turn and murmur, "I understand."

But I don't understand. He has options here. He told me himself he had two offers on the West Coast. At the time, California sounded too far away for me to consider pursuing something serious with him, but compared to fucking Israel, it's only a six-hour flight from New York to San Francisco. At least it's on the same continent. We could have flown to see each other. I could have worked remote. I would have moved. I would have uprooted my whole life for him. But he's leaving. He's leaving me again. After considering it for less than twelve hours.

I feel ill. I rise to my feet, but he grips my forearm and pulls me back down. "Gabriella, I'll miss you so much, but we'll stay in touch."

What's the point?

But I hate to let him down, so I say, "Maybe."

He reaches out and touches my face. "I have one week. I have a lot to do before I go, but I want to spend more time with you."

I lift my eyes to his. Are they watery, too, or is it my wishful thinking? I open my mouth to answer him, but I'm at a loss for words.

"Should I stay now or go?" he asks.

Stay here with me. I love you. I've loved you for years.

"You should go," I say before turning away.

I would have given you everything, but you didn't even ask.

I walk toward my front door, hoping he'll follow me and just leave me here to cry, to scream, to wonder why the hell I keep doing this to myself.

He walks to the front door and stands there, waiting for me to say something. *What can I even say?*

I settle on, "Be safe," then kiss him on the cheek, and he pulls me into a hug. I allow myself to savor it—even though I know later I'll regret it—because deep down, I know this is the end of our story.

The Jewish High Holidays That Fall

Up in Smoke

Gabby

Since Ben left, it's been … rough. Thank God for a huge project at work that has kept me focused on something else besides all of my regrets and my own naivete. Still, my life is a depressing dichotomy of work and missing Ben.

Last week, I was forced out of my self-imposed hermit state when my mom informed me that my attendance at synagogue during Rosh Hashanah was mandatory. Aaron invited Ilana to spend the holiday with us, so we're driving to Glen Rock together on Rosh Hashanah Eve when she asks me out of nowhere whether I told Ben goodbye before he flew to Israel.

"I know he and Aaron hung out a couple of weeks ago right before he left," she remarks.

I glance at her, unable to utter a word, but I conveniently—and guilti-ly—start crying.

"Oh, geez," she says. "Pull over. You can't drive like this."

"I'm fine," I say, but after a minute, I have to admit that I am anything but fine.

She gives me a moment to calm down and takes an audible breath. I brace myself for questions I don't have the strength to answer, but her voice is soft, kind. "Why did you do it to yourself? You knew he was going away."

I suspected she knew—Marissa must've told her immediately—and here's the proof. *Did she tell Aaron?*

"I knew he was leaving," I say, "but I didn't know he'd be ten thousand miles away. I thought ..."

I thought he'd be closer. That he'd ask me to come with him. That it was finally our time.

But I can't say that to Ilana. I meet her eyes, her face blurry through my tears.

"He's always had this ... place in my heart. Around him, I just ... become weak. It's been this way since I was fifteen. I'm so pathetic."

"You're not pathetic," she says. "That's how it is with someone you love."

My mouth drops, and that statement right there makes me cry even harder. Too bad he didn't love me half as much as I now understand I love him. But it doesn't matter because he's gone. Our chance for something has passed. Love or not, I have to let go.

She hugs me, and I wipe my eyes. "We need to get going." I put the car in drive and pull back onto the freeway.

"Why didn't you want anyone to know?" she asks.

"I was worried that things would turn out ... exactly as they have, and I thought it might be easier if I didn't have to talk about it with the whole world."

"I thought you might've been seeing each other," she admits.

"You did?"

"Well, Marissa was saying you had some sort of summer romance going on, and I noticed that you, um, couldn't stop looking at each other during that dinner at his mom's house," she says with a small giggle.

I snort. That's certainly a diplomatic way of saying he had his hand up my skirt half the night.

"So I had kind of put two and two together, and then Marissa told me she saw you guys out at 333."

I nod.

"I figured when you wanted to share, you would. I didn't mention it to Aaron."

She didn't?

"But you might want to talk to him now," she says. "He loves you. He'd want to know if you're going through a hard time."

I exhale. "I'll think about it, but I'm not in the mood to talk much right now, okay?"

"Okay."

"But if you want to tell him, you can. Just tell him I don't want to talk about it."

At Rosh Hashanah services the next morning, I try to do some soul-searching. It's the closing of one year, and the start of a new one. Have I learned anything from repeating the same mistake—Ben—for at least the third time in my life? But, accompanied by the plaintive melody of "Avinu Malkenu," I'm distracted from beating myself up inside every time my mom points out all the young, successful, attractive suitors back home visiting their families for the Jewish High Holidays. And every time I brush her off—"Yes, Ima, Jonah Feldman is handsome, but I'm trying to pray"— Aaron side-eyes me.

I guess Ilana told him.

By the time Sukkot rolls around two weeks later, I'm more emotionally stable. I have mostly stopped having dreams about Ben, and I have started working out again. My mom didn't even have to guilt-trip me into coming down for an outdoor dinner in the *sukkah* tonight.

We've finished our meal, and Ilana just took a load of dishes inside where my mother is already stationed in the kitchen. Aaron and I are alone in the *sukkah*, gathering up the tablecloth and remaining dishes. I take the water pitcher, bundle the cloth napkins in my hands, and start to walk inside when Aaron says quietly, "Gabby Cat?"

"Yeah?" I say, turning around.

"You all right?"

"Of course," I say, forcing myself to smile at him. My cheek twitches.

My happy muscles must be out of practice. He scrunches his brow.

"Why?" I ask, not quite ready to volunteer any information.

"Listen, I know that you and Ben spent a lot of time together this summer, and I thought you might be ... missing him?"

"I don't want to talk about Ben or—"

"I warned you to stay away from him," he says.

I clench my jaw. "It's none of your business what I do, and if you think—"

"Stop," he says. "I'm not trying to tell you what to do."

But I'm already upset.

"Mind your own fucking business, Aaron!" I yell, slamming the pitcher down on the table and throwing the bundle of napkins in his face.

I stomp into the house, startling my mother and Ilana in the kitchen, and head straight upstairs to my old room. After slamming the door behind me, I flop down on the bed and squeeze my eyes shut, but I'm bombarded by painful memories. Images of Ben's face. The last night we spent together. The hard days and weeks afterward, wondering whether he was thinking about me as much as I was thinking about him. Me, picking up my phone a thousand times, typing a text to him, only to think that I would feel like a loser if I caved and told him how much I was missing him, how much—*fuck*—I needed him.

But I don't need him. That's what I tell myself, like a mantra. It's what I tell myself when I prepare for Friday night dinners without him. It's what I tell myself when I roll over in my bed and stare at "his" side of my bed, the place he claimed closer to the window, so the sunlight wouldn't wake me on weekend mornings.

It was only two months, Gabby. Quit being so dramatic. But my response to that more practical, less patient Gabby in my head—the response from real-life Gabby whose heart has been crushed one more time by Benjamin Fucking Adler—is a sob, which I attempt to stifle by burying my face in a decade-old Squishmallow.

There's a light knock on the door, and I turn over in my bed to face the wall. My makeup must be a mess, and I'm pretty sure I have snot smeared across my face. But just like when he was a kid, like brothers do, Aaron simply comes in without an invitation.

"Get out of here!" I half-yell, half-sob.

"No."

"Seriously, I can't deal with your shit right now." I bury my face again.

"Gabriella."

That makes me look up. He never calls me by my real name.

"I'm your brother. I love you. I don't want to see you suffering," he says in a tone appropriate for defusing a hostage situation.

"What?" My voice comes out weak, wet.

Perhaps heartened by my response, he strides across the room and sits on my bed. Before I know what's happening, he's pulled me into a hug.

Aaron has hugged me before, of course, but it's never been an embrace quite like this. One that encompasses me and somehow listens to the words I can't find the courage to say. I let my body relax into his and cry for a bit longer.

When my sobs slow, he says softly, "I don't know all the details, but I'm sorry, okay? I'm your big brother, and I should've taken better care of you."

That sends me into another round of crying, but in the end, I laugh.

"What's funny?"

"I'm twenty-five years old. It's not your job to take care of me."

"Well, I don't know about that, but if Ben were here right now, or anywhere in the continental United States, I'd kick his ass for you."

"Ohhhhh, Aaron," I say. The idea of my fun-loving, goofy brother kicking anyone's ass is enough to send me into peals of laughter.

"Why are you laughing?" he asks, fake-riled up.

"He didn't do ..." *Sniff.* "Anything wrong." *Sob.* "He ... went after his dreams. And I guess I wasn't one of them," I say in a volley of tears and sniffling.

"He's an idiot, Gabs. You ..." I look up. He smiles. "*You* are the best there is. You're smart and successful and kind-hearted, and you have amazing dreams. And I've heard from other people you're pretty ... when you're not a blubbering mess." He holds out his sleeve for me to wipe my nose, but I won't let him ruin his shirt, and I lean back to grab a tissue from the box on the nightstand while I let out a halfhearted laugh.

I wipe my eyes and my nose and then my eyes again. There's a lot to wipe.

"Listen to me. He made the wrong choice, but if that's the one he made, then he doesn't deserve you."

I exhale. "That might be the nicest thing you've ever said to me."

"Well, it's completely true, and I was an asshole to you for at least half our childhoods, so I guess I'm making up for it now."

A soft knock sounds on the door. "Gabby?" Ilana's voice says.

"Come in," I say.

She peeks her head inside and the look on her face is so kind I almost start crying again. "Oh, sweetheart."

She looks at Aaron. "Can we have a minute?"

He squeezes my hand and stands, vacating his place and letting her sit next to me on the bed. "Why don't you help your mom finish up the dishes?" she suggests.

He nods and shuts the door on his way out.

"How are you doing?" she asks.

I gesture at my puffy face and my streaked mascara.

"Dumb question, huh? I have an idea."

"What?" I ask.

"You wanna go out and get wasted?" she asks with a huge grin.

"Looking like this?"

"You still look hot. If you want, I'll smear my makeup, too, and we'll make Aaron drive us so we can drink and dance 'til 3:00 a.m."

"You don't even like drinking that much," I say.

"For you, I'll do it."

I laugh. "You know what? Yeah, let's do it."

"Yesssss ... Get dressed, and I'll go change."

Two hours later, we're in a karaoke bar, and Ilana and I are having a blast. I'm not so sure about Aaron, but he's being a good sport and has made friends with another guy whose girlfriend is drinking and dancing with us.

"Gabs, what are we singing?" Ilana asks after taking a swig of a beer.

"'Firework' by Katy Perry?" the girlfriend suggests, looking through her phone.

"Too fucking happy," I reply.

Ilana shoots me a look, then explains to the girlfriend that I'm pissed at a guy.

"'You Oughta Know' by Alanis Morissette?" she suggests.

"I don't think I know that one," I reply. I think for a moment. "Ooooh, I know." I march up to the guy to give him my request. I pick up the microphone and gesture to Ilana *come hither* with a curled index finger.

She joins me. "What are we singing?" she asks, as the first measures of "We Are Never Ever Getting Back Together" by Taylor Swift come on.

"Noooo," she says, looking at me and then at Aaron, who has already gotten his phone out to record us and is gesturing for her to grab the other microphone.

"Yessssss," I say and start clapping.

And we kill it, though, in all fairness, I do the heavy lifting. Aaron films the entire thing while trying to stay upright despite laughing his ass off.

When we sit down, after the crowd goes nuts, I knock back a glass of water.

"Gabby, that was amazing, but it was kind of 'basic bitch,'" Aaron says.

I shoot him a nasty look. "Well, you have a small dick."

He spits out his drink like a cartoon character, cracks up, and reaches over to put me in a headlock.

Ilana's eyes go wide—she wouldn't be the first friend to see us rough-house, though it has been a good ten years since our heyday—and remarks, "I'd say his dick's actually quite a nice size." Aaron and I both snap our heads up, pausing our halfhearted wrestling, then fall over laughing.

"Why are we talking about my brother's dick?" I howl.

"You're the one who brought it up," she replies, curtly, and then sits on his lap and kisses him on the cheek.

When we get back home, it's late. We try to be quiet as we come in, but

Ilana is doing a drunken rendition of "Firework" by Katy Perry, the last song we heard at the bar. Our new friend finally got her way. Aaron and I exchange a look.

"I'm gonna put her to bed," he says, helping her up the stairs.

"I'll bring you some water," I say and go to the kitchen.

When I come upstairs, he's leaving his room and shuts the door softly. "Too late, she's already out," he says, taking the glass of water from my hand and going back in to set it on the nightstand near his old bed.

"She's gonna be dead in the morning," he says, as he comes out the door, shutting it softly. "She barely drinks."

I grimace. "Sorry."

He shakes his head. "Nah, she wanted to raise your spirits. She loves you. We all do."

He walks me to my room, and we sit on the bed while I take off my boots.

I lean into him and rest my head on his shoulder. "I love you, too. Thank you for ... I don't know. Going out with me. Trying to help."

He puts his arm around me. "I'm always here for you."

"I know."

"And I'm sorry things between you two didn't work out."

"Deep down I knew it wouldn't," I admit, "but I just ... *hoped* it would."

"I know," he says, softly.

And then, in my frail state, I find the guts to ask him, Aaron, my brother who has known Ben since he was eleven years old, who has known *me* my whole life, "Why didn't he choose *me*?"

He holds me out and looks at my face. "I don't know. I think he's ... He's had a lot of his own shit to deal with. Maybe what he experienced growing up with his parents? And it's messed up, but this has more to do with him than it does you. He's still ... finding himself if that makes any sense."

"I hope he finds himself choking on a falafel," I say.

He snickers. "You'll get over him, and you'll end up happy. I know you will."

Maybe. One day.

At some point, I lie down on the pillow, and he leans back against the wall. In the morning, I wake covercd by a blanket and don't even remember Aaron leaving, which I think means he stayed by my side until I fell asleep. I still feel like shit, but knowing my big brother has my back makes me feel just a little bit better.

Ben

As I traverse the maze of stone alleyways of the Jewish Quarter of Jerusalem's Old City, buzzing with life and tourists from all over the world, I think of New York City. And when I think of New York City, I think of Gabby.

Everywhere I look, there is a twenty-something woman who could be her, but then she turns her head and my daydream bursts. I imagine roaming these streets with Gabby, holding her hand as we get lost in the labyrinth of the market in the Christian Quarter, and then, somehow making it out of the Old City, sitting in a rooftop café somewhere, to have a late-night coffee and deep conversation.

"Ben, this way," Avi calls. My new roommate gestures to me from across a courtyard teeming with people. Six-foot-three and built like a tank, he's easy to spot. I joke with him sometimes that he should've been a football player, only for him to correct me, "Rugby, you American."

I jog over to meet him.

"Get lost again, professor?" he teases and pats me on the back.

I pat him on the back, even harder. "Maybe you just walk too fast, you ginger ogre."

He barks out a laugh at my latest description of his shockingly red hair, and I grin.

"You ever been here?" he asks as we continue our way down a crowded pathway.

"I did my bar mitzvah at the Western Wall, but it's been a while," I say.

"Well, you're in good hands. You've got an almost-certified Israeli tour guide with you," he says.

"With a British accent," I add.

He snorts. "Precisely."

Originally from England, Avi abandoned his cushy job and London flat a year ago to pursue his lifelong dream of living in Israel. He was fresh off a few months of army basic training—in case he's called up for reserves—and in search of a roommate when I showed up looking for a place close to Weizmann.

The added perk of his new career aspiration—to become a tour guide—is that he's already begun forcing me to get out and travel, which is how I've ended up in Jerusalem for a few days.

"We're almost there," he says, and I look around.

We're at the top of a tall stone staircase, and suddenly, it all seems familiar. As we descend a few hundred stairs, I gaze out—eastward—and take in the southernmost point of the Temple Mount. The gray dome of the Al-Aqsa Mosque is visible, and beyond it, the Mount of Olives cemetery. I consider taking a picture. *Maybe my mom would want to paint it, or maybe ...*

"This way," Avi calls, and I continue down the stairs. We pass through the metal detector pavilion at the entrance to the Western Wall plaza as the sun is setting. Thousands of people are milling around—some praying, some taking pictures.

"I'm going to do evening prayers. Coming?" Avi asks, gesturing with this head to the men's side of the plaza.

"I'll stay here," I say. "You know me. Full-blown heretic."

He laughs and tells me he'll be back soon.

I take in the myriad of people before me from all different cultures and backgrounds. It's one of the holiest sites for Jews, but it draws people from all over the world. What are they looking for? God? Spirituality? The history and the culture of this place are what interest me. With all the people here trying to speak to God, though, who knows? Maybe even an atheist like me might get some divine inspiration and figure out what the hell I'm doing.

I'm sitting, thinking about my past, present, and future all at once when Avi comes back. "You're kind of ... thoughtful."

"Moreso than usual?" I ask.

He laughs. "Yeah. Everything okay, man?"

"Just thinking about someone in particular," I say.

He raises an eyebrow.

"A woman. This girl back home I was hoping … I dunno …"

"Gabby?" he asks.

Have I mentioned her?

His look answers me. I must have.

"I was hoping she'd ask me to stay, but she didn't."

He nods and smiles softly. "Well, there *are* a lot of Jewish women in Israel."

"Don't know if I can find another one like her, though."

He sits next to me. "You can always try," he jokes. "I'm heading to First Station to meet some friends for a drink. You in?"

I consider it for a moment. No. "I'll walk back to the apartment." We're staying in his relative's flat in the Rehavia neighborhood for a few days while he's traveling abroad.

"You sure?" he asks, standing.

"Yeah," I say and follow him toward the exit.

We part ways at the metal detectors, and I walk back up the stairs and through the Jewish quarter, choosing a quiet place to stop and call my mom.

"Benny," she answers. I can imagine the smile on her face. "How are you doing, sweetheart? Over the jetlag?"

"Mostly. I'm … okay."

"I talked to your sisters over the weekend," she says in a bright tone. "They're planning to come for Thanksgiving."

"I'm sorry I'll miss it," I say.

"I miss you already," she says. "I guess we didn't realize you'd end up so far away, but … it kind of worked out, didn't it? You being home for the summer?"

I liked being home with my mom. I liked—loved—spending time with Gabby, and I'm not so far removed from my own feelings to miss that the heaviness in my chest is the weight of regret.

Is it the fact I left? Or the fact that I let everything happen with Gabby to begin with?

I'm in the middle of a strain of unhelpful thoughts when I zone back into what my mom is saying. "—and when Marci brought over some of the extra food, she asked how you were doing."

"How are the Feinmans?" I ask, hoping my mom will drop some tidbit about Gabby.

"They're fine. I sat with them at synagogue on the second day of Rosh Hashanah. Aaron was there with Ilana. She's so friendly, isn't she? And Gabby ... she looked beautiful in her white dress. Well, she's always beautiful, isn't she?"

"She is."

We're both quiet for a moment. Then my mom says, "She looked a little sad for some reason."

Sad. For some reason.

I'm sad, too. For some reason.

I stand and begin winding my way back to Jaffa Gate. I should have told her how I felt. After thinking about it for the past few weeks, I'm sure that I would have stayed in America for us to be together. If she had ever told me she loved me, that she was willing to give me—us—a real chance, I would have told her right back.

But she didn't. And neither did I.

"Ben, are you there?"

Huh? I've stopped beside a small shop, and there's something inside that Gabby would love. The shopkeeper is gesturing at me through the window to come in.

"Sorry, Ima. Um, is it okay if we talk tomorrow?"

"Of course. Call me when you have time. Be careful. I love you."

"I love you, too."

On my daily bus ride to the university, I think about Gabby. When I left, we didn't lay any ground rules for how much we should communicate, or even *if* we should communicate, but I send her emails and texts from time to time. Here and there, she responds with a simple message wishing me well that reveals little to nothing about how she's doing or what's happening in her life.

One afternoon, I'm sitting on my elderly neighbor Idit's balcony, checking Gabby's Instagram once again, when she returns from inside with bourekas and offers me one.

"These look delicious," I say, taking a cheese-filled pastry from the tray.

She sits across from me and wraps her hands around her mug. "Who's that girl you were looking at on your phone?"

I open my mouth to speak, then close it, not sure I want to reveal all of my secrets to my new friend. She waits patiently, so I tell her Gabby's name.

"And who is Gabby?" she presses.

"Someone …"

"Someone … *nu*?" So? "Who is she?"

I smile. Idit reminds me of Gabby's neighbor, Evelyn Friedberg.

"She's someone I … care about a lot," I finally admit.

"I could tell by the look on your face when I came out." *I guess that hasn't changed at least.*

"She's very pretty," she says, looking pointedly at the phone on the table.

I wipe my hand on a napkin. "You're right. She's beautiful, inside and out," I say.

Idit smiles softly, then mercifully changes the topic. "How do you already know Hebrew so well?"

"My mother's Israeli," I share.

"And what brings you here now?"

"A post-doc program at Weizmann."

"And you came here instead of doing an American program?" she asks.

"Weizmann is excellent," I say.

"I know that. Everyone knows that." She presses her lips together and thinks for a moment. "And what did Gabby think about you leaving?"

I narrow my eyes at her. *I've only known this woman for a month. Why is she acting like my mom?*

I cobble together a non-answer answer. "I don't know." I'm lying. I saw the surprise and then the disappointment in Gabby's eyes when I broke the news to her, but I was too afraid to ask the only question I needed to: *Do you want me to stay for you? For us?*

Because what if she had said no? I'm a damn coward, which is what Idit tells me now with a soft snort. "I bet you *do* know."

I do. But it's too late to do anything about it now.

The morning before Hanukkah starts, a plate of elaborately decorated *sufganiyot* catches my eye in the bakery near my bus stop. The flavor of the day is something with cream and strawberries on the top, and I take a picture, wanting to share it with Gabby. *She doesn't want to hear from me, though.*

Aaron told me about a month ago that I needed to give her space. He explicitly said that if I wasn't going to come back, then I needed to let her move on. I'm not sure when he found out about us, but he wasn't even mad that I'd kept it from him. He just sounded sad. I shove my phone back into my pocket and board the bus to Weizmann.

Later that evening, Avi and I are on our way to celebrate with some of his relatives in Modi'in when he admits belatedly—fifteen minutes before our arrival—that part of the reason he invited me is to set me up with his cousin.

"What?" I ask. "Dude."

"Dude," he says in his best impression of an American accent. "You'll like Meital. You're both biologists."

"Is that all it takes?" I ask, laughing. "A mutual love of studying living organisms?"

"You never know," he replies.

Oh, man.

"She's doing her master's at Tel Aviv University," he adds, "And she's pretty."

I'm skeptical but try to be open to the idea. *You gotta move on, man.*

When Avi parks the car on the street, I look up and take in the large apartment complex. Built with Jerusalem stone, it's simultaneously fortress-like, with its limestone façade, and modern, due to the beautiful lighting.

"Damn," I say, getting out of Avi's small Volkswagen Golf. It's a comical choice considering his size, but it gets the job done.

"Hell of a lot nicer than our place," he comments as he extracts himself from the driver's seat.

"Or my shitty apartment in Ramat Gan," adds a young woman coming down the stone stairs.

Her curly, light brown hair is pulled back in a ponytail, and her red sweater sets off her bright green eyes, even in the dim light.

She's cute. Short, too, but her platform shoes add a couple of inches, though she still has to stretch to hug Avi.

"It's been forever, Avs," she says in a slight British Accent, surprising me.

The woman turns to me and holds out her hand. "I'm Meital, and you must be Ben?"

I nod and shake her hand. "Nice to meet you." A friendly smile lights up her face, and the look in her eyes tells me that she's been briefed on this setup, too. It's been a minute, but I know that expression. *She likes me.*

She ushers us up the stairs to her parents' apartment and invites us in. Inside, Avi introduces me to his huge extended family. A woman around my mom's age is bustling around the kitchen, and a teenage girl is helping her set the table.

She turns and comes to greet us. "Avi, introduce us to your friend."

"Aunt Esti, this is Ben Adler, my flatmate in Rehovot. Ben, Esti."

"Hi Esti, it's so nice to meet you," I say. "Thank you for the invitation."

"We're so happy you could join us. Avi's told me a lot about you."

"Where did you make *aliyah* from?" I ask.

"We immigrated from London *many* years ago," she says with a smile. "Come. We'll light candles and have dinner."

After lighting the Hanukkah candles, we sit down to a feast. The table is filled with all sorts of Middle Eastern salads and dips, baked salmon, bourekas, and, of course, latkes. *Some things are the same the world over.*

Conversation around the table is loud and fast-paced, and there are a lot of laughs. The food and the company make me miss home—especially Miri and Ariella. Despite the happy noise, during the meal, Meital and I make small talk, and every once in a while, I catch Avi—seated next to me—listening in and looking pleased.

"So you think you'll end up in academia or in the industry?" Meital asks.

"Still not sure," I say, "but I have another year and a half to figure it out."

"So you'll be here a while?" she asks, her green eyes sparkling.

I consider all the possibilities the future holds. For the first time in a while, they don't seem daunting, and I smile. "Looks like I will."

Dinner wraps up, and Avi asks if I want to go outside to the patio. As soon as we sit, he asks, "So what do you think about Meital?"

"She's nice," I say, noncommittally. "But I don't know what I'm doing right now."

"What does that mean?" he asks.

"It means that ... I don't know," I say, not ready to admit much to him.

He narrows his eyes at me. "You're still hung up on your girl back in the States."

"Nah," I lie.

"I never hear you talk to her."

True.

Before Avi can press me further, Meital opens the sliding glass door. "Want a hot drink?"

"I'd love some tea," I say. It's cold out here.

"Maybe hot cocoa?" she offers instead.

I nod.

When she goes back inside, Avi says to me, "She likes you."

I give him a confused look. "How do you know that?"

"Hot cocoa. Give me a break. We're adults, man," he says, laughing.

"I guess it is sort of a kids' thing," I say.

Meital returns with a tray with three mugs. She sits next to me on the patio sofa and hands me a mug. The taste, the warmth, takes me back to a night many years ago, the night I sat on Gabby's bedroom floor drinking hot cocoa while confiding in her about my parents fighting. How many years has it been? *Over a decade*, I realize with a start.

And despite the fact that I'm sitting next to a beautiful woman, some-one with whom I have a lot in common, I can't shake the feeling that I'm here with the wrong person. *You're supposed to be moving on, remember?*

How can I move on, though, when every time I close my eyes I see Gabby's face? The hurt, but not entirely surprised expression on it when I told her I was leaving for Israel—choosing this over her.

The morning after that terrible conversation, I'd opened my phone and found a text:

Gabby

I hope Israel is everything you want it to be. Stay safe. Stay you.

It wasn't anything that special, but I'd screenshotted and marked it as a favorite. From time to time, I open up my photos and look at it. Then I usually end up digging a small box out of my bedroom closet, my paltry collection of mementos—a picture of me and my mom from my first trip to Israel when I was three years old, a more recent picture of me and my sisters, and Gabby's drawing of a bird on a piece of stationery from our weekend away in Point Pleasant.

It was one of the only times she ever woke up before me. When I'd opened my eyes, I found it on the pillow next to me. A few minutes later, she'd come back with hot coffee for both of us and a warm smile. *Hey, early bird*, she'd teased before leaning down to kiss me.

My stomach twists as I think about what that drawing is currently folded around, the gift I bought for her right after I moved here. I'd seen it and immediately knew it was for her. I don't know if I'll ever have the chance to give it to her, though.

I take a deep breath and exhale, opening my eyes, to find both Avi and Meital looking at me, with similar looks of amusement on their faces.

"Thought you fell asleep for a second," Meital says.

"Ben's a thinker," Avi says by way of explanation.

"What generally occupies your thoughts?" Meital asks.

I note the way her eyes crinkle at the corners when she smiles.

"Usually experiments I'm working on," I lie.

Avi's phone rings. He glances at it and indicates with his head that he'll take the call inside. Meital and I are left on the patio, looking at each other in slightly uncomfortable silence.

"Would you want to … hang out this weekend?" she asks. "We could go out in Tel Aviv?"

I nod, not feeling wholly comfortable with the idea. Meital herself is fine. Friendly, smart, attractive. It's the fact that she's not, well … *Times change*, a sober voice somewhere in my head reminds me. Gabby's ten thousand miles away, and she doesn't want to hear from me.

"Let's do it," I say, more bravely.

Her smile widens. "You seem like a good guy."

"I'm just alright," I respond, and she laughs.

"Why don't you let me determine that? Give me your phone."

I hand it to her, and she puts in her number and texts herself so she'll have mine.

"Can I see your photos?" she asks.

"Um," I hesitate.

"You don't have any … inappropriate selfies on there, do you?" she asks, amused curiosity evident in her tone.

No, all those were deleted immediately after I sent them to Gabby over the summer.

I shake my head. But what I do have on there are lots of pictures of Gabby. By herself. With me.

"I'm not hiding anything, but, well, I have a lot of pictures of my ex on there. Stuff I haven't deleted yet." *I can't. I don't want to.*

"Ah, I get it. I have some of those pics, too. Did you break up because you came here?"

I shrug, not sure what to say, but certain that I don't want to get into a long, drawn-out conversation about it with Meital.

"You don't have to go out with me, you know …"

Yeah, I do, if I ever want to forget about her.

"I didn't say *yes* because I felt like I had to. I want to," I say, trying to sound genuine.

"Okay, I'll text you on Friday with a plan."

"Sounds good. I think we'll head out soon," I say. I stand and so does she.

"Bye, Ben," she says, leaning in for a hug.

"Bye." I lean in and kiss her on the cheek.

It's almost midnight, and I'm in a loud club in Tel Aviv with Meital and some of her friends. I've had a few drinks, and much to my surprise, I'm having a good time. I've been avoiding fun experiences since I've been here. Major self-penitence was more my *modus operandi*. But it's not healthy to be sad for so long. Here's my chance to be more proactive about the future of my love life.

So here I am, dancing with a sexy woman who is very into me. Without any warning, Meital pulls me down into a kiss. Her lips reach mine, and in a moment of clarity, I realize that I'm truly in the present. No thoughts of loss or what could have been, no thoughts of anything, except this very real, very hot woman whose arms are wrapped around my neck. She presses her body up against mine, and I slip my hands down to her hips, appreciating her curves.

"Are you having fun?" she says in my ear.

I look at her. "*You* are fun."

"I know I am. Biologists are the best at parties."

I laugh. She kisses me again, more deeply, and grabs my ass, then slips her hand into my back pocket to take out my phone.

"Finger?" she says, holding it out to me to unlock it with my fingerprint.

I do so and raise an eyebrow, curious. She taps on the camera and takes a selfie of us. "It might be time for you to start filling your phone with new photos."

I look down at her. She's short, but she's got a big personality. Her hair is curly, full, and wild tonight. It—like her—has energy.

"Yeah, maybe," I reply, leaning down to kiss her again, this time with more intention. I part her lips with my own and slide my tongue into her mouth. It's different than kissing Gabby, but it's not bad, not at all.

Her mouth is warm—inviting—and she tastes like the mango cocktail she drank before we started dancing.

"You taste good," I say in her ear.

She turns her head quickly and catches my lip between her teeth.

"You like mango, huh?" She runs her hands through my hair which I've let grow out since coming here. "Your hair's as wild as mine," she says, laughing.

"*Your* hair is beautiful," I say, catching a curl between my fingers and admiring it.

"You wanna go somewhere quieter?" she asks.

I know what happens if I leave here with her because I've done this a lot. This newfound "good guy" act I've been playing the last year or so isn't who I used to be. But the question is not who have I been up until now, but rather, who do I want to be? Am I a guy who's finally tired of being stuck on the same girl for the last ten years, a guy who's ready to move on? Or am I a guy still grieving a loss, a not-quite-man, despite my age, holding out, holding on, to someone I'm not ready to part with?

"Ben?"

"I need some water," I say, and I walk away to give myself a minute to think. I head to the bar, and after drinking down a glass of water, I slip out a side door.

Quiet. Air. I exhale and pull out my phone. In the selfie Meital took of us, I see my own smiling face, next to hers. *Can I be this guy?* The one who finally accepts that a childhood crush on his best friend's sister is just that. Am I ready to let go of whatever dreams I might've had about what Gabby and I could've been?

I scroll through some pics until I find the one I'm looking for. Me and Gabby lying in bed. We'd woken up and lay in her bed one Saturday morning this past summer, not quite ready to get up and start the day. She'd looked well-rested—eyes bright and cheeks flushed—so heartachingly beautiful I had to take a picture of her. Looking at her now, my stomach clenches.

Meital comes outside and finds me looking at my phone. "Everything okay?"

"I'm really sorry, but ... I think I'm gonna head home."

"So early?" she asks.

"Yeah, it's been fun, but ..."

She comes closer and kisses me on the cheek. "Why don't you call me when you're ready?"

I nod at her. Three or four years ago, I'd already be on my way home to a very good time with her, but something in me has changed. Something in me is ... broken.

On the way back to my place, I alternate between berating myself for giving up a chance to see where the night might have gone with Meital and being proud of myself for having grown as a person. But I'm still stuck. It's not hard for me to understand what—or rather, whom—I'm stuck on.

I walk in the door and go to the bathroom to splash water on my face. Looking in the mirror at myself, I give myself a pep talk. *Ben, get your shit together. Just tell her how you feel.* But it takes me a few minutes when I sit down at my laptop to begin typing. How do you put into words everything you've felt for someone for the last decade? I'm tempted to give up before I even start, but I place my fingers on the keys and will them to move.

`Gabby,`

`It's been a while. The last time we talked was awful. I shouldn't have broken the news to you the way I did. I know that now, and I'm sorry.`

I wish I could go back and try again.

`I noticed you're not posting as much on Insta. I hope it just means that you're busy, that your life is full of good things.`

Have you moved on? Because I haven't. I can't.

`Things are okay here. I'm getting to know my mom's side of` the family better. My cousin Ariel took me out last week in Tel Aviv, and I got a hamburger and fries, but then I had to order a milkshake (to dip the fries, of course). You'll be happy to know I got strawberry (didn't want to be accused of being unimaginative). I probably shouldn't tell you I drank the milkshake WHILE I ate the burger, but Ariel was eating a bacon cheeseburger, so I guess I'm an okay Jew in comparison. I even went to synagogue with my roommate Avi last week.

I didn't pray, though. During the silent prayer, all I could think about was you.

Sometimes I walk down the sidewalk here, and I wish you could see what it's like, especially on Friday nights. You hear families having Shabbat dinner together and hanging out, and it makes me miss home.

It makes me miss you.

I need to tell you …

That I think about you. I think about you when I wake up alone in the morning and when I go to bed at night. And many, many times in between.

Do you think about me, too? But I don't ask her that. I veil my longing in words that only scratch the surface of what I feel for her.

I need to tell you … that you'll always be my bestie. You're always with me, even though you're not.

My finger hovers over the Delete key. But I leave it. This small truth I'm able to share. *Will she understand it for what it is?*

It's almost New Year's, and I can't believe I've already been here a few months. I hope the new year brings you

health and happiness and everything you want.

I sign it "Always, B," click Send, and close my eyes for a moment. I'm not sure how I can sleep with a hundred-pound weight on my chest, but I brush my teeth and fall into bed, curled up with a blanket, wishing it was Gabby instead.

When I wake in the morning, I check my phone immediately and find Gabby's reply in my inbox. *Deep breath.*

Hey B,

I was surprised to hear from you. It's been a while, but maybe that's a good thing. It gave us both some time to sort out some feelings. I felt like there was a lot you weren't saying in your email.

Hearing that you were moving to the other side of the world came as a huge surprise, and I've asked myself if I'd have done things differently had I known. I'm still not sure. I already told you that this summer was one of the best. Ultimately, I'm glad I spent it with you, my bestie. You've meant a lot to me over the years, and every time we've been together, it's been special for me.

My heart pitches at her words. *Does she mean ...?* I continue reading.

But I think I'm getting at least a little wiser with age. I've always enjoyed our time together, but it's also never ended well. Every time we come together, sparks fly, but then the fire goes out. It fades away, and I'm left wondering whether it even happened at all.

I don't think I can keep doing this and not be permanently
scarred by it at some point. Maybe that point has already
passed. I want the best for you, but we shouldn't get too
close again.

*Did she hesitate before she wrote that part? Before she told me that, in
essence, we're done?*

Like you wrote, it's almost the new year—an opportunity
for a reset: a new year, new expectations, and new,
emotionally healthy behaviors.

Be well, Ben. Be safe.

Always, G

Her email is so Gabby. Honest, open, but kind. God, she let me down
kindly. But she … let me down. *I've fucked up one too many times.*

I close my laptop and go to my closet to get dressed to swim. As I snatch
a t-shirt off the shelf, my box with her drawing and my gift for her topple
to the floor. I stare at it for a minute, then shove everything back inside
and get ready to leave.

• ❤ • ❤ • ❤ • ❤ • ❤ •

When Avi invited me to a hotel in Eilat for Passover break, I jumped at the
chance to snorkel in the Red Sea. After swimming both in the sea and the
pool this morning and eating my weight in chicken shawarma and fries,
I'm seeking refuge from the heat on the covered balcony of our hotel
room.

I know I shouldn't, but I allow myself to daydream about Gabby, imagining one of the times we had sex last summer. But instead of in her

apartment, we're here in Eilat. Instead of her couch, we're going at it on a chaise lounge on a hotel balcony. Funnily enough, since it's my own daydream, I'm the one warning her, "People might see, let's go inside," and she's the one telling me not to worry. *She runs her hands up my torso, touches my pecs, and then leans down to kiss me, pressing her breasts into me. It turns me on even more, knowing that she wants me bad enough to risk all the beachgoers seeing us up here.*

A man shouts something at his friends on the beach, and I open my eyes. *It's gone. She's gone.*

I grab my phone. 3:00 p.m. here which means 8:00 a.m. there.

I don't want to force her to live in the past, but I'm also desperate as hell to hear her voice, to know how she's doing, to know whether she thinks about me even a fraction as much as I think about her.

I wish she were here, lying beside me in that crocheted bikini of hers that's just this side of scandalous. I can picture her, looking over at me with lustful eyes. *What would make her respond to me?*

A selfie—a thirst trap, specifically. Not being the selfie expert Gabby is, I do my best, then choose the one where my head is tilted and my hair is in my eyes. Something tells me she'll like it. Maybe she'll even respond.

Me

> It's hot as hell here in Eilat. I might even resort to eating strawberry ice cream to cool down.

I check it one more time, then press Send.

Gabby

My phone pings, and I roll over in bed to check the time. 8:03 a.m. Lior grabs my waist and leans over to kiss it and then my bare hip.

"*Boker tov,*" he says with a sexy, half-sleepy smile on his face. *Good morning to you.*

He tries to roll me back in his direction. "Stop," I whisper, but I giggle. I don't *really* want him to stop, but we're in my parents' house. We came for the Passover *seder,* then stayed here last night.

We've been dating since last month when Leah introduced us. He's a computer programmer like me—a colleague of her boyfriend's. We went on a blind date, and it's been going well. He's a front-end developer at a startup, and our conversations are a nice mix of tech topics, culture, and getting to know each other. We see each other a few times a week, and when we're not together, we text a lot. I like that he says what he's thinking—no games. I need a guy who doesn't play games, like, well …

This weekend was the first time Lior met my family, and my mom, happy to see me dating someone Jewish, Israeli no less, and willing to bring him to Passover, didn't even bat an eye when he put his overnight bag in my old bedroom. Last night at dinner, Aaron and Ilana got along well with him. He's different from what I'm used to, but he's charming in his own way and attentive to my needs. Just the type of guy I need right now.

I open my phone and see that the message is from Ben. Not just a text. There's a thumbnail of a photo.

"I'll be back in a second," I whisper to Lior and get up, grab a robe, and head to the bathroom.

I haven't heard from Ben in a few months, not since I sent him an email telling him that I'm moving on. It was hard to write, hard to tell him that anything that might have been is never going to happen, but I'm glad I did it. My conscious efforts, my restraint, are paying off. Little by little, I've become more future-oriented and less focused on the past. Past equals Ben and his stupid games. Lior is part of my present. Who knows? Maybe even my future.

I close the bathroom door quietly and lean up against the vanity to unlock my phone. It's a photo of him. He looks happy. Happy and—*damn it*—hot as hell.

His tanned, shirtless chest looks edible, and his hair has gotten longer than I've ever seen it, falling into his hazel eyes, which seem to be staring right at me.

Should I respond? Yes, but what?

Me

> Looks like you're having fun. There with friends?

A girlfriend, perhaps?

Ben

Just my buddy Avi.

I haven't seen you in a while. Selfie?

I shouldn't, but I've never been able to deny him. *It's harmless. He's 10,000 miles away.* But I don't even believe myself. I know how slippery of a slope it is to fall back in love with him, and I keep letting myself get dragged back in.

Deep breath, Gabby.

I glance at my reflection in the bathroom mirror and find I look surprisingly good for having just woken up. The Israeli boyfriend treatment must be good for my complexion. Not to mention my "fucked well last night" hair. Makes sense, since I was.

I wonder if a "harmless" selfie is the best approach with Ben, but I don't want to hurt him. *Who am I kidding? Maybe I do.* Maybe the fact that I'm doing perfectly fine without him is *exactly* what he needs to know.

I put my elbows on the bathroom counter and prop my phone up. My robe falls open, emphasizing my cleavage and a small mark from Lior's teeth on my collarbone. *Perfect.* I inch my finger forward to snap the close-up selfie.

"This could've been yours" is what I want to type, but instead I send:

Me

It's still cold here, but I have someone to keep me warm. <kiss emoji>

There. Just right.

Lior and I were doing well, but in July, he accepted a job offer in Silicon Valley at an up-and-coming medical diagnosis startup run by some young Jewish couple I read about on *Hacker News*. We parted with a promise that I'd come visit him right after he got settled which is how I find myself on a beach in Carmel-by-the-Sea in August.

"Let me take a photo of you," he says, pulling my phone from his pocket.

He's holding it for me since half my shorts are wet from the freezing wave that doused me earlier.

"I'm all wet and covered in sand," I say.

"But you're sexy," he says, smiling. "Stand right there. You look beautiful."

I smile. "*B'seder*," I say. *Okay.*

"You're so cute when you speak Hebrew."

"And you are verrrry cute when you speak English," I reply, in my best Israeli-speaking-English impersonation.

He laughs and takes the picture, and I reach out to take his hand while we continue our stroll down the beach.

"I missed you the last few weeks," he says, leaning down to kiss my cheek.

"It's been fun seeing your life here in California," I say.

"It's beautiful, huh? The sea and mountains remind me of Haifa in some ways." He showed me pictures from his parents' balcony on the Carmel mountain, overlooking the Mediterranean, and he's right.

"Maybe I'll visit there one day," I say, off-handedly. Somehow, even the mention of Israel shifts my mood, and I quiet.

"What do you want for dinner tonight?" he asks. "There are a lot of good restaurants."

"Maybe Italian?" I suggest.

"Sounds good."

I look down at my sandy clothes. "I need to shower first."

His eyes track down and take in my body. "Maybe I'll join you."

And he does, and we decide that dinner can wait while we indulge ourselves in an extended afternoon session of slow, relaxed lovemaking. Afterward, he falls asleep, and I curl up under the covers and look out the glass-paned door that leads to the room's balcony, watching the birds land on the railing.

Eventually, I grab my phone from the nightstand and scroll through photos from the last couple of days: a selfie of both of us with the Golden Gate Bridge in the background, a photo of me smiling broadly near sea otters at the Monterey Bay Aquarium, and the most recent one, the picture Lior took of me this afternoon—wind-blown and damp—on the beach. Behind me, shades of orange, red, and pink on the horizon as the sun starts to set bring out my recent highlights. I post it on Instagram with the hashtag #CaliforniaGirl. I look happy—or at least content.

Maybe Lior and I should see where this goes despite being so far away from one another. He enjoys being with me—he shows it, he says it—but it's only been a few months, and I can't be sure if it's worth moving here. I could work remote for a while, maybe even find a job out here. I thought I wanted to be near my family, but for the right person, I'd go further afield.

Is he the right person? Maybe I'll know by the end of this trip, but that's quickly approaching. I'm okay with letting things happen naturally with him, but generally, I've begun to feel that I need ... someone.

Getting closer to Ben last summer flicked a switch in my brain. I began to feel differently—about Ben, for sure, but also more generally about my desire to find someone to build a life with.

My phone vibrates—a notification of a few likes on my Instagram post. My friend, Leah, and then ... Ben.

I check the time, then do the time difference math—5:00 a.m. in Israel. Despite my better judgment, I text him.

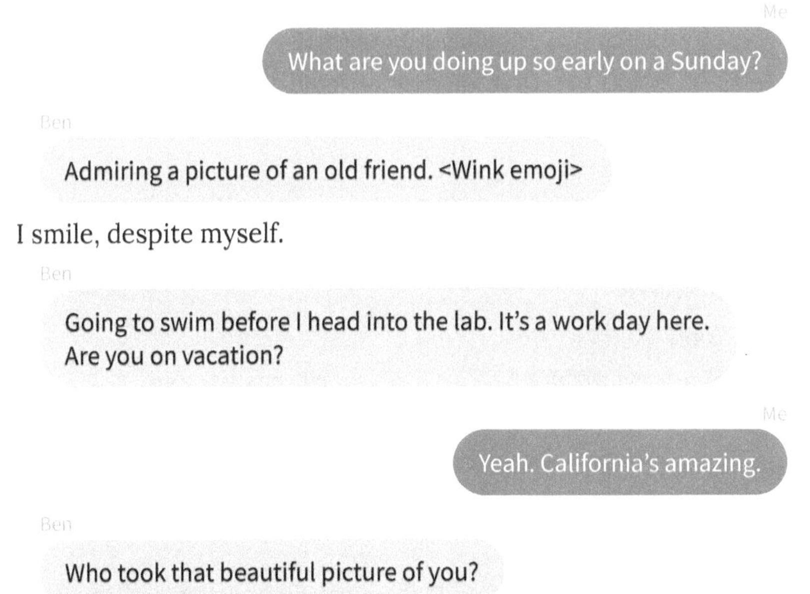

I smile, despite myself.

What is Lior to me? For all intents and purposes, he's my boyfriend. Do I tell Ben that? I can text him back whatever I want or nothing at all. After a moment's hesitation, I type my response, feeling guilty toward Lior but desperate for myself.

Me

A friend.

Ben

A friend like me?

There's no one like you.

Ben

Can I call you?

I'm typing out *It's not the best time* when my phone starts to vibrate. *Shit.*

I could reject the call, but I haven't heard his voice in months. Longer. *How has it been a year?* I slide out of bed, pull a robe from the closet, and slip out onto the balcony as quietly as possible.

"Hey," I say.

"Why are you whispering?" he asks.

His voice. It takes me back in time—to pain, to ecstasy, to longing, to … fuck, love. A broken, sad, doomed type of love.

I take in a ragged breath and close my eyes as I exhale as quietly as possible. "Someone's sleeping."

"At 7:00 p.m.?"

"We had a long day in the sun," I reply.

He hesitates and then says, "Got it." He knows I'm with someone. So be it. "How are you?"

"I'm … okay."

"I'm sorry for everything," he says, his words rushing out.

I catch myself before I reply that it's okay. It's not.

"I should've said this months ago," he says. "I just, I saw that picture of you and everything from the past year came rushing back, and I'm really, really sorry."

"I know," I say. My chest tightens from hearing his voice after so long.

He's not a terrible person. He's a scared animal—coming close, tempted by curiosity or the scent of good food, then running away in fear. I don't know *why* I've never been able to convince him I'm trustworthy enough—no, simply *worthy* enough—to win his love. But we've known each other for years, and the whole time, his heart has been good. He always tried to do the right thing, even if he sometimes fucked up.

He's quiet, so I speak up. "How is it there? Is it everything you hoped for?"

"It's paving the way for the rest of my career," he says without much emotion. As if on cue, the small, blue-feathered bird I was watching on the railing earlier lifts off. *He was always meant to fly away.*

I sigh.

"Ask me how it is otherwise," he says in a voice that sounds like he's close to tears. I must be imagining it.

"How is it otherwise?" I ask in almost a whisper.

"It can get lonely. I have friends, but ... I need something, someone, more than that."

I close my eyes and sit in silence, listening to him take a deep breath on the other end of the line, so far away. Downstairs, a cat wanders down the ivy-lined alley near the bed and breakfast.

"I get that," I say on an exhale. *How can we be on the exact same wavelength sometimes, yet so far from being able to make it work?*

"G, do you ever wonder what would've happened if I'd stayed in the US last year?"

"Ben—"

"I'm—I'm not trying to derail you again. I know I've done that ... too much. I ... I just ... do you ever think about me?"

I should say "never" just to serve him right.

No. I can't—won't—lie. He's been careless, but he's never intentionally hurt me.

"I think about you sometimes." *More than I should.*

I see movement inside. Lior rolls over and notices me outside. He gives me a curious look, and I smile and hold up two fingers to tell him I'm coming in soon.

"I have to go," I say.

"Sure," he says. "Have a good trip. And, uh … don't think about me a lot—"

I sniff out in amusement.

He laughs softly. "But …"

"Yeah?"

"Try not to forget me?"

As *if* I *ever could.*

"Never," I say. "Bye, Ben."

I'm booked on an afternoon flight from SFO to New Jersey tomorrow, so Lior and I take advantage of what I'm slowly figuring out will be our last night together. After a dinner of pasta and expensive red wine, we walk back to the beach and sit for an hour, listening to the waves, kissing, and enjoying each other's easy company.

Maybe this is how it's supposed to be. Easy. Lior is a smart, generous, and fun boyfriend. He hasn't caused me a moment of pain or suffering.

"Is everything alright?" he asks.

"Everything's fine."

But it's not. My call with Ben earlier shook me. He and I are not meant to be, but after all these years, there is still … something. And it's not fair to use someone else as a distraction from my still-unresolved feelings for h im.

We start our walk back to the hotel, and somewhere on the way, I make a decision. I need to take a break—from Lior, from dating more generally. I need to do some mental and emotional work on myself to be truly ready for the next stage in my love life—or maybe just life in general.

After I wash my face and change into pajamas, I slip into bed next to Lior where he's reading something on his phone. He sets the phone down on the nightstand and runs his hand down my shoulder to my waist. "I'm glad you came to visit me."

"I've had a great time." It's true. I have. But …

"Do you think we'll see each other again?" he asks.

His question startles me.

"What do you mean?" I ask, but it's clear he's picked up on whatever vibe I've been sending out.

"What's going on, Gabby?"

"Well, um, I'm not sure. I mean, you're great. And we ..." I gesture with my hand back and forth between us and raise my eyebrow, indicating our physical compatibility. "We're great together. And it's been ..."

"Great?" he asks, smiling.

I nod and open my mouth to speak, but I don't know what to say. I sit up. I try to understand my own feelings and put them into words. It would be too harsh to admit everything I've been feeling, so I offer him an excuse.

"But long-distance is awful, and I'm not sure if I want to move so far away from my family to live out here."

He nods. "I understand." His intake of breath leads me to believe he might have something else to say, maybe some attempt to convince me otherwise. I might not think I'm ready to pursue something more serious with him, but maybe I'm wrong. Maybe *he* thinks what we have is the beginning of something special.

In that pause between his inhalation and what could be a word coming out, I half-hope he'll say, *Are you sure? We could try to make it work. You're worth the long flights and sacrifices.*

All he does, though, is press his lips together and give me a tight smile. The cheerful eyes I've become accustomed to over the last few months suddenly seem less warm. In an instant, everything between us cools.

He doesn't fight for me. He doesn't try to convince me. And that is as clear of an answer as any. To his credit, he also doesn't pull away when I put my arms around him and snuggle into him to fall asleep.

When I wake in the morning, I pull on some warm clothes and go downstairs in search of coffee. My flight back isn't until later in the day, so I let Lior sleep in. I take my coffee from the dining room and find a spot outside on a patio, trying to find some peace—rather than gloom—in the fog that has drifted off Carmel Bay.

Twenty minutes later, half-frozen by the cool morning air, I stand to head inside. Lior is holding the door open for me.

"Breakfast?" he asks with a sleepy-looking smile and the smallest pang of uncertainty flits into my thoughts.

I nod and follow him inside.

While we eat a breakfast quiche and fruit salad, we talk about our work and plans we're both looking forward to later in the year. Over the course of the night, our fate has been settled, and our futures no longer involve each other.

The fact that neither of us feels strongly enough to reexamine our potential as a couple is evidence enough that it was the right decision. Our tight, but short hug goodbye at SFO is a beautifully-tied bow on a present nobody truly wanted.

On the flight home, I indulge in my melancholy by listening to acoustic versions of all the saddest songs I know, but too many piano covers in a row drag my thoughts back to Ben.

It's been a while since I've allowed myself to wish things with him would have turned out differently. But hearing his voice last night brought back all the feelings I only allow myself to acknowledge in the dead of the night when I'm lying awake in bed, unable to fall back asleep. *Why didn't it work for us? Why wasn't I worth fighting for?*

Sitting here, thirty thousand feet in the air, escaping my latest breakup with a guy who too easily let me go, I look out the window and squeeze my eyes shut, trying not to let the tears fall.

Is there anyone in this world who would fight for me? Anyone who would try to convince me that he simply can't live without me?

Ben

We're sitting in a café on the beach in Caesarea. The waitress arrives with the cappuccino Aaron ordered, then places my bottle of Goldstar on the table in front of me.

"She couldn't come," Aaron says when I ask why Gabby didn't come on their family trip to Israel.

"I thought maybe she'd want to join you." *Or maybe she'd want to see me.*

"She'd already planned her trip to Paris for Thanksgiving break before we decided we were coming here. She couldn't take even more time off after her trip in August."

"To California?" I ask.

"Yeah, to see her boyfriend."

So they're still together.

"Ex," he adds.

"They broke up?" I ask, choking on my beer.

Aaron shoots me a knowing smile. "He was a nice guy. But, uh ..."

I raise my eyebrows, indicating he should go on.

Ilana walks up and sets a small shopping bag on the table. "I got the cutest little necklace for my mom at that booth over there. Do they always have these artists's booths here, Ben?"

"Huh?" I ask.

She raises an eyebrow at me. "Why do you look like that?"

"Like what?"

"Your face," she says. "It's like you're happy but also being tortured?"

Damn, she's good.

Aaron laughs. "He's trying to get me to spill why Gabby broke up with Lior." He leans toward her, and she ruffles his hair.

She smirks. "Why so interested?"

"Why did they break up?" I ask Ilana directly.

Aaron answers instead. "He moved out to California which was the beginning of the end."

Ilana shoots him a sharp look and clears her throat. "And then there's the *real* reason."

"Which is?" I ask.

She sits on Aaron's lap, and he wraps his arm around her waist to keep her from falling.

"Do you know how long Aaron waited for me?" she asks me. "How many times he asked me out and heard me say 'Give me a little more time to get over my breakup?'"

I shake my head.

"A lot. And you know what that showed me?"

I offer an educated guess. "That he thought you were someone really special?"

She nods. "And he wasn't afraid of a little hard work."

I nod, focusing on the bottle of beer in front of me. The label is peeling from the condensation, and I pick at it with my fingernail.

"Ben," Ilana says softly, and I meet her eyes. "Gabby's amazing—smart, beautiful, a huge heart. I don't have to tell you that."

No, she doesn't.

"She's simply reached the point in her life where she knows she's worth fighting for. And he didn't."

So I'm not the only idiot.

"She *is* worth fighting for," I say after a moment.

I glance at the stray cat wandering past and toss a piece of cheese from my mostly finished salad on the ground for him. He nabs it and runs off. All of a sudden, the afternoon sun is too bright for me. My skin prickles, and I grab a glass of water from the table and down it in one shot. *I've lost her.* She knows she's worth fighting for, and I didn't.

"You gotta call her, man," Aaron says in a voice that sounds as sad as I feel.

"It's not enough," I say.

"So offer to meet her in Paris."

I'd love to see her, better yet to see her in Paris, losing her mind over the art and culture. I'd go in a heartbeat, but she would think I came for a hookup, something temporary.

I meet his eyes. "Why are you helping me? I hurt her so much. She's your sister. You told me last year that she was broken, pissed off."

"Oh, she was. She told me she wanted you to choke on a ... what was it, baby?" he asks Ilana.

"Falafel," she replies with a smirk.

I snort. It sounds just like Gabby—full of rage but still able to crack a joke.

"Didn't you also tell me you were just waiting to be in the same country as me to beat me up for dating your little sister and then breaking her heart?"

He sighs. "I've been doing some contemplation."

I narrow my eyes at him. "What do you mean?"

Aaron glances at Ilana, and as if they've communicated telepathically, she kisses him on the cheek and gets up. "I'll go find your mom," she says. She smiles at me. I can feel her trying to read my thoughts, but she simply squeezes Aaron on the shoulder and walks off.

"So?" I ask.

Aaron looks at the ground. "What if I'd never told you to stay away from her?"

"What?"

"When we were kids. I knew you guys liked each other, even back then."

What?

"Don't give me that look," he says. "I knew you had a crush on her senior year. Your jaw was on the floor the night of prom when you saw her in her dress. I've never gotten confirmation from either of you, but I'm pretty sure you guys hooked up that night."

I cough and avoid his gaze.

"But before that," he continues, "I also told you any senior guy who touched my sister would be sorry."

I remember.

Aaron dips his head and cracks his knuckles. *Am I about to be sorry?*

He looks up at me and takes a deep breath. "I didn't mean you. At the time, well, you weren't exactly the man-whore you became in college ..."

I roll my eyes. "I don't sleep around anymore, bro."

"I gathered that."

"I stopped a while before Gabby and I ... got together last summer, and since then ... well, I don't want any other woman."

He sighs. "You *did* break her heart. I wasn't exaggerating."

I stare at my hands for a moment, then meet his eyes. "I beat myself up for it daily, okay? I regret ... so much. But you keep going back and forth. Are you here to punch me or to try and match-make, Feinman?"

He leans back in his chair and surprises me by laughing. "I regret stuff, too. I-I feel bad that you're both still unhappy. Gabby seems to have recovered from your disastrous attempt at a relationship last summer, but I … God, I've become such a sap. I love Ilana, and we're so happy together. I want to see Gabby happy. You, too, man."

I nod, sadly.

"So what if you hadn't felt like you had to stay away from her? Maybe you guys would be one of those high school sweetheart couples who found each other and fell in love early."

Damn, Feinman. Right in the feels.

"Or maybe," I reply, "I would've fucked it up anyway."

"She loved you, man."

"Did she tell you that?" I ask.

He smiles. "She didn't need to. It was written all over her face. It took me some time to figure out—well, Ilana told me—but once I knew, I realized that she'd been glowing the whole summer. You made her *glow*, dude."

I sigh.

"Why don't you have a girlfriend?" he asks. "A fuck-buddy? It's not like you not to have somebody, someone—"

"Because I don't *want* anybody else," I say, interrupting him.

He smiles. "I get it. Now that I'm with Ilana, I understand love a little bit better. You and Gabs have known each other for years. And from what I've seen, I think … I think you've loved each other, in some way, for a long time."

He's right.

He gives me a sad look. "Man, we've been friends forever, and I know you have some doubts about long-term relationships and maybe even yourself. But you're a good guy. I know that. Gabby knows that. People mess up, but I think real love can overcome it."

But is what we have real? Even if it is, what am I supposed to do now?

"When does she go on her trip?" I ask.

"End of the month."

"Hopefully, she doesn't meet some Parisian guy who sweeps her off her feet."

He raises his eyebrows at me. "You know that's a possibility. As much as I hate to admit it, my little sister is very charming."

"I know," I spit out. "But thanks for making my somewhat unrealistic fears more tangible."

"Eh, don't worry too much," he says. "She has a real 'girls run the world' vibe now. She's gonna do an art class while she's there. She said she wants some alone time to re-evaluate her life. If any guy hits on her, she'll probably turn him down. Her French isn't that good, anyways."

I don't point out that it's not exactly her French that attracts guys.

He levels a stare at me, and I meet his eyes. "You gonna do the right thing, Adler?"

"I'm gonna try."

"Good." He stands, and I join him, pulling out my wallet and throwing a couple hundred *shekel* notes on the table for the bill.

I look at my phone to check the time and see a few *Y-net News* notifications. "You guys are getting out of here just in time."

"What do you mean?"

"Things are heating up in the south. My roommate might be called up for reserves."

Ilana returns. "I'm gonna head out," I say. "Have a safe trip back, and maybe ... tell Gabby I say 'hi?'"

"You could always tell her yourself," she suggests. I smile and give her a quick hug, then lean in to hug Aaron.

He grips me hard and doesn't let me pull back right away. "Stay safe, man," he says in a low voice. "We're all waiting for you."

"What?" I ask, but he just winks at me and turns to walk away with his arm around Ilana.

I head in the other direction and wander on the beach, taking in the Mediterranean Sea and thinking of Gabby back in America. I replay as many moments from the previous summer as I can. When I run out of memories from last summer, I go back further in time, remembering all the times I messed up with her, but also—thankfully—many of our good times.

How many times had she tested the waters with me and I missed it? When had my childhood friend become so much more than that to me? I can't even pinpoint the exact moment my heart became tethered to hers, because it was such a gradual process.

There hasn't been a day over the past year and a half that I haven't thought of her. I run my hands over my face, then take in the sunset over the water. The horizon is on fire—the exact color orange Gabby loves so much. I'm half a world away, but I feel her—always—because ... because she is *my* fire.

In. Hold. Out. Wait. In. Hold. Out. Wait. In. Hold. Out—

"Is this your first war?" Idit asks, her gravelly yet comforting voice breaking into my thoughts as I sit on the scratchy carpeted floor of the bomb shelter trying to remember the right breathing pattern for a panic attack.

The amused expression on her time-weathered face brings a small, much-needed smile to my own. "I guess you could say that."

"This isn't *really* a war, you know," Avi comments.

And I'm not really *having a panic attack.* I know that. But it's still damn scary.

I look up at Idit for a response and see her hide a small smile. Like a queen, she surveys the cramped room from her throne of a cheap folding chair. Her grand scepter is a modest wooden cane on which she rests one of her frail arms.

Someone's phone clatters to the floor, and I startle. Idit's cloudy blue-gray eyes meet mine. "It's okay, Benny." She reaches out the hand closest to mine, and I squeeze it, inexplicably comforted by her cool, papery skin.

Of course she's calm and collected. This is far from her first rodeo, and my mind darts for a fraction of a second to the story she told me the last time I joined her for tea. Her father escaped from the Radom Ghetto, survived in a Polish forest until World War II ended, and boarded a ship for the land that would become the State of Israel.

I consider my own situation: scared but safe inside of a bomb shelter in

Rehovot with a banged-up but functional iPhone that still has reception. *Yeah, I suppose it is okay.*

I close my eyes, lean my head back against the concrete wall, and try to block out the muffled sound of the air raid siren somehow filtering through the thick walls. I'm taking deep but what I hope are not entirely dramatic breaths—in and out, in and out—when the sound of a muffled explosion makes the hairs on my arms stand up.

"*Kipat Barzel,*" says the young father sitting across from me. *Iron Dome.* His little girl is curled up with her blanket on the floor, her head resting on her father's lap, just under her baby brother's chubby legs, and I consider how my own childhood might have been different if my mom had stayed in Israel and I had grown up here.

I've heard her stories and read the news, but this is the first time I've been woken from a deep sleep to an air raid siren myself, trudging down the stairs at five in the morning to the shared safe space at the bottom of the building.

Idit squeezes my shoulder again, and I meet her eyes. "Think of something—*someone*—that makes you happy."

I uncross my legs and prop my elbows on my knees, letting my head drop between my legs. The little black Shih Tzu someone brought down to the shelter shimmies under my knees, looking up at me expectantly. I pet his head, grateful for the physical connection, and catch sight of my phone on the floor, resting face-up. Somehow, it's open to the photo I was admiring before I fell asleep.

My heart falls into my stomach. I stare into the face of the most beautiful woman I've ever met, the one who kept my heart beating when it felt like the world was falling apart. I imagine what she would tell me if she knew where I was right now.

"*Breathe, Benji. You'll be fine.*" I can almost feel her hand on my chest, just over my heart.

I close my eyes, and from the depths of my memory, her face comes to me, the last time we made love. She was quiet, fully focused on the moment, the connection between us, and I had fallen, completely and deeply into her dark brown eyes.

Why didn't I stay? Why didn't I tell her how I felt? Why didn't I—

Avi bumps his knee against mine. I turn my head and look at him. He glances down at my phone. "You miss her?" he asks.

I barely have the time to roll my eyes at him—he *knows* I miss her—before Idit replies behind me, "Of course he misses her."

Who needs your own Jewish mother when you've got someone else's? Plenty to go around in this country.

Avi snorts. "Keep scrolling through your photos. It'll keep your mind off—"

"Death by Kassam rocket?" I offer dryly.

"You're not gonna die today, dude." He turns to Idit and yell-whispers in Hebrew, "It's like it's his first war or something."

"I hear you," I say. "You're not *actually* whispering, and I speak Hebrew."

"With an accent," he says.

"A slight accent," I say, correcting him. "And so do you."

He shrugs, knowing I'm right. I hear another muted boom and raise my eyebrows.

"It works. Mostly," he says.

"So I'm not gonna die today?" I ask.

"Not today, *ahi*." *My brother.* I smile at him, but before I can respond, there's a quick, loud explosion, then a slight tremor of the floor.

Avi's eyes widen, and Idit takes a raspy, deep breath. "But you will one day," she says.

I turn to her, and she looks pointedly at my phone, still open to the picture. "For the life of me, I can't figure out why you're here getting rockets rained down on your head when Gabby is out there."

She's right. I'm here, and she's ... there.

"What if I died today?" I whisper to Avi.

"I told you you're not gonna—"

"What if I did, though?" I ask, cutting him off. "What if something happened to me before I told her how I feel?"

He meets my eyes. "What would you say to her if she were waiting outside that steel door when you walked out?"

I open my mouth to speak, but he stops me. "Don't tell *me*. Think about it, then figure out a way to tell her."

I sigh and close my eyes. "*You're the one,*" I'd say, *taking her into my arms.* "*You're the only one who has ever had a place in my heart. You're the beginning, the end, and everything in between.*"

I open my eyes, and my pajama-clad neighbors are beginning to shuffle out of the shelter. With the door now open, I can hear the siren of an ambulance or fire truck—God knows—sounding nearby.

"We can go back up to the flat," Avi says.

I stand, and he pats me on the back. "You know, iPhones send texts. Probably even make calls."

I blink at him as he helps Idit stand. "I'll be up in a minute."

"I'll make you some Nescafe," he says.

I don't need coffee. I'm more awake now than I have ever been.

My hands shake as I type out something I should have admitted the second I walked out of Gabby's door last year.

Me

I miss everything about you.

I press Send, then step outside. It's winter. There's still an hour until sunrise, and the twilight—that eerie time between what has been and what could be—chills me more than the freezing morning air. *It's time. I'm ready.*

Gabby

My first few days in Paris are dream-like, and I quite stereotypically visit as many art museums as possible and drink wine with every delicious meal. On the first day, I sketch in my small notebook and brainstorm what I might want to work on during my art workshop.

On the third day of my trip, I sit down before a large canvas and take a deep breath. I already know what this painting will be. In the hours I traversed the streets of Paris, I felt someone with me. From the vibrant red tulips I spotted in the Île de la Cité flower market to the Eiffel Tower light show, the magic of this city was something I found myself wanting to share with ... him. He's not here, but with each day that passes, the boy, the man, I've loved for years starts to take shape on my canvas. In a dark green shirt, he sits on a stool, partially turned away from me. I can't see his whole face, just a hint of that smirk I know so well, but I know it's him. I know his body, his build. He sits, relaxed, as if he's about to turn his head and ask me whether he can give me a foot massage that will surely turn into something more.

"No," I whisper to myself. *I don't think that's a good idea. We're done now, remember?*

But I can't help but notice how much imaginary me wants to say, *Fine, one last time.* Try as I might to deny it, there's a small part of my heart that will never be done with Ben. He was there at the beginning, and he'll be there at the end.

That night I dream of him. He sits, painted on my canvas, except now, I'm inside the painting with him. When I look down at my arms, they're the same, splotchy texture as his visage.

"I'm sorry, beautiful," he says, as he approaches me and reaches out to me. Tears threaten to spill from his eyes. "I hurt you, but you need to know, it hurt me more to leave you."

"Then why did you go?" I whisper.

"Did you ever love me?" He locks eyes with me and waits for my answer.

"Of course I loved you. How could you even ask—"

There's a loud crash, and he turns back to the position he held in my painting. I wake up shivering.

I never told him. I swallow a sob. *I never told him.*

I sit up and grab my phone from the bedside table. It's 7:00 a.m., and I missed a text message from Ben a few hours ago.

Ben

> I miss everything about you.

What? It's been months since we last spoke. *Why is he texting me now? Why was he up so early?* I squeeze my eyes shut and take a deep breath to calm my pounding heart.

Me

> Are you ok?

Yeah. Just been thinking a lot. You know me.

I do know you.

Having fun in Paris?

He's either talked to Aaron or checked my Instagram.

It's beautiful here. Heading home today, unfortunately.

Did you go with friends?

So transparent.

I just enjoyed my own company and drank too much wine.

I'd love to see you drunk and talking about art. <smiley emoji>

Me? Never <laughing emoji>

Have a safe trip home.

Happy Hanukkah. And stay safe.

You, too.

I could sleep another hour before I need to get ready to leave, but I'm already wide awake and there's construction going on outside my hotel. I decide to do some last-minute shopping before heading to the airport. I spotted a beautiful scarf a few days ago that would make the perfect Hanukkah gift for my mom. When I arrive at the shop, I'm lucky to find it's open early.

While browsing, I catch sight of a men's scarf that makes me think of Ben. I run my fingers over it, enjoying its softness and thinking how much the forest green would bring out the flecks of green in his hazel eyes.

"It's beautiful, isn't it?" the stylishly dressed shop owner says in English tinged with a French accent.

"It is," I say. I could buy it and send it to him in Israel. *Maybe I shouldn't.*

"In that case, why not get the matching one for you? I have a beautiful one with a pattern, for a woman. They would go nicely together."

"We won't be wearing them togeth—" I try to explain.

But she wraps them together, and I don't protest. Maybe I'll drop them both at his mother's, and she can wear the second scarf.

Later in the day, as I wait at my gate to board my flight, a text from my mom comes in.

Why is she asking?

A rocket hit an apartment building in Rehovot last night, a few streets over from where he lives.

What the hell? Why didn't he say anything?

I quickly open my Israel news app. One of the breaking news items jumps out at me: "Direct hit on Rehovot apartment; one critically injured."

I feel sick to my stomach. *It wasn't him,* I remind myself. *But it could have been ...*

I *never told him* plays on repeat in my head.

No, *he didn't.*

But before I can text Ben again, a Google Chat message from my manager pops up.

```
Hey Gabby, Hope Paris was great. I put time on your
calendar for Thursday about something Artem is cooking
up. He wants to poach you to his team. I told him "hell
no," but if you're interested, we can work something out.
How do you feel about Zurich?
```

How do I feel about Zurich? It's beautiful, but I'm not moving there.

I write him back:

```
I liked working with his guys last month, but let's talk
more about it when I'm back. Paris was great but not sure
I want to move to Europe.
```

The flight crew announces that my group is boarding, and I get in line. I write Ben a text.

The flight attendant asks for my boarding pass, and I swipe to it on my phone.

Does his apartment have a safe room? Was he in a bomb shelter? Why didn't my Red Alert app notify me? It's supposed to ping me if a rocket is fired toward his city.

Oh, Ben. I check my phone at least twenty times before we take off, and I have to switch it to Airplane Mode.

You heard from him. He's okay.

But I'm not. My chest tightens, and I dig out the tissue paper-wrapped scarf from my bag and clutch it as the plane takes off, wishing he were here beside me, so I could see him, touch him. I wish I could tell him exactly how I feel.

I miss everything about you, too.

· ❤ · ❤ · ❤ · ❤ · ❤ ·

Waking up jetlagged at 3:37 a.m. this morning hasn't done any favors for my tired eyes. But my family has been worried about me lately, so I spend extra time getting ready for my parents' Hanukkah party. *I'm perfectly fine,* my burgundy A-line skirt conveys. *Single does not equal sad,* my cat eyeliner proclaims. *You don't fuck with an empowered woman,* my heeled boots declare. I might have failed at my Paris mission to clear my head of memories and regrets, but they don't need to know that. I haven't heard from Ben since my last text, which means he was just feeling lonely and sentimental. *How very, very typical.*

And stupid me? I let myself get carried away by fear. It was simply the latest instance of us slipping back into old, bad habits. It doesn't mean anything because he is there, and I am here. And *I'm perfectly fine.* I repeat it like a mantra the entire drive to my parents' with intermittent breaks for inspiration from my new musical guru, Eden Golan.

When I walk through my parents' front door, my father is hustling around. My mom calls an order from the kitchen, "Marc, get the napkins! I forgot them in the dryer."

I drop my gifts near the stairs and kiss my dad on the cheek. "I'll go. Tell Ima I'll be right down."

My dad shoots me a grateful look. "I missed you, honey."

"I missed you, too, Aba," I call back as I run up the stairs.

After gathering the cloth napkins, I head back downstairs just as Tzipi comes in from the cold. *Perfect.* I'll give her the scarf I bought in Paris and ask her to give the other one to Ben the next time he comes home.

So imagine my surprise to find out the next time Ben will be home is … now? And later, when I dumbly mention my peace offering—the scarf—he thinks that wrapping my legs around his neck while he gives me his own Hanukkah gift is a *much* better way to keep warm.

This Hanukkah ... Again

Burn It Down

Gabby

My body is in the wrong time zone. Full stop. It's 4:07 a.m., and if I weren't hiding in bed under a weighted blanket woven entirely from my own regrets and uncertainty, I'd be fully capable of starting the day.

I pull the covers over my head—a cocoon of shame—and the look on Ben's face as he burst out my parents' front door last night, right before I'd thrown my car in reverse to make my escape, comes hurtling back to me.

I try, in vain, to lull myself back to sleep with some deep breathing and relaxation exercises. It's too early to be awake. My body feels it, but my mind is already racing. Defeated, I pick up my phone, but before I can even unlock it, a text flashes on the screen:

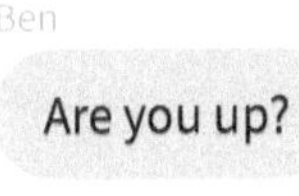

Ugh.

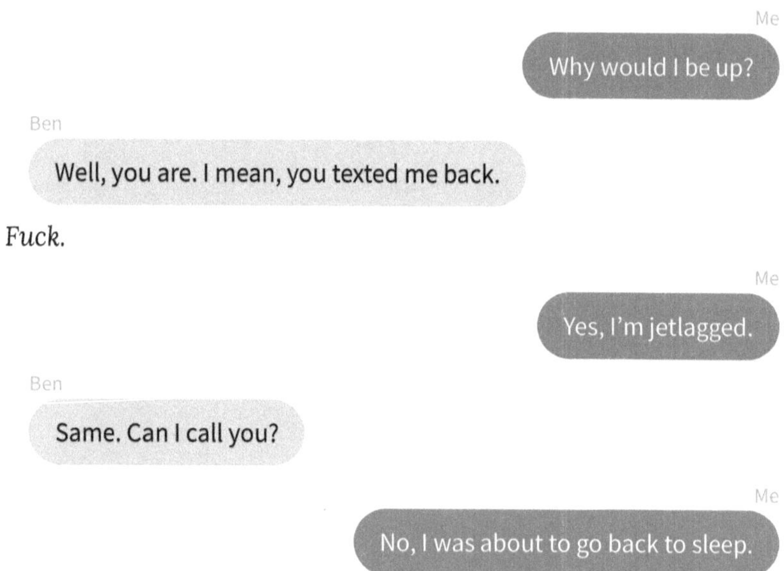

I set my phone to "Do not disturb" and toss it across the room just in case I'm tempted to look at it.

Damn you, Ben, for making me go back in time. I've been doing it anyway, but it was in my own safe space, my mind. Having him here, having to make actual decisions—and, as usual, making the wrong ones—is doing a number on me.

I curl up in the fetal position and pull the covers back over my head. I must fall asleep at some point because when I hear a soft knock on my front door and glance at my clock, a couple hours have passed.

I drag myself out of bed and head to the bathroom. On my way, I trip over my phone in my zombie-like state and pick it up. Three missed calls, all from Ben.

And a text.

Someone is certainly determined this morning.

Can I come over?

Aren't you in NJ?

I'm close by. I promise to bring something yummy when I come.

Sigh.

Fine.

When I hear a knock on my door three minutes later—he really *was* close by—I look through the peephole to find an unshaven, slightly rough-looking but still smiling Ben holding a to-go coffee cup in one hand and a paper bag in the other.

Thankfully, I've brushed my teeth, and I quickly run my fingers through my tangled hair, hoping for a miracle. I rummage through my bag on the hook next to the front door and quickly swipe lip gloss across my lips before shoving it back into the bag. I'm still buzzing with annoyance at him showing up last night and being just as damn endearing as he always has, but I'm determined to show him that his charms have no hold over me.

I open the door.

"Good morning," he says, handing me the coffee cup. His eyes track down quickly to my lips. *Shit. He noticed.*

He smiles at me. "Latte?"

"Thanks. Come in," I grumble, holding my hand out to take the cup.

He's wearing a thick black hoodie and a beanie. When he takes it off, his hair explodes from it.

"Have a bad night?" he asks.

"Honestly, I don't even know how to characterize my night." I sit at my kitchen table and take a sip of the coffee. It's not super hot, but it's still good.

"I brought you breakfast," he says, offering me the paper bag and sitting next to me.

I peek in the bag, and it's a breakfast burrito. Despite the fact that I'm annoyed with him for ... well, existing ... it's a pretty strong play. Apparently, his charms *do* have a hold over me.

"Thank you." I unwrap the burrito and take a bite. It's also good, but no amount of coffee or burritos is going to settle my stomach or my nerves.

I set down the burrito. "It's ... nice to see you after a year, but like, what are you doing here?"

"Here in America or here in your apartment?" He gives me a questioning smile that would have charmed the pants off me a couple years ago. *Not today, Mister. I'm fresh off the Regrets Valley Express Line.*

I shrug impatiently.

"I don't know. I guess I'm just ... here. It was so good seeing you at your parents' last night."

Seeing me. That's one way of putting it.

"It was ... a surprise," I say. "To see you there."

"Your mom didn't tell you?" he asks, but then looks like he didn't mean to say it.

"My mom *knew*?" I ask. I immediately begin drafting a mental membership list for the Meddling Jewish Mothers Club, Chapter President: Marci Feinman.

"I, uh, saw her yesterday, and I asked if you'd be there," he replies.

"Hmmm," I huff out.

"I was *hoping* I'd see you," he admits.

The caffeine in the coffee must have revived me, and now I have questions. "Why?"

He runs his hand through his hair, then looks up at me. I narrow my eyes at him. *What?*

"I wanted to talk to you."

Oh, here we fucking go.

He opens his mouth, but before he can utter a word, I speak. Frustration that's been building in me since we hooked up last night—as if our physical contact ignited a long fuse and the fire has finally reached the bomb—bursts from my mouth.

"No."

"No?"

"Exactly," I say, setting the coffee down hard on the table and some of it dribbles out of the top. "No. You had plenty of opportunities to talk to me last year, the first … what … seventeen years we knew each other, but you chose to leave, to *run away*. You left last year, and I wished you well because I … am a good person. And I want you to follow your dreams—"

"Thank—" he starts to say.

"But I was a wreck for months," I say before he can continue. "I had to get over you for my own mental and emotional health."

I stand and move away from him. "And I'm finally … over you." *Well, something like that.* "And then you start texting me again and showing up here and …"

Still sitting at the table, he looks at me, his expression teetering back and forth between confusion and … sadness?

"Why didn't you tell me that you were in a bomb shelter when you texted me the other night?" I almost shriek.

His mouth drops.

"Yeah, I found out."

He stands, moving closer to me. "I didn't want you to worry."

I close my eyes and take a deep breath. He draws closer to me and rubs his hand down my arm, and I open my eyes and pull away, shaking my head.

"Listen, we slid back into an old pattern last night. It wasn't a good decision … for either of us," I say, looking down at the floor.

I'm surprised it's not shaking because that's how unstable I feel. Ever since I got that text from him, ever since I found out where he was and what made him send it. I've been worried about him since he left last year, and having him show up here now, it's too much.

"Hey—" he starts to say.

"You need to leave," I say, interrupting him. "I held it together last night because people were watching me—and then, the other part, I got swept up … in the moment." *In him.* "But it was a mistake." I take a ragged breath.

"I can't do this now. Just ... go."

He reaches out to touch me again, but I snatch my arm away before he can.

"Please leave."

His face scrunches up in pain, but I look away.

"Go."

Ben

Shit, I think as I head down the stairs from Gabby's apartment. I've been up since 2:00 a.m., and I still haven't recovered from the twelve-hour flight two days ago. I'm exhausted, but I'm also a man on a mission. Namely, get Gabby to talk to me.

I catch myself in the reflection of a window. My long hair is escaping from my beanie. I should have gotten a haircut. Then again, it felt so fucking good when she tugged on it last night when I was ... well ... My clothes are rumpled, too, from hanging out in my mom's car until I got too cold and took refuge in the diner a couple blocks down. Then fate, in the form of a tiny little *bubbe*, intervened. Evelyn Friedberg walked by the window just as I happened to look up and invited me up to her place to wait for Gabby to wake up.

Sitting at Evelyn's place, telling her what had gone on the last year gave me the time I needed to build up the courage to knock on Gabby's door again. Then, she'd texted me.

"Thank you, *maideleh*," I had told Evelyn as I left. She shared with me once that before her husband passed away, he always used to call her that because they had known each other since they were kids. Sitting in her kitchen, I remembered that little fact, and it had heartened me as I knocked on Gabby's door for the second time that morning.

Leaving Gabby's place now, I could feel defeated, but I don't. I feel exhilarated. She couldn't resist kissing me last night. She said it was a mistake, but I've heard Gabby tell all kinds of lies over the years—to her parents, to her brother, and to me. Sometimes, she's even said things she might *think* she believes.

That look on her face when she told me it was a mistake? She was forcing herself to say the words, struggling to do something she knew deep down was wrong. She doesn't hate me. She might even have it in her to forgive me.

The last year, I've longed to hear her voice, I've pined for her, but I never thought I had a chance. Seeing her last night, though, and this morning—*ah, beautiful Morning Gabby*—I'm full of hope. I've got five days to convince her that I'm worth giving one more chance.

In the Dying Embers

Gabby

Once again, I've woken up too early. It's dark and quiet—a deadly combination when you're trying to avoid thinking about the one that got away. The one who *ran* away. Except the one that got—or ran—away keeps texting me and asking me to call him.

I'm not ready to talk to Ben, but he'll be leaving again soon—and I don't want to have any regrets. Who knows when I'll see him again?

Early mornings mean tired afternoons, and I snuck out early from work today. My manager caught me getting on the elevator.

I gave him a sheepish look. "Sorry, Phillip. I'm exhausted. I'm useless here. I'll get back online later, after a nap."

"Eh, you're more productive asleep than most people are fully awake. Get some rest, but I wanted to let you know that Artem's ready to move if you are. He said he'd make you a team lead if you're interested in moving there."

Moving there? The whole commute home, I told myself there's no way I'm moving to Europe, but a small part of me kept pushing back. *What if change is exactly what I need right now?*

I'm still mulling it over, but also looking forward to a power nap as I arrive home and unlock my apartment door.

Before I can go in, Mrs. Friedberg pops her head out her door. "Gab-by-leh, how are you?"

"I'm fine, Mrs. Friedberg. Happy Hanukkah."

"Happy Hanukkah to you," she replies. "Would you like to light candles together tonight? I know you probably have friends to visit or a boyfriend..."

"No, no plans tonight. No boyfriend," I add. I want my pajamas, a nap, and Netflix for the rest of the night while I contemplate major life decisions like a relocation to Switzerland. She looks at me, waiting for an answer, and I consider that her children live in Connecticut, and she'll be alone if I don't say "yes."

"Sure," I say. "Let's light the candles together. Your place or mine?"

"Why don't you come over? I'll make us a light dinner."

"No need," I protest.

"I'd love to. Benny told me once you like kugel. Maybe I'll make that."

"When did you talk to Benny—Ben?" I ask, correcting myself.

"The other morning," she says. "When he came to visit you."

That's how he got here so quickly.

"What a lovely young man," she says, putting her hand over her heart.

"He is," I say, begrudgingly.

"Come over at six?"

"See you then," I say.

I'm setting Mrs. Friedberg's dining room table when there's a knock at her front door.

"Are you expecting someone?" I call to her in the kitchen.

"That must be Benny," she says, coming into the dining room.

Excuse me?

My surprise must show on my face because she adds, "Did I forget to mention he's coming tonight?"

Are you freaking kidding me? I take a deep breath and add Mrs. Friedberg to my list of old Jewish ladies who need to mind their own damn business.

She checks the peephole and opens the door to Ben, who has gotten a haircut since I last saw him. It's not as short as I'm used to, but it's less wild than a couple days ago. *Shame,* I think before I chastise myself for being wooed by his stupid wild hair and his stupid cute smile and the stupid way he's crouching down, almost bending his tall frame in half to lean down and hug her with warmth and—

Stop, Gabby.

He's shaved, and he looks less tired than the other morning. I try to smile at him, but he barely glances at me before focusing his attention back on the little old lady in front of him. He procures a bouquet of flowers he was hiding behind his back up until this moment, and she begins fawning over him again. *When did these two become best friends?*

I figure I might as well be useful, so I continue setting the table. Mrs. Friedberg bustles into the kitchen to fill a vase with water, and Ben comes up beside me and whispers in my ear, "Don't be jealous. She's a little old lady. I bet she doesn't get flowers that often."

I glance up at him and roll my eyes. "I buy her flowers almost every Shabbat."

"You do?" he asks, the corners of his mouth turning up.

"Yes," I admit. "I kept doing it after you left last summer."

He looks down. "I do the same thing for the old lady in my building in Israel."

"Look at you. Enchanting grandmas the world over."

"Are you upset I'm here?" he asks.

"Honest answer?"

He nods, and I drown—momentarily—in his beautiful eyes.

"I was ... when you walked in the door. You know I don't like surprises." *Ambushes.* "But ..."

"Yes?"

"Now, I'm not. I shouldn't have thrown you out the other day. I was overwhelmed."

"It was a lot at once." He looks like he wants to say more but instead heads into the kitchen and asks Mrs. Friedberg if he can help her.

I finish with the dining table, and Mrs. Friedberg calls me into the kitchen. "Gabby, come, darling. We'll light the candles in here and then we can sit in the dining room to eat."

I join them, and Mrs. Friedberg offers Ben the box of matches in her hand. "Would you like to do the honors?"

"Sure." He catches my eye. "Help me?"

I nod and come closer. He smiles, then strikes a match. I expect he'll start the prayers and I'll need to jump in quickly since he doesn't know all the words, but when he confidently sings the beginning of the blessings, I realize he *does* in fact know the words. I sing softly so I can hear his rich baritone voice. I haven't often heard him sing. When he finishes the second prayer, he hands me the *shamash*, and I put it into its place.

I lean into him. "I thought you didn't know the words, *Benjamin*."

"I spent the last year and a half speaking Hebrew, *Gabriella*. I *know* the Hanukkah blessings," he says with a goofy grin.

"Why didn't you tell my mom that?"

"Because she wanted to hear your beautiful voice and so did I."

"You both have lovely voices," Mrs. Friedberg chimes in. "I used to love singing with my Benjamin."

Her Benjamin?

"Your husband's name was Benjamin?" I ask, suddenly realizing I'd only ever thought of her as Mrs. Friedberg and her husband, whom I never knew, as Mr. Friedberg.

She smiles at me and nods. "I guess that's why I took a liking to *your* Benjamin."

My Benjamin? I can't help but smile.

"You know," she continues, "we also met when we were kids. In a singing group together. His voice was much better than mine, but he always insisted that mine was better. That's what you do when you love someone. You see the beauty in them, despite their faults."

My eyes lock on Ben's when she says it.

"Let's eat," she says, saving me from muttering something embarrassing. "Do you two mind bringing the food in? I'd like to sit down."

"Of course," I say quickly, ushering her into the dining room and getting her settled. I go back to the kitchen to take the food.

"You look good tonight," Ben says, as he hands me the kugel.

"Thank you."

"I was talking to the kugel," he jokes. "I love a good kugel."

I roll my eyes at him and snort softly.

"Did you know her husband's name was the same as yours?" I ask before walking back to the dining room.

"I did."

Of course he did. He's always been a good listener.

Dinner is lovely. Good conversation, good food, and good company. Mrs. Friedberg—Evelyn, she told me I must call her now—and Ben have such a rapport. I had no idea how much they must have bonded the year before. He makes references to stories about her husband and her children and her life that I had no clue about, and for the time it takes us to eat our meal, I can almost see him through her eyes.

After dinner, I make tea for her, and Ben and I clear the table and wash the dishes while she sits in the living room.

When it's time to go, Ben leans down to hug our hostess goodbye. "*Maideleh*," he says. "Thank you for a lovely evening. I haven't had a nice dinner with two such beautiful ladies in a long time."

I stand in the doorway and watch them.

"Benny," she says, "come closer. I want to tell you something."

He crouches down, and she leans in to whisper something in his ear.

I go back into the kitchen to give them privacy, but I overhear her "whisper."

"She needs you as much as you need her. That boy she dated earlier this year, he was fine, but he wasn't her *beshert*, her match, like you are."

My mouth goes dry. I can't do this.

I walk to the doorway. "Mrs. Fri—Evelyn, thank you so much. I'm going to go to bed. I've had a long day." I walk over to her quickly and kiss her on the cheek, then head to the front door and walk out.

While I fumble with my keys, Ben leaves her apartment in a rush and comes closer. "Can I come in? Just for us to talk?"

"I-I can't. We can't."

He looks at me for a moment. I'm sure he'll ask again, but he doesn't. "No worries."

I stand there, looking at him. Do I kiss him on the cheek? Do I hug him? Do I wrap my arms around him and ask him to stay forever? Before my brain can arrive at an answer, he asks, "Can I see you again before I leave?"

"Of course."

He steps away, head bowed, and looks up at me through his dark lashes. "It was nice seeing you tonight," he says before turning and walking down the stairs.

For the past thirty minutes, I've been sitting on my couch, looking at the vase of flowers on my kitchen counter. Shortly after Ben left, Evelyn knocked on my door, flowers in hand, and insisted I take them. I'm staring at them, wondering if he knew she would end up giving them to me when he chose them—orange tulips are my favorite—when I get a text from Aaron: a GIF of a dreidel dressed like Dr. Dre. He is appropriately named "Dr. Dreidel."

Hmmmm.

I call Aaron. Without even saying "hello," I jump right in. "I can tell you, but I suspect you already know. I lit candles tonight with my elderly neighbor and Ben."

"What?" he asks.

"Yeah, since he came to the Hanukkah party the other night—which by the way, our mother totally knew he was going to be there and conveniently failed to mention it to me—he's been ... I don't know, trying to talk to me and tell me he's sorry." I sigh. "It's all putting me in a weird place emotionally."

Aaron's quiet for a moment. "He needs some sort of resolution, Gabs."

"Do you understand how hard it is for me to be around him?" I ask.

"And just why do you think that is?"

I can't find any words to respond.

"Do what you need to do, but ..." He takes a deep breath. "If you feel like you can protect yourself—your heart—maybe see him one more time before he goes."

"I already told him I would," I say. "I just haven't figured out when or how or ..."

"Well, you're coming to Ilana's Hanukkah party on Saturday night. She'll invite him, too, and you'll get to talk, but it'll all be low-key. No pressure."

I need to. We both need closure.

"I can do that. I'll see you then."

Ben

"Ariella?" I say when I come down the stairs on Friday night for Shabbat dinner and see my oldest sister coming in the door. She doesn't even take off her long coat before rushing up the stairs to pull me into a rib-crushing hug.

"I missed you so much," she says, not letting go of me.

"Ari... ella, I can't breathe," I say, and she loosens her grip.

She holds me out at arm's length, dark eyes trained on me. "Are you here for the reason I think you are?"

I nod. Ariella knows all my secrets. She's the one I've been confiding in the last year about my feelings for Gabby and whether or not—she claims not—I'm an asshole like my dad.

She smiles broadly, and for a second, she looks exactly like our mom. "So where is she?" she asks.

"I ... didn't exactly tell her yet?"

Her eyes bug out. "Ima said you're leaving on Sunday. What the hell are you waiting for?"

I grimace. "It's been more complicated than I expected."

She looks at me beseechingly.

"I know," I say. "I'll see her tomorrow. I'll talk to her."

She shakes her head. "You've loved this girl for years. Cut the bullshit already."

Miri comes in the front door with my dad, just as Ariella says the word *bullshit*.

"Bennnny," she says, bounding up the stairs. "What's cracking, Holy Brother from the Holy Land?" She hip-bumps Ariella out of the way and gives me a hug. "I've missed you."

I snicker. "I've missed you, too."

"So where's Gorgeous Gabby?" Miri asks, looking around, as if I'm hiding her behind me or downstairs in the living room.

Ariella levels a stare at me and rats me out to Miri. "She's not here because Ben is a pussy and didn't tell her yet."

My eyes widen. I had no idea Ariella even knew the word *pussy*.

"What?" Miri exclaims.

"I know," Ariella says.

"You three, down here. *Yalla*," my mom says, and I notice my dad has come in from the cold.

My sisters and I smile at each other over my mom taking charge, and I head down the stairs to hug my dad.

"It's so good to see you, Benjamin," he says. "I've ... missed seeing your face. Missed hearing your voice."

It's not like my dad to use such words, and I step back and take him in. Something about him is different. I glance at my mom, who is carefully watching our interaction.

She then hugs him herself. "Come, let's have dinner," she says.

After my sisters light the Shabbat candles, we bless the wine and the challah. I start to stand to help my mom bring in the food from the kitchen, but my dad stands first.

"Ben, sit. I'll help your mom."

My sisters and I exchange glances.

As soon as my parents walk into the kitchen, my sisters pounce on me. "Why haven't you told her yet that you love her?" Ariella says at the exact same time that Miri asks, "What are you waiting for, you idiot?"

"I tried," I say in a low voice. "I've seen her a few times. The first time, we even kissed—"

"That's not what I heard," Miri says with a rude hand gesture.

"Stop it. The point is, I've tried talking to her, but she's pissed off. I think giving in and making out with me made her even more pissed off—"

"At herself," Ariella interrupts. "She's pissed off at herself for giving in which is a good sign."

"It is?" I ask, trying to understand what she's saying.

"If she had sex with you—"

"We didn't have sex—"

"Fine, 'made out,'" Ariella says, doing quote fingers.

"Anyways, if she did ... whatever she did ... after all the times you jerked her around—especially last summer—and she agreed to see you tomorrow, she still has feelings for you," Miri says.

"Oh, she has 'feelings,'" I say, thinking of some of the choice words she shared with me this week.

"You can dislike and love someone at the same time," Ariella says.

"It's like when you call me an asshole, but I'm still your favorite sister," Miri says.

Ariella kicks me under the table, dramatically, so Miri can see and says, "Exactly how *Miri's* your favorite sister, Ben."

"You're *both* assholes," Miri says, as my parents come back into the dining room with the first course.

"Jonny, look how much our children love each other. We did such a good job," my mom jokes.

He smiles at her warmly and remarks, "You did an amazing job. I just helped."

I can't remember the last time we had such a calm, comfortable conversation at a family dinner. Everyone is full of questions about my time in Israel, but what shocks me the most is my dad's curiosity about my life, my work.

My mom and sisters move to the living room, but I stay at the dining table answering all his questions. I can't leave. It's the best conversation I've had with him in years. When it starts to get late, though, Ariella says she needs to head out. Miri and my dad offer to help with the dishes.

"No, it's okay. I'll do them," I say. "You guys head home. It's a long drive." Miri has been living with my dad while she does her medical residency at PMC.

They prepare to leave, but before my dad walks out the door, he tells me, "Ben, I, uh, was thinking about coming to visit you when you get back to Israel. Maybe sometime in January or maybe even for Passover?"

"That would be great," I say, surprised.

"I'd like to spend some quality time with you. It's ..."

"What?"

"I haven't always been ... what you needed, but I want to try to do better. If it's not too late?"

I swallow and meet his eyes. "No, Aba, it's not too late."

He pulls me into another hug. "I love you. I want you to know that."

"I know. I—"

"Whatever you need, I'm here for you. Do you know that?"

I'm not sure I did until this moment. But I look into his eyes. They're brown, sincere—like Gabby's.

I nod. "I know, Aba. I know."

"So who's gonna be there?" I ask Aaron on Saturday, as we drive into Manhattan for Ilana's Hanukkah party. I keep pressing Aaron for more information, but he's run out of answers.

"I don't know. Like, a lot of people. Ilana's friends, some colleagues, Gabby ..."

"She's barely talked to me, and I'm starting to think this is going to be more of a long-term multi-phase project. Your sister is stubborn."

"My sister is an intelligent woman who knows her worth, Adler."

"Both things can be true at the same time, Feinman."

He chuckles. "You're right. But you're leaving tomorrow, so I humbly suggest you get your ass in motion, *Adler*."

"Yes, I've already been advised by *multiple* people that time is running out, *Feinman*."

"Exactly. So, like, use the tools in your toolbox, man," he says in an exasperated tone.

"Meaning?"

"You're gonna make me say it?" he asks, flinching.

What is he talking about?

"She's my sister, dude."

"What are you trying to say?" I spit out.

He groans. "For the record, I'm *only* saying this because I'm certain your intentions toward my sister are pure."

Not entirely, but okay ...

He exhales loudly. "I know you know how to hit on chicks, so now's the time to pull out the big guns."

"Are you making a reference to my dick?" I tease. "You know, I always thought of it as an instrument of love, not a weapon, but that's an interesting take on—"

"Shut the fuck up, dude. No. I mean, you are ... smooth, I guess. You used to be a grade-A dork, but something changed when you went to college. Harness the force, man. Whatever you used to charm women in college and afterward, I'm giving you permission to use it now. Get it d one."

Get it done, huh?

He parks the car.

"Alright, I guess it's time to ... get it done."

Ilana recently moved back in with her parents, and they agreed to go away for the weekend and leave her the place for the party.

When we walk into the large apartment near Riverside Park, Ilana greets us, kissing Aaron on the cheek and opening her arms to me for a hug. I lean in to hug her, and she says quietly. "I'm glad you're here. You *needed* to come back."

"Well, your boyfriend's a very convincing man." Her eyebrow twitches upward, and she fixes her face after just a hint of a mischievous smile. *How involved was she in this whole plan?*

Before I have time to wonder, she leans in and whispers, "Gabby's not here yet, but let me introduce you to some people." She guides me over to a small group of well-dressed women. The look one of them has in her eyes is unmistakable interest, and I widen my eyes in alarm at Ilana. She winks at me in response.

I introduce myself to Sarah, Rebecca, Rachel, and … Coco. *You gotta be kidding me.* As they continue their chitchat, I feel completely out of place talking to these beautiful women decked out in designer brands. In my head, I compare my crappy apartment in Rehovot to this fancy home in the Upper West Side, and I would 100 percent rather be there now having a low-key Shabbat dinner with my roommate or sharing a coffee with Idit on her balcony. Except Gabby isn't there. She's here.

And now is not the time for a lack of self-confidence. *Harness the force,* Aaron said.

Coco, my newest friend, works in the fashion industry. "That's so interesting," I say. *It's not interesting to me at all.* "I could tell right away you must be in fashion. You're really stylish." I give her what I hope is a charming smile. I'm a little out of practice, but it seems to work.

"That's so nice, Ben," she says, touching my arm. "You know, most men—well, most straight men at least—can't appreciate good style."

Well, most men are not trying to resurrect their stale come-on tactics in the five minutes before their ex arrives at this party.

It takes longer than five minutes for Gabby to show up, but it's in my favor. By the time she arrives, I have at least three women listening to me raptly about the time I broke up a fight between two elderly men in a supermarket in Israel.

"You are so funny," Coco exclaims, just as Gabby steps from the foyer into the room in which we're all talking. Her eyes flick in my direction, and she quickly turns away as if trying to hide the fact that she noticed me and my growing entourage of single Jewish women in their twenties.

While she and Ilana hug, I admire her from afar. She's wearing a mini-skirt with leggings underneath and knee-high boots. She has on some sort of velvety top that accentuates her curves, and she looks drop-dead gorgeous. I must not be the only one of that opinion. Two guys in the corner have also taken note of her arrival.

I don't think so, fellas.

"Excuse me," I tell Coco. "I need to go say hi to a friend."

Before she can respond, I join Aaron who has just finished hugging Gabby, and I lean in for my turn.

"Is this what women are wearing to Hanukkah parties these days?" I ask her, tracing my eyes down her body.

"What's that supposed to mean?" she whispers in my ear.

"It means that you look beautiful, of course." I lean back from our hug, but then I take a gamble and lean back in. "And utterly fuck-able."

She gasps and quickly darts her eyes around, checking if anyone has overheard our exchange. I catch her eyes, and she's trying, but failing, to withhold a smile. I hold her eyes for one second longer, and she cracks.

I mouth the word *fuck-able* at her, and she laughs out loud. Then her eyes flick in the direction of the front door.

"Oh, hey, Matt," she says, escaping to greet a guy who's just arrived. He hugs her and leaves his hand on her waist. *What the hell?*

"We said we'd meet up when you got back from Paris," this guy Matt says, "but I didn't know it'd be this soon. Nice coincidence, huh?"

"Indeed," Gabby says.

"How was your trip?" he asks.

"Lovely. Cold. Romantic." I bristle at the tone of her voice. I've been flirting with this girl for a decade, and—*damn it*—she's in full-on flirting mode.

"I loved Paris. I was able to check off the Mona Lisa from my famous art bucket list," Matt says. *Trite mother fucker.*

"Oh," she says, her voice going up just the slightest. I bite my lip to hold in a smile. Gabby thinks it's cliché to mention the Mona Lisa at the Louvre, too.

"The Mona Lisa is impressive," she says, "but I hope you got to see some of the other exhibits, too?"

"Oh, obviously," he replies, trying to course-correct.

"I fell in love with this small museum," she shares. "I can't remember the name. It was mostly Monet's works. It was pretty empty the afternoon I went, and I stayed until they finally kicked me out."

She laughs, then he laughs, and I glance out the second-story window to my left, wondering if I can just run right through it.

I take a deep breath and glance away, but not before noticing her unbutton the top button on her top and fan herself. "It's so hot in here, isn't it?"

Seriously, Gabby. Stop it. I get it.

Ilana greets Matt. "Hey, you made it. Want something to drink?"

"Sure," he says, distracted by Gabby fanning herself with her own top. *Fuuuck.*

Aaron catches my eye, then Ilana's, and walks quickly over to Matt with a drink in his hand. "Hey man, I've been meaning to ask you about that new project you're working on. Come tell me about it." He ushers him over to a couch on the other side of the room.

Aaron Feinman is playing wing-man for me … for his sister. I never thought I'd see the day.

My eyes flick back to Gabby as she leans in to say something to Ilana. Ilana whispers, "Down the hall, third door on the right. Whatever you want." Gabby walks down the hall, and after a moment, I follow her.

Gabby

I head to Ilana's bedroom to change out of my hot blouse. The pre-party glass of wine I had to calm my nerves is taking effect—not the one I intended—and I'm feeling way too warm with Ben's eyes on me and talking to Matt.

I'm rifling through the tops in Ilana's closet when I hear the door open behind me.

"Gabriella?"

"Benjamin," I reply sternly, turning around. "What are you doing in here?"

"I came to talk to you."

"Well, as you can see," I say, gesturing at my bare torso, covered only by my red lace bra, "I'm busy."

His eyes track down, and his mouth parts. He closes his eyes and turns away. "Sorry. Get dressed."

"I don't need your permission," I spit out, turning back to the closet. I yank a lighter-weight top from a hanger and pull the shirt down over my head.

I turn back around, noticing only then that it's partially see-through. *Shit.*

I cross my arms over my chest. "What do you want?" I ask at the same time he asks, "Are you dating that guy?"

I scoff. "None of your business."

His jaw clenches. "Why can't we just have a normal conversation?"

"You want a normal conversation?" I ask. The sheer gall of him to act as if everything is fine. This whole week, he's been hounding me to talk to him, but I don't *want* to talk to him. I thought I'd forgiven him, but the frustration bubbling out of me right now is indication enough that I haven't. I'm not sure if I ever will.

"Yes, I do," he says. "I want a normal conversation."

I stalk toward him, fists balled up, see-through shirt be damned. "Here's your normal conversation, you JFB—"

"JFB?"

"Jewish Fuckboy," I spit out. His mouth drops open, and I launch into my tirade. "You've come back. You're acting nice like you did last year, and you're hanging around, trying to get on everyone's good side. Why? So you can get on my good side again? I told you already. We hooked up, and it was a mistake. I don't know what you want from me."

"I—" he starts to stay.

"I am trying to be a strong, adult woman, who knows what she wants and doesn't live in the past, but when you are around, it drags me back to memories, to better times, and—"

"Gabby—"

"No." I take a deep breath. "I. Loved. You. I have loved you, in one form or another, since I was a teenager, and last year, we spent the summer together. We got closer, you became even more special to me than you were before, and then you left. You just … left."

A tear slips out, but I don't wipe it away. My arms are locked at my sides. He closes the distance between us and reaches out his hand, but I swat him away.

He opens his mouth and starts to say something, but I blurt out, "I don't want you to talk."

"Well, I'm going to," he says in a defiant tone. "I am a total shit for so many things. For taking you for granted. For leaving. And maybe even for coming back into your life now. Is that what you want to hear?"

I shake my head and then nod. It's a good—confusing—question I don't know the answer to. If he tells me how sorry he is, how much of an idiot he's been, will it make me feel any better? Or would I rather not talk about it, bury it deep down with the feelings I thought I'd worked through, but I'm now discovering might be hiding somewhere inside?

"I'm so, so sorry." He reaches out now and pulls my stiff body into a hug. "If I could take it back, I would."

The tension in my body rushes out of me, and I relax into his arms.

"What would you take back?" I ask between tears.

"Where do I even start?" he whispers.

Someone knocks on the bedroom door. "Gabs, everything okay?" Ilana asks through the door. "We're gonna light candles soon."

"Fucking Hanukkah," I say, feeling completely deflated. But then I look up at him, and his expression—a mix of amusement and familiarity with my, well, sometimes dramatic antics—takes the edge off. *How does he do that? Build me up and destroy me all at once?*

I call to Ilana in as normal a voice as I can muster, "I'll be out in a second, okay?"

She pads back down the hall, and he touches my face softly, guiding my eyes to his, then swipes his thumbs gently across my cheeks to wipe away my tears. "You look so sad, but also beautiful. How do you do that?"

I shrug. "I guess I'm complex."

"That you are," he agrees. "Do you need a minute?"

I nod.

"G?"

When was the last time he called me that?

"B," I say, softly.

"We need to talk, like, really talk. I have a lot of things to say sorry for, and I've only just gotten started."

I sigh. I don't want to have the conversation, but we *need* to have the conversation.

"Later, okay? We will."

He opens the door but turns. "You should wear the blue one there... if you want?"

I turn and see the top he means. "Blue's your favorite color," I say simply.

"Especially on you," he says, meeting my eye, then closing the door.

I come out a few minutes later wearing Ilana's blue top. Ben takes note of my choice and smiles. I point at my top and then waggle my finger at him. Not *for you*, I mouth at him. He laughs, and I press my lips together to hide my own smile.

A few different *chanukkiot* with candles sit on the table, waiting to be lit. Aaron has taken on the master of ceremonies role and begins to recite the prayers. He lights the *shamash* and holds it out to Ilana to light the candles. They're a beautiful couple, so in sync with one another. I close my eyes for a second, sending up a small prayer for their wellbeing. Maybe we'll have a wedding in our family this year.

When I open my eyes, I notice Ben watching them as well with a huge smile on his face.

·❤ · ❤ · ❤ · ❤ · ❤·

After candle lighting, I hustle into the kitchen to help Ilana uncover all the food and begin serving everyone. When I finally take a plate of food and go in search of a seat, I find Ben having a conversation with my friend from work, Marissa.

Before I can head into a different room, Marissa calls me over. "Gabby, join us."

I sit, and Marissa grins at me. "I was just jogging Ben's memory that we met last year at 333," she says. "I mean, it was loud, so we didn't get to talk much. But it looked like you guys were having a great time."

"Yeah, last summer was … a good time," I say and take a sip of my drink.

"What have you been doing since?" Marissa asks Ben. "You live in the city?"

Ben looks at me, then answers her. "No, I've been in Israel working on my post-doc the last year."

"Wow. Are you planning on staying there?" Marissa asks.

"I don't know where I'll end up," he says, "but I've begun applying for positions closer to home."

Excuse me?

"I miss my family … and other people here. I have to think about where I really want to be in order to be happy for the long term. Work is important, but other things … the people you build your life with …" He glances at me. "That's much more important."

Ben's chest rises and falls, and he rests his eyes on me. After an awkward beat, he says that the post-doc has been hard—time-consuming but hugely interesting. "I've learned a lot over the last year about cancer research but also about myself. What I want. What I need."

He's coming back to the US soon? He's prioritizing his personal life over work?

I'm sure Marissa has begun to sense that he's no longer talking to her, but to me, and being an odd combination of pot-stirrer-slash-aspirational do-gooder, she pipes up, "Talk about bad timing. Gabby's actually considering—"

I touch her arm, and she stops, looking at me curiously.

I stand abruptly. "I need to excuse myself for a minute. You two enjoy."

Ben's mouth opens, but when he turns back around, I meet Marissa's eyes and shake my head emphatically. I hear her change the subject as I walk off.

I walk into the living room and find a seat next to Matt on the couch.

"I was wondering where you went," he says. "I was telling your brother about my work." *Still?*

"Yeah, what exactly is a hedge fund anyways?" I joke. I lean back into the couch and drink down the rest of my wine.

"Oh, we pool investors' money, and we try to get big returns. I had no idea you were interested in hedge funds."

"Well, I used to love *Sonic the Hedgehog.*"

"What?" he says, smiling and laughing awkwardly.

It was just a dumb joke, dude.

Ben

I'm making my way over to sit near Gabby when I hear her tell Matt a corny joke. He completely misses her intention—to make him laugh, or maybe to get him to stop droning on about *his* work and show some interest in hers—and fumbles the play. She gets embarrassed. Her finger taps the empty wine glass she's holding, and I can see the thought bubble above her head: *I'm gonna need more Cab Sav for this conversation.*

I pour a new glass of wine and observe them like an anthropologist examining the mating rituals of chimpanzees. *Man, this guy really doesn't understand smart girls, does he?*

With a slightly frozen smile, he turns, awkwardly, back to Aaron to continue their conversation.

I slide in next to Gabby, offer her the glass of wine, and whisper in her ear, "Sonic sucks. Zelda's where it's at."

Her stiff posture loosens, and she smiles at me. "You were never very good at Zelda, though. You need nimble fingers."

"I'm good at other things with my fingers," I say, pausing for effect, "so it doesn't matter."

She snorts loudly. *Is she drunk?* That *would* explain her bad joke from before.

"May I?" I ask, gesturing at the wine glass in her hand.

Her brow furrows, she offers me the glass, and I take a huge swig, drinking more than half of it in a large gulp.

"Hey," she says. "Didn't you just give *me* that?"

"I did, but then I remembered you get a wine headache when you have too much."

"You're right. I do. Life is so unfair." Her fake-sad eyes lock on mine, and she sticks out her bottom lip. *God, she's adorable.*

"Do you want water instead?" I ask, grabbing a water bottle from the coffee table in front of us.

As I lean forward, I shoot Aaron a meaningful glance. Reading my mind, he invites Matt to see something in Ilana's dad's office. They get up, and I crack open the bottle for Gabby. She drinks half of it, and when she's done, a drip trickles down her chin. I wipe it with my thumb, and she smiles at me.

"Tell me about your trip," I say. "Did you paint while you were there?"

"Yeah," she replies dreamily.

"*What* did you paint?"

She sighs. "I painted my dreams."

"That's beautiful. I thought you were a visual artist, not a poet."

"Sometimes you're so inspired—or so destroyed—you have to resort to more than one medium."

I nod. "I know it's hard for you to be around me, but could we go for a coffee or something after this?"

"Hot cocoa?" she suggests.

I sniff out. "No whipped cream or marshmallows?"

"Sounds perfect," she whispers.

I stand but then lean back down. "I think you were at Musée Marmottan Monet ... the museum in Paris you mentioned before. I went there once with my mom."

"You're right," she says with a smile. "That was it."

Eventually, the crowd dwindles to only me, Gabby, Aaron, and Ilana. I guess both Matt and Gabby discovered that their initial attraction to one another was not supported by any actual shared interests.

Aaron has his arm around me and keeps squeezing my shoulder. "You bulked up the last year," he says.

I narrow my eyes at him. "Are you okay?"

"No," he whispers. "Every time I offered that guy Matt a drink, I had one myself. I should've stopped two drinks ago."

Ilana rolls her eyes at me.

"I guess that means I don't have a ride home?" I say.

"Slumber party?" Ilana suggests.

I'm not sure what I'm going to do, but I'm sure as hell not staying here listening to Feinman have sex with his girlfriend in the next room. There are some things a best friend does not need to know, or at least, to experience firsthand.

Gabby returns from the bathroom and pulls Ilana into a hug. "Thank you for a lovely party. As soon as I find my phone, I'm ordering an Uber and getting out of here."

Time for action.

"I could take you home. I'll take Aaron's car, drop you at your place, and then drive home."

Gabby shrugs. "Okay, thanks, Benji."

Aaron has removed his hands from my body and is grabbing Ilana from behind to dance with her. He kisses her neck and slides his hands down to her ass.

"Aaron, God," Gabby groans. "Cut it out. Wait until we leave."

"Seriously," I say. "Restrain yourself for another ninety seconds while I get Gabby's boots on."

"My boots are off?" she asks.

Ilana and I exchange looks and laugh.

"What did they drink tonight?" she asks.

I shrug.

Ilana wrestles herself away from Aaron and tells him to go get ready for bed and she'll join him soon. She orders Gabby to sit and works one boot onto Gabby's foot, while I do the other.

While we're both kneeling down, she says to me, "You're gonna take care of her?"

"Of course I will. Don't worry."

"Text me when you're *leaving* her place," she says.

I raise my eyebrow. "Give me some credit."

"I'll give it to you when you earn it."

Touché.

Gabby

We spend most of the drive to my place singing songs from our teenage years. It's dangerously nostalgic for my current state of mind, but I'm allowing myself just one more walk down memory lane before Ben leaves and I won't see him again for … well, as usual, I don't know when I'll see him again.

The minute I walk in the door to my place, I collapse on my couch and yank my boots off. Ben sits down next to me, and I whisper in his ear, "Remember what we did on this couch?"

He looks at me intently. His gaze shifts down to my lips, then he swallows. "It would take me a lifetime to forget what we did on this couch."

I sigh. "That's my problem, too. I can't forget."

He opens his mouth to say something, but I blurt out, "You broke my heart." His face falls, and a tear slips down my cheek. "You broke it, and I don't know if I'll ever find someone who loves me." I cover my mouth. *No. Shit. I did not want to say all this to him.*

"Don't stop talking," he says. He touches my fingers, pulling my hand from my mouth. "Tell me … how you were feeling. Tell me how you *are* feeling. We need a clean slate."

And so I do, but what results is less a clean slate and more a battlefield strewn with casualties—a true, yet sometimes brutal recounting of the last decade of our lives. The countless number of times my feelings for him have been rekindled only for me to have to tamp them down again.

"You left," I say, "just when I felt like we were on the cusp of something real. But then I realized you must not have felt the same way I did. You made the decision to leave the country in less than a day. You didn't even ask me if I wanted to try something—something long-distance, something ... anything ..." I sigh and look down.

"I didn't know you felt the same way as me," he says in a ragged voice. "You never told me. You never told ... *anyone* we were together."

He's right.

I take a deep breath. I want to go to bed.

"I'm sorry," he says for the twentieth time. *Should I apologize, too?*

But I simply shake my head. "I'll be fine. Don't worry." I stand, and he joins me.

"The slate," I say, smiling sadly at him, "is now clean."

He looks down at me, not saying much. Most of the conversation was just me rambling.

"I need to get ready for bed."

"Can I stay for a few minutes?" he asks.

I nod. When I finish brushing my teeth and washing my face, I change into a t-shirt and pajama pants in my bedroom. I come out to find him folding up a blanket and putting a few of my belongings in their place.

He glances at me. "New shirt?"

It's a *very* pink t-shirt of a guinea pig in a convertible with the phrase, *The horrors persist, but so do I.*

"My Hanukkah present from Ilana last year," I say. "She thought it would encourage me."

"It's cute," he says.

"You sure you're okay to drive?" I ask.

"Yeah, but would you ... want me to tuck you in?"

"What?" I ask and a resistant smile sneaks its way onto my face.

He walks with me to the bedroom. "Get under the covers. Lie down."

I raise an eyebrow.

"I was thinking about you being sad last year—after we talked now—and I want to spend a few more minutes with you now before I go. Time that's not us talking about all the bad stuff."

I slip under the blankets—deep down wishing he was under them with me—and he sits down next to me on the bed and caresses my hair.

"Do you want a lullaby or a bedtime story?" he asks.

I snicker. "You know I like stories."

He starts by telling me funny little stories about things that have happened to him over the last year living in Israel. The time he visited the Western Wall and wheeled an old man in a wheelchair up to the wall because his daughter couldn't enter the men's section. The night he ran into a wild boar while walking back from a bar to a friend's place on the Carmel Mountain. The three-hour traffic jam he and his roommate got stuck in, which they survived by drinking wine and eating chocolate in the backseat of their friend's car. Listening to his stories, I get a sense of Israel and what he did while he was there, his daily life, the challenges, and the high points.

"Why didn't you tell me you were in a bomb shelter when you texted me last week?" I ask, realizing after I've uttered the words that I've already asked him.

"I told you," he answers, rubbing my back, then pulling the blanket up over my shoulder again. "I didn't want you to worry about me."

"I've worried about you every single day since you moved there," I admit.

I close my eyes so I won't have to interpret the look in his, and he tucks some hair behind my ear.

"Tell me another story, B," I whisper. "Just one more before you go.

Ben

"How about this?" I ask. "One Shabbat, a friend of mine invited me to stay in Jerusalem. The vibe was more religious than I'm used to, but I thought I'd give it a try. We went to one of those Carlebach *shuls*. Where it doesn't even matter if you know the words—"

"But I bet you did know the words," she interjects, opening her eyes and smiling sleepily.

"I knew most of the words, but I sang 'nai, nai, nai' anyway. It's what you do in that type of place."

I wait for her to make a comment or ask a question, but she just looks at me with heavy-lidded eyes. What I wouldn't give for her to ask me to lie down next to her, to hold her in my arms. But she doesn't, so I do my best to hold her in my words.

"We were staying with a family my friend knew, and we went back to their place for Friday night dinner. There were fifteen, maybe twenty, people there, and I ended up next to a guy who was an interesting combination of hippie and rabbi."

"Like my uncle Aryeh?" she asks, smiling.

"Come to think of it, maybe it was him," I joke. I reach out, unable to stop myself, and trace my pointer finger over her jawline, realizing a second too late it's something I used to do the summer we spent together. She leans into my hand. Her eyes are closed, but I don't know if she's fallen asleep or is simply resting.

"We had dinner, and between each course, someone would share a Jewish teaching. After the main course, this Uncle Aryeh-lookalike shared a story from the Zohar, and he put me on the spot. Asked why such a good-looking, smart young man like me was there without a wife."

I wait to see if she'll say anything, and she doesn't. Maybe she *has* fallen asleep. I lower my voice for the rest of my story.

"I shied away from answering him, but later that night, he told me not to worry. He said that Jewish mystical texts teach that a husband and wife are one soul, and they're only separated when they descend into this world. When they're married, they're reunited and become one again."

Telling Gabby the story now, I don't mention how, when he said that to me, I felt a little shaky.

"I asked him, 'So why haven't I gotten together with my soulmate yet?' And he told me that only when they're both righteous, ready, do they gain the privilege to meet and become one again with their true match."

Gabby's breathing slows and I lean in to kiss her softly on her temple. *I need you. I'm ready.* But I can't say the words. *What if I hurt her again?*

"Did you kiss me?" she asks in a sleepy voice.

"Yeah, I'm sorry," I whisper.

"It's okay."

"Can you ever forgive me?" I ask. "For all the times I—"

"I have," she whispers. "You can go back to your new life now."

My heart drops into my stomach. *I only want a life with you.*

I sit there for a few more minutes, unable to tear myself away from watching her. She's so close, but so far away from me.

You are the other part of me, I tell her in my head. Will I ever have the chance, the courage, to tell her for real?

I turn off the bedside lamp, then place one last kiss on her soft, sweet-smelling hair. *Good night, my love.*

It's past one in the morning when I get to my dad's, but he comes outside to meet me and pulls me into a hug. I'm an inch or two taller than he is, but I relish the embrace. I didn't get quite enough of these growing up.

"I'm glad you called," he says, guiding me inside. "You hungry?"

"You made food?"

"I can make you a sandwich," he says, chuckling.

That sounds right.

We head inside and make a couple of pastrami sandwiches. I'm not actually hungry, but it seems important to him that he be able to offer me something.

He drinks a cup of coffee while I eat, and after some pleasantries and questions about how my visit has been so far, he leans back in his chair. "Did I tell you I've been going to therapy the last few years?"

"Really?" I ask.

"I know. I was shocked at myself, too. After everything fell apart with your mom, it took me a while, but I had to try to figure it out. I spent at least a couple of years thinking about it and couldn't make sense of it. Well, that's not entirely true. I knew it was mostly *my* fault, but I couldn't handle feeling that every day either. All the guilt. All the regret."

"And how do you feel now?" I ask.

"Well, I still feel guilty. I put you kids—mainly you—through a lot. But

I'm also learning some forgiveness for myself, and I'm trying to be a better person. I've apologized to your mom."

"You did?" I ask.

"It was during the time you were away at Cornell. We met for coffee, and we sat there for three hours while I apologized to her. She had some apologies, too, but she didn't need to. It's a shame I didn't figure things out earlier and see a therapist—with your mom, by myself—that could've helped. But fear is a strong emotion. It can limit us from doing what's best. Fear of rejection. Fear of failing."

"Fear of disappointing you pushed me down a pretty successful path," I blurt out.

He winces, then presses his lips together. "I haven't told you enough, but I'm so damn proud of you. And your sisters. But I wish I could have done a better job of inspiring you through love and not ... not from a negative place."

I sigh. I wish that, too. "I know you did your best."

It's true. I know how hard I'm trying to make things right with Gabby after a lot of avoidable mistakes. Sometimes, you do your best within your specific emotional limitations.

He looks down and gives me a curt nod. "So you were at Gabby's tonight?"

"Yeah."

I hear footsteps on the stairs and a pajama-clad Miri comes into the kitchen. "I didn't know you were coming over tonight."

"I didn't know I was either, but, uh ..."

"Ben was looking for some relationship advice, and he thought he'd come to the master."

Miri snorts, and I follow suit.

"So you still haven't told her?" Miri asks. "Aren't you leaving tomorrow?"

I nod.

"What are you waiting for?" she asks.

I shake my head. "She is ... tough and ..."

"She's smart, is what she is," Miri says, sitting down and grabbing the uneaten half of my sandwich. "And you are a scared little boy—"

"Hey," I say.

"But you're fucking lovable, man."

I roll my eyes at her.

"And you really love her, don't you?" she asks.

I meet her eyes. "I really love her."

My dad takes a sip of his coffee and looks at me carefully. "Why haven't you been able to tell her?"

"Miri's right. I've been scared. It's not just about me, though. I don't want to put her in a bad place. I also don't want to hurt her again."

"So don't," he says.

"Don't tell her?"

"No, don't hurt her. Ever again. Be there for her now and in the future—if she'll have you. Make a promise and keep it," he says, surprising maybe even himself with his passionate words. "Benjamin, don't make the same mistake I did. Because what I had with your mother, with our family, I'd give anything to have it back."

Miri and I exchange a look.

"I've messed up so much with Gabby," I say. "I don't even know if she has it in her to give me another chance."

"You were always a kind, generous kid, who wanted to do his own personal best and help others. And you're no different now. You've also always been brave and not afraid of a challenge."

"That's what you think about me?" I ask.

"That's what I *know* about you," he says, grabbing my hand and squeezing it.

Miri stands and smiles. "Me, too, Baby Bro," she says, calling me the nickname I always hated. I stand, too, and tower over her, smiling at her smugly.

"You think you intimidate me?" she says. "I work in a New Jersey ER, buddy. Nothing intimidates me anymore."

My dad smiles proudly.

"You have to talk to her before you go back to Israel," she says, "Doctor's orders."

"Two doctors' orders," my dad agrees.

I snicker.

They're right. Time is running out.

One Match is All You Need

Gabby

I woke up this morning feeling strangely rested, especially considering I drank too much wine last night. I look at my nightstand and see the glass of water Ben brought when he tucked me in. *God, when was the last time someone tucked me in?*

Physically, I'm okay, but my heart feels hungover. An overindulgence in Ben time this week, and then it'll be back to nothing. So maybe not a hangover, but a sort of prophetic withdrawal. It's a visceral reminder that what the heart wants and what it *needs* can be two very different things.

I drag myself out of bed and head into the kitchen for coffee. *Sufganiyot?* There is a box of Hanukkah jelly doughnuts, leftovers from the party last night, sitting on the kitchen counter. I vaguely remember walking up all the stairs, one of Ben's hands on my back to make sure I made it up, the other balancing the box. Despite the oil spots showing clearly on the white cardboard box, I decide hot coffee and a somewhat stale *sufganiyah* are just what the doctor ordered for me this morning as I nurse my tender heart.

After my highly nutritious breakfast, I figure I can either wallow in memories, contemplating what could have been, or commit—actually commit—to moving forward. Buying some healthy groceries for the week to balance out the twenty thousand calories of fried Jewish holiday foods I've eaten this week seems like a good start to my first-ever post-Hanukkah resolutions, so I head out. While I'm at the supermarket, Ilana texts me.

Ilana

> Soul Cycle or yoga today?

I groan, but I know she's right. We have a semi-regular habit of exercising on Sundays to start the week off right.

Me

> Yoga, I guess.

Ilana

> 2pm at Brooklyn Flow?

Me

> See you then.

I stop at home to grab my yoga mat. I'll need to hurry since it's already 1:20. When I arrive at the yoga studio, Ilana tells me that Aaron is still nursing a hangover from last night.

I grimace. "Well, I drank some coconut water this morning. I heard it's supposed to help."

"Guess we'll find out soon, won't we?" she says, laughing and pulling me inside the studio. As we set up our mats, she asks me if I had a good time last night.

"You know," I say, sitting on my mat and beginning to stretch my tight muscles. "I think I'm okay. Seeing Ben this week set me back, but being in Paris and working things out with him last night was good."

"You worked things out?" she asks, and I note the surprise in her voice. "What do you mean?"

"We talked after he took me home, and ... There's still a small part of me that will always love him, but ..." She looks at me intently, and I pause and glance away. It's more than a small part, but I'm chipping away at that big part that used to be my whole heart. I steel myself and look back at her with a fake-confident smile. "Maybe we could have been together in some alternate universe or something. Our personalities—our history—they would have been great together, but our paths diverged."

She nods. Is that sadness or something else—simple understanding—in her expression?

The yoga teacher comes in and welcomes us all. "Namaste. I'd like for you to think of an intention for your practice. You can keep it to yourself. But I'll share with you, so those of you who may be new have an example. Today, my intention is courage of the heart. I must face something difficult this week that requires a little extra bravery, and therefore, that will be my focus."

Courage. There are so many intentions I could choose: forgiveness, acceptance, recovery, self-love. Courage, though, hits me in my core. As I sit in lotus position and breathe deeply, in and out, thinking about what energy I need to bring into this week, into the rest of my life, courage sounds perfect.

The yoga class isn't the hardest one I've done, but I find myself simultaneously exhausted and energized by the end as if I've done not only a physical workout but a mental and emotional one, too.

"Did you bring extra clothes, like I suggested?" Ilana asks as we roll up our mats.

"You wanted to shower here?"

"Let's go out for a late lunch," she suggests.

"Sure," I say. We both shower and change. It's pretty cold outside, so I use the hair dryer at the studio.

"You look beautiful," Ilana says as I walk out to the lobby, where she's sitting serenely on a modern gray couch. "You like that place Miriam?"

"Sure," I say. "I need to eat a salad or something after this week."

She laughs. "You and me both."

We leave the studio and walk a few blocks to the restaurant.

"So what did you concentrate on today during the practice?" she asks.

"I went with courage, like the teacher."

She smiles brightly. "Sometimes a little courage is all you need."

I arch an eyebrow at her.

She glances over my shoulder, and I turn my head to see someone who looks an awful lot like Ben smiling at me.

I swivel my head back toward Ilana. "What's going on?"

"Have courage, Gabby," she says and grabs me by the elbow to steer me in Miri's direction.

"Gabby, hey," Miri says.

"Hi, what are you doing here?" We're standing right outside the restaurant bearing, well, her name.

"Well, I live in New Jersey," she explains, "but I always go for lunch at—" She checks her watch. "3:46 on a Sunday afternoon in Brooklyn."

"So why'd you come for lunch in Brooklyn *this* Sunday afternoon?"

I take her in. She looks great with her short haircut and bright smile. *She has the same smile as Ben.*

"I thought we should talk," Miri says.

My eyes dart between Miri and Ilana, who looks quite pleased with herself. *It's a setup.* Goosebumps pebble on my skin as I follow them into the restaurant.

We get a table, and Miri doesn't even wait for our drink order to arrive before jumping in.

She leans back in her chair and rubs her lips across her teeth. Amusement dances in her eyes. "I've heard you're very accomplished at work at a relatively young age which makes me think you're the type of woman who doesn't wait for life to happen *to* you."

I fold and unfold my napkin, waiting for her to complete her obviously unfinished thought, then glance at Ilana who has barely made a peep since we ran into Miri on the sidewalk.

Miri meets my eyes. "I'd bet money that you're the type who makes things happen the way *you* want them to."

Maybe I am.

The server arrives at our table with our drinks and asks if we're ready to order. I haven't even looked at the menu, but Ilana orders a Jerusalem Breakfast for me and granola for herself.

"You want anything?" she asks Miri.

Miri shakes her head and jumps into the reason she's here.

"He's leaving today," she says simply. "Have you two … talked?"

I half-nod, half-shrug. "Kind of, but maybe I haven't told him … everything. I have to protect myself."

Miri reaches out and squeezes my hand. "It's hard putting yourself out there. And he's clueless and scared. But trust me, he's fucking lovable, and he is *worth it.*"

I know he is, but my heart still hasn't healed from the last time.

I blink my eyes quickly, trying not to cry.

"Don't cry, Gorgeous Gabby."

I sniffle but smile at her, then gather up the courage to share something that has always perplexed me about Ben. "He's got all these people who love him. He's so good with every woman in his life. His mom, you, Ariella, every freaking *bubbe* he meets. How is he such an open, kind person to all of you but he breaks *my* heart?"

"Isn't it obvious?" Ilana asks, breaking her silence. "You matter more than any of those other women, and for you, he has to make himself vulnerable. He's scared as hell."

I look at Ilana, then to Miri for confirmation. She nods. "I think he's ready."

"How do I know he's ready, though?"

"Why the hell do you think he flew halfway across the globe? To have sex in your parents' bathroom?" Miri asks, laughing.

"We did not have sex," I say before I can catch myself.

"That's not what we heard," she says, a smug smile on her face. "From my mom, your mom, your brother, my sister—"

"Stop," I say, wanting to crawl under the table.

Ilana starts to giggle, unable to hold it in.

Miri starts again. "My point—"

"Yes, get to it," I plead.

"Is that he loves you, and he's finally grown up."

Miri glances at her watch. "Double G, you don't have a lot of time."

She's right. Ben and I have wasted so much of it.

I stand and grab my bag, psyching myself up. *I can do this. I will do this.* I stride quickly toward the exit before stopping in my tracks and turning back.

Ilana locks eyes with me. *Courage,* she mouths.

"You got this," Miri calls out. "He's yours … *if* you'll have him."

If I'll have him. First, I have to find him.

·❤·❤·❤·❤·❤·

I make my way back to my apartment as quickly as I can with a gym bag on my shoulder. It's gotten colder and the jeans and thick sweater I brought for after our yoga class are doing nothing to save me from the bitterly cold breeze.

I make it up the stairs to my place, unlock my door, and dump my bag inside. *Phone. Where's my phone?*

I've made seven calls since I left the restaurant and only one of them has been answered.

I tear through my gym bag until I find my phone in the side pocket, where I must have stuffed it the last time my call went to voicemail. Just as I'm about to unlock my phone, there's a knock on my door. I look through the peephole. *Evelyn Friedberg?*

I open the door, frazzled. "Hi, how are you?"

"I need your help with something, dear. If you don't mind."

"Is it urgent?" I ask. "I have something important to do right now."

"It is. The electricity in my apartment is off. Is yours?"

I flip the switch next to the door up and down. "Working fine. Um, why don't you stay in my place and we'll figure it out when I get back? Or I'll call the superintendent, and he can work it out for you? I *really* have to go."

"I'm sorry to inconvenience you, Gabby dear, but I'm a little under the weather. I'd love to make some tea and rest in my own home."

Oh, geez.

"Okay, of course. I'll be right there. I just need to make a quick call, okay?"

She shuffles back to her apartment and goes in.

I call one more time. *Fuck. Voicemail again.*

I call Ben's mom, but she doesn't answer. I call my mom. She, too, doesn't answer. Then I think that maybe Aaron can help. At this point, I'm unsurprised that his phone, too, goes to voicemail.

As a last-ditch effort, I send a misspelled text to Ben. There just isn't time. He's getting on a plane to fly to the other side of the world.

> Bean, I dont know y ur not answering ur fone, but please call meat b4 you leave. I need 2 talk 2 u.

Shit. That won't do. Breathe, Gabby.

> Benji, I've left a few things unsaid, and I need to speak to you ASAP.

> Please call me and tell me where you are.

I quickly text Ilana.

> Send me Miri's number. I need to find out Ben's flight details. I'm going to Newark Intl to find him.

I glance at the time. I've kept Mrs. Friedberg waiting for seven minutes and go to knock on her door.

"Just a moment. I'm coming." Then I hear footsteps. But they don't sound like the shuffled footsteps of an old woman. They sound like—

"Ben?" I gasp, as he opens her door.

"I was thinking of going by 'Bean' now."

A half-exhale, half-burst of laughter escapes my mouth, and I put my hand on the door frame to steady myself. He looks at me, concern on his face. "Okay, okay. Call me 'Ben' if you must."

I look at him with watery eyes.

"Would you like some tea?" he asks, gesturing toward the table, where Mrs. Friedberg is comfortably seated before two teacups and... of course, a bouquet of flowers.

I step inside. "No, thank you, *Bean.* I don't need any tea right now." I walk toward Mrs. Friedberg. "So I guess this means your electricity is back on?"

"Oh, yes, dear. On my way out of your place, I saw Benjamin here and asked if he could help. And he even brought me flowers."

I turn to look at him. "Of course he did."

"*Maideleh*," Ben says to her, "if it's okay with you, I need to speak with Gabby. I was planning to see her ... after I delivered your flowers."

"Of course. In fact, maybe Gabby should keep the flowers. They're beautiful, and she needs some beauty in her young life."

I sniff out. I lean down to kiss her cheek. "You keep them, Evelyn." I wink at her, and she smiles back.

Ben and I leave Mrs. Friedberg's apartment, and the moment the door closes, I turn on him. "What are you doing here? You're gonna miss your flight."

He reaches up and cups my jaw. "For such a smart woman, you miss a lot sometimes."

"What's that supposed to mean?" I ask.

"It means, I'm not getting on any flight today."

"Why not?"

"Should we do this in the hallway, or do you think we can go inside?" he asks, amused.

"Of course." I unlock the door, and we step inside. *What is going on? He's not leaving? Why is he here?*

Then it hits me. *He's here for me. He's. Here. For. Me.*

"You're here for me?" I manage to utter.

He smiles and puts his pointer finger on my nose.

"I've also left a few things unsaid." He pulls me by the hand to sit on my couch, then turns toward me. "Gabby."

"Ben."

He smiles. It's a smile that I've known—and loved—for a long time. The sweetest smile in the world because it belongs to him.

He takes a shaky breath. I've *never* seen him this nervous. "I ..." He glances away, then looks around the room. "Wait, you haven't lit the candles yet?"

I shake my head. "I was … I was in a rush. I was on my way to …"

He raises an eyebrow.

"To find you."

"Really?" he asks.

I nod, and the corner of his mouth curls up the slightest.

"Should we light them together?" he asks.

I stand, take his hand, and guide him to my bedroom, where I usually set them up to face the street.

He places the candles, one by one, in the silver *chanukiah* my grandma gave me for my bat mitzvah, then looks at me, waiting. I strike a match to light the *shamash* and start the first blessing, and he joins in. After lighting the first four candles, I hand him the *shamash* to light the last four.

When he has arranged the *shamash* in its holder, we both take in the beauty of a fully lit, last-night-of-Hanukkah *chanukiah*. Then, he grabs both of my hands in his. "Why do you celebrate Hanukkah, G?"

I scrunch my brow at him. *Really?*

But he's not deterred. "Tell me."

"Fine," I say. "Because the oil lasted eight days, and against all odds, the tiny band of Maccabees defeated the powerful Greek army."

"You definitely went to Jewish day school," he says and snickers. "So, in short, miracles?"

I nod. "People kept their faith, and things that didn't seem possible suddenly became … possible."

He squeezes my hands, and warmth spreads throughout my body. I look at the flames of the candles in the menorah next to us, then turn and meet his eyes.

"*You* are my miracle, Gabby. The fact that I found you so early in life—a warm-hearted, intelligent person who reached out to me when I needed it, who continues to give me chances even when I don't deserve them."

"I—" *I don't know what to say.* I want to believe in miracles. I want to believe in the possibility of us. Despite all the positive feelings my heart is stirring up being close to him now, though, my mind is at work here tonight, too. It hasn't so easily forgotten the bad times.

"I love you, Gabriella."

I stop breathing for a second. I'm sure of it.

"Ben—"

"My heart has been breaking the last year not being with you. Our summer together was the best few months of my life, and I ... left you. You are a smart, kind, hot-as-hell woman, and I walked away from you for no good reason."

He caresses my jaw and looks straight into my eyes, but I close them. It's too intense, being this close to him—hearing him say these words.

"I'm still here," he says softly. *But am I?* My soul might have left my body for a second.

I open my eyes. "I've cared about you for a long time, too. I even loved you—last year, when you left, I was *in love* with you—"

"You never told me," he whispers. "If you'd told me, or if I'd told you, things could have been so different now."

He squeezes my hand and turns it over in his, palm up, and traces the lines of my hand with his thumb.

"But they're not," I reply. "You made your decision, and we've both lived our lives in the meantime. We can't turn back time."

"But *we* determine how things will be going forward. Gabriella ..." *God, I love the sound of my name on his lips.* "You bring light to my life. You bring me happiness and warmth, and it can probably be considered a Hanukkah miracle you haven't dropped my sorry ass and kicked me out of your life altogether."

"Well," I say, sitting down on my bed and looking up at him. "You're fucking lovable."

He gives me a strange look.

Uh, oh.

"Did you ...?"

He knows.

"I had lunch with Miri today," I admit. *Well, something like that.*

"You did?" He sits next to me on the bed.

"I was coming out of yoga class with Ilana, and we bumped into her."

"Bumped into her? What was she doing in Brooklyn?"

"She and Ilana fancy themselves matchmakers, apparently, and I guess she felt it was time to, uh, drop some knowledge on me."

He cocks his head.

"She said you've loved me since we were kids."

He smiles.

"She also said you can be a bit clueless ... and scared."

"She told you I'm clueless and scared?" he asks through a laugh.

"Yeah, but she also said, and I quote, 'fucking lovable.'"

He looks at me, a question in his eyes.

"I agree. You are. You always have been. It was easy to develop a crush on you as a teenager, and it was ..." I start to cry. "It was too easy to fall in love with you later."

He pulls me into a hug. "I've hurt you so much, and you're the last person in the world I want to hurt."

"Because you love me," I say. Saying it out loud sends a shiver through my body.

He nods. "Because I love you."

"But ... are you ready?" I ask. "Like the story you told me last night?"

"You were awake?" he asks, surprised.

"I don't remember being awake, but then this morning, I knew this story, and I realized you must've told me. You did, right?"

"I did, and I'm—" He blinks his eyes fast. "I'm so ready," he utters in a voice filled with emotion.

I touch his face. "Neither of us was honest enough about our feelings last year. I'd like to give it—us—another chance. Like, a real chance?"

He nods.

"It'll take a lot of planning and thinking and logistics," I say, "but you said you've started applying for positions in the US?"

He nods eagerly.

"And ... well, I have an opportunity, too. With the Zurich team."

His face falls. "Zurich?"

"I caught the director there today—between trying to find you and calling every person we know ..."

His eyebrows raise.

"And, well, he said I can work in any company location in a similar time zone."

Understanding dawns on his face. "Like Tel Aviv?"

I nod. "Like Tel Aviv. I'd like for us to try … to be together, for real. To be boyfriend and girlfriend." I swallow and feel my heart in my throat. *Say something. Now. Before I faint or cry.*

"G, I'm not asking you to be my girlfriend."

Oh no, oh—

"I'm asking you to be my everything."

Everything?

He reaches into his back pocket and pulls out a folded piece of notebook paper. As he unfolds it, I realize it's the picture I sketched for him on our trip to Point Pleasant. Before I can even express amazement that he kept it, I notice what was wrapped up inside. It's a ring. *Oh my God. It's a mother-bleeping wedding ring.*

He places it in my hand and closes my fist around it.

My mouth drops open and goosebumps pop up on my skin. "Are you serious?"

"Don't freak out," he says in a reassuring voice. "Just give me sixty, maybe ninety seconds to say something?"

Can a person die from not breathing for ninety seconds?

"Do you remember that the first time we met you called me Benji?" he asks.

"When I was … nine?"

"How old are you now?" he asks.

"Twenty-six," I say.

"So it's been seventeen years. Can you find it in your heart to give me another seventeen? Another *seventy* to make it all up to you?"

He reaches out and puts his palm over my heart. I do the same to him with my free hand, and I feel his heart pounding beneath my hand.

"Maybe you need some time to get used to me again," he says. "Or to be comfortable with the idea, so consider this ring an offer, a promise, that when—if—you want to accept it, I'm all in. For you, for us. I will *never* break your heart again."

Is this real? Is this really happening?

"I will cook for you, I will cherish you, and I will sex you up whenever you ask. I—"

"Can you stop talking for a second?" I manage to say.

He nods.

I open my fist and look carefully at the ring. It's simple, white gold, and inscribed inside is a message: *Ani l'dodi, v'dodi li* in Hebrew. *I am my beloved's, and my beloved is mine.*

"How long have you had this?" I say, trying but failing to hold my tears in.

"You won't believe me if I tell you."

I lock eyes with him and wait.

He takes a deep breath, then answers me. "Right after I went to Israel last year. I was in the Old City in Jerusalem in the Jewish quarter one night, and I came upon this jewelry store, and I ..." He stops, looks down, and pinches the bridge of his nose. "I was thinking about you, what you mean to me. I didn't know if I'd ever have the chance to give it to you."

He bites his lip and looks at me.

"'I am my beloved's and my beloved is mine.' *Are* you mine?" I ask, looking into his eyes which, if I'm not mistaken, look a little misty.

He pulls me into a tight hug and whispers in my ear, "If you want me."

I want you. I want you so much. But I'm terrified. I take a shaky breath.

He kisses me on the forehead. "I know you weren't expecting me to show up here and profess my love to you."

"You've had more than a year. What made you come back now?" I ask.

"Some people have to feel like the world might end in order to get their priorities straight. You gain a lot of clarity sitting in a bomb shelter listening to rockets fly over your head. Kinda makes you evaluate your life decisions."

I nod, tears falling freely down my cheeks. "The moment I found out I... I couldn't stop imagining the worst. What if something had happened to you?"

"But it didn't," he says.

"But it could have." I take a deep breath. "Something clicked in my mind, too, that day."

He wipes my tears with the edge of his sleeve. "I was sitting there, my roommate and our little old lady neighbor—"

Of course his story involves a grandmother. I smile, and he smiles back at me.

"Idit told me to think of something that makes me happy, and you're the first and only thing that came to mind. You're my happy place, G. I don't believe in God, not really. I've been in a lot of so-called holy places, the last year, but the holiest place I've ever been ..."

He glances away.

"What?"

"It's in your arms."

"That's ..." I start to say.

"Cheesy?" he asks, laughing softly.

"A little," I admit, "but it's also pretty powerful." I squeeze his hand. "So you just ... flew back? And came to a Hanukkah party at my parents' and hoped for the best?"

"It's naive, isn't it? To think that you'd give me one last chance?"

Do I tell him that he's had a free pass to my heart for a decade? But no, no—

"No," I say. "I mean, I need to think about this."

"Do you want like a week, a year, or a decade?"

I laugh. "Let's start with me taking a long bath."

"Am I invited?" he asks.

"I'm sure it would be a lot of fun," I say, "but I think I'll do this one solo."

"Solo, huh?" he asks, reaching down and rubbing my fingers.

I push him on his chest. "Get your mind out of the gutter, Adler."

"Impossible when you're around." He winks at me. "Should I stick around? Like, in case there are any follow-up questions? Or you need someone to help you wash your ..." His eyes glide down to my chest, then back up. "Hair?"

I snort. "Stay."

"Have you had dinner?" he asks.

"I was a tad busy planning how I'm going to get to Newark International in record time and begging my boss for a relocation to Tel Aviv."

"You were really going to come find me?" he asks.

"I was until a certain *maideleh's* electricity went out. We might've missed each other," I say, still in awe at the timing.

He lets out a ragged breath. "I'm tired of missing you, G."

I'm tired of missing you, too.

Ben

I knock on the bathroom door softly. "Gabby, the food is ready, whenever you are. No rush ... on anything."

"What did you make for dinner?" she calls softly.

"Your favorite," I call through the door.

"Borscht?"

"No, *shakshuka* cooked way too done, the way you like it. Since when do you like borscht?"

I hear her giggle. I open the door quickly, covering my eyes, and she shrieks. "Hey, I'm naked."

"That's why I'm covering my eyes."

"Why? You don't *want* to see me naked?" she says enticingly.

"There is literally nothing else in the world I'd rather see than your body naked, but I'm trying not to overstep my boundaries here."

"Says the guy who showed up a week ago unannounced and just proposed to me."

She has a point.

"Fine, overstep any more than I already have," I admit.

"Come sit next to me. I'm covered by bubbles anyways. You can open your eyes."

I open them a slit and see her head popping up above a thick layer of bubbles. I sit on the floor next to the tub and lean my head back against the wall.

She turns to me, the water sloshing. "Are you nervous?" She props her elbows on the edge of the high tub, and the top curve of her breast draws my attention.

My heart is beating so wildly it just might fly out of my chest. "You could say that."

"Do you trust me?" she asks.

"With my life," I say, without hesitation.

"And you love me?" she asks, smiling.

God, I want to kiss her so much.

"More than you know," I say.

"Close your eyes."

I close them and hear her stand up. I stand, too, to give her space to get out of the tub. It takes superhuman willpower not to peek, because my God, if there is anything better than a naked Gabby, it's a *wet* naked Gabby.

The towel brushes across my hands as she takes it from the floor near me. "You doing okay, there?" she asks in a husky voice.

I take in a shaky breath. "Me? I'm ... fine." I am decidedly *not* fine. The scent of her combined with the heat of her body close to but not touching me is about to send me over the edge, but I manage to choke out, "How are *you*? What are you doing?"

"Oh, just drying my hair before dinner." She turns around. I know because her hip bumps me and then her—*Oh, God, her naked ass is up against me.* I clench my eyes shut and ball my hands into fists.

"You still okay?" she teases.

"Totally fine." I back up, giving myself some space. "We should have dinner, right?"

"Yes, we have some things to talk about, and it feels a little imbalanced, you standing here dressed and me in my birthday suit."

"I could take my clothes off, too," I jokingly offer.

She turns and runs her hand down my chest, and I bite my bottom lip. "I'm afraid the things we do together naked would unfairly influence my decision."

I exhale audibly and stop her hand from going lower. "You're right. I'll go. You'll join me soon?"

"I will," she says, kissing me on the cheek.

"This is counter to every principle I have in life," I say, fumbling for the doorknob behind my back.

"What?"

"Leaving a beautiful naked woman behind," I answer as I slip out the door. I start to close it but then pop my head back in to peek.

"Ben!" she yells, and I wink at her before shutting the door again.

Gabby

As I sit eating Ben's delicious *shakshuka* and salad—*Man, I've missed his cooking*—I watch him watching *me*.

"What?" I ask, as I stab a cherry tomato and put it in my mouth.

"Nothing," he says, smiling. "I ... missed you. A lot."

I reach out and touch his hand. "Me, too. I'm glad you're here. I'm sorry that I made you feel otherwise. When you were here last summer, it felt *almost* perfect. That's why I didn't understand how you could leave, but at the same time, I knew you had a once-in-a-lifetime chance. I couldn't stop you."

He sets his fork down and looks at me intently. "I would've stayed ... for you. I would've figured out something else for work. I should've told you. If you had said anything to me—or if I had been brave enough to say something to you..." His breath catches in his throat.

"You did tell me," I say.

"What?" he asks.

"You told me—with your actions—when you were here. All this time, I thought you'd never said it, and you didn't, not with words, but you said it in so many other ways. And I suddenly realized today that you've ... always had a hard time asking for what you need."

He narrows his eyes at me as if he's not quite convinced.

"But I always held out my hand and helped or gave you what you needed," I say. "Maybe I should have done that last year?"

He shakes his head empathically. "No. At some point, a man just has to tell the woman he loves that he ... loves her, that he's willing to put her before anything else. That's what I'm here for now."

I look down at my plate and an old memory surfaces. "You remember the time we volunteered at the high school track meet and then it started raining, and we got soaked trying to get all the scoresheets and stuff inside?"

He nods. "Afterward, we collapsed in the school breezeway and just listened to it pound down on the metal roof."

"I was cold," I say, "and you put your arm around me."

He scoots closer and puts his arm around me now.

"But your hair kept dripping onto me," I say, laughing and leaning my head on his shoulder.

"I remember," he says. "I wanted to kiss you so much then."

I look up at him. "You did? I remember *wanting* you to kiss me."

"Why'd you think of that now?" he asks.

"What you said about putting the person you love before anything else, you said something like that then, too. We got to talking about your parents' divorce—"

"As one does when trying to make a move on a pretty girl," he jokes.

"I guess so," I say. "Anyways, you said that your dad needed to put your family and your mom before himself."

"I said that?" he asks.

"It makes sense you'd have forgotten. It's ancient history."

He turns my chair toward him and his eyes lock on mine. "I don't want you only to be a piece of my history. I want you to be part of my future, too."

I squeeze his hand, then stand up and walk to the bedroom. I slide down and sit on the floor, leaning my back up against my bed and looking down at the floor between my legs.

Ben comes into the room and his feet come into view below me. I look up at him, towering over me. "It's a lot to process."

He slides down next to me and leans up against the bed, then turns his head to smell my hair and thread his fingers through mine. After a minute or two, I relax into his body, leaning my head on his shoulder.

"What's worrying you?" he asks.

Here goes nothing.

I meet his eyes. "I do love you."

The corners of his mouth turn up.

"I should say, I *still* love you. I have for a while. Since last summer for sure, but on and off for years. In the way clueless young people love. Not knowing any better."

He nods.

"What's worrying me is that we've been together before and you left, or life … dragged you away. I can't lose you again. If I do, I won't be the same. I—"

Tears slip from my eyes, and he pulls me onto his lap, straddling him.

I lay my head on his shoulder, and he strokes my back and caresses me with his fingertips on my cheek, my neck, wherever he can reach me.

"Look at me," he says.

I shake my head.

"Fine, don't." He pulls me in closer, wrapping his strong arms around me. "But are you listening?" he whispers in my ear.

I nod and try to calm my breathing.

"I love you. Nothing will drag me away from you. Ever again."

He leans me back and looks directly into my eyes. "The starting point is you. It was always you, but it took me some time to figure that out. It took even more time for me to be brave enough to say it out loud."

You are my starting point, too. I've felt it for years, but I was also scared to admit it.

He runs the back of his fingers down the side of my face, then smiles. "I want to support you. I want to love you the way you deserve to be loved. I want to see you grow and develop professionally and conquer your fears and achieve your dreams. I …" He chews on his lip, then smiles at me nervously. "It's a little hard to open up when I know how much is at stake."

I hug him again and whisper, "Tell me."

He nods. "When you're ready, I want us to be a family—a small one—and then for us to, well, make a bigger one. When I say I want you in my future, I mean that I want us to create a beautiful one, together. I never allowed myself to imagine what life with a partner might be like. But with you, I can't *not* imagine it. When I close my eyes at night, I see us together. I see you in a white dress and me holding our first child. I see us ... doing it all."

Doing it all.

"Wow," I whisper. "That's a lot."

"Too much?" he asks.

"No, I think, I think it's just right."

I look at his mouth, the one that uttered those lyrical, life-changing words, knowing that if I kiss him, I've truly forgiven him. But more than that, I'm opening all of this up again, opening *us* up again for something real. Something I've dreamt of.

"It's our time?" I whisper.

"It's our time, G."

I touch his face, and he closes his eyes and rests his head in my hand. My heart melts, seeing the look of calm and happiness on his face. As I lean in, he opens his eyes and pulls me into the sweetest, most serene kiss we've ever had together. He is a melody, I am the chords, and the song we create together is one of indescribable beauty.

I wrap my arms around him. "I'm never letting you go."

He laughs.

"You can't leave this apartment for at least a couple days. I need to make sure I'm not hallucinating, and after that, well, I'm sure we'll find something to keep us busy."

His mouth twitches. "If I have anything to say about it, shit's about to go down, girl."

I crack up. "I've missed your sense of humor."

"I've missed your laugh."

I stand up and offer my hand to him. We crawl into bed, and we each lie on our sides, facing each other.

"So what happens now? Gabby-Ben 2.0.? 3.0?" I ask.

"Well, 2.0 is that we plan how we make this happen in reality. I have some opportunities in the works in the US, but I'll take whatever works for you for your job, for both of us to be together. But before we get to logistics ..."

"Yeah?"

"I have a few ideas," he says, trailing his fingers up my back.

"What are these ideas?" I ask, giggling.

"You've shed a few tears the last few days, and I'd say it's time to feel good. We have the best reason in the world to feel good."

I nod.

He leans in and kisses my forehead. "You know that when you orgasm, your brain produces dopamine …" He moves down and kisses my jaw. "And oxytocin." A kiss, then a nibble on my neck. "And endorphins." And then a long, drawn-out kiss on my mouth. "And serotonin."

"What're you trying to say?"

"That you're gonna feel fucking fantastic in about ten minutes, baby." He unties the belt of my robe and the cool air hits my bare skin. "Happy and turned on and then calm and relaxed. It's science."

"Who am I to question a biologist about science?" I say.

He rolls over to turn off the lamp, and we're lit only by the candles in the window.

"I thought I had your body memorized, but you're even better than I remember." He kisses me lightly on the lips.

"Candlelight makes everyone look better."

"You look great in any light," he says, running his hand up my torso and aligning his fingers to my rib cage. "I know you have a range: gentle, dirty, fun. What's it gonna be, the first time after a *long* time?"

"How about we just get started and see where the night takes us? I only have one condition: You. Naked. Now."

He jumps up and starts shedding clothes in such a haphazard manner that I laugh.

"Come here."

He lies back down on his back, and I roll over to straddle him, letting my hands explore and caress his bare chest.

"Fuck," he breathes out. "I have missed this. It's been so hard without you."

I lean in and whisper in his hear. "How did you manage all this time, huh?"

He nips my ear, before whispering back, "I read some of those smutty books you like so much."

I sit up. "Really?"

His eyes track down to my bare breasts, then back up to my eyes. "They were very ... educational."

I giggle. "And what exactly did you learn?"

"That women like men in gray sweatpants."

I snort. "Is that it?"

"Oh, I have all sorts of new ideas for us to try, G."

I roll my hips over him and feel him hard beneath me. "I like the sound of that."

His grin fades.

"Everything okay?" I ask.

"Actually," he admits, "I read them because they made me feel close to you."

I smile. "Reading smut made you feel close to me?"

He nods, the look on his face hopeful, honest.

I run my hands over his chest, his abs, and back up his body to his face. "You were always close to me, in here," I say, taking his hand and placing it over my heart.

He pulls me down for a deep, lingering kiss.

When I come up for air, I sigh. "You know, missing an international flight to propose to a woman is quite the romantic gesture."

"I'm not romantic," he says. "I'm just hopelessly in love and can't live without you."

"I love the beautiful words coming out of your mouth, but I think it can be put to better use."

"In other words, stop talking—"

"Stop talking," I say, "and put your fucking mouth on my body."

Ben

"Ohhhh, yessss."

That's what I like to hear.

I raise her hands over my head so her breasts are in my face and take her nipple in my mouth. I pull my mouth away for only a second to switch sides.

"More," she says.

"Patience," I reply and flip us over so I'm on top. I run my hands over her full breasts and return my mouth to her, licking, sucking, and teasing her.

"We have a lot of lost time to make up for," she says breathlessly.

Yes, we fucking do.

Her hands in my hair are driving me almost as wild as her grinding herself onto my hard cock with her legs wrapped around my waist. It has been a *very* long time since I've had sex, but everything is in working order as she reaches down and grips me with perfect pressure.

I suck in my breath, through clenched teeth.

"What do you want, baby?" she asks. "I missed going down on you."

I will last less than four seconds if she does that.

I'm above her now, pressing myself into her hands and kissing her mouth, and it sounds amazing, the idea of coming in her sweet mouth. But we *just* got back together. I might not always make the best decisions, but that for sure isn't the right move.

I shake my head. "I want to look into your eyes and kiss you while we make love. I've been dreaming about this for a long time, and I want it to be right."

She locks eyes with me, and the look she gives me indicates I've said the right thing. *About damn time.*

I press my chest into her perfect breasts. "Oh my God, you're so soft, so much better than I remember," I say. "You fit me so well."

I roll to my side and caress her body, starting at her neck and then moving slowly down. I stop for a moment or two to pay some attention to her nipples, which are already hard, and take one in my mouth. She arches her back into me, and I let my hand trail down between her legs. While I kiss her breasts, I find to my pleasant surprise, she is already slick. I press one finger into her and imagine that soon I will be inside of her, showing her through touch how much I've missed her—how much I love her. While I kiss her and pleasure her with my hand, she wraps her hands around my cock, moving them up and down.

"Do you wanna come, baby?" I ask.

"B, I want you inside of me. I need you now," she says. She pushes her hips into me, rhythmically, seeking pressure, seeking release.

"You want me to come in you?" I ask, verbalizing something I've imagined countless times since the last time we were together.

"Yes," she says, breathlessly.

"Soon. Let me help you, first. I want you to feel good, then me."

Her eyes are closed, her lips parted, and I can't help but lean in and kiss her, taste her. While we kiss, I slip a second finger in and then move back down to kiss her breasts, biting her nipple lightly. "You like that?"

"Mmmm."

"Tell me you want me," I say.

"I want you so much."

"More."

"I want you hard in me."

"More, G."

"I want you to come ... oh ... in me."

"How do you want it, baby?" I ask.

"Just like that, baby," she says as I use my hands and mouth to bring her closer and closer to release. "Just ... like ... that." Her breathing speeds up, and she begins to whimper. "Yes. Oh my God. Yes," she cries out as she c omes.

Simply watching her would be enough to make me orgasm, too, but I hold off and move my hands to caress her body while she recovers. I rest my head on her stomach and hold her.

"That was ... intense," she says when she finally catches her breath.

I close my eyes and smile. Her fingertips dust my jaw, then trail down the side of my neck. "Your turn."

"Nah, I could wait," I joke.

"Let's go to sleep, then. Maybe tomorrow," she teases.

"No way," I protest, crawling up her body. "I'm so hot right now, you're lucky I didn't come on your sheets." She exhales a tired giggle, and I bite the side of her neck. The sound from her throat almost sends me over the edge.

My hard-on feels like a steel rod at this point, and I slide into her unobstructed like my body was built for hers.

"Oh, that's my man," she moans. Her eyes lock on mine. "I forgot just how good this feels."

"Let me remind you," I say, pumping into her slowly. "Want me to start off easy?"

She shakes her head decisively. "I want it hard. Show me how much you missed me."

There's no way I can express how much my heart longed for her, how much my body craved hers. But we have each other—finally. We have time. We have the rest of our lives.

When I wake in the morning, I roll over to find Gabby looking at me with sleepy eyes.

"Hey, there," she says.

I take her in, well, what little of her is visible. The blanket is pulled up to her chin and only her head is popping out.

"*Boker tov*," I say. *Good morning.*

"Listen to you with your nice Israeli accent," she says, scrunching her nose. I lean in and kiss it.

"You're so beautiful," I say before I can help myself.

She scoots closer to cuddle with me. "Oooooh, you're so warm, my own personal heater."

I laugh into her hair, kissing her there, too. I need to kiss her as many times as I can. So much wanting can't have been expended in one night alone. She must feel the same because she has her arms wrapped around me tightly. I slide my hands under the blanket and caress her soft, bare s kin.

"You kissed me a lot last night," I say, "but you never answered me. Not really."

"Didn't I?" she says.

I narrow my eyes at her. *What is she playing at?*

"I mean, the answer you gave me," I say, squeezing her ass, "was pretty good, but I'm not sure if it was the answer to my question."

"This *question*?" she asks, twisting her body away from me to grab the ring from the nightstand.

I nod. "That one."

She looks at me carefully, her lips pressed together. "So here's my answer. If ... sorry, *when* next Hanukkah rolls around, and we're still together, I'll marry you."

I had guessed it was a "yes," but hearing it confirmed, a veil of calm and rightness falls over me. "You want a winter wedding? A Hanukkah wedding?"

"We've tried a few summers," she replies. "I think winter's our season."

"We do like hot cocoa," I say, nuzzling her neck and kissing her near her ear. She threads her fingers through my hair, and I inhale her scent. *I love this woman.*

She rubs her pointer finger over the outside of the ring, currently resting on her thumb, and I take it from her. "Do you even like it?"

"I like you," she says.

"So you *don't* like the ring?" I chuckle.

"I like the ring, Ben, but it's a wedding ring. I can't wear it now."

"I'll get you an engagement ring then. Something you like."

She looks at me with so much love in her eyes that it almost takes my breath away. "I like the boy who gave me the ring. That's what matters. You keep it safe for me until the big day, and just ... stay with me, always?"

I set the ring on the nightstand, roll back over, and pull her into me. "Always."

She rubs her warm hand over my heart, and I do the same to her. I can feel it beating, softly, beneath the skin.

"Mine feels like it's in one piece again," I say. "Does yours?"

"It feels complete with you here," she says.

Yeah, it does.

Gabby

We cuddle for a while and make love again. This time slow, lazy kisses, with murmurs of how much we've missed one another. We dream about how this could be our new normal—lazy, sex-filled Sunday mornings. Except when I suggest that, Ben reminds me that it's Monday.

I groan, and he laughs. He kisses me on the forehead, then untangles his body from mine and slides out of bed to pull on his boxers.

"Why don't you lie here a few more minutes, and I'll make you breakfast in bed?"

"Mmmm. Can you write 'breakfast in bed' on a *ketubah*?" I muse.

"I was at a few weddings this year in Israel. I never heard anyone mention breakfast in bed on the marriage contract, but it can be arranged."

"This deal is getting sweeter by the minute," I say.

He leans down to kiss me. "I'll be back in ten with breakfast."

While Ben opens and shuts cabinets in the kitchen, surely searching for his favorite frying pan, I take a shower and pull on a comfy but work-appropriate top and some pajama shorts. How I'm supposed to work today after what has occurred in the last eighteen hours, I'm not sure, but I'll eventually have to get online. I come up behind him in the kitchen and wrap my arms around his waist while he puts the finishing touches on what looks like a savory crepe.

"I was going for crepes, but they came out more like filled pancakes," he says, grabbing one of my hands and kissing my fingers.

"I love pancake-crepes," I say, pouring two cups of coffee and taking them to the table. "Let's eat together here."

As we dig into our first breakfast together as an official couple, Ben asks me, "Doesn't it feel weird to eat at a time like this?"

I set my fork down. "Yes, but what are we supposed to do? Maybe tell our families?"

His eyebrows go up.

"Well, Miri and Ilana already know something is up, right?" I say.

He emits an obviously fake cough, and I cock my head. He responds with a tight smile.

"Which means Aaron knows, and therefore my parents, and likely *your* parents ..." I continue.

He presses his lips together.

"Does anybody *not* know?" I ask.

"Nobody knows you said 'yes?'" he offers up.

"This has been quite the ruse."

"More like ... inexpert execution of a well-intentioned plan."

"What does that mean?" I ask.

He glances to the side, then meets my eyes. "Well, when your family was in Israel a couple weeks ago, it might have been a little obvious how I feel about you. Aaron and then Ilana, and then your mom ... pretty much everyone but your dad told me that I was an idiot for leaving you here."

"And my dad?" I ask.

"He saw how miserable I was, and he felt sorry for me."

I sigh. My dad is such a softie, and he's always loved Ben.

"So you only came back because my family forced you to?" I tease.

"Not at all," he says emphatically. "They just gave me their blessing if I decided that I wanted to, you know, grow up, stop feeling sorry for myself, and treat you the way you deserve to be treated by the man who loves you?"

I reach out and touch his hand, and he scoots closer to me.

"I called your mom," he says, "and told her that I'd made the biggest mistake of my life when I left without telling you how I felt, and I wanted to come back and talk to you."

I imagine for a second the conversation they must have had. Ben, love-sick and nervous, spilling his guts to my mom, and my mother, realizing that her time to shine as a matchmaker had finally arrived.

"She said it would be best for me to take it slow," he says.

She did?

"That if I showed up and professed my undying love for you right away, after everything we've been through, you'd get super-pissed off and refuse to speak to me ever again."

Does my mom know me or what?

"So that's why she planned the Hanukkah party for us to meet up nonchalantly," he explains.

I laugh. "And do you consider almost screwing me in my parents' guest bathroom nonchalant?"

"That wasn't *exactly* part of the plan," he says, smiling awkwardly, "but I'm not sorry we did it."

"Me either," I admit. "But you know everyone in our family has been discussing our sex lives and all related matters, right?"

"It certainly didn't help that my mom found your red thong in my bedroom last winter."

Oh my God.

"She finally had tangible proof for her theory we'd been hooking up all summer. In case you're wondering, *that* was an awkward FaceTime." He's cracking up but trying to hold it in. I'm not sure whether to cover my face in embarrassment or crack up right alongside him.

He kneels in front of me, wrapping his arms around my waist in a tight hug and looking up at me sweetly. "Does it bother you that they know we're in love?"

I gently yank his hair and he laughs, then kisses me full-on. When he breaks away, he says, "Anyway, our moms have been plotting this for years, so ..."

"They're probably in cahoots with Mrs. Friedberg," I say.

"She owes you a lot of flowers," he comments. "Those flowers last night, well, all the ones I gave her last summer, too, were for you."

I furrow my brow.

"I was ... too nervous to give them to you," he starts to explain, "so I gave them to her instead."

"I made you nervous?"

He smiles. "You've been making my butterflies drunk for a *very* long time, Gabby."

"Maybe she can sponsor the flowers for the wedding," I say, with a snicker. "She'll be a guest of honor for helping all of this come together."

He grins and nods. "Ilana deserves honorable mention, too. Did you see her cock-blocking Matt the other night?"

I snort. "Yesterday, I had *no* idea what she had up her sleeve. And Miri. How did *she* get involved? Did she even *know* Ilana before yesterday?"

He shrugs. "I mean, Miri's been staying with my dad, and I saw him late Saturday night. You know—well, *now* you know—she kinda just ... takes charge of situations."

"I noticed. I bet they all have some group text I'm not on," I comment. "Thank God, I didn't accidentally send my cleavage pic to *that* thread."

"We have women all over the world rooting for us," he says.

"What does that mean?"

"Idit," he says. "My neighbor in Rehovot. I need to let her know ..."

"Let her know what?" I ask.

"That you love me," he says simply.

I kiss him on his forehead. "I do." I sigh and smile.

"What?" he asks.

"I'm kind of grateful that Jewish mothers can't mind their own damn business," I say.

"Me, too."

"Well," I say, "if everyone already knows, then we're off the hook in announcing it for a bit, which means we can just kiss and ... you know..."

"No time for that, Ms. Feinman. We have to plan the rest of our lives together."

"No time for *that*?" I ask in shock.

"I'm joking, obviously. There's *always* time for that," he says, running his hand up my thigh.

I take his hand in mine. "It's crazy how quickly everything can change."

"Quick? This right here is years in the making," Ben says.

He's right. We met for the first time on Hanukkah seventeen years ago, which reminds me ... "I have a present for you."

"Is it the scarf you promised me?" he asks, kissing me on my neck and then sinking down between my legs and wrapping his arms around my waist. "I already told you, baby. Your legs are the only thing I need wrapped around my neck."

He lifts one of my legs and props it on his shoulder, then slips his hands into the legs of my shorts and massages my butt. Nudging up my top with this nose, he kisses my bare stomach.

It's tempting to let things run their course, but I lift his head with my hand. "Later, B."

I wriggle past him to stand. "I have something for you. Wait here, okay? Come into the bedroom when I call you."

"Ohhhh, it's that type of gift?" he asks as he starts to remove his t-shirt.

"Put your clothes back on, you nut," I say and swat him on the butt and walk to the bedroom.

Ben

"Okay, you can come now," Gabby calls.

When I walk into the bedroom, she's kneeling in front of the bed looking at something. I come closer and see it's a canvas sheet unfurled on the bed.

"I told you I painted my dreams when I was in Paris," she whispers and looks up at me.

I drop to my knees and join her to examine the painting up close. My breath catches in my throat. It's ... me—me the way Gabby sees me. The colors are muted. The whole tone seems ... heavy. Was it created with love or sadness? I'm no art critic, but it's hard to mistake the message in this. I'm facing away from the beautiful soul that created this vision of me. I left her.

I look at her. "I turned away from you. I'm so sorry."

She shakes her head. "No. At first, I thought that, too. But I think ..."

I wait for her to continue.

She smiles at me shyly. "I think it's the second, maybe the millisecond before you turn back to me to tell me you love me, maybe to ask me if we can take a bath together, or just walk and hold hands outside while spring flowers begin to bloom."

It's not her disappointment in me. It's her longing for me, for an *us*. It's a love letter to me—in one of the languages she speaks most fluently.

I swallow and reach out for her hand. I have to touch her. "*I'm* one of your dreams?"

"I guess *we* are one of my dreams. A life together."

I stand and pull her up to embrace her. "It's— *You* are so beautiful. Your heart and your mind and ..."

She looks into my eyes and brackets my face with her hands. The feel of her fingertips on my skin takes me to a higher plane of existence. This past year, not knowing if I'd ever feel her touch again created a hole inside of me that her presence this past week has only started to fill.

"I don't even deserve you," I say.

"You deserve me," she says. "And I deserve you." She smiles and indicates with her head for me to look at the painting again. I take in the details more carefully this time. In the corner are her initials, G.F., scrawled in her curvy hand.

She leans over and rolls up the bottom corner where there are a few more hastily written words. I lean down and find in her handwriting the words, *Nice Jewish Boy*.

I exhale a laugh. "It's called 'Nice Jewish Boy?'"

Her mouth twists in a smile.

"*I'm* your nice Jewish boy?" I ask.

"I always told you I'd end up with one," she says, unable to hide her satisfaction.

My chest tightens, but it's no longer a feeling of sadness, longing, or regret. It's ... happiness. "This is the second-best Hanukkah gift I've ever gotten."

"Second?" she asks, surprised. "What was the *first*?"

"It's too cheesy to even s—"

"Me?" she asks with a huge grin on her face.

I pull her into a hug. "Yeah, you. The first—"

"The best," she interrupts, correcting me.

I smile. "The best ... was you."

Epilogue

Gabby

I carefully unwrap the small box covered in pastel watercolor wrapping paper. "You painted it, didn't you?"

"I couldn't help myself," Tzipi says. "I knew it would get ruined, but I wanted it to be special."

"But why a gift?"

"Because I love you," she says as she touches my arm.

I look at her. "But you already gave me the *best* gift, your wonderful son."

She smiles. "Still, a gift is in order. You're my *kallah*, my bride," she says as she smooths my hair back from my face. It's clear that Ben inherited his ability to radiate love with a simple glance from this special woman standing before me.

I open the small jewelry box. Inside lies an intricately designed silver *hamsa* necklace with a small sapphire in the center.

"It's beautiful," I say, tracing the delicate hand-shaped charm.

"I made it for you."

"You *made* it?" I ask.

"I learned a few years ago, and this piece was always meant to be yours. Maybe Ben was, too."

Oh.

"Wear it to keep you safe and healthy," she explains.

I smile at her. "Would you put it on me?"

She takes the necklace, then moves behind me to secure it around my neck. Placing her hand on my shoulder, she says softly to me, "He'll mess up sometimes ..."

I turn to her.

"But he loves you ... deeply, and he's going to make you the happiest woman in the world. I know it."

"I know," I whisper, hugging her tightly. "I'll take care of him. You don't have to worry."

"Why would I worry? *You're* in charge now," she jokes. "And don't let him forget it."

I laugh.

We part, and she tells me, "Go join everyone. It's your engagement party, after all, but I wanted to tell you that I will *always* be here for you. You've gotten yourself another mother, whether you like it or not."

"Thank you," I say, squeezing her hands. "Shall we?"

She nods and we join everyone at the table in the other room.

Ben is talking to someone on FaceTime, and I give him a confused look.

"Avi," he explains.

"Your roommate?" I ask.

"Flatmate," Avi says, correcting me. Ben aims the phone camera at me. "Hey, Gabby. *Mazal tov!*"

"Thank you," I say.

"Avi, we'll talk later, man," Ben says.

Before he can disconnect the call, Avi shouts, "See you soon, roomie!"

I roll my eyes good-naturedly, and Ben adds, "*Your* roomie, too, at least for a couple weeks until we find a place together."

I smile and sigh. This whole moving-across-the-world thing is not for the weak-willed.

"When we get back, it'll almost be Tu B'shvat. I'll take you on hikes in the Negev, and we can see the flowers blooming in the desert."

"The desert?" I ask.

He nods, and his eyes glitter with excitement. "And we can go to the beach together, and the market, and get great coffee and—"

"You know he'll keep on going if you don't stop him, right?" Miri says, interrupting him.

I touch his face, then lean down and kiss him on the cheek. "I can't wait."

"So," Miri says, "he convinced you to move to Israel for him, Double G?"

She can't decide if her favorite nickname for me is "Gorgeous Gabby" or, the shortened version, "Double G." I roll my eyes at her but grin straight away. Miri says Ben is "fucking lovable," but so is she.

"He didn't have to convince me of anything," I reply. "I had a work opportunity, and I turned it into a broader … *life* opportunity. I'm the kind of woman who makes things happen the way I want them to."

Miri winks at me. "You are."

Ben turns and pulls me into his lap. "What she's saying, Mir, is that she *loves* me, and she couldn't wait to come woo me and get in my pants and—"

I smack him on the chest. "Will you shut up?"

"But it's true," he replies.

I shake my head at him, but I'm still on a love high from the past week of Ben pampering me and cooking for me and, well, proposing marriage. Nothing can put a dent in that kind of happiness. "It is true. I feel better when I'm around you."

He whispers in my ear, "Me, too, baby."

I catch Aaron's eye, and he smiles. "So where you gonna live?" he asks. "When are you coming back? What's the plan?"

Ben looks at me, and as if we've practiced it, we both say, "We'll figure it out."

He leans in to kiss me, and the younger half of the table groans, while my mom and Tzipi exchange looks as swoony as my own.

Ben shoots Aaron and Miri, the two loudest groaners, a sharp look. "I've been waiting a long time to kiss this girl in front of you, and now you're all gonna have to deal with it."

I laugh, then slide into a chair next to Miri, and bump shoulders with her. "I found out the rest of the story," I say to her quietly. "You, going all detective at 3:00 a.m. and finding out my Sunday schedule. Concocting that harebrained restaurant plan with Ilana."

She grins. "Well, our little Benjamin needed help. He certainly wasn't making things happen on his own. I mean, he's been in love with you since he was at least sixteen. I don't know if Bubbe has *another* ten years to wait. I just got things moving."

Ariella leans in. "But how did you get Ben to postpone his flight? To actually go after her?"

Miri glances to the side, and Tzipi smiles, apparently already listening in. "She called in the big guns for that one. Right, Marci?"

Marci exchanges a glance with Tzipi. "Jewish mothers and Jewish mothers in training," she says, leaning her head toward Ilana's, "can be very convincing."

"Oh, it didn't take any convincing," Ilana says, joining the now table-wide conversation. "He just needed reassurance that Gabby would say 'yes.'"

Ben shoots her an appreciative look, then mouths, *Thank you.* She responds with a bright smile.

"Hey now," Aaron chimes in. "Let's not downplay the role of *others* in this whole thing. I think I deserve the title of 'honorary Jewish mother' at the very least."

"What for?" I ask.

"For getting him drunk and sending him off to propose?" Ariella asks, and we all laugh.

"You don't get drunk from one shot of Manischewitz wine," Marc replies.

"You didn't," Marci laughs.

"Ima, geez," Aaron says. "This isn't the Catskills in the 1950s. We sat him down, let him sip some good bourbon, and dropped him off at Gabby's."

"We?" Marci asks.

"Me, Aba, and Jonathan," Aaron says.

"Aba?" Ariella asks, glancing at her dad.

"I went along for the ride," Jonathan answers. "Ben and I had already talked. I knew he had it in him. He's a good man."

Tzipi looks at Jonathan, and he gives her a striking look—intimate—and I glance away, but hear him say, "He's loving and compassionate, just like you."

She shakes her head shyly. "He takes after you, too. He's determined. The fact that he and Gabby are together. That's the result of not giving up, isn't it?"

The song on the playlist changes to something from a bygone era, and Jonathan stands, offering his hand to Tzipi for a dance.

I turn back to the table, just in time to catch Miri asking Ilana, "So when are you two getting married, huh?"

"Miri!" Ariella says. "Mind your own business."

"My track record is pretty good lately," she says. "I'm gonna strike while the iron is hot."

Aaron glances at Ben's parents dancing. His mom is laughing, and his dad twirls her. "In that case, you might want to spend some time with those two."

"No need," I tell Aaron. "They're both flying to Israel in March to visit us, and they've rented a place in the Ein Hod artist village for a month."

Ben watches his parents for a moment. "My dad said he wanted to indulge my mom in 'an environment that inspires her to create.'" He looks at me and says quietly, only to me. "I want you to have everything you need to flourish, too."

I touch his face. "We'll create it together."

"I have no doubt," he says, standing and offering me his hand. "You ready, G?"

I place my hand in his and stand as he pulls me into a hug. "For what?"

"For everything. For all of it?"

I meet his eyes and nod. "As long as I'm with you."

Author's Note

"God gave Adam a secret—and that secret was not how to begin, but how to begin again." —Elie Wiesel

For months, I went back and forth on whether to include the above quote at the beginning of this novel. Why in the world would I start a feel-good steamy romance with a quote from Elie Wiesel, one of the world's most well-known Holocaust survivors and authors? But from the moment I came across these words one Yom Kippur in the special prayer book for the Jewish high holidays, they were engraved in my heart and thoughts.

There is something so beautiful to me about forgiveness. Without it, there is no hope for true, long-lasting connection or love. I love the idea that we *are* not—and *cannot*—be perfect, but we can always strive to be so. That striving is the human experience—to try, to sometimes fail, and to begin again. And so I began writing a book, once again, about forgiveness.

The idea for this book started from a simple, halfway-comical thought I had a couple years ago: "There are so many Christmas romance books; there need to be a few more Jewish holiday romances." Sure, Jewish holiday romances exist (thank you to the wonderful authors writing them!), but in a sea of red and green, they are still the exception, not the norm. Starting this book was the perfect opportunity to ramp up the level of humor from my previous books, and I set out to write *Light It Up* (originally titled "Burn It Down") as a rom-com. I was well on my way, too, when the October 7, 2023 massacre was carried out in Israel on the Jewish holiday of Simchat Torah. And the world—for me, for Jews everywhere—was turned upside down.

It was hard to focus in all areas of my life, especially writing. "What is the point?" I asked myself. I wondered, "How can I ask people to buy and read my silly little love story when so many people were massacred, when there are hundreds of hostages, when there is a war?" But in early 2024, those close to me—those in whom I had confided that I had something beautiful and Jewish and heartwarming in the works—told me, "We need those silly little love stories right now. We need those big-hearted, different love stories that either distract us from the horrors of the world or remind us what's possible when love—light—pushes out the darkness."

So, I dove into *Light It Up* again with fresh eyes that had seen horror but also resilience. My aspirational rom-com became far less comedic and more heartfelt, and I began to weave in more tidbits of Jewish and Israeli culture and history and even some comments on anti-Semitism. [Note: Some readers might have noted that I included the names of a few well-known universities, which at the time of publication are failing miserably to address unprecedented levels of hate speech, intimidation, and outright violence toward Jewish students and faculty. I considered omitting these university names to avoid somehow "giving a pass" to these institutions that should be doing everything they can to create safe spaces for all students and faculty. Ultimately, I chose to use their real names, since I believe it is an accurate portrayal of the American Jewish experience: to know that we will face challenges in certain academic, professional, or social situations, ranging from a simple lack of understanding all the way to fear for our safety, and still put ourselves in (emotional, mental, or physical) harm's way in order to pursue our dreams.]

But being Jewish is so much more than the hardships we face, and I wanted to shine a light on Jewish life and culture for those who know and love it already ("You are seen"), as well as share it with those who might find interest and commonality with the collective human values and experiences shared by all of us. Now, more than ever, the world needs to see expressions of Jewish joy and Jewish values. Exposure to the Jewish people—even if only through creative works—is sorely needed for others to understand us just a bit better.

In some ways, this is a very Jewish book, and in others ... it's a regular old romance novel, where miscommunication and vulnerability and swooning and pining and intimacy and all the regular stuff happens. After all, all humans love. We all make mistakes, we all grovel, we all suffer and mourn, we all lust, and we all dream ... We all just live. Jews are a bit different, sure, but we all just live.

The Jewish experience encompasses aspects of burden and suffering alongside love and continuity. The small piece of wisdom from Elie Wiesel I chose to share perfectly encapsulates this complexity. Things *will* go wrong, on a smaller or grander scale, at some point in our lives, and sometimes, the only choice we have is to begin again.

In a conversation between the two main characters of this book, Ben says to Gabby, about the societal issues Jews face in contemporary times, "That's what we do, right? Stand up in the face of hardship, bigots, I don't know, and focus on the right thing." So, if I can end on any point, maybe this is the right one: We cannot—must not—ignore those who seek to do us harm or steal our joy and our purpose, but we must always remember that *we* define our values and our identity. Stand strong, remember who you are, and make your own light brighter to push out the darkness.

Acknowledgments

It goes without saying (but when have I ever gone that route?) that writing a book takes time. Creating a book that people want to read—a work that might have come from my brain but one that also resonates with others—takes even more time and a good bit of collaboration.

I always start by thanking my husband. While none of my books up until this point have been biographical, the fact that I can channel feelings of true love and all the other emotions related to a close relationship is due to the fact that I have someone I really love. As far as *Light It Up* goes, he didn't quite understand Ben's inability to make a decision or commit to the woman he loves early on. In fact, he told me quite bluntly, "When I liked you, I didn't mess around." Thank goodness!

Thank you to my wonderful editor, Jen Boles, who is thoughtful beyond description, seems to take ownership of my characters almost as much as I do, and always helps me figure out where to dive deeper. Her careful attention to structure, pacing, what's lacking in a scene, and what's non-essential makes me a better writer. And she gets a lot of my jokes, which is always a plus.

Thank you to Hannah Gordon-Teller for the beautiful cover art. It was important to me to take a different path with this book's art, since Gabby is an artist. The feelings between Gabby and Ben are long-held, deep, and rich and the cover art reflects the beauty in their love story and my appreciation for (though complete lack of skill in) visual art.

Thank you to all my early readers, in no particular order (well, my mom comes first): Linda Till, Allie Goldberg, Kendra Tarbrake, Erika Travan, Kacie Douglas Leicher, Leah Krauss, Tal Israeli, Sorcha Mildiner, Avital Samet, and Samantha Martin. Thank you for your time and energy reading, contemplating, taking notes, and giving me feedback. I aspired to write my first unapologetically Jewish story, but it was important to me that this book be entirely accessible to non-Jewish readers. You told me what worked and what didn't. You opened your hearts and minds to my story in its various phases and gave me your real feedback about the parts you loved (Gabby's strong FMC voice), the parts you didn't ("extended soliloquies are kinda Ben's jam - cut!"), and your true thoughts on whether it's okay to mention Jewish ritual in the same chapter as spicy bedroom scenes.

It would be impossible for me to list all the people who contributed to my Jewish upbringing, learning, and identity along the way, but I'll name a few who deserve special thanks:

Dad, your lessons on Jewish ethics, often imparted on a fishing boat or in a woodshop, have guided me every step of the way. Being a *mensch* and always striving to make the world a better place through my interactions with others is something I am so grateful to have learned from you.

To my big-hearted mom and generous step-dad, who spent not a few hours in a house of prayer different from the ones they knew in order to support my Jewish education from a young age. I have never taken for granted your openness to my chosen spiritual journey in this life, and I love you so much for being the people you are.

Dear Janet, you were a wonderful step-mom and a true ally of the Jewish people, and I miss you every day.

To my dear parents-in-law, who have contributed in so many ways to my life, my successes, and my family.

To Rabbi Andy Koren and countless other Jewish educators, who nurtured my love for Jewish learning, spirituality, and Israel.

And now, for those of you who contributed professional, academic, and cultural knowledge, thank you:

To Dr. Sivan Sizikov, for answering all my questions about biology,

PhDs, post docs, and cancer research.

To Anna Abramzon, for answering my questions about everything art-related and for introducing me to a beautiful new artist, Hannah Gordon-Teller.

To Lawrence Szenes-Strauss, for your input on the "plaintive" nature of the Jewish high holidays melodies and all sorts of other Jewish questions.

To Kalika Rogers, for input related to cultural sensitivity and respect.

A special thank you to those of you who have read my previous books (The Startup Love series: *Ship It* and *Pitch It*). Your feedback, reviews, online conversations, and book clubs have helped me improve as a writer, and I hope to continue along this joyful, challenging, frustrating, and rewarding journey for a while longer.

Thank you to Eri Nelson of She Shed Studios and Jamie of Page Me Podcast for hosting me on your podcasts, to the indie bookstores who currently stock my books, and to all the readers and fellow writers out there on Bookstagram, Booktok, and other bookish communities who hype up and support indie authors.

Thank you to some amazing indie authors who are always psyched to hype me (it goes both ways): Samantha Renee, Elle M. Stewart, J.A. Merkel, and Eli Gardner.

And to the wonderful *Jewish Women Talk About Romance Books*, *Artists Against Antisemitism*, and *Never Alone Book Club* communities: My courage to publish this book and, hopefully, future ones featuring Jewish characters, settings, and storylines is strengthened by these communities who support and encourage Jewish creators and readers.

Glossary of Hebrew and Yiddish Terms

Aliyah – Literally, "to go up." To "make *aliyah*" means to move to Israel. An additional meaning of *aliyah* is to be called upon to read from the Torah.

Chanukiah – The special menorah (candelabra) used on Hanukkah. The *chanukiah* has nine branches, one for each of the eight nights of Hanukkah and an additional branch for the *shamash* candle (see definition below).

Hamotzi – The Jewish blessing recited over bread.

Ima / Aba – Mom / Dad in Hebrew, commonly used by Jews all over the world.

Kippah – Yarmulke (Yiddish) or skullcap.

Maideleh – Yiddish word for "girl" or "young woman."

Shabbat – The Jewish Sabbath, which starts on Friday evening and ends on Saturday evening (note: Jewish holidays begin at sundown).

Shamash – The candle used to light the other candles of the *chanukiah* (i.e., the Hanukkah menorah).

Shul – A Yiddish word for "synagogue."

Sufganiyah; pl. Sufganiyot – A fried jelly doughnut eaten during Hanukkah.

Sukkot – The Jewish fall harvest festival. Many Jews observe this week-long festival by building a *sukkah*, a temporary hut topped with branches, and eating (and sometimes even sleeping) in the *sukkah* during the festival.

Evie grew up on the beautiful Florida Gulf Coast, and after finishing her bachelor's degree, she decided to explore the world and move to Israel, where she lived for almost a decade. While there, she earned a master's degree in political science, worked in academia, founded her own translation and editing business, and married a pretty awesome guy.

Their path led them to the San Francisco Bay Area, and Evie found her way into the world of high-tech. She has helped found and grow a hardware startup, been part of a successful software startup exit, and participated in an IPO.

After reading approximately a million romance novels during the COVID-19 pandemic, she tried her hand at writing contemporary romance. She published the first novel of her Startup Love series, *Ship It*, in 2022 and followed it up with a sequel, *Pitch It*, in 2023.

Pivoting a bit with *Light It Up*, she set out to write a fun and endearing Jewish romance novel that expressed the beauty and meaningfulness of the Jewish experience with the hope that both Jewish and non-Jewish readers could connect to and enjoy it.

Evie's a friendly, always-supporting-bookish-endeavors kind of gal, so make sure to connect with her @evieblumauthor on Instagram and TikTok or visit her website at www.evieblum.com

Also by Evie Blum

www.ingramcontent.com/pod-product-compliance
Lightning Source LLC
Chambersburg PA
CBHW031845310726
48972CB00005B/1414